Praise for
The Cross Examination of Oliver Finney

"Randy Singer's *The Cross Examination of Oliver Finney* is that rarest of novels—a thrilling story that makes the reader think as well as feel. A cigar-smoking, plain-talking Christian judge goes on a reality TV show to defend his faith and finds his life threatened in the process—it's a great concept, and Singer has pulled it off with entertaining aplomb. I couldn't put this one down, and you won't be able to either!"

—ANGELA HUNT, author of *Magdalene* and *The Novelist*

"Randy Singer has done it again! He has produced a first-rate legal thriller written from the perspective of a Christian worldview. Intrigue, suspense, and mystery capture the reader's attention. But in the context of unraveling a thoughtful whodunit, a dynamite case for Christianity is articulated. Saint and skeptic alike will find *The Cross Examination of Oliver Finney* to be an informative, intriguing, and challenging must-read. Singer's fictional work is sanctified imagination and informed apologetics at their best."

—DR. PHIL ROBERTS, president of Midwestern Baptist
Theological Seminary

"Randy Singer is a talented writer with an incredible ability to bring relevant topics into page-turning fiction. *The Cross Examination of Oliver Finney* is a must-read for all Singer fans and will bring him new fans, too. I thoroughly enjoyed it."

—RENE GUTTERIDGE, author of *Boo, Boo Who,* and *Boo Hiss*

THE
CROSS
EXAMINATION
of OLIVER FINNEY

THE
CROSS
EXAMINATION
of OLIVER FINNEY

RANDY SINGER

WATERBROOK
PRESS

THE CROSS EXAMINATION OF OLIVER FINNEY
PUBLISHED BY WATERBROOK PRESS
12265 Oracle Boulevard, Suite 200
Colorado Springs, Colorado 80921
A division of Random House Inc.

Scripture quotations or paraphrases are taken from the following versions: The Amplified®
Bible. Copyright © 1954, 1958, 1962, 1964, 1965, 1987 by The Lockman Foundation.
Used by permission. (www.Lockman.org). The Holy Bible, English Standard Version, copy-
right © 2001 by Crossway Bibles, a division of Good News Publishers. Used by permission.
All rights reserved. Holman Christian Standard Bible®, © copyright 1999, 2000, 2002,
2003 by Holman Bible Publishers. Used by permission. Holy Bible, New International
Version®. NIV®. Copyright © 1973, 1978, 1984 by International Bible Society. Used by
permission of Zondervan Publishing House. All rights reserved. New King James Version®.
Copyright © 1982 by Thomas Nelson Inc. Used by permission. All rights reserved.

Suras from the Koran are taken from www.hti.umich.edu/k/koran, an electronic version of
The Holy Qur'an, translated by M.H. Shakir and published by Tahrike Tarsile Qur'an Inc.,
in 1983.

The characters and events in this book are fictional, and any resemblance to actual persons
or events is coincidental.

ISBN 1-4000-7166-6

Library of Congress Cataloging-in-Publication Data
Singer, Randy (Randy D.)
    The cross examination of Oliver Finney / Randy Singer.— 1st ed.
      p. cm.
    ISBN 1-4000-7166-6
  1. Death—Fiction. I. Title.
    PS3619.I5725C76 2006
    813'.6—dc22
                                    2006002431

Printed in the United States of America
2006—First Edition

10 9 8 7 6 5 4 3 2 1

To Jeanine Allen and David O'Malley,
two extraordinary friends who each heard
these coveted words in 2005:

"Well done, good and faithful servant!"
Matthew 25:23, NIV

∾

PART 1

AGENDAS

I'm not afraid of dying. I just don't want to be there when it happens.
—WOODY ALLEN

They could have done better with an axe.
—GEORGE WESTINGHOUSE, after witnessing the first use of the electric chair

Chapter 1

There must be some mistake.

The room started spinning as soon as the Patient heard the words. *Inoperable brain cancer. Frontal lobe.*

He gripped the arms of the chair and began the denial process immediately. He never trusted this doctor in the first place and now…he could swear the doctor smirked when he told him. All doctors, even highly paid oncologists, envied the Patient. Hated the Patient. The doctor was wrong, his judgment blurred by a subconscious bias. Men the Patient's age do not get brain cancer. Especially men who run three times a week and drink one glass of red wine every evening.

Do not. Cannot.

In the ensuing days, the Patient would get a second and third opinion. The top oncologists at the best hospitals in the country, all singing from the same song sheet. "We're sorry, there's nothing we can do. Chemo might slow the spread of the disease, but you probably have less than a year." They ticked off symptoms like a parade of horrors: behavioral changes, impaired judgment, memory loss, reduced cognitive function, vision loss, partial paralysis.

The Patient worked quickly through the stages of acceptance. Denial turned to anger. Tragedy seemed to stalk the Patient's family. His mother died from a stroke when the Patient was in college. His sister lost a teenage son in a freak motorboat accident. A first cousin died before her thirty-fifth birthday. And now this. But anger eventually gave way to grief and then ultimately resignation—all within a span of four weeks. Yet he wasn't prepared for the last stage, and he couldn't shake the irony of it.

Remorse. Nearly a billion dollars in net assets that he couldn't take with him. Today he would trade all of his wealth for one additional year. All the eighty-hour weeks, jetting around the country, the dog-eat-dog world he faced every day, the enemies he had made—everything he did to build the net wealth so he could one day retire early and enjoy life. And now he had twelve months.

He started getting his affairs in order. He signed a living will and durable power of attorney, spurred by the knowledge that he might lose his sanity before he drew his last breath. He changed his last will and testament a dozen times but eventually lost his enthusiasm for disinheriting the estranged children of his first and second wives. For the most part, they were young and firmly in the clutches of their overbearing and greedy mothers. No sense punishing the children. He changed it one final time and made each child a millionaire, even his rebellious fourteen-year-old daughter who reminded him way too much of her mother.

The one thing he couldn't prepare for preoccupied his thoughts day and night, night and day. He wasn't ready to face whatever lurked on the other side of death. He tried praying to some vague notion of God but just felt silly. What kind of God would listen to a man who had spent his whole life denying that God existed? Yet the thought of stepping into the darkness of death without solving life's greatest mystery scared the Patient most of all. If he were God, he would judge his own life harshly. Sure, he had accumulated vast amounts of wealth, but what *good* had he done? Who would say that life on earth was better because they had known him?

The sad and honest truth kept him awake at night and haunted his daytime thoughts. Maybe there was still time. A lot could be done in twelve months. But even if he wanted to curry favor with God, how could he do that? He still didn't really believe that God existed. And if God did exist, which of the gods worshiped on planet Earth was the true God?

It hit him while watching *Survivor,* nearly four weeks after the initial diagnosis. Life's greatest reality show! It seemed like such a deliciously good idea that it was either a stroke of genius or the brain cancer deluding him ahead of schedule. Powerful advocates for each of the world's major religions would be chosen as contestants. Their faith would be put to the ultimate test on a remote island. They would be forced into the trial of their lives: defending their faith against all challenges. The winner's god would gain a whole raft of new adherents, including the Patient. He would donate millions to the right causes. The ratings for the show would be spectacular.

The losers' gods would be exposed as impotent—powerless frauds in the face of death.

CHAPTER 2

Nikki Moreno leaned around the folks in the back of the long line at the Norfolk Courthouse metal detector, propped her sunglasses on top of her head, and caught the attention of one of the sheriff's deputies. She flashed her famous Moreno smile, and he waved her to the front. D. J. Landers, a sleazy defense attorney who had caught up with Nikki in the parking lot, followed hot on her heels. Too hot, in Nikki's opinion. He had already hit on her twice, and now he chattered in her ear as if they were best friends, undoubtedly realizing that Nikki was his ticket to the front of the line.

"I'm five minutes late already," Landers said. "But as fate would have it, my hearing's in front of Judge Finney, and I just happen to bump into his beautiful and talented law clerk this morning in the parking lot." Landers made a little "tsk-tsk" noise to emphasize what an incredible stroke of luck this was. "Hey, maybe she'll cover for me. Tell the judge she insisted I fix her breakfast after last night."

Nikki snorted without turning around. "We've got to get you off those mind-altering drugs," she said, placing her briefcase on the belt. She sashayed through the detector, content to let the deputies ogle every inch of her long legs and masterfully designed body. Landers, on the other hand, gave her the creeps. She could feel his beady little vulture eyes drilling into her from behind, and she wanted to slap him.

"I've got this one," said one of the beefy deputies. "Total pat down. She looks dangerous."

"You have no idea," Nikki shot back, picking up her briefcase as she graced the deputies with another smile. These guys were her buds, enjoying the friendship that develops between a law student clerking at the courthouse and the deputies who guard it. An *attractive, young* law student, that is. One not afraid to push the upper limits on skirt length or make a fashion statement with ankle and shoulder tattoos.

Before heading away from the guards, Nikki turned to address the annoyance who had slithered through the metal detector behind her. Landers was tall and bony, forty-five or so, with a spray-on tan, a thin black mustache, and jet-black Grecian Formula hair slicked straight back. His face was all angles and bones, and Landers somehow always managed to look like he hadn't shaved in a day and a half—no more, no less.

"Good luck on your prisoner lawsuits," Nikki offered, referring to the well-known practice of prisoners suing the sheriff's department for alleged abuse. Landers looked stunned. He hadn't said a word about any kind of prisoner suit. "A huge verdict might put an end to using Tasers altogether," Nikki continued. "I had no idea how dangerous they were."

"Huh?" Landers said, reaching for his briefcase. But a deputy already had a hand on it.

"Better run this through again," the deputy said. "And sir, I'll need you to step back through there as well."

The other deputy winked at Nikki as she took off down the hallway. She felt safe with these guys around.

"Have a great day," Nikki said over her shoulder, never doubting that the eyes of the deputies would follow her down the hallway as far as humanly possible.

∽

Judge Oliver G. Finney opened the proceedings in Courtroom 3 with a five-minute tongue-lashing of Landers for being late, topped off with a fifteen-hundred-dollar fine—a hundred bucks per minute. "And that's generous," claimed Finney. He motioned to the prosecutor. "Mr. Taylor's time alone is worth twice that much."

Landers gave Nikki a "Say something" look, but Nikki immersed herself in the papers in front of her that suddenly required immediate attention.

Just before court, Finney, who in his spare time wrote test questions for the puzzles and games section of the Law School Admissions Test, had given her some sample questions to try. "You know I stink at these," she protested.

"Precisely why I give them to you," Finney replied. "If you get more than twenty-five percent of the answers correct, I know the questions are too easy."

Landers tendered his check, and Finney got down to the real business at hand. Nikki had glanced at the docket sheet earlier and knew that the defendant, a guy named Terrel Stokes, faced several drug charges that could earn him twenty years minimum. He slouched low in his seat at the counsel table, his movement restricted by handcuffs and leg irons. Despite the restraints and the orange jumpsuit that identified him as just one more accused felon, arrogance leached from the man like body odor.

"We are here today," said Finney, "because the government's key witness in this case was brutally murdered. The prosecution wants to use a prior written statement from the witness at trial, and the defense objects. Does that about sum it up, gentlemen?"

As the lawyers voiced their agreement and discussed procedural issues, Nikki turned her attention to the impossible word puzzle Finney had given her about where certain people sit on a bus given certain parameters. *Arlene never sits next to Bill but will always take a seat beside Carli or Daphne. Daphne always sits in front of either Ella or Carli. If Carli sits next to the window in the second row and Daphne sits across the aisle, then Ella must sit…*

Nikki thought about it for a few seconds, grunted in frustration, and circled choice D. Last time, she had gone with straight Bs, and Finney had accused her of not trying. This time, she would vary her answers.

Finney brought her back to the present with one of his increasingly common coughing fits. He held up his hand to the lawyers, managed a "Hold up a second," then dipped his head and started hacking away. It was a deep and phlegmy cough, and it worried Nikki. A few seconds later, he regained control, though he still wheezed a little as he sucked in air.

Nikki's judge was fifty-nine and starting to show his age, though his lean face still carried vestiges of the sharp and handsome features Nikki had observed on old Bar Association portraits. Finney had lost most of his hair on top, but you hardly noticed the long forehead because the deep-set blue eyes demanded your attention, sparkling with mischief when Finney smiled or slicing you like lasers when he frowned. The eyes were rimmed by thick auburn eyebrows laced, like Finney's hair and long side-burns, with distinguished amounts of gray.

Finney was forever an enigma to Nikki—battle-tested and demanding in the courtroom, but an everyday Joe outside. He wore his hair longer than most men his age, so that it curled out a little at the ends, the only part not flattened into place by an old John Deere cap Finney insisted on wearing outside court. If you ran into Finney on the street, you might guess he was a NASCAR fan, but hardly a judge.

"You okay?" asked Mitchell Taylor as the judge regained his composure and took a big gulp of water.

"Fine, fine," said Finney with a flick of the wrist. But Nikki knew that the coughing spells were increasing in both regularity and intensity. She wanted to strangle the judge for refusing to give up cigars. "Continue," he said.

Mitchell Taylor looked down at his notes and picked up at the precise spot where he had left off. Always prepared. Never flustered. A buttoned-down prosecutor who had recently transferred to Norfolk from Virginia Beach. He would have been near the top of Nikki's hottie list but for the fact that he was happily married.

"The facts for this hearing are essentially undisputed," said Mitchell.

He picked up an enlarged photograph mounted on poster board. "This is Antoine Carter," he said, waving the life-size picture of a face caked in blood. "The coroner says he choked to death on his own blood." Mitchell placed the photo facedown on his counsel table while Landers furiously scribbled notes. Stokes sneered at Mitchell, his lips curling slightly upward with a maddening nonchalance, as if he had a Get Out of Jail Free card.

But Mitchell was a pro, too battle hardened to give the defendant even the satisfaction of a glance. "Marks on the victim's wrists and ankles, and around his chest and neck, led the coroner to conclude that he was bound hand and foot and forced to lie on his back, duct-taped to a table, while blood pooled in his throat and ultimately his lungs."

Now Mitchell unveiled another picture, one that made even Nikki divert her eyes, though she had pretty much seen it all. Finney didn't flinch.

"This is a closeup of the victim, Antoine Carter, with his mouth propped open," said Mitchell. "As you can see, his tongue has been cut out."

The deputy sheriff assigned to the courtroom turned her head, and the court reporter went pale. Only Detective Jenkins, a homicide investigator who had accompanied Mitchell to court in case the judge needed testimony, appeared as unaffected as Finney. Nikki forgot all about where her hypothetical passengers might have been sitting on her hypothetical bus. *Who would do such a thing?*

As if reading her mind, Mitchell grabbed a third blow-up from his counsel table. Even as her stomach tightened, morbid curiosity forced Nikki to keep her eyes glued to the young prosecutor and what he might reveal next. "We believe this killing is gang related. This is a picture of Mr. Carter's chest," Mitchell said, his voice tense with anger. "As you can see, the initials BGD are carved into his skin. The blood that coagulated around these cuts indicates Mr. Carter was still alive when they did this.

"BGD stands for the Black Gangster Disciples," said Mitchell, who firmed his jaw and turned to the defendant. "It's one of the strongest gangs operating in Norfolk right now, and we have reason to believe that the defendant, Terrel Stokes, is its leader." At this Stokes grunted his disapproval, then narrowed his eyes and slowly shook his head at Mitchell, sending a chill up Nikki's spine along with an unmistakable message: Mitchell would be next.

Undeterred, Mitchell turned back toward Finney. "The victim was scheduled to testify against Stokes in the defendant's upcoming drug trial. We had flipped Mr. Carter, promising him we would take his cooperation into account at sentencing. We have a full written confession about his involvement in a drug ring headed by Stokes, and we want to use the confession at trial, since the witness himself is no longer available. That's why we filed this motion *in limine.*"

D. J. Landers rose, arms spread wide. "And we object, Your Honor, because it's classic hearsay and violates the defendant's constitutional right to confront the witnesses."

"Looks like he already did that," said Finney.

"My client was in jail when Carter died," protested Landers. "And the commonwealth doesn't have one shred of evidence that my client was involved in his death. You can't try a man for drug offenses based on written statements from dead witnesses."

"You can when the defendant orders their death," snapped Mitchell, still standing like a marine in front of his counsel table. "You waive your right to confront your witnesses when you kill them—"

"*If* you kill them," interrupted Landers. "Which, of course, didn't happen here." He turned to Mitchell. "You think my client killed your witness? File murder charges."

Mitchell didn't respond, his stare saying what words could not. Nikki knew that Mitchell had been criticized for taking cases too personally. It's what she liked about him—passion.

"You won't indict him for murder, because you don't have any evidence," Landers continued. His air of self-satisfaction curdled Nikki's stomach. "So why don't you spend your time looking for Antoine Carter's killer instead of harassing my client with this baseless drug charge?"

The muscles in Mitchell's neck tightened. "We searched the apartments of other suspected gang members. We found letters Stokes wrote from jail, telling a gang member that Antoine Carter would be testifying for the government. A few days later, Carter's dead. What more do we need?"

"Those letters, written by my client, show that he didn't believe Carter was a threat," Landers explained, his voice even. "They show my client believed that Carter would never cooperate with the government."

"Right," scoffed Mitchell. "The letters go out the week of April 4. The very next week—April 11, to be precise—Carter dies, losing his tongue in the process. What a lucky coincidence for the defendant."

Landers stiffened, fired back a retort, and the insults flew. For the next few minutes, Finney let the lawyers spar themselves out, his chin resting on his hand like a spectator at a chess match.

Finally he banged his gavel. "Gentlemen, that's enough." They both looked up at him, two schoolboys who had been prematurely untangled from a fight, seething to get back at each other.

"Let me see the letters," ordered Finney.

"I object," said Landers, his tanned face flushing.

"On what grounds?" asked Finney.

"They contain impressions of my client about his own lawyer," Landers said, crossing his arms and taking a half step away from his suddenly poisonous client. "Those allegations are untrue, and the letters themselves are privileged communications."

"Oh, come on," Mitchell blurted, obviously sensing blood. "The letters are written by a prisoner and sent to a fellow gangbanger on the outside. How can they possibly be privileged?"

"I'm just saying—," started Landers, but Finney cut him off with a wave.

"Pass 'em up," Finney said. "We'll take a brief recess while I study them. And don't worry, Mr. Landers. I'm not going to form any opinions about you based on what your client says in those letters. I'm perfectly capable of forming those judgments on my own."

"Thank you, Your Honor," said Landers, though Nikki was pretty sure the judge hadn't meant it as a compliment.

Chapter 3

I n the judge's chambers, a messy office that reeked of cigar smoke, Nikki finished her work on the LSAT questions while Finney studied the letters. He took off his reading glasses, rubbed his forehead, and picked up the half-smoked Phillies cigar from his ashtray. Nikki glanced up and frowned her displeasure. She knew he wouldn't light up in front of her, but he still had a nasty habit of chewing on the cigar and spitting little bits and pieces into the trash can.

He cleared some phlegm from his throat and thrust the letters toward her. "Take a look at these," he said, "and let me know what you think."

"I think you ought to flush those cigars."

"About the letters," said Finney.

Nikki rose from the worn leather couch and started toward the desk.

"And let me see your answers," Finney added, pointing to the LSAT questions she had spread out on the coffee table in front of her. "If you get them all right, I'll quit cold turkey."

"Like that's going to happen," she muttered.

They traded documents, and Nikki settled back onto the couch, arranging the letters before her in chronological order. The first one, written in neat block letters from Stokes to a man nicknamed Juice, was dated April 4.

4/4/2006

Juice,

Got to get me a new mouthpiece. Landers did me greasy, wants to plead. What about that piece who repped you last year? What's his price? Landers is just yanking my chain and rippin me off. Paid the man 15, now he's jackin me

for 10 more.

    I ain't no Trump,

    Stokes

Nikki chuckled to herself as she thought about Landers's futile attempt to keep these letters from the court. No wonder. She loved the phrase "did me greasy"—it perfectly described the way Landers practiced law. She turned to the second letter, obviously written the next day.

4/5/2006

Juice,

    Word up that my man Carter's on the G-man witness list. They

say he's ready to snitch. Claim he's a gangbanger with the Black

Gangster Disciples. Ever hear of them? But Carter's ace kool. He won't drop

a dime on nobody. Carter just playin with the Man.

    Keep it real,

    Stokes

The defendant, acting like he'd never heard of the Black Gangster Disciples, obviously had a penchant for sarcasm, thought Nikki. Still, this letter seemed to indicate that Stokes wasn't worried about Carter's testimony, just like Landers claimed. Maybe that's because Stokes knew the Disciples would take care of Carter before he ever made it to the stand.

There was one more letter from Stokes.

4/6/2006 and 4/7/2006

Juice,

    Hey, my man. Bring my old lady by and tell her to bring a crate.

I'm buggin out in here and time is crawlin. BGD had a blanket
party last night for one of the new fish. As shot caller, I
had to break it up and confirm my boy was still breathin.
They punked him good.
    The Peacemaker,
    Stokes

Nikki just shook her head at this one. Even in jail, Stokes was calling the shots, practically chuckling as his boys beat a new inmate within an inch of his life.

The last letter was a return letter from the gangbanger named Juice, obviously intercepted by the deputies at the jail.

4/12/2006

Stokes,
    Business is good. My suit Crankston charges $10k per count. The
man is dirty but real slick. Landers is dirty, period. Your old lady left
V-town last week for a few days. Should be back on Friday. They got
nothin on you, that's why they want to get a deal done. Don't bite.
    Juice

Nikki finished reading the letters and looked up at Finney.

"Well," he said, the cigar dangling out the side of his mouth. He held her LSAT answers in his right hand. "Guess I'll be able to enjoy these babies a little while longer." He licked the end of his cigar and placed it in the ashtray, coughing as he did.

"How bad?" asked Nikki.

"One out of twelve. You would've done better if you had just put the same letter for every question."

Nikki grunted, swallowing a few choice words for the old geezer, and shrugged. "I did that last time. You said I wasn't trying hard enough."

"It's not easy getting *less* than twenty percent right," said Finney. He leaned back in his chair, crossed his legs, and locked his hands behind his head. "What do you think?"

Nikki stacked the letters and placed them back on the judge's desk. "Guilty."

Finney raised an eyebrow.

"It's just like Mitchell said," Nikki insisted, standing in front of the judge's desk. "Stokes doesn't have to order the killing of a witness in plain English. He just has to mention to his gangbangers that one of their own is ratting him out, and they take care of the rest. You've got to allow the written statement into evidence."

"Really?"

"Yep." Nikki stood her ground and crossed her arms. She could see he wasn't buying it, but she was ready to fight for this one.

"So every time an inmate mentions a witness to someone outside the jail, and the witness later dies, we just flush the defendant's right to confront the witness in court?"

"Not every time, Judge. But here you've got proven gang connections and the timing—one week after the letter the witness is dead. And the whole tongue thing."

Finney stood and started putting his robe back on. "You'll make a good prosecutor, Nikki. But I'm not being paid to be a prosecutor. Sometimes a judge has to hold his nose and still make the right ruling, especially when a constitutional right is at stake."

"Judge," protested Nikki, following him out of his office. "You can't be serious. This guy had a gangbanger cut out the man's tongue…"

"All rise," said the deputy as Finney entered the courtroom. Nikki trailed half a step behind, veering toward her seat next to the wall. But first she made one last plea.

"His tongue, Judge. They cut out his tongue."

CHAPTER 4

In a move that surprised Nikki, Judge Finney said he would rule after he asked Detective Jenkins a few questions. He swore the witness in and took him through a series of background questions about the letters. Stokes seemed to be uninterested in the proceedings, glancing around the courtroom and occasionally sneering at the witness. Nikki couldn't believe the judge was even thinking about putting this man back on the street.

"Are you familiar with gang activity in and around the Norfolk area?" Finney asked.

"Very familiar, Judge."

"What can you tell me about the Black Gangster Disciples?"

Jenkins described the criminal activities of the Disciples in a no-nonsense tone that made him eminently believable. Under prompting from Finney, he testified about the dominating presence of the BGDs in the jails throughout the state, including the Norfolk City Jail. Many of their outside gang activities, according to the detective, were directed by leaders presently incarcerated.

"Leaders like Mr. Stokes?" asked Finney.

"Objection," called out Landers.

"Overruled."

"Yes," said the witness. "Leaders like the defendant."

"Now, take a look at that third letter sent by Mr. Stokes," instructed Finney.

While Jenkins studied the handwritten note, the defendant glared at the witness.

"What's the date on top of that letter?"

The detective hesitated. "It actually has two dates: April 6, 2006, and April 7, 2006."

"Does that strike you as unusual?" asked Finney. The judge's tone caught Nikki's attention.

The detective stared at the letter for a moment. "I'm not sure what you mean, Judge."

Finney leaned back in his swivel chair, twirling his glasses. "Well, it seems to me that it's an awful short letter to take two days to write. Maybe—what?—five total lines?"

"I guess so."

"Detective, read that letter into the record. And tell me if it sounds like the kind of letter that was actually written over the course of two days."

" 'Hey, my man. Bring my old lady by and tell her to bring a crate…,'" Jenkins read. As the detective worked his way through the letter, Finney caught Nikki's eye and graced her with a wink.

When Jenkins finished, he looked up at the judge. "Short letter," he said. "Seems to me like it was all written at the same time."

"The same thing I thought when I first read it," said Finney, looking at the defendant. "So I started asking myself, 'What's going on with the dates?' "

At this, Stokes whispered something angrily to Landers. Landers shook his head without looking at his client. In response, Stokes whispered again, angrier than before, jabbing a finger at a legal pad.

"So here's what I want you to do," said Finney. "Start with the first letter and assume that the date is more than just a date. In fact, assume that the date is an encryption key to help you decipher what these letters are really saying."

The detective studied the first letter and looked up at the judge, still confused.

"For example," continued Finney, "just for the fun of it. If the date is 4/4/2006, go to the fourth line of the message and the fourth word of that line and write it down. Then for the next letter, which I believe is dated 4/5/2006, go to the fourth line and write down the fifth word. Then for the last letter, dated 4/6/2006 and 4/7/2006, write down both the sixth and seventh words of the fourth line. Then use the same method on the reply letter. Does that make sense?"

The detective nodded, already working on his task. Landers and Stokes argued in loud whispers, and Nikki could feel a motion for a change in legal counsel coming. Mitchell turned and glanced at Nikki, the glint of victory in his pupils. And Finney, the smartest judge Nikki had ever known, sat impassively watching the detective, as if nothing more were at stake than the answers to an LSAT question.

"Okay," said the detective, working hard to maintain his professional demeanor. "I think I've got it."

"What does it say?" asked Finney.

"We object, Your Honor," said Landers, though Nikki could tell his heart wasn't in it.

"On what grounds?"

"Uh…this is total speculation. And highly prejudicial."

At this, Finney actually grinned. "How do you know it's prejudicial, Counsel? The detective hasn't even read it yet."

Stokes grabbed the arm of Landers, causing the lawyer to bend over so Stokes could unleash another tirade into his reddened ear. Landers shook it off and rose again to face Finney. "We have to assume it is, Your Honor, based on the tone of your questions."

"Overruled," snapped Finney.

Landers sat down.

The detective looked to the judge for permission to proceed.

"Go ahead," said Finney.

"Here's what I get when I apply the methodology you suggested," said the proud detective. "Stokes's letters say: 'Off Carter and confirm.' The reply of Juice, one day after Carter's murder, simply says: 'Done.'"

Finney stroked his chin and studied Stokes and Landers. After a painfully long wait, he spoke into the silence. "Another amazing coincidence, Mr. Landers?" He paused until the silence became uncomfortable. "I'm not only going to allow the confession of Antoine Carter to be submitted as evidence in the drug case, but I'm also going to suggest that Mr. Taylor seek that murder indictment you mentioned earlier."

Stokes suddenly bolted to his feet, shackles and all, causing the deputy to stand up and place a hand on her gun. "I want a new lawyer," the defendant spit out. "One who's not always stoned."

"Sit down!" Finney barked.

Stokes glared at the judge, then flopped back into his seat.

"You'll get a new lawyer," said Finney. "But no more pen pals. I'm ordering the defendant held in solitary confinement pending trial. No mail privileges, no visitation."

Then Finney turned his attention to a crestfallen Landers. "And if I were you, Counsel, I think I'd watch my tongue."

CHAPTER 5

Wow!" Nikki said when she and Finney retreated to his chambers. "How'd you figure that out?" She had grabbed the letters from the judge's bench on her way in and was even now counting the words.

"Elementary, my dear Watson."

"Huh?"

Finney shook his head. "It's Cryptology 101. These inmates all think they're Einsteins, but the code in those letters is as basic as it gets."

Nikki watched as Finney walked over to his bookshelf and pulled down a small hardback with a brown parchmentlike cover and maroon lettering. The cover featured a ghosted picture of Christ wearing a crown of thorns. Finney handed it to Nikki. "Ever see this before?"

The book was entitled *The Cross Examination of Jesus Christ,* written by some guy Nikki had never heard of. She flipped through a few pages. "I don't think so," she said.

"Not many people have." Finney gave her a cockeyed smile, then grabbed his Bible off the corner of his desk. The black leather cover was tattered and well worn. Nikki had caught him reading it on a few occasions.

As the judge searched for the right page, he started in with one of his coughing fits. He turned his head, covered his mouth, and hacked like he might spit his lungs out at any moment. Eventually he stopped coughing and started turning pages again as if nothing had happened. "Did you know that the Old Testament scribes encrypted a few words in the biblical text using a Hebrew substitution code called the *atbash* cipher?"

"Uh, no. But I'm not exactly a Bible scholar," Nikki admitted. "I think I did hear something about Bible codes once, though."

"I'm not talking about that nonsense," said Finney. "Here." He rotated the Bible for Nikki to see. "Jeremiah 25:26. See that word 'Sheshach'?"

Nikki nodded.

"That's really a Hebrew code word for Babel, or Babylon, produced using the *atbash* cipher. Someday I'll show you how it works."

"Thrilling," Nikki mumbled.

The judge put the Bible back on his desk and reached for *The Cross Examination of Jesus Christ.* "I wrote this book," he said, taking it from Nikki. "I used a pen name because a lot of people might think it inappropriate for a sitting judge to be writing a religious book like this." He opened the book to the introduction. "It's tells how Jesus handled the hostile questions of the lawyers, the Pharisees, and ultimately Pontius Pilate. You ought to read it sometime."

Nikki didn't know what to say. She knew that her judge was a religious man, but she had been working for him almost a year and never realized he had written a book. "Sounds interesting."

"Oh, it is." Finney's eyes sparkled with mischief, and he became more animated. "Christ's answers are masterful on so many levels. Every time you think you've got Him figured out, there's another whole layer you're completely missing. So I decided to add an element to the book to symbolize that."

"Of course," said Nikki, trying to remember how they had started talking about this. "Which is?"

"I've encrypted hidden messages in the book," responded Finney. "I figured if the Old Testament scribes could get away with it, so could I. Like this one in the introduction. See these hidden letters?"

Nikki looked at where the judge was pointing. She probably wouldn't have noticed the small letters on her own. But even now, as Finney pointed out the faded images that seemed like part of the page design, it looked like a haphazard jumble of meaningless letters, like trying to figure out who was sitting where on the bus all over again. "I don't get it," she said after enough time had passed so the judge would think she had tried.

Unfortunately, he picked that moment for another coughing spasm. When he finished, his eyes watering, he handed the book back to her. "Figure it out and I'll buy you lunch," he announced.

Don't hold your breath, Nikki thought, though you couldn't really speak that way to a judge. "You're not going to tell me?"

"Nope. I don't give away my secrets. I just wanted you to see this so you'd know why Stokes's method was mere child's play."

Now Nikki was curious. And she had zero chance of figuring it out on her own. "Why would you go to all the trouble to hide these messages in your book and not tell anybody what they mean? What if nobody figures them out?"

"Somebody will." Finney plopped down in his desk chair, looking tired from his coughing fits. He placed his cigar in the ashtray. "John Wesley once said that there are things hidden so deeply in Scripture that future generations will always be drawing out new truths. In some small way, I wanted this book to symbolize that—hidden truths yet to be discovered by future generations."

Nikki paused to think about that, struck by the effort the judge had put into these codes. In some ways the codes were like the judge himself. A family man who never reconciled with his son. An outspoken Christian who wouldn't stop smoking. A puzzle. A walking contradiction. "Really, Judge? That's why you did this?"

"Nah," said Finney. "Actually, I just like puzzles."

CHAPTER 6

The Honorable Lester Madison Banks III did not look so high and mighty as he sat naked in his Jacuzzi, his eyes bugged out with fear at what he saw on the small monitor on the bathroom counter. In fact, to the Assassin, the sixty-six-year-old judicial despot looked more like a prune than a powerful state court judge. Except that the old man's wrinkled skin was pasty white, the only purple coming from his shivering lips and the round Gorbachev birthmark on the front half of His Honor's mostly bald scalp.

"Pronounce the sentence," demanded an anxious voice into the Assassin's earpiece. The Client. Someone the Assassin detested even more than the judge shivering with fear in front of him. A control freak. Consumed by revenge. With only one redeeming quality.

Money. One point two million, to be exact. For a high-risk hit involving a judge, one million dollars. For the privilege of watching via videophone, an extra two hundred thousand.

The Assassin kept his gun leveled at the judge though he knew it was no longer necessary. "Remind him how merciful we're being," the Client's voice continued with a mixture of stridency and delight. "We're sparing his grandchildren and will be executing him in a certifiably humane fashion."

"I'll stick with the script," the Assassin said in return. He should never have allowed this guy to monitor the execution. Even by the Assassin's standards, the Client was bizarre.

"I want to watch him die," the Client had insisted when he first hired the Assassin. He asked to actually come along, as if this were some kind of theme-park ride that he could enjoy while sitting next to the Assassin. The Assassin vetoed the idea but, for the extra cash, agreed to bring along the videophone device that now sat on the bathroom counter, transmitting every moan and grimace from the embattled judge.

Next to the camera sat a small monitor, the sole reason the judge had earlier gone from being demanding and arrogant, even at gunpoint, to being compliant as a whipped puppy. The monitor showed a real-time video of the judge's youngest grandson, sleeping blissfully in his own house, less than half a mile from the judge's home. The young boy was barely distinguishable in a room illuminated only by an Aslan nightlight.

After the Assassin bragged that he had planted an explosive device that could be detonated by remote control (a small but necessary lie), His Honor became very good at following orders.

Banks had disrobed and filled the Jacuzzi with water just as the Assassin instructed. Before climbing in, the judge turned on the bathroom television, located on a custom-designed wooden shelf above the Jacuzzi. The judge seemed to shrink as he slid into the water, the FOX News commentators babbling in the background.

"He looks pitiful," the Client said, as if the Assassin needed a running commentary. Ignoring him, the Assassin recited the indictment against the judge. In a steady monotone, the Assassin reminded the judge of the most egregious mistake of His Honor's celebrated judicial career. It had cost a young woman her life. And now it was time to pay. An eye for an eye. A tooth for a tooth. A life for a life.

He pronounced the old man guilty and asked Judge Banks if he had any final words. But the judge didn't answer, keeping his eyes glued instead to the monitor showing his grandson. The judge seemed to be drawing strength from the image of the boy.

"Not even an apology," sneered the Client.

Which made the Assassin respect the judge, if only a little. But the Assassin still had a job to do.

"Before I carry out the sentence, Your Honor, my client wants me to remind you of your own opinion, twelve years ago, in *State v. Vincent*, when you delivered a stirring defense of the constitutionality of the electric chair. Do you remember that case, Judge?"

His Honor ignored the question.

"You want your grandson to survive this?" the Assassin asked, his voice flat.

Banks nodded, still transfixed by the monitor.

"Then answer the question. Do you remember the case?"

"Yes."

"You ruled that the electric chair was not cruel and unusual, right?"

"That's correct."

"Do you remember the testimony of the doctor hired by Mr. Vincent's lawyers?"

The judge shuddered, perhaps at the thought of the testimony, perhaps at the specter of his own impending death. He took a furtive glance at the Assassin and then turned back to the monitor, breathing sporadically.

"Make him answer," the Client demanded. But the Assassin tuned out the voice in his earpiece.

"The doctor testified that death by electrocution is an extremely violent and painful affair," the Assassin said. "He testified about watching an inmate squirm as he died in the chair, the veins on the inmate's neck standing out like steel bands. He said the temperature of the brain would have approached the boiling point of water and that when the coroner performed the post-electrocution autopsy, the liver was so hot it couldn't be touched by human hands. Do you remember all that, Judge?"

His Honor gave the slightest, smallest nod. The imperial power of the bench reduced to this—a shriveled and trembling old man.

"How did you rule, Judge?"

Silence. But the Assassin didn't have time to wait him out.

"How did you rule?" he asked more sharply.

"I rejected the defendant's motion."

The Assassin took a step toward the television. Two days ago he had broken into Banks's home and replaced the GFCI outlet with a faulty one that wouldn't trip the circuit when the water seeped into the high-voltage block on the back of the picture tube. Thirty thousand volts. He had replaced a few other outlets as well, so it would look like a case of faulty wiring, and he loosened the screws on the wooden brace supporting the television shelf to complete the accident scenario.

All of this, he knew, would be considered entirely too coincidental for the city's homicide detectives. But the Assassin believed in redundancy— a belt *and* suspenders approach—so he left two false leads. The detectives would pride themselves in ruling out an accidental death and suspecting foul play. But then they would immediately focus their investigation on the La Familia gang, concluding that this was a retaliatory strike for the contemptuous way Banks had sentenced a gang leader to death just last week. It was retaliatory, all right. But who would suspect an eight-year-old case?

An eye for an eye. Wait until a judge crosses a gang noted for violence and you can literally get away with murder.

The Assassin placed his free hand on top of the television and stared down at the judge. "You still believe the electric chair is not cruel and unusual?"

"Don't hurt my grandson. Please."

The Assassin felt a small pang of sympathy but quickly extinguished it. He had learned to suppress every emotion. "I've got no desire to harm the boy, Judge. Provided you're ready to face your death sentence like a man."

"Don't tell him that," the Client hissed into the earpiece. "That's not in the script. He needs to die wondering."

"You know, Judge," the Assassin continued, "they say that when Jesse Tafero was executed in Florida, witnesses saw him clench his fists and convulse for about four minutes while smoke and sparks shot out of his death mask. Something about the sponges on his head not being properly placed." There was more, but the Assassin was suddenly weary of this scripted approach to the old man's death. The Client was sick. The judge just needed to die.

"Any last words?" asked the Assassin. He placed his hand firmly on top of the television, preparing to send it and the shelf crashing into the Jacuzzi.

"What are you doing?" the Client asked. "That's not the end."

Without warning, the judge gasped and clutched at his chest. His eyes went wide as he convulsed and jerked back in the Jacuzzi, fighting for air. "Push the television!" the Client barked. "Push the television!"

But the Assassin pressed the End Call button on his cell phone, turned his back on the thrashing judge, and walked calmly over to the bathroom counter. He powered down the video monitor of the judge's grandson and the video feed for the Client. When he looked back over his shoulder, the judge had stopped moving, slipping peacefully down the side of the Jacuzzi, all but his head and shoulders submerged in the water.

A heart attack. Fate had intervened and spared the judge the electric chair. The La Familia scapegoat wouldn't be necessary. The Assassin began the tedious process of sanitizing the crime scene, focusing on the work at hand while trying to keep the guilt and emotions at bay. But the Assassin knew the emotions would eventually catch up with him. Only Hollywood hit men feel no remorse. In real life, the emotions eventually bubble to the surface.

Like the last job. A true family man. Two days after the killing, the nightmares started. The Assassin almost lost his mind, saved by prescription drugs and a new job that demanded total focus. This one.

Now, to preserve his sanity, he would immediately begin focusing on the precision planning required for the next job. One last high-profile hit and another big payday. Afterward, he could put this behind him forever. It was only fitting that his final assignment would be the most complicated and daring of his entire career, making Judge Banks's carefully orchestrated death seem like child's play. The elaborate machinery of death for the Assassin's final unsuspecting victim was already well under construction.

CHAPTER 7

Oliver Finney felt ridiculous. A grown man, sitting in a big New York conference room straight off the set of *The Apprentice*. He was the only one wearing a sports coat and tie; these television folks all dressed like a bunch of burglars—black on black. At the time he applied for a slot on *Faith on Trial,* it had seemed like a good idea. But he never really dreamed he'd be sitting here...

"We really like the idea of a judge on this show representing the Christian faith," said the man in the middle on the opposite side of the table. In Finney's mind the guy fit to a T the stereotype for a director—like maybe this guy had himself been selected by central casting. The man pulled his gray hair back in a ponytail and looked over wire-rimmed glasses at Finney. He had on a ratty black T-shirt that covered a soft little gut but exposed two skinny arms and one forearm tattoo. He wore a left earring so everybody would know he wasn't completely out of touch with the younger culture. The others in the room all nodded vigorously when he spoke, as if their jobs depended on it.

"Christians are always complaining about the judges who run this country," the director continued. What was his name? Something McCormack—Bruce or Barry or one of those B names—but a little different. Finney had never been good with names. "Now they'll be cheering for one."

The room became quiet for a moment as the production team considered the delicious irony they were about to foist on Christians everywhere. A young woman at the end of the table practically smacked her lips while McCormack finished shuffling through Finney's application. He put the papers down and stared at Finney for a moment—a director's feeble attempt at intimidation, Finney supposed.

"You're my first choice, Judge. But I've got a couple of concerns. My first has to do with your reasons for being on this show. Your application is not entirely clear."

"Other than a million dollars for my favorite charity?" Finney asked. But they both knew that wasn't the reason.

"Yes. Other than that."

Finney slid forward in his seat. The situation called for blunt honesty, his specialty. "When you sit where I sit and see what I see, you get concerned about the next generation." Finney surveyed the group, practically daring somebody to give him one of those patronizing media-elite smirks, the kind that try to make you feel stupid for defending traditional values. "Gang rapes. Crack heads. Last week I sentenced a fifteen-year-old kid for stabbing another kid thirty-seven times with a Phillips head screwdriver. The victim was fourteen."

Finney let out an exasperated breath. Even talking about this could be depressing, the relentless march of wasted lives. "You know how many of the kids that I've sentenced in the past two months have fathers living at home?" he asked McCormack.

The director shook his head. "Not many?"

"Try none," said Finney. "Not one time did I have a father come to court and stand up for these fifteen- and sixteen-year-old kids. So what do I do? Hand down long prison sentences. Warehouse more and more of these kids in places where they learn how to become career criminals. Somehow we've got to break this chain. Somehow we've got to reach these kids. Maybe a few of them will watch this show. God knows, most of them will never set foot in church."

Finney realized he had silenced the room with his sanctimonious lecture, but he didn't care. McCormack had asked the question. Finney was too old and too sick to worry about what other people might think.

McCormack jotted a few notes while the silence hung in the air. "Fair enough," he said when he had finished. "Which leads me to the second issue." He paused, apparently at a loss about how best to phrase this. "It says here you've got metastatic lung cancer."

The "c" word sucked the remaining air out of the room. Though they all knew the facts, McCormack's saying it out loud made the youngsters stare at Finney as if he were already a ghost.

So Finney decided it was time to loosen things up a little. The last several months had taught him how awkward it could be for healthy people to be around a cancer patient. "Oh," Finney said, glancing around, "I must have the wrong show. I didn't know I'd stumbled into the WWE studio."

Nobody grinned. "It's not championship wrestling," said McCormack matter-of-factly, "but it's not *Jeopardy!* either. *Faith on Trial* will test you spiritually, intellectually, emotionally"—he paused so the point would not be lost on Finney—"and physically."

"Such as?"

"You know I can't provide details."

Finney was tired of playing games. He wasn't accustomed to meetings he didn't control. And he felt another coughing fit coming on.

"Is it something a fifty-nine-year-old cancer patient can do or not?" he asked.

The director hesitated for a second or two, just long enough to convey his concern. "I think so."

"Then where do I sign?"

McCormack looked to his left and his right. Nobody registered an objection. "Congratulations, Judge Finney," he said, sliding a sheaf of papers across the table. "It looks like the future of Christianity is resting squarely on your shoulders."

"Thanks," said Finney, though the word was cut short by a cough. He put his fist over his mouth and hacked away while the others watched wide eyed as if he might kick the bucket at any minute.

"I think it's getting better," Finney said.

The paperwork was preposterous. According to the documents, Finney released the show, the producers, and anybody associated with the enterprise from any and all claims of whatsoever kind or nature. There was a full page listing all the dire consequences that would develop, including lawsuits for injunctions and a two-million-dollar liquidated damages payment, if the contestants divulged any information about the show's results before all of the episodes had aired.

The release went on for pages, explaining all the dangers facing the participants and all the reasons they couldn't sue the show—not for injury or death or fraud or deception or breach of contract or loss of consortium. Finney laughed out loud at the last one. "Loss of consortium" would be the loss of a spouse's companionship and physical affections due to an injury. Some New York lawyer obviously had too much time on his hands. Finney had been a widower for several years.

"Is this a reality show or a POW camp?" Finney asked.

"Lawyers," McCormack said as if that explained everything.

Finney skimmed quickly through the boilerplate, content in the knowledge that most of this stuff wouldn't hold up in court anyway. He flipped to the end and found the place for his signature.

"You don't want to read it?" asked McCormack.

"I know what it says," Finney responded. Actually, he was rushing to sign because he felt yet another coughing spell coming on. "Basically, I'm signing my life away."

McCormack's mouth formed a thin line, and he didn't say a word. He didn't have to. Finney had spent the last twenty years reading the eyes of witnesses. Compared to the cons Finney dealt with on a daily basis, McCormack was an open book.

You have no idea, McCormack was saying.

CHAPTER 8

We lost the rabbi?" Cameron Murphy repeated in disbelief. The executive producer of *Faith on Trial* ran his fingers through close-cropped brown hair, then subconsciously rubbed the stubble of his beard. "How can we lose a rabbi?" He stood and shook his head. "What else can we mess up? This is our last preproduction meeting, folks. We've got one week. One week!" He cursed through clenched teeth.

Everyone around the table except Bryce McCormack winced. Bryce had known Murphy too well for too long. He had known the producer would explode when he learned the news. In fact, Bryce had secretly counted down the seconds as the casting assistant stammered through the news. *Liftoff,* he thought just as Murphy exploded.

Halfway down the conference table, the assistant casting director spoke softly. "The Anti-Defamation League got to him," she said. "They've been making a lot of noise about how inappropriate this show is—fosters competition and hate among religions, the Jews have suffered enough from religious bigotry, that type of thing. Rabbi Demsky wanted some assurances we couldn't give him."

"Like what?" sputtered Murphy. "What was he asking?"

The young woman fumbled through her notes for a second. McCormack thought about bailing her out but decided against it. If she planned on being the lead director someday, she'd have to learn how to take the heat. "Not allowing the contestants to denigrate one another's faiths. No proselytizing people of other faiths. Plus, he wanted a complete dossier on the Muslim contestant—"

Murphy strung together a creative string of curse words and then apparently remembered that a fair number of the folks around the table were Jewish. He shook his head and stood to get a refill on his coffee. "Why didn't he just ask to direct the show? We could have given him Bryce's job." Murphy reached the counter and poured himself a cup. "This is reality TV, not a scholarly symposium at the Guggenheim."

Murphy returned to his seat without further profanity (a minor miracle) and turned to the assistant casting director again. "Who's the backup?"

"Rabbi David Cohen," the woman said hopefully. She passed a file down the table to Murphy. "Rabbinical studies at Hebrew University. Law degree from Columbia."

"And how do we know the Anti-Defamation League won't get to him?"

"We don't know for sure. But he doesn't seem the type to be intimidated by anybody."

Murphy took a sip of black coffee and glanced through the file. "I remember this guy," he said tersely. "Too old. We've already got the judge and that Buddha dude. We don't need another old guy." He shot a look at Bryce, who stared back over wire-rimmed glasses. Bryce was two years older but hadn't aged as well as Murphy, a fact that Murphy brought up whenever possible. Unlike Murphy, Bryce let nature take its course—no hair color, no plastic surgery, no LASIK surgery. The cumulative effects cost him the appearance of ten years. "No offense, McCormack."

Bryce McCormack showed Murphy his middle finger. He was one of the few folks around the table who could get away with it.

The assistant slid another file toward Murphy. "Levi Katz is thirty-three and an up-and-comer in a big New York law firm. A little weak on religious studies but very camera friendly."

Camera friendly. A euphemism for young and good looking, words that nobody used for fear of getting sued. Except for Murphy. After all, he was the producer. Laws for mere mortals didn't apply to him. Murphy glanced at the young Levi Katz's picture.

"What'd you think of this guy?" he asked Bryce.

"Orthodox Jew," Bryce said, sounding bored. "Serious about his faith. I don't remember what skeletons he had in his closet."

Murphy checked the file. "Fooled around on his wife," Murphy said. "Don't we already have one of those?"

Bryce hitched a shoulder. "It could still serve its purpose."

Murphy didn't look convinced. "What kind of medical condition does this Levi Katz have?" he asked, flipping through the file again. "All I see in here is a blood condition he's taking medication for. How does that qualify as life threatening?"

This time the casting assistant was barely audible. "That's all he's got, Mr. Murphy."

Murphy sighed, a signal that these people could never get anything right. "That won't work," he barked. "A life-threatening medical condition—we've had that requirement in place from day one."

The table grew silent. The casting crew were apparently fresh out of Jewish candidates with life-threatening medical conditions; theological training, a shameful secret, and if possible, a legal background.

For the next half hour, they discussed whether to do the show with three older contestants or to conduct an expedited search for a suitable replacement. It was Bryce McCormack who finally came up with an idea that could turn this setback into ratings gold. The *Passion* principle, he called it—a lesson from the extraordinary success of *The Passion of the Christ.* "Embrace the controversy," he lectured. "Tell the world that we won't back down. We believe in a free marketplace of religion with no rules that would interfere with a robust debate. But just to show what great egalitarians we are, we will agree to give Rabbi Demsky five full minutes on our first show to tell the world why they shouldn't watch us."

Heads turned toward McCormack as if he'd lost his mind. Who had ever heard of such a thing? But they all had to admit that embracing the controversy had worked for Mel Gibson.

Before the meeting was over, they agreed to recommend it to the suits. "I hope you know what you're doing," Murphy said to Bryce after the others had dispersed.

"Controversy," said Bryce, smiling like a madman, "is a reality show's best friend."

∞

The Assassin checked and rechecked the final punch list Friday night. Professional killers don't operate on emotion or instinct. They plan. Then they check every detail of the plan. Twice. Then they execute, pushing aside every emotion. Otherwise, they don't survive.

He had survived the last job better than most others in his profession would have. The coroner had ruled the death accidental. The Assassin had even thought about going to the funeral, but he knew investigators would be there surveying the crowd. The mental images of the old man croaking in the Jacuzzi had lasted only a few weeks. Soon the Assassin was consumed with planning his next job, sweating over every detail and developing backup plans for every contingency.

That's why the Assassin's services didn't come cheap. The down payment for the *Faith on Trial* job had already been confirmed. He would get five hundred thousand dollars up front, wired to an offshore bank. The Assassin would transfer the funds at least three times before they reached their final destination. Another two hundred thousand would come once the Assassin reached the island. The rest of the money—eight hundred thousand—would be paid after the successful hit.

The total of one-point-five million dollars, though it might sound like a lot of money to most people, was actually low for a job like this. High exposure meant high risk. And what could generate more exposure than death on a high-profile reality show? A federal investigation would follow. After the job, the Assassin would have to undergo a complete makeover—nose, chin, eyes, hair, weight, everything. Plus, the expenses would be substantial.

But the Assassin wasn't complaining about his fee. After all, one-point-five million dollars was more than the prize money for the winner's charity of choice.

The Assassin would earn every penny.

PART 2

CONTESTANTS

Strive mightily, but eat
and drink as friends.
—SHAKESPEARE

No wise combatant underestimates
their antagonist.
—JOHANN WOLFGANG VON GOETHE

CHAPTER 9

At least the show is transporting us in style, Finney thought. He climbed on board the network's Gulfstream IV with the other *Faith on Trial* contestants, preparing to leave Teterboro Airport in New Jersey for a top-secret set location that the producers took great pains to conceal. Cameron Murphy joined them a few minutes later.

He introduced himself to the contestants and collected watches, cell phones, computers, and PDAs. He cleared his throat and made a few curious announcements.

"You've got a long flight ahead of you, so relax and get some sleep," he said, looking from one contestant to the next. "You're going to need it.

"We'll explain the official rules of the game when we're on location, during our first day of shooting, which is when the game starts. However, from this point on, pretty much everything you do or say will be recorded on camera. You need to wear your microphones at all times, except when you're sleeping or in the bathroom." As Murphy spoke, a couple of cameras were already running, one focused on him and one scanning the contestants. "Everything we catch on film is fair game for the show. And I do mean *everything*."

At this, Murphy looked at the younger contestants, including a young female scientist named Victoria Kline. She had introduced herself to Finney with a firm handshake and a hard gaze. Apparently, Murphy felt no need to lecture Finney about extracurricular activity.

"While we're shooting, you'll be prohibited from interacting with camera or audio crews or your director, Bryce McCormack, or myself. It will feel awkward at first, but after a while, you'll get used to ignoring us and you'll feel like the cameras are not even there."

Murphy hesitated for a moment, as if he wasn't sure how to phrase this next part. "As you know, you'll be required to defend your faith over the next two weeks, and I think all of you will be very persuasive. But you need to know that *Faith on Trial* is not just about defending your faith; it's also about living your faith under the most stressful circumstances imaginable. So if you're not ready to do that…this is your last chance to opt out."

None of the contestants moved, including Finney. He knew how reality shows worked. He would be ready for anything they threw at him.

"I'm scheduled to leave on another plane a little later, so I'll see you on location," Murphy said. "I'm not going to ask if you've got questions because I know you've got a ton of questions I can't answer. That's something you'll just have to get used to."

The man had an arrogance that Finney didn't like. What was it with these TV people? A cocky producer. A surly director. And Finney thought lawyers were bad!

Murphy turned toward the door, but Finney blurted out his question anyway. "Is this a nonsmoking flight?"

Victoria groaned and the others looked at Finney as if he'd just proposed a suicide mission.

"Yes, Judge Finney. I'm afraid it is."

∽

At forty-one thousand feet, Finney met his match in the person of the young man sitting across from him—Skyler Hadji, or Swami Skyler Hadji, as the kid called himself. Finney almost laughed when they first shook hands. The guy couldn't have been a day over thirty. With his shaggy blond hair, light blue eyes, slender build, and serious tan, the "Swami" had California surfer dude written all over him.

"I'm not a real swami," he confessed almost in a whisper. "It's just a nickname my friends gave me."

Turns out the Swami was the chosen advocate for Hinduism, a passionate convert who embraced the faith after his acting career hit the rocks. He legally changed his name and traveled to India for two years to study with a leader of the Bhakti sect of Hinduism, then returned to California enlightened and focused. He attended the University of Southern California Law School and graduated near the top of his class. His goal, he said, was to represent the workers in India being abused by corporate America. As soon as he won this reality show.

After a few hours of boredom on the flight, the Swami suggested a few hands of Texas hold 'em. He talked two cameramen into playing and, after the other contestants refused, Judge Finney as well.

A half hour later, the chips were piled high in front of the Swami, who always seemed to know just when to hold and when to bet. Finney started chewing on the stub of a cigar, but it was apparently no match for the Swami's serious card karma, as he called it. Though Finney was losing, he couldn't help but like this kid. The other contestants seemed to be taking themselves seriously, but the Swami was obviously intent on going with the flow.

"All but one," said Finney as he pushed a large pile of chips to the middle of the table. The two cameramen each raised an eyebrow and folded, but the Swami barely moved. He closed his eyes, cards held in front of him, and hummed in a low voice. He uttered Vishnu's name a few times—something he had done on every major hand ("You ought to try it, Judge O")—and then opened his eyes to glance at Finney and the cameraman standing behind Finney, one of two who had been filming the entire game.

The Swami smiled and started counting Finney's chips. "I'll call," he said, shoving a big pile of his own chips to the middle of the table, "and raise you one." Finney flicked his last chip in as well. The only reason he had held it back in the first place was so that the Swami would have to reveal his cards first. It would make the look on the kid's face that much sweeter.

Finney liked his chances. There were five cards showing on the table: two aces, a jack, a ten and a deuce. In his hand Finney held another ten and a useless six, meaning that the Swami would have to beat two pairs—aces over tens—or lose the biggest hand of the night.

The Swami laid down the cards in his hand—two *queens*. His aces and queens were more than a match for Finney's hand. The Swami raised an eyebrow and shrugged. "You've been a good sport, Judge O."

But before Finney could reveal his own hand, he started coughing. He pulled the cigar out of his mouth and placed it on the table, covering his mouth with his free hand as he turned his head and hacked. His other hand, the one holding his cards, dropped down near his lap.

"You okay?" the Swami asked. "I'm not real good at CPR."

"Fine, fine," said Finney as he brought the coughing under control. He cleared his throat a few times. "Where were we?"

The Swami pointed to the table. "You were just about to concede defeat, Judge O."

"Oh yeah," said Finney. He laid down the cards in his hand. An ace and a ten! A miraculous full house. The useless six was nowhere in sight.

"Whoa," said one of the cameramen.

"Nice play, Judge O," said the Swami. Finney had just outcheated the Swami, and the Swami knew it. But the Swami's face gave nothing away, not even a flicker of surprise or annoyance.

As the Swami started shuffling for the next hand, Finney smiled and 'fessed up. "I can't take your money," he said, pulling the six of hearts from under his leg and placing it on the table. "When I figured out that you were looking into that camera over my shoulder and reading my cards, I slipped an ace out of the deck and waited for just the right hand."

The Swami matched Judge Finney's smile with his own, a much brighter smile with the perfectly aligned teeth of an actor. "I know," said the Swami. "You pulled it out four hands ago."

Finney tried not to show his own surprise. And it was at that moment, looking directly into the Swami's eyes, that Judge Oliver G. Finney knew he would be up against a formidable opponent in the days ahead.

"I was still planning on making a little comeback, Judge O, before we called it a day."

Then, still smiling, the Swami reached down next to his own leg and placed a pair of kings on the table.

"Whoa," said the cameraman again.

"Sometimes Vishnu needs a little help," explained the Swami.

CHAPTER 10

Though he had plenty of time, Finney had less luck getting to know the other contestants. They were not exactly the kind of folks you'd invite to a cocktail party. The Muslim advocate, Kareem Hasaan, seemed determined not to let friendship get in the way of victory. It appeared to Finney that the show's producers had intentionally played into the stereotype of the combative and foreboding Muslim. Kareem was the largest of the five contestants, a good two or three inches taller than Finney, with ripped muscles that made his black T-shirt look like a Batman costume. Finney guessed the man was about thirty-five, with thick and curly black hair and the dark features of the Lebanese—the identity of his native country was one of the few things Kareem had disclosed during the plane ride.

"Isn't that where the Hezbollah are from?" whispered the Swami.

But the other thing Finney learned about Kareem didn't seem to fit the stereotype. He described himself as a "human-rights lawyer," representing clients who had been discriminated against, including criminal defendants. A Muslim human-rights lawyer. It made about as much sense as a cigar-smoking judge representing Christianity.

If Hasaan won the award for intensity, Dr. Victoria Kline won the prize for aloofness.

"What religion do you represent?" asked Finney.

"None," replied Dr. Kline.

Finney waited for further elaboration but none came. "All right then," said Finney. "Wonder what movie they're showing on this flight?"

"I'm a scientist, Judge Finney," Kline replied. "I'll be advocating the position of science, not religion."

"Didn't know they were mutually exclusive." Finney said it with a smile, but a thin one.

"Let's leave the advocacy for the show, shall we?" Kline asked.

"It's a good thing she's pretty," the Swami whispered later. " 'Cause she doesn't stand a chance at Miss Congeniality."

The final contestant seemed to fit the mold of his religion better than anyone else. Dr. Hokoji Ando, a bald Asian with heavy glasses, couldn't have been more than five foot six. "A pint-sized Buddha," according to the Swami, who claimed he'd never seen a Buddhist priest so thin. Though Ando walked with a distinct limp, he still managed to carry himself with a soft-spoken dignity that oozed wisdom. He was the one person on the show older than Finney, though Finney would have bet his life savings on the fact that Ando would live longer. *Those Eastern guys never smoke, and they eat all that seaweed,* thought Finney. Ando could live to be a hundred.

Most of the trip, Dr. Ando sat alone and meditated.

Not to be outdone, Finney stared out the window and prayed. He prayed for God's will in this game—a noble prayer but also one he knew would mean victory for his cause. When he finished praying, Finney pondered again his reasons for doing this. The whole experience still seemed so surreal. But he was committed now and knew there was no turning back.

What he had said to McCormack and the others was true—Finney hoped this show might be a vehicle to reach a few members of the next generation. But he had other motivations as well. Part of it was the intrigue. Finney liked nothing better than the competition of a challenging intellectual problem, and what could beat this? But it was more than that. Finney was tired of seeing Christianity represented by those who gave Jesus a bad name. Screaming televangelists. Judgmental legalists. Uncommitted believers who shirked the tough sayings of Christ. He believed a reformed lawyer-turned-judge like himself could do better—or at least no worse.

More important still was the updated diagnosis he'd received just a month ago. The lung cancer had metastasized to his liver. It was, Finney knew, a death sentence with no appeal. "You have six months at the outside," his doctor said. "Maybe a year with the right kind of chemo." But Finney passed on the chemo. He wanted to make the last six months count. And that's what was really driving this; that's why he was here.

The pilot interrupted Finney's thoughts with an announcement: "Fasten your seat belts and draw your window shades." The Gulfstream was about to begin its descent. The contestants, explained the pilot, were not supposed to know where the plane was landing.

After a smooth touchdown, the pilot asked the contestants to stay seated until they received further instructions. A few minutes later, Murphy and his production crew boarded the plane. Murphy surveyed the five contestants, obviously relishing the fact that he knew what would happen next and they had no idea. Finney decided he might as well get used to it.

"I hope you had a comfortable flight," Murphy said. "Thanks for your patience. We are almost to our destination."

In his hand Murphy held several black blindfolds. He gave one to each contestant. "The location of our set needs to remain undisclosed for a number of reasons. So you'll need to put these on until we arrive."

Finney took a blindfold from the producer and felt stupid. He had signed up for a sophisticated reality show analyzing the world's great religions, not pin the tail on the donkey.

"Cool," said the Swami, snapping his on.

Kareem Hasaan frowned and turned the blindfold over in his hands as if he might quit on the spot. "Is this really necessary?" the civil-rights attorney asked, his eyes clouding over.

"I'm afraid so," said Murphy with as much authority as possible. He probably didn't expect a contestant uprising quite so early. "We'll make sure your luggage arrives safely on the island with you."

Kareem looked at the other contestants and then at Finney. Finney shrugged and pulled the elastic over his head.

"Do we get a last cigarette?" the Swami wanted to know.

Murphy thanked the contestants for their cooperation, and then some assistants helped Finney down the steps of the Gulfstream and onto the paved runway. Finney tried to look out the bottom of the mask but could see nothing. He felt the hot and sticky air of some kind of tropical island—no surprise there. The show's producers had told them to dress casually for the trip and said that the outside temperatures could reach the nineties. It felt to Finney, who was wearing jeans, a T-shirt, and his John Deere cap, as if they had underestimated by twenty degrees.

"We're going right over this way," someone said, pulling Finney along. The humid tropical air smelled like jet fuel. Unknown persons loaded Finney onto an aircraft and placed him in a seat next to someone who used too much aftershave.

"Can we take these off now?" he heard Kareem ask.

The answer, in a deep voice that Finney hadn't heard before, was a gruff "No. We'll tell you when to take them off."

Finney's seat started rumbling as an aircraft engine fired up, and he heard the whir of helicopter blades overhead. The temptation to remove his blindfold was nearly overwhelming, but Finney decided to be a good soldier and leave it on. Before long, he could feel the helicopter rising into the air.

"This is stupid," said Kareem loud enough to be heard over the roar of blades and engine. But since nobody joined in the complaining, he didn't say another word the rest of the trip.

Finney estimated that the trip took less than thirty minutes before the helicopter landed. Somebody helped Finney off the helicopter and whisked him away from the bird. This climate seemed identical to that of the last stop, perhaps a few degrees cooler. Finney felt a strong blast of wind as the helicopter took off again and then listened intently as it retreated into the distance.

The stillness engulfed him. For a moment it felt as if Finney were all alone in the warm island breeze. The sounds reminded him of the Virginia Beach inlets on a quiet summer night—the chirping of some kind of cricket, the faint rhythm of ocean waves marching to the shore, the wind rustling through the trees.

"You can remove the masks now."

Finney's eyes adjusted quickly to the light as he gaped at his new environs. Blue sky. The beautiful green hue of the ocean. White sand and palm trees a few hundred yards down the hill from the landing pad.

"Awesome!" exclaimed the Swami. "This place rocks!"

Even Kareem let a small smile crease his lips.

"Welcome to Paradise Island," said their slender host, a woman whom Finney had met before leaving New Jersey. Her name was Tammy something or other. Or it might have been Jamie; he couldn't remember. She had on a short skirt and a low-cut blouse—a sure sign that the producers intended on using this piece in the first program. Even taking into account the well-known fact that television tended to add ten pounds to a person's physique, Finney thought their host could stand to put on a few pounds and would still look just fine. A woman's collarbone should not stick out that much, in Finney's humble opinion.

Sure enough, the cameras whirred away, recording the contestants' reactions. Only Dr. Ando seemed not to be excited. He looked around with the same level of detachment you might expect from a Gold Medallion traveler surveying another Holiday Inn hotel room.

"I hope you enjoy your stay here over the next two weeks," said their host.

"What's her name again?" Finney whispered to the Swami.

"Tammy," said the Swami without taking his eyes off the woman. "Awesome name."

The director shot Finney and the Swami the same look Finney used when people whispered in court.

But Tammy didn't seem to notice. "As you know, you've each been selected—all except one of you, that is—because of your firm commitment to your faith. The nation will be watching to see how your faith

stacks up when you encounter"—she paused like an amateur actress trying to manufacture drama—"trouble in paradise."

Finney thought the line was cheesy, but what did he know about television production? He did know that this moment was staged, and he
hated to ruin it, but he just couldn't help himself. When you've got to
cough… He tried swallowing it and choking it down, but that only made
his face red and made the urge overwhelming.

He cleared his throat, turned his head and hacked away, spitting up
phlegm in the process. When he stopped, all eyes and most cameras were
trained on him.

"Allergies," he said.

"Let's roll that one again," said McCormack with no small amount of
annoyance in his voice. "Would you guys mind putting your blindfolds
back on?"

❦

It took them four takes just to get the opening scene right, and Bryce
McCormack was ready to pull his hair out, long gray strand by long gray
strand. Between Finney, who always picked the worst possible moment to
cough, and Tammy, who overdramatized every line, the cast would turn
Paradise Island into a director's worst nightmare. There were naturals in
the acting business; these folks were not among them.

Tammy had been Murphy's choice, and Bryce didn't have the heart or
the will to veto her. She had originally garnered her fifteen minutes of
fame as a contestant on the fourth season of *The Bachelorette*. Within six
months, the romance that budded on that show fell apart, and Murphy
decided to give her a second shot at the spotlight. "A great gimmick," he
told Bryce, "a reality-show contestant hosting another reality show."

It sounded clever at the time. But they had both been regretting it
ever since. Next time, Bryce would insist on hiring a professional.

CHAPTER 11

The next hour consisted of the Paradise tour, as Murphy dubbed it. The property consisted of several buildings, all nestled around a picturesque cove with some of the clearest ocean water Finney had ever seen. He had spent most of his adult life sailing the waters around Tidewater, Virginia, so the ocean was nothing new. But comparing the Atlantic at Virginia Beach to this body of water was like comparing his dingy Norfolk courtroom to the U.S. Supreme Court.

This was the ocean as God had originally colored it—translucent green, a color Finney had seen only on postcards. The sand along the half-mile stretch of beach was pure white, with loungers and a large Hobie Cat sailboat calling Finney's name. Two double-seated Wave Runners and a surf kayak sat next to the Hobie.

"There's a Hobie Cat, if you like to sail, as well as snorkeling gear and a kayak," Murphy said, pointing toward the shed at the end of the beach. "The snorkeling fins, masks, and life jackets are inside the shed. The kayak paddle is right next to the kayak. For safety reasons, please stay inside this large cove if you sail or kayak. The Wave Runners are reserved for our security guards."

The Swami groaned about not being able to use the Wave Runners, but the tour continued. A sidewalk and a manicured lawn connected the beach area to the main building, which contained two floors of condo units—about forty in all, by Finney's estimation. Each contestant would have his or her own condo. Pink and yellow flowers in full bloom bordered the path. The whole island was lush, its rolling volcanic hills covered in dark-green vegetation. This little resort was the only sign of civilization as far as Finney could see.

He had expected more primitive accommodations, the kind you see on *Survivor.* But this stuff was all first class—more like a converted five-star resort.

"Is this some kind of vacation property?" Finney asked.

"Like Tammy said, it's paradise," Murphy replied. "And that's about all we can tell you."

A small but stately restaurant—the Paradise View—was built on a rocky ledge that overlooked the cove. "This is the mess hall," quipped Murphy. The sun streamed through the floor-to-ceiling windows on the ocean side, and Finney could only imagine how nice this place would be at sunset in a few hours, with white linen covering the tables and the chandelier providing dim interior light.

The only place that didn't have a view was a large ballroom in the main building that the producers had converted into a library. It now had a large conference table in the middle, a few comfortable chairs and reading lamps spread around, and rows upon rows of bookshelves. Fittingly enough, it smelled musty. "We've collected nearly five thousand books on the major world religions," Murphy said proudly. "Even a few authored by the folks in this room."

Finney wondered if they had his book. He had mentioned it during his first full-blown interview when McCormack and a film crew came to Norfolk to see how well the judge performed on camera.

The centerpiece of the resort was a large stone-and-masonry building with a Spanish-tile roof and two impressive archways on the front porch. The interior smelled like freshly cut lumber and varnish. Finney guessed that, a few weeks ago, the building might have been some kind of chapel. For the next two weeks, it would serve as the Paradise Courthouse.

"Dinner will be waiting for each of you in your condos," instructed Murphy. "Our camera crews will, of course, be following you, so feel free to engage in any type of religious ceremonies that might be appropriate before or after you eat. We will need you back at the courthouse in two hours." He reached into his backpack and returned everyone's watch.

"We have reset your watches so that we're all on Paradise Island time," he explained. "You need to be back here at 9:00 p.m. sharp. Tammy will be explaining the rules, and you will be getting your first assignment on camera. So dress appropriately."

On the way to his condo, Finney fell in step beside Dr. Kline. She looked like she was born for island life—her sunglasses smacked of island cool, and she had piled her blond hair on top of her head, exposing her perfectly tanned neck. Finney, on the other hand, was already sweating. "Where do you think we are, Doctor?" he asked, not loud enough for the others to hear.

"I don't know. We were blindfolded, remember?"

Two weeks of this, thought Finney. "Yeah, but you must have a guess. I'll tell you what." Finney made a show of glancing around. They were a few steps ahead of the others. Dr. Kline hadn't seemed to notice that Ando had a hard time keeping up. The cameramen were carrying their cameras at their sides. "You tell me what *you* think, and I'll give you *my* guess."

Dr. Kline sighed. "All right. Based on the white sand beaches, palm trees, sea grape trees, cacti, agave, and coral reefs as well as the direction of the trade winds, the range for a Gulfstream IV with a full fuel tank, and the oleanders and royal poincianas growing along this path—I'd say we're somewhere in the eastern South Pacific. Probably near the Galápagos chain."

The Galápagos. Charles Darwin. Evolution. Just the kind of melodramatic location the producers might choose.

Just then an iguana darted across their path, startling Finney. "Not to mention the iguanas," said Dr. Kline. "Native to that band of islands as well."

They walked on a few steps in silence. What Dr. Kline said made sense, except for the style of the architecture. Somehow it seemed out of character for a Pacific island.

"And your guess, Judge Finney?"

"I was going to say we were on an island too," said Finney. It was important to keep the poor country lawyer routine going as long as possible. "Somewhere in the middle of an ocean—most probably the Atlantic or Pacific." He glanced at Kline out of the corner of his eye. It was possible that somewhere under those large-framed sunglasses the pretty eyes were smiling, but he doubted it. "But I'll tell you one thing: it's way too hot for paradise."

CHAPTER 12

They gathered back at Paradise Courthouse a few minutes before nine. Finney had stuffed two suits and one sports coat with matching slacks in his suitcase. For his first court appearance, he wore a two-button suit coat with a blue windowpane pattern and pleated pants that Nikki had begged him to leave in Norfolk. "You'll lose everybody under thirty with those pants," said Nikki. But based on what he'd seen so far of the other contestants, the under-thirty crowd was going to be hard to win no matter what.

The inside of the courthouse could have been transplanted from Norfolk, or just about any other jurisdiction in the Commonwealth of Virginia, except that the hardwood floors had been recently varnished and showed no signs of wear. The harsh television lights bounced off the flat surfaces of the judge's dais, the counsel tables, and the floor, creating a kind of antiseptic glare that Finney found disconcerting. Still, it was a courtroom and it therefore felt like home.

Finney had been assigned to sit at the table on the right side of the courtroom, next to the ever-serious Kareem Hasaan. *A bad spot,* thought Finney, since Hasaan had him beat in both the physique and clothing departments. The Arab's suit screamed money, a dark-gray pinstriped three-button model with a matching pocket square and wide lapels. A monogrammed shirt, cuff links, the works. No pleats on this guy, of course. Finney leaned away from his tablemate—no sense making it easy for the cameramen to get them both in the same shot.

The other three contestants shared the opposite counsel table—a real mishmash of styles. The Swami opted for casual chic, with a wrinkled sports coat and open-collar shirt. Dr. Ando apparently decided to dress the part of a Buddhist monk, his one-size-fits-all robe swallowing his pint-sized body. And then there was the stunning Dr. Kline.

Finney stole a few sideways glances at Kline, not the way a younger man might look, not the way he noticed the Swami stealing glances, but the way a lawyer sizes up opposing counsel before a case, wondering how much the natural beauty will convert to jury appeal. Kline had large blue eyes, accentuated by dark eye shadow, and a slender nose. She had a broad mouth and pouty lips, and she wore her blond hair pulled back in a tight ponytail. Even when she was in a skirt suit, you could tell that Victoria didn't miss many days at the gym—there was no hiding the definition in those calf muscles.

Finney thought about the young men watching the show. Maybe he should have brought Nikki Moreno to argue for Christianity. Except, of course, that she wasn't a Christian yet. But the judge was working on it. Another reason, he reminded himself, for doing this program. Nikki had promised to rally support and handle PR for the judge's cause. For Christ's cause. To do so, she would have to watch every minute of every show.

It would help Finney define his style. He'd be speaking to a lot of folks just like Nikki, so he would pretend that she was his only audience. Every speech he made, every question he asked, every answer he gave would be articulated with Nikki Moreno in mind. If he could convince Nikki, he would probably end up reaching thousands of others as well.

Before they started rolling, McCormack filled them in on a few logistics. They would be on Paradise Island for two weeks. A week from Friday, everybody would be sent home except the two finalists, who would be asked to stay for an additional day. The method of choosing the finalists would be revealed later.

As with other innovative reality shows, the network was running a pilot during the summer months to see what kind of ratings the show would generate. If it did well, a sequel would follow next year.

Throughout the month of June, the show would air twice a week—

Tuesdays and Thursdays. After those eight episodes, they would skip Tuesday, July 4, and the final episode would be aired on Thursday, July 6. They would be filming something most every day, and editing would be tight. Most reality shows were recorded weeks or even months before they aired. But not this one. They had considered doing the whole thing live, but it would have cost too much to keep everybody on the island for five straight weeks. So they would be doing the next best thing. The first two weeks of the show would air while the contestants were still on the island. The last three weeks would air immediately afterward. McCormack reminded everyone that they had signed a confidentiality agreement promising they wouldn't divulge any aspects of the filming or results until after the final episode aired.

It would not be unusual for segments shot one day to be edited and aired the next. The contestants should treat this like live television, because that's essentially what it was. In fact, if the contestants messed up royally, they could be pretty certain that their mistakes would be featured in the next show, since that kind of thing makes for good television. Even Finney's stomach got a little riled by that comment—the prospect of the entire nation watching his biggest faux pas.

Without asking for questions, McCormack stepped aside and started counting down the seconds. Tammy toed her spot at the front of the courtroom, looking glamorous but stiff as she addressed the contestants.

"Each of you has been chosen to represent one of the prominent faith groups in America," she said on cue. "You've been selected because you have a rare combination of theological and legal training and because you are passionate advocates for your faith. In addition, your various life experiences demonstrate that your faith can help you survive the worst of times."

Tammy paused and turned woodenly, looking into a different camera that apparently represented the viewing audience. "Each of those traits will be put to the test in the upcoming weeks as these advocates defend their faith in this courtroom and try to live their faith on Paradise Island.

We will put the advocates through a literal hell on earth because we know that Americans are not just looking for a faith that makes sense but also a faith that survives when everything else is falling apart.

"The rules are simple. Each week you will see the contestants advocate for their faith in this courtroom. And in each episode, you will see the advocates confront the issues that an authentic faith helps us address—temptation, injustice, trauma, sickness, shame, forgiveness, and love."

Tammy turned to face the contestants again as Finney wondered what the producers had up their sleeves that could address all of those issues. His mind flashed back to the release he had signed—maybe he should have read it with more care.

"This show will use an innovative combination of two types of verdicts. The first verdict will be delivered by a judge here on Paradise Island—a certified agnostic whom you will meet in a few minutes. That verdict will be revealed immediately following the courtroom activity for that week. Our viewers will learn of this verdict when the show airs on Tuesday nights. A second verdict—a *jury* verdict—will be rendered by the viewers themselves. Our viewers will vote by phone following the airing of the Tuesday night show for a period of four hours. Their jury verdict will be announced on the Thursday-night show.

"For each judge and jury verdict you receive, *Faith on Trial* will make a donation of fifty thousand dollars to a charity of your choice. In addition, two finalists will be chosen to compete on the very last show through a method that will be revealed later. The overall winner will be awarded one million dollars for his or her favorite charity."

Finney could hardly imagine a better scenario. Even if he performed miserably and never obtained a verdict from the agnostic judge, he was pretty sure that the Christian viewers, who would far outnumber the viewers from the other faith groups, would grant him a jury verdict nearly every show. But just as he was thinking about his charity of choice, Tammy turned to another camera and flashed a nervous smile.

"There is, of course, a twist," she said. "We want to see how persuasive our contestants are, not just gauge the number of viewers watching from any given faith group. Therefore, we've conducted an independent poll of television viewers who said they were planning on watching the show." While Tammy was talking, a large flat-screen monitor automatically lowered from the ceiling behind the judge's bench, and a chart appeared on the screen.

"Judge Finney, we found that seventy-four percent of potential viewers labeled themselves as Christians already. Mr. Hasaan, four percent of potential viewers said they were Muslim. Mr. Hadji, one percent are Hindu..."

"Cool," said the Swami.

"One percent Buddhist, Dr. Ando. And Dr. Kline, when we subtract our Jewish viewers, that leaves approximately fifteen percent who are either agnostic or belong to some other religion not already mentioned."

Victoria Kline nodded, looking determined to double that number before the show was over. Finney coughed, but nothing major, just a polite little smoker's hack.

"To win a jury verdict, you must show you are making converts," said Tammy. "Which means that you will be judged based on the percentage of viewers *above* this baseline percentage who are calling to support your cause."

Finney stared at the percentage for Christians as if by sheer willpower he could reduce that huge number to something more reasonable. Seventy-four percent? Either the show's producers had surveyed every Christian in America, or a lot of nominal Christians who hadn't seen the inside of a church in years answered the survey. Or they had rigged the show.

"All rise!" shouted the court clerk. "The Honorable Judge Howard Javitts presiding. All those with pleas to enter and arguments to be heard should now draw near. God save this honorable court." The clerk looked at Dr. Kline and smirked. "Assuming, of course, there is a God."

"You may be seated," said His Honor.

Javitts glared at the contestants as if daring them to challenge his authority. His square face featured wrinkle lines that creased deep into his forehead when he scowled, which was most of the time. His broad and flat nose gave him the appearance of a former heavyweight boxer who now took out his aggression in the courtroom. The man was probably gunning for his own judge show when this stint was over, reasoned Finney.

Javitts lectured the contestants on the rules of decorum, his bass voice filling the courtroom. Javitts had the voice of God, thought Finney, though not His visage. Finney preferred a smiling Jesus, One who enjoyed us too much to be constantly frowning.

Javitts finished his lecture and immediately dished out the first assignment. Court would reconvene tomorrow morning at 9:00 a.m., and each contestant would give an eight-minute opening statement—not a minute more, because the judge himself would be keeping time. Were there any questions?

Hearing none, the judge adjourned court for the day, and the cameras stopped rolling for a moment. "That's a wrap," said McCormack.

Murphy strolled to the front of the courtroom with his hands in his pockets to address the contestants. "Most of you have probably already discovered that we've placed a desktop computer with Internet access in your room. We want you to feel free to use that computer for research, for notes, whatever.

"However, keep in mind that your Internet access will be monitored and, in fact, filtered. Any attempts to access video of the shows already aired, or to access press stories or other information about the shows, or to communicate with anyone outside of Paradise Island about any aspects of the show, will result in your immediate dismissal. The computers are provided for the purpose of doing research about the various faith issues involved in this reality show and for that purpose only. Are there any questions about that?"

Nobody raised a hand, so Murphy continued. "The camera crews will be following you back to your condos and shooting some footage tonight. Plus, as I'm sure you noticed, there are wall-mounted bubble cameras in every room of your condo except the bathroom. Feel free to go through the same types of prayer or meditation ceremonies that you would on any other night. It wouldn't hurt if we caught some of that on camera to use as B-roll."

This, Finney reminded himself, was what he hated most about television. Everything was so phony. *Stage a little prayer time for me,* Murphy was basically saying. Viewers might be fascinated to see the Swami burning incense and performing rituals in front of some small shrine, or Kareem on his prayer rug facing Mecca, but Finney's prayers were much less exotic. Besides, he didn't like the idea of praying for show.

Jesus must have seen a day like this coming. When you pray, don't be like the hypocrites who pray standing in the temple and on the street corners, Jesus had warned. *But when you pray, go into your private room, close your door, and pray to your Father in secret.*

The problem on Paradise Island was the lack of a private room. There was no place to pray secretly except... Wait! There was one place where the cameras wouldn't follow him. A bathroom is not exactly the first thing that springs to mind when you think of a prayer closet, but then again, privacy is privacy.

Chapter 13

What do you think about Skyler Hadji?" Bryce McCormack asked. He took a swig from his iced tea and eyed the beer in Murphy's hand. There was a price to pay for being an obsessive perfectionist as a reality-show director. Part of it was not drinking on nights during the shoot.

"Are you kidding?" replied Murphy. "He's perfect. Makes me want to convert to Hinduism." He took another pull on his beer and set it down on the patio next to his cushioned lounge chair. "Assuming they can drink."

"They say his condo already looks like a Hindu temple—idols everywhere, incense, the whole works," Bryce said.

Murphy didn't respond.

"What about Finney?" Bryce asked.

A pause as both men studied the night. "Reminds me of my old man," Murphy confessed, looking out at the ocean. The offhand comment surprised Bryce. There were a few things the two men didn't talk about, an unwritten rule. Murphy's domineering father was his forbidden subject; for Bryce, it was a daughter's suicide.

But there was something about the island breeze and the Jimmy Buffett music that caused a man to let his guard down. Bryce could feel it too, and he was stone-cold sober.

"You think he's that bad?" Bryce asked.

Murphy considered this for a moment. "Nobody's that bad. Plus, Finney's too cagey to come across looking anything like my old man. But he's got a lot of the same characteristics."

"And never got along with his own son," Bryce added, knowing this was going through Murphy's mind as well.

"Imagine that."

Bryce let the silence hang for a few minutes. He had met Murphy five years ago, long after the man had changed his first name, last name, drug habits (mostly), and occupation. They started doing reality shows together, and the two developed a solid friendship. He knew enough about Cameron Murphy's father not to push the issue. Bryce's own father had been proud of his son's brief Hollywood success and even the reality shows Bryce now found himself directing. But Pastor Ronald Martin had not merely withheld approval; he'd actually led a boycott against his son's most recent reality-show offering. It didn't help when *Marriage Under Fire* got dumped after its first season.

"What's New York think about the buzz?" McCormack asked, sensing they needed a change in subject.

It was dark, but he could hear the smile in Murphy's voice. "This thing is hot, Bryce. The Anti-Defamation League is fired up, screaming loudly. After our teasers, the right-wing fundamentalists are thinking about joining them."

My teasers, Bryce thought. Murphy was the producer, but Bryce and a screenwriter friend had brainstormed the concepts for the spots. *Temptation, trials, and faith.* One of the teasers featured Tammy in the smallest of bikinis, which promised to test the resolve of the male contestants to keep the faith. The spots made *Desperate Housewives* promos look like teasers for *Father Knows Best.*

Murphy burped, his way of rubbing in the fact that he was enjoying a beer while Bryce played the prude. The thing that drove Bryce nuts was that *he* ended up with the beer gut while Murphy's incredible metabolism burned away every ounce of fat on his body.

"Christians are so predictable," Murphy said. "They're saying it doesn't treat faith with the proper respect. Another example of the Hollywood crowd being out of touch. All that crap. Our network execs pulled the ads right on schedule, promising a show respectful of our valued religious diversity. Or some nonsense like that."

The whirlwinds of controversy, Bryce thought, *blowing money right out of the trees.* You couldn't buy this kind of publicity. They were fast becoming *The Passion* of the reality-show genre. Or perhaps *The Da Vinci Code* was a more apt analogy—something the Religious Right could denounce while they all read it.

"I even sent my old man an anonymous letter with a copy of the promo tape for the show," Murphy said. "He'll probably be leading the charge."

Bryce smiled at the thought but also grasped the underlying desperation that it signaled. "Murph, this show's gonna work," Bryce said. "And if it doesn't, we'll bounce back. We always do."

"No," Murphy said, barely loud enough to be heard above Jimmy Buffett. "There's no second chance this time. This one's *got* to work."

McCormack sighed and finished his iced tea. Murphy was a talented producer but one who had lost the fun of the business a long time ago. Ratings and reputation meant everything to Murphy. Lately, he hadn't had much of either.

And even for Bryce, his one cult-following hit on the big screen seemed like a lifetime ago. These days, he scrounged around with Murphy on the scrap pile of reality TV. What did that one guy call it? "The vast wasteland of television" or something like that.

There was another thing Bryce needed to get on the table, and this might be his last chance to bring it up. "Murph," Bryce said softly, "we don't need any miracles here. We've got enough juice without manufacturing anything."

He sensed Murphy stiffen. "We've been through this," Murphy replied.

"It's not right, Murph. I mean it's your call. But if it were up to me, I'd play the Muslim guy straight up. And I'm not one to shy away from risks." Bryce knew the show would receive intensive scrutiny. Why set up a fake healing and risk getting caught?

"Hasaan needs our help," Murphy replied. He shifted in his lounger, sitting forward. "We're just leveling the playing field a little. Americans prejudge all Muslims these days. You know it's true, Bryce, and that's why you chose Kareem in the first place—fits the stereotype perfectly. Even though he didn't meet the sickness criteria."

Bryce didn't bother responding. He'd learned that often the best way to argue with Murphy was to bite his tongue. When Murphy realized he could get his way, he would start feeling bad about pushing too far. Before long, Murphy would start back-pedaling on his own.

But not tonight. "He's your guy, Bryce. *You* talked *me* into putting him on the show," Murphy continued. "I never liked the idea of the staged medical tests in the first place. Sooner or later, our boy finds out that he's fine, and then we're toast. I'm just saying, let's preempt all those problems by discovering right on the show that he's been healed." Murphy paused, perhaps to see how well this was being received. "The show giveth and the show taketh away. Blessed be the name of the show."

Murphy lifted his beer in a solitary toast to his own wittiness, then drained it. He set down the empty and burped loudly, as if he were a judge banging his gavel to seal off further debate. Case closed.

Further argument tonight, Bryce knew, would only cause Murphy to dig in deeper. Instead, Bryce would come back to it later from a different angle.

His apparent acquiescence allowed the tension to seep out of the air as Jimmy Buffett gave way to Kenny Chesney. The two friends soaked up the night in silence, each lost in his own thoughts.

"Well," said Murphy a few minutes later, "better head back to my place. Big day tomorrow."

"Yeah," said Bryce.

They walked into the condo, and Murphy threw his empty bottle in the trash. "Any predictions?" he asked on the way out.

"Name calling, controversy, boycotts, and high ratings," McCormack replied.

"No. I mean about who's going to win."

"You know who my favorite is," said Bryce.

Murphy turned and looked at him. "Not a chance," scoffed Murphy. And they both knew he wasn't talking about the show. "She's way out of your league."

"What about you?" asked Bryce.

Murphy shrugged his shoulders, turning to leave. "Anybody but Finney."

∽

Finney snuffed out his cigar, jotted a few more notes on his yellow legal pad, and looked up a verse of Scripture. He glanced up at the camera on the wall again, feeling conspicuous, ever mindful of the fact that he was being watched. He thought about how boring this would be for the person who had to review the tapes. Finney had watched a few other reality shows, and the characters were always doing something interesting, usually hooking up with a member of the opposite sex. But here he sat. Smoking cigars and reading his Bible.

This experience was a lot different from what Finney had thought it would be. He wasn't sure what he had expected; he just knew it wasn't *this.* The other contestants were all so much younger, except for Dr. Ando. Only Kareem and Finney appeared to have much courtroom experience. But Finney sensed that courtroom tactics would be a small part of what it would take to win this contest, though he didn't have the foggiest idea what else might be required.

For some reason, meeting the other contestants had made him less focused on winning. Yes, he still wanted to represent his faith well. But he didn't want to embarrass or humiliate the others on national television. Before today, the show was just a fascinating intellectual challenge, one that Finney thought could dramatically advance the Christian message. But now real people were attached to these other faiths. People who, for the most part, Finney already liked.

He put his Bible down and stood up to face the wide-angle bubble camera mounted on the wall. He scratched the back of his neck and frowned. No wonder he had never tried acting. He cleared his throat and got a little cough out of the way before proceeding.

"This is not going to be easy," he told the camera. "But I'm not going to attack the advocates for the other faith groups. I'm committed to the truth, so I'll have to point out where their beliefs are wrong, but I'm going to keep the focus on Jesus and try to act like He would if He were in my shoes. And I don't really think it serves any useful purpose to attack their faith as opposed to showing them why they should believe in mine."

He hesitated for a moment, though he was not sure why. It wasn't as if the camera was going to respond. "Well, that's about it. I'm going to pray and then try to get a little rest."

Finney returned to his chair, took off his John Deere cap, and placed his elbows on his knees, bowing his head. All he could think about was that blasted camera filming the top of his mostly bald head.

After a few minutes, he stood and decided to address the camera one more time. "God hears me whether I pray out loud or silently," Finney lectured. "It's not like I've got to slit my wrists and yell real loud to get His attention."

Not long afterward, Finney turned off the lights and crawled into bed. He was dog-tired but knew he would have a hard time falling asleep with the bedroom camera focused on him, its red light reminding Finney that the entire nation might enjoy watching him snore. He rolled over so that his back was to the camera and began to pray in earnest. Before long, he had forgotten about the one-eyed monster. The bravado was gone now too. Finney had learned a long time ago that false fronts don't work well with God.

"Please don't let me embarrass Your name tomorrow," he prayed.

Chapter 14

adies and gentlemen of the jury," Finney began. He thought it was clever that the show's producers had asked the set extras to sit in the jury box along with some employees of the Paradise Island resort. It gave him somebody to focus on, somebody to think about other than the four contestants shooting daggers at him from their counsel tables.

Finney had drawn the short straw. Somebody had to go first.

"I could talk to you today about the contrasting philosophies of the various religions. Or I could explain the historic tenets and doctrines of the Christian faith. Or argue about ways that Christianity has made the world better. But this occasion is too important and my time is too short to spend it that way."

Finney leaned forward on the podium that separated him from the jury. Judge Javitts had said the advocates could pace the courtroom if they liked, but Finney believed in protocol. If the jury wanted flamboyant, they would be hearing from the Swami soon enough.

"Instead, I want to talk to you about a man named Jesus. Because to accept Him is to accept the Christian faith, and to reject Him is to reject the Christian faith. And because He is, with all due respect to the other religions represented here today, the single-most-important figure in world history."

Out of the corner of his eye, Finney could see Kareem bristle, but he couldn't worry about hurt feelings. Eight minutes was not a lot of time.

"Nobody taught like Jesus," Finney said. And he waited a few seconds for that to sink in. "Two thousand years ago, in a chauvinistic and intolerant society, Jesus broke down longstanding barriers based on sex, nationality, and occupation. His followers included a tax collector and a former harlot. He ministered to the 'untouchables' of His day, those with leprosy. A few years after His death, the leading advocate for the early church, a man named Paul, summed it up this way: 'There is no Jew or Greek, slave or free, male or female; for you are all one in Christ Jesus.'

"But that's not all. In a society characterized by 'might makes right,' at a time when His own people expected Him to lead a military revolt against the Roman Empire, Jesus taught His disciples to turn the other cheek. He told them to love their enemies and pray for those who persecuted them. He told them that great leaders must first be humble servants. And He washed the feet of His disciples."

Finney turned and walked to the counsel table where Skyler Hadji sat between Drs. Ando and Kline. He gestured toward Hadji, the only one who seemed to be enjoying the judge's performance. "Even one of this man's icons, Mahatma Gandhi, recognized the inspired nature of Jesus's teaching. 'It is the Sermon on the Mount that endeared Jesus to me,' Gandhi once said. And on another occasion, speaking about the Christian religion, he said, 'I like their Christ; I don't like their Christians.'

"And many times, Mr. Hadji, I have to agree with him." Finney thought he noticed a slight nod from Hadji. Could it be this easy?

Emboldened, the judge made a sweeping gesture toward the others. "What man or woman here would say that Jesus was not an inspired teacher, an enlightened prophet, light-years ahead of His time both morally and ethically?" Finney waited in silence, each second driving home his point, until finally he turned back to the jury.

And then it hit. The worst timing possible. He reached for the glass on his counsel table and took a quick drink of water, but nothing could stop it. Finney had been finding it increasingly hard to catch his breath during these coughing spells, and today was no exception. He coughed and hacked for a moment, his face flushing with the effort, until at last he regained his composure and smiled at the jury.

"Sometimes I even choke myself up," he said, but only one or two even gave him a token smile. How many times had he told lawyers that the courtroom was no place for humor?

"Where was I? Oh yeah—nobody taught like Jesus. Nobody lived like Him, either. Jesus was a prophet who backed up His teaching with His life. But there's more to Him than that. Because nobody died like Him."

Finney settled in behind the podium again as he talked about the suffering and death of Jesus. He briefly explained the horrible Roman practice of crucifixion and the reason that Jesus willingly took His place on the cross.

"What other founder of a world religion died so that His followers might live? Others died in a state of meditation or from an unexpected sickness, but who else allowed Himself to be nailed to a tree so that His followers might find favor with God?"

"Four minutes, Mr. Finney," said the voice of God from the judge's bench.

That guy needs to go to judge school—learn a little courtroom decorum.

"Yes, Your Honor," said Finney.

"And nobody rose like Jesus," Finney continued, gathering steam as he approached his final point. This would be his strength—his specialty, if he had one. Finney had always believed that the one thing that distinguished Christianity was the ironclad proof of the Resurrection. He had devoted a whole chapter to it in *The Cross Examination of Jesus Christ.* "It all rises or falls with the third day," Finney sometimes said, though he knew better than to use anything that hokey in this setting.

He mentioned a few factors supporting the reliability of the gospel witnesses—the archaeology that confirmed the gospel accounts and the twenty-four thousand ancient manuscripts, including more than five thousand five hundred Greek manuscripts, that contained and verified various portions of the New Testament records. Plus, Finney said, the gospel accounts have the "ring of truth—the ragged edges that reflect the way things happen in real life."

"Why else, at a time when women were prohibited from testifying in a court of law, would the gospel writers say women first discovered the empty tomb? Why else would they paint the disciples as scared and skeptical followers of Christ—men who returned to their jobs after Christ died, not believing that He would actually come back from the dead?"

Finney's questions started flowing faster as he noticed the judge glance down at his watch. "Did you know that for more than sixteen hundred years nobody even suggested the tomb was not empty? How could the early church have started in Jerusalem, just a stone's throw from the tomb, if Christ's body were lying in the grave? Peter's powerful sermon on the day of Pentecost, when three thousand souls were saved in one day, would have been categorically refuted by the decaying body of Jesus Christ in a nearby tomb."

Finney stopped and caught his breath, moved out from behind the podium, and lowered his tone. "Those who contest His resurrection today tend to gravitate toward one of two theories. Some say the whole Resurrection thing is a legend, cooked up by the church years after the life of Christ. Others say it is a conspiracy or fraud, cobbled together by the disciples so they could take their place at the head of a major world religion.

"The legend theory is easy to refute. Some distinguished scholars have spent their entire lives studying things like the length of time that it takes for a legend to develop. According to their research, it takes a minimum of two generations, *with no written documentation in existence,* for a legend to develop that will supersede the actual facts.

"Think about it in a context we can more readily understand. Let's say I've never argued a case in front of the Supreme Court. If somebody wanted to create a legend about me, saying I won twenty straight cases there, would they be able to do it within thirty years of my death, at a time when thousands of people who knew me were still alive?

"The first gospel account was written within thirty years of the life of Christ. When that account was written, many witnesses to the death and resurrection of Jesus were still living. According to the experts, there is no example of a legendary tale in ancient history that developed in so short a period of time. None. Ever."

"Two minutes."

Finney shot the judge an annoyed look before turning back to the jury. "And this theory that it was just a conspiracy by the disciples..." Finney shook his head, hoping the jury was with him. "I've tried enough cases to see every kind of conspiracy imaginable. I've seen men and women lie to make money, to further their own reputations, to gain political power, or to save their own skins. But I've never seen men and women lie so they could be tortured and burned at the stake. I've never seen them conspire so they could be crucified like their leader. Death has a way of revealing truth. Why would the disciples die for a lie?"

Finney surveyed the jury and noticed a woman in the back row fighting to keep her eyes open. How could she sleep through *this?* He was discussing the most significant event in the history of the planet. He wanted to throw something at her.

He decided against it.

"Imagine for a moment that you are the apostle Peter. You've either seen a resurrected Jesus or you're making it all up—one big practical joke on all mankind. You are hauled before the Jewish rulers—the Sanhedrin—and ordered not to talk about Jesus and the Resurrection. But you keep preaching. You see your friends stoned, whipped, and jailed for the faith. But you keep preaching. Emperor Nero of Rome declares himself the 'enemy of God,' and you see Christians tied to posts, covered in wax, and set ablaze to light the Roman roads at night. But you go out and convert others to take their places, telling everyone you see about the Resurrection.

"You are arrested and thrown in the Mamertine prison in Rome—a death cell where you are chained upright to a post and made to stand in your own urine and excrement for nine long months. Your only exposure to light comes when the guards haul you out of prison to torture you.

Renounce Christ and you will go free. But you refuse to become a traitor to your faith.

"Finally you are hauled before Nero to face execution. There you see your beloved wife, whom you have not seen since the day of your arrest nine months ago. If you renounce the Resurrection now, she will be spared. And you will be released."

Finney paused and studied the jury. They were all with him, all except one…and as long as she didn't snore.

"But you hold firm and Nero announces your penalty—crucifixion for you and your wife. Do you renounce now, at the last possible moment?

"No!" Finney slapped the jury rail, and the lady in the back snapped to attention, a possible whiplash victim. "Your resolve strengthens. You insist on being crucified upside down because you are not worthy to die like your Savior. And as you are being led away, you look over your shoulder and make eye contact with your trembling wife. 'Oh thou,' you say, 'remember the Lord.'

"Can anyone seriously believe that Peter did this for a hoax? for a conspiracy? Or had he seen the resurrected Christ with his own eyes and felt Christ's power in every sinew of his body?

"Peter didn't ask to be crucified upside down because he was a ringleader in some plot to deceive. He asked because he had heard Christ teach and he had watched Christ die and then he had seen Christ come back from the dead. It was the most important event in history, with the most important Man who ever lived at the center of it.

"And Peter had seen it all with his own eyes."

"Your time is up, Judge Finney."

"Thank you, Your Honor," said Finney. He felt almost breathless, but he was satisfied that he had given it his best shot. He turned to sit back down.

"Not so fast," said the big, booming voice.

Huh?

"I do have two quick questions for you."

Finney faced the judge. "Okay."

Javitts looked down at his notes. "In your understanding, is it ever permissible for a Christian to kill another human being?"

Finney thought about this for a long moment. Where did that come from?

"Mr. Finney?"

"Sorry, Your Honor. Jesus said to love your enemies, not to seek revenge. So I would say an individual should never take the life of another except in self-defense. But sometimes the state must do so through its citizens, including Christian citizens, in order to punish wrongdoers or defend its national interests."

Judge Javitts showed no reaction. "Okay, then, let me ask you this: Is it ever permissible for a Christian to take his or her own life?"

The judge had his pen poised over his legal pad, as if it was the most natural thing in the world to ask these questions and take a few notes. But Finney hadn't said a thing about suicide during his entire opening statement. *Where are these questions coming from?*

"No, Your Honor. Most Christians believe that doing so would usurp the prerogative of God. And we also believe that life is always worth living—that God gives grace sufficient for even the most drastic circumstances. Committing suicide is wrong, but it doesn't somehow negate a person's faith. A Christian who commits suicide is still a Christian."

"I see," said Javitts. "Thank you, Judge Finney."

CHAPTER 15

adji was next. What he lacked in courtroom experience he more than made up for with enthusiasm. "Man, that dude is smart," he said, shaking his head and embarrassing Judge Finney. "How do you follow an act like that?"

He shoved his hands into the pockets of his jeans. If he had been a lawyer in Finney's court, he would have spent the night in jail for wearing jeans and a blue blazer to court, but this was TV.

"I've got no problem with the Resurrection," he said casually.

The admission floored Finney. He scribbled a note, hoping the jury was paying attention.

"I mean, I wasn't there and neither was Judge O, so we'll probably never know, but a truly advanced yogi could do something like that."

Finney blinked. The Swami had a way of just conversationally saying mind-blowing stuff, and the jury looked like they were swallowing every word of it. "In fact," he continued, "some Hindus believe that Christianity is just modified Hinduism and that Jesus lived in India between the ages of thirteen and thirty-one."

The Swami shrugged. "I don't know about all that. But let me tell you a few things I do know about."

For the next several minutes, the Swami painted an appealing picture of Hinduism, explaining the concept of Brahmin, the supreme god, the ultimate reality, the world soul. He talked about karma, and Finney had to admit that this kid had more than his share of good karma. And then, in his ever-so-casual way, the Swami moved on to the issue of samsara.

"Did you ever wonder why bad things happen to good people—or why good things happen to bad people, for that matter?"

A few of the jurors actually nodded.

"Did you ever think that you must be missing something? Well, turns out you are.

"You're just looking at one snapshot in time," said the Swami, "and so life sometimes seems unfair. But all souls experience samsara, or transmigration, a long-lasting cycle of births and rebirths. When you look at someone and judge what's happening to them based only on this life, you're missing a big part of the motion picture of their soul's migration."

The jurors looked a little confused, and the Swami must have noticed it. "If that's hard for you to understand, it's okay. You'll figure it out in your next life."

It did Finney good to see the Swami's jokes bomb too. And Letterman thought he had tough crowds.

"Have you ever experienced a sense of déjà vu? I've been here before. I've done this before. But you know for certain that this is the first time it's happened in *this* life. Where do you think that sense of déjà vu comes from?"

Next to Finney, Kareem was grunting his disapproval. "Are we having fun yet?" asked Finney.

"You smell like smoke," said Kareem.

The Swami decided it was time for show and tell. He walked behind his counsel table and emerged with a small carved image. To Finney, it looked like an Asian monk, sitting yoga style, with multiple arms and multiple heads.

The Swami placed the idol on the rail of the witness stand. "People say that Hindus worship hundreds of gods, thousands even. Gods like this one—Vishnu."

Kareem shot to his feet. "I object, Your Honor." Finney didn't even know you *could* object. What were the rules for game-show trials?

"On what grounds?" asked Javitts.

"Idol worship," insisted Kareem, as if the rules for trials prohibited such a thing. "There is no god but Allah. This man"—he pointed an accusatory finger at Hadji—"should not be allowed to subject the rest of us to the worship of one of his thousands of gods."

"Overruled," said Javitts. "You'll have your turn."

Kareem didn't try to hide his displeasure.

Hadji turned to face his adversary. If Kareem was trying to throw Hadji off stride with his objection, it didn't appear to be working. "It's not idol worship when I just place Vishnu on this rail," explained Hadji calmly. "I'll let you know when we start the actual worship." Kareem glared at the man. "And we don't actually believe in thousands of *gods,* Mr. Hasaan. There is only one transcendent force—Brahmin—but this supreme being manifests himself in an infinite number of ways. Think of it as a billion snapshots of one supreme god rather than a billion different gods."

Hadji then walked to his counsel table, ignoring the simmering Kareem. He paused for a drink of water.

"Four minutes," said Javitts.

"I cannot drink this water directly; I need a vessel to help lift it to my lips. So it is with Brahmin and our idols. The mind sometimes needs a tangible thing to help direct our adoration of an intangible supreme being. Other religions do the same thing, with a cross or a temple or a prayer rug."

"Objection!" shouted Kareem, on his feet again. "Now this man accuses *me* of idol worship!"

"Mr. Hasaan, sit down!" Javitts ordered.

Kareem remained standing.

"Mr. Hasaan."

"Your Honor, it is one thing to argue for your religion. It is quite another to do so by denigrating and mischaracterizing the religions of others. With all due respect, if the court's not going to say something about it, then I must."

Finney watched the lines on Javitts's face tighten. This was a direct challenge to the court's authority, and all the alpha males in the courtroom

knew it. Finney had dealt with this type of thing himself many times as
a judge. Some litigants, like Kareem, turned every minor skirmish into
World War III. It really came down to this: who will run the courtroom—
the judge or the lawyers?

"Overruled, Mr. Hasaan. *Sit...down!*"

When Kareem still didn't move, Finney knew that the man's anger
was just a strategy. The issue that had caused the objection was merely an
excuse for an early showdown. Hadji's case had been effectively interrupted, and the Muslim had made *his* point—if you mess with the advocate for Muhammad, you'd better be ready for a fight.

"You're risking contempt," Javitts warned.

"I don't recall a prison on the Paradise Island tour," Kareem said.
Finney saw a flash of panic from a judge whose bluff had been exposed.
Then Javitts's face flushed in anger, and Kareem, totally in control, slowly
pulled out his chair and took his seat.

Round one, Finney thought, *for Kareem.*

∽

Once Kareem had made his point, Hadji completed his opening without
further incident. Afterward, Kareem delivered his own thunderous opening, extolling the merits of Islam while being careful not to malign the
other religions. When he concluded, Judge Javitts posed the same two
questions he had asked Finney and Hadji.

"In your faith, is it permissible for a Muslim to kill another human
being, Mr. Hasaan?"

Kareem smiled thinly, then scowled. "That is, of course, the question
Americans have been asking me since 9/11. What is a jihad? Do Muslims
believe that the hijackers were justified?"

Kareem zeroed in on Javitts, his face taut. "I condemn those actions in no uncertain terms, as do all true Muslims. Ours is a peaceful religion. The 9/11 terrorists hijacked our religion as surely as they did those airplanes. Nothing in the teachings of Muhammad legitimizes the killing of civilians."

Kareem took a deep breath and continued. "But with that said, the answer to your question is an emphatic yes—killing for the right cause can be just. Do you need me to cite the Koran verses? 'Fight those who do not believe in Allah, nor in the latter day.' That's Sura 9:29. Or how about, 'Surely Allah loves those who fight in His way in ranks as if they were a firm and compact wall'? That's Sura 61:4.

"And then there are the promises that Allah will grant special favors for those who die in a holy war. We do not shirk from these teachings, Judge Javitts."

Kareem let the silence linger to emphasize his point. He presented an imposing figure as he stood there unblinking in front of the judge.

"But to judge my religion on the basis of the hijackers is to judge Christianity on the basis of David Koresh or the Ku Klux Klan.

"Do not the other religions represented here talk about 'just wars' as well? Judge Finney cleverly disguised the issue, saying that Christians are not allowed to kill as individuals but may be called on as part of an army to defend national security. That is nothing more than a polite way of saying that people of Judge Finney's religion are killing people of my religion every single day. And they're doing so for political reasons and to protect oil reserves—all in the name of justice."

Kareem motioned to the other counsel table. "And then, of course, there is Dr. Ando's religion, considered by many to be a religion of peace. Did not the Zen priests during World War II train the Japanese kamikaze pilots? Did they not tell them that they would gain improved karma for the next life by their suicide missions?"

He turned back to Javitts. "We all have our suicide bombers, Your

Honor. But that doesn't change the fact that Islam is a religion of peace that only justifies killing in the context of a just and holy war and never justifies the intentional killing of civilians."

"What about suicide?" asked Javitts. "Is it ever permissible for a Muslim to take his or her own life?"

"Only in the context of sacrificing one's own life to save the lives of others or to advance the cause of Allah. In times of war, we call that heroism."

"Thank you, Mr. Hasaan."

∾

Kareem's argument was followed by a smooth presentation from Dr. Kline. After another break, so that the production crew could discuss camera angles and lighting, Judge Javitts gaveled the proceedings to order and called the name of Dr. Hokoji Ando.

The Buddhist advocate rose slowly and limped to the jury box. He stood there stiffly in front of them, his hands folded together. "Pardon my slowness," he said, "but I have fibrodysplasia ossificans progressiva, commonly referred to as FOP. It is a rare and incurable disease that causes bone to form in my muscles, in my tendons, and in my ligaments. There is nothing the doctors can do except monitor the spread of the disease. My body is literally forming a second skeleton, a bone-shaped prison of its own making."

Ando spoke so softly that Finney had to lean forward to hear him. It occurred to Finney that everybody had stopped fidgeting, taking a cue from the unmoving advocate in front of them.

"The average life span of a person with FOP is forty-five years. I have cheated that number by nearly two decades. People with this disease literally turn into living statues—their bodies welded into position like a plastic doll. We suffocate because the bone growth restricts our breathing, literally strangling us."

He paused, letting the full weight of his condition sink in. Finney noticed no sadness in the man's eyes, just a stoic resignation to his lot in life. "What explains this?" Ando asked. "Is it the Christian God of love who saddled me with this condition even before I was born? Or was it Allah, the god of perfect justice, who decided to punish me before I even drew my first breath?"

"Objection!"

Finney couldn't believe that Kareem had the audacity to object at this moment. Didn't he understand anything about sympathy? Didn't he know anything about the subtleties of trying a case? Staking out your turf early was one thing, but this was just plain stupid.

"Overruled," said Javitts without even glancing in Kareem's direction.

Finney leaned over to Kareem. "You're not helping yourself with all these objections," he whispered.

"You try your case; I'll try mine."

And look like a jerk in the process, Finney thought.

"Does science explain it?" continued Ando. "Am I just another mutation in the endless march of the human race to evolve into a higher form? Look at me—am I a higher form? Are two skeletons better than one?"

He stared evenly at the jury, oblivious to the other contestants, the words falling softly from his lips like the hiss of incoming missiles.

"Who explains this? Only Buddha explains this. Only Buddha makes sense of a world steeped in suffering.

" 'Life is suffering,' Buddha said. 'Suffering is caused by our attachments to the world. We can end suffering by developing nonattachment and following the Eightfold Path.'

"What is the body, really? What more is it than a skin bag filled with bones, flesh, muscle, organs, and fluid? Free yourself from the body. Settle the mind. I will show you how even an old man with FOP can find enlightenment. I will invite you to follow me there."

Ando concluded less than four minutes later and turned to the judge. Javitts had asked each of the contestants, except Dr. Kline, the same two questions he had sprung on Finney earlier in the day. Ando didn't wait. "The answers are no and no, Your Honor." Then he limped back to the counsel table and took his seat.

I have underestimated my Buddhist friend, Finney realized. The little man's dignity filled the courtroom.

PART 3

CROSS-EXAMINATION

*The first to state his case seems right
until another comes and cross-examines him.*
—PROVERBS 18:17

*Witness: You want answers?
Lawyer: I want the truth!
Witness: You can't handle the truth!*
—FROM THE FILM *A Few Good Men*

CHAPTER 16

F inney felt like a common criminal. The room was sparse and undignified, an ancillary space in the back of the Paradise Courthouse building. Because Finney had given his opening statement first, he was also the first contestant Javitts sent to the "cross-examination room."

The room felt cramped and musty. A worn hardwood floor had so many layers of varnish on it that the wood appeared almost black, except in the middle of the room where the harsh spotlight turned the floor a yellowish white. Three of the walls consisted of yellowed and blistered Sheetrock, with no windows. The fourth wall was a bank of mirrors, meaning that Finney had spectators on the other side. A fan rotated slowly overhead. The room seemed to be shut off from the building's air-conditioning circulation.

Finney had been instructed to sit in the black wooden chair directly under the spotlight in the middle of the room. He removed his suit coat and hung it on the back of the chair. Between the spotlight and the heat, Finney wondered how long it would take before he sweat straight through his T-shirt and white dress shirt. He took a seat and rolled up his shirt sleeves, loosening his tie. He coughed. A man who introduced himself as Dr. Armond Zirconni, a polygraph expert, took his place next to Finney and hooked up the polygraph machine.

"There's a reason they don't allow these things in a court of law," Finney said.

Zirconni saw no humor in the comment. He gave the usual instructions and started right in.

"Is your name Oliver Gradison Finney?"

"Yes."

"Do you serve as a judge in Norfolk Circuit Court?"

"Yes."

"Do you smoke cigars?"

"Yes."

"Have you ever had any impure thoughts toward your law clerk, Nikki Moreno?"

Finney hesitated. Zirconni glanced at Finney over the top of his glasses.

"I refuse to answer that question."

Zirconni sighed and placed his pencil on the table. "You can't refuse to answer questions."

"I just did."

"Look, Judge Finney. I'm just trying to get a baseline of responses. None of these questions will be shown on the air."

"Choose another question," said Finney. "Nikki's like a daughter to me, not some kind of sex object. So the answer to your question is this: it's none of your business."

∽

On the other side of the one-way mirror, Murphy chuckled. "Finney's a little feisty today," he said.

Bryce McCormack didn't respond.

"I can't wait to see how Kareem Hasaan reacts to the baseline questions we throw at him," mused Murphy.

"Shh," said McCormack, focusing intently on the scene before him.

∽

Finney and Zirconni eventually worked through the baseline questions, though Finney held his ground on the question about Nikki. Just because he signed up for a reality show didn't mean they could insult him.

"Did you just deliver an opening statement in the Paradise Courthouse defending the Christian faith?" Zirconni asked.

"Yes."

"Are you familiar with the concept of proof beyond a reasonable doubt?"

"Yes."

"Did you listen to the opening statements of the other faith advocates?"

"Yes."

"Now, Judge Finney, I'm going to focus your attention on the opening statements of each of those other advocates. I want you to tell me whether listening to them created any reasonable doubt in your mind whatsoever, no matter how small, about whether your faith is the correct one. Do you understand what I'm asking?"

"Yes." The spotlight glared in Finney's eyes, causing him to squint. He could feel the sweat breaking out on his forehead. His shirt undoubtedly had rings under the arms already.

"Did the opening statement of Skyler Hadji create any reasonable doubt in your mind?"

Hadji *had* surprised Finney with his acceptance of the Resurrection. And the statement about déjà vu made Finney think. The kid was sharper than he let on. But still, he hadn't shaken Finney's faith.

"No."

Zirconni made a little check next to the answer. Had he done that before? Finney couldn't remember. "Did the opening statement of Kareem Hasaan create any reasonable doubt in your mind?"

"No."

"Did the opening statement of Victoria Kline create any reasonable doubt in your mind?"

"No."

"Did the opening statement of Hokoji Ando create any reasonable doubt in your mind?"

Finney licked his lips, suppressed a cough. "No."

Out of the corner of his eyes, Finney saw Zirconni make another check.

"All right, now I want to change direction a little bit."

"Hold up," said Finney, turning his head to the side for a brief coughing spell. "Okay."

"Do you believe that your God can perform miracles?"

Without hesitation, "Yes."

"Do those miracles include healing people from physical diseases?"

"Yes."

"Do you believe that your God hears your prayers to Him?"

Finney paused for a moment, not because the question gave him any trouble, but because he didn't like where this line of questioning was headed. It was an old courtroom trick: never ask the real question directly, just imply the condemning information through a series of tangential yes-or-no questions.

"Yes, and He always answers my prayers. But it's not always the answer I want."

This brought another over-the-glasses look. "Just answer yes or no, please. Do you believe that your God hears your prayers to Him?"

"Yes, of course."

"Have you been diagnosed with lung cancer that has metastasized to your liver?"

"Yes."

"Have you been told that there is nothing the doctors can do about liver cancer?"

"Yes."

"Have you also been told that you have less than a year to live?"

"Yes."

"Thank you, Judge Finney, that's all I have."

CHAPTER 17

Finney stopped by the rest room after his interrogation. He found Kareem at the sink, washing his hands and wrists. Finney headed to the urinal. "You're gonna love the cross-examination room," he said.

"I am pure. They can ask me what they wish."

"It's a lie detector," Finney said. "You ever been hooked up to one before?"

"No."

Finney finished and stood behind Kareem at the sink. "It monitors your heart rate, breathing, and other vital signs. The theory is that they can tell when you're lying because—"

"I know what a lie detector is," Kareem snapped. "I'm a lawyer, re-member? I've seen dozens of lie-detector tests administered to my clients. I never trust them." He rinsed out his mouth and then held some water in his palm, sniffing it up his nose.

"Me, either," said Finney, watching Kareem with curiosity.

In silence, Kareem washed his face from his forehead to his chin and from ear to ear. Finney realized that this was probably part of Kareem's purification process for his midday prayers. Either that or the man was some kind of compulsive neat freak.

"You mind if I slip in there?" asked Finney.

Kareem was in the process of washing his forearms. Without respond-ing, he shook the water off and stepped aside.

Finney washed his hands and then stepped out of Kareem's way to dry them. Meanwhile, Kareem wet his right hand and passed it over his thick black hair.

"How often do you have to do this?" asked Finney.

"Five times a day," said Kareem. He breathed in deeply and then stopped for a second, looking at Finney in the mirror. "If a pure river ran to your door and you took a bath five times a day, would I notice any dirt on you?"

"What kind of soap?"

Kareem ignored the response. "Of course I wouldn't. The same can be said for the five prayers by which Allah annuls evil deeds."

"I admire the passion of your beliefs," said Finney. "But I'd hate to see your water bill."

Kareem shook his head and resumed his washing.

"Good luck," said Finney as he opened the door to leave. As soon as the words crossed his lips, he wished he could take them back.

"I do not believe in luck," said Kareem.

∽

Finney didn't believe in luck either when the drawings took place later that afternoon. At least not good luck.

With cameras rolling, Tammy gave them their next assignment. After two false starts and one quick break to reapply her makeup, she managed to get it right. In two days the contestants would start the next phase of the trial process. They would each be asked to cross-examine one of the other contestants about the weaknesses in the other's belief system. Tomorrow and the next day would be for research and preparation. Three contestants would go Thursday; two contestants would go Friday. Highlights would run on next week's show.

Dr. Kline drew first. She picked a card from Tammy's hand and turned it over. "Kareem Hasaan," she announced.

"This means that Mr. Hasaan draws next," Tammy said with a smile.

Kareem drew the next card. "Judge Finney," he announced. He shot

Finney a triumphant look. Finney winked, then stood to draw the next name.

"Hokoji Ando," he said. *Darn it!* Every lawyer knew it was toughest to cross-examine a witness who elicited sympathy. Finney would have to handle Ando with kid gloves.

Ando then drew Hadji, and Hadji was left with Dr. Kline.

"We may need to spend some time together in private preparation," Hadji suggested. Victoria Kline gave him a look that could melt steel.

∽

Before they left the courthouse, Judge Javitts turned to the day's final order of business. To Finney's surprise, Javitts told the contestants that he was prepared to render his verdict for the opening statement episode and that it had been heavily influenced by the jury members. He explained that he had purposely selected a diverse jury composed of several production crew extras—"runners" in the lingo of the trade—two security guards, the cook from the Paradise View, and two members of the resort lawn crew. After the contestants had finished, Javitts had discussed the opening statements with the jury in another room while the contestants took their turns with the lie detector.

"Contestants, please stand," ordered Javitts. Finney knew the protocol—this is what criminal defendants and their lawyers did at the end of a criminal case. "Based on my consultation with the jury and my observation of the opening statements, I am rendering my first verdict in favor of"—Javitts looked from one contestant to the next in standard reality-show staging—"the Buddhist advocate, Dr. Ando."

Finney looked to his left and watched the shy Dr. Ando nod in thanks. Finney did his best to mask his own disappointment. It's not as if Ando didn't deserve the verdict, Finney told himself. And Finney had been around courtrooms long enough to know that a lot could happen between opening statements and final judgments.

But he also noticed that the warm and fuzzy feelings he had last night toward the other contestants, particularly Ando, had largely disappeared. Finney wasn't used to losing. As a trial lawyer, he had put together a remarkable won-lost percentage. As a judge, of course, he lost only on those infrequent occasions when the appellate court didn't see things his way. He reminded himself that this was undoubtedly a sympathy verdict. After all, he still had truth on his side. And even in a court of law, that ought to count for something.

Ando could have his fifty thousand dollars. Finney had his sights set on a million.

∾

"That's just unacceptable," Murphy lectured. "I watched the tests myself."

Bryce McCormack leaned inconspicuously against the wall with his arms crossed. He was staying out of this one. He didn't even join the men at the table.

The air of confidence that had accompanied Dr. Zirconni's first announcement of his polygraph results had long since dissipated. The man appeared to be shrinking by the minute under Murphy's assault.

"Why'd we fly you all the way out here for this?" Murphy asked. "Bryce, do we have enough footage for the first show without the polygraph tests?"

Bryce shrugged. They both knew they would never cut the polygraph segment. Murphy was just trying to pressure this guy by threatening his few minutes of fame.

Zirconni placed his glasses on the table. "I don't know what you want me to say. I don't give the answers, I just interpret them."

The problem, as expressed by Murphy, was that Zirconni had ferreted out few doubts among the advocates about their cases. Ando admitted that reasonable doubt had crept into his mind when he heard both Finney and Dr. Kline. Zirconni also concluded that Dr. Kline, despite her denials, had reasonable doubt when she listened to Ando and Finney. But none of the other advocates—Finney, Hasaan, or Hadji—harbored any doubts at all.

"Wouldn't it be more interesting if the advocates were struggling a little themselves?" Murphy asked. "I just can't believe that these guys all think they've got a monopoly on truth. I watched Finney with my own eyes. The guy was sweating like a pig."

"It's not my job to make it more interesting," said Zirconni.

"Yeah, but can you sit there and tell me that there was no difference at all between Finney's answers when you asked him about Kline and Hasaan, on one hand, or Hadji and Ando, on the other?"

Zirconni pulled in a long breath and glanced at Bryce McCormack, apparently hoping for a bailout. When none came, Zirconni picked up his graphs, put on his reading glasses, and studied them again.

"I'm not saying there was *no* difference," Zirconni explained. "I'm just saying that Judge Finney denied he had reasonable doubts, and with respect to Ando and Hadji, the data is inconclusive. I *can't* say he was lying."

"All right," countered Murphy. "But that means you can't say he was telling the truth, either. Am I right?"

"I suppose."

"Okay, now we're getting someplace. With respect to Finney, why don't we just show his response to those two questions on camera and let you explain how the heart rate and breathing increased a little, though the results were inconclusive."

Zirconni considered this. "I guess I could go that far. Just as long as I say the same thing about Hadji with regard to his answer when I asked him about Ando."

Murphy looked at Bryce, who shrugged his acquiescence. "Works for us," Murphy said.

After a few more minutes of discussion, Zirconni left the room.

"Is that part of the ABF plan?" asked Bryce.

"The what?" said Murphy.

"The ABF plan—anybody but Finney."

Murphy scowled. "He was lying, Bryce, and you know it. He just knows how to beat the machine."

"Justice on Paradise Island," Bryce said sarcastically.

CHAPTER 18

On Tuesday night Nikki Moreno hosted her first Oliver Finney Victory Party. Well, she didn't exactly host it *herself.* But she was the one who did the heavy lifting—passing out invitations, calling a local television station and the newspaper, and dropping major hints to lawyers thinking about not coming that the judge had a long memory when it came to these sorts of things.

She rented out Norfolk's Finest Sports Bar at the Waterside complex and gave the owner strict instructions to have every television tuned to *Faith on Trial* at exactly 9:00 p.m. She placed several donation containers at the front door (this was, after all, a religious ceremony of sorts) to offset the expenses. She made herself conspicuous next to the containers in the hour before the show started, just as the main crowd rolled in, pretending to take casual note of how much the patrons contributed to the worthy cause. It was amazing how many attorneys reached into their pockets and plunked in a twenty. The judges, of course, didn't put in a dime.

The crowd was loose by the time the show started, and they hollered like crazy when Finney's face graced the screen during the show's opening. After a commercial break, however, things became much more subdued as the Jewish advocate who had resigned in protest, a young rabbi named Samuel Demsky, recounted all the reasons the show was a bad idea.

Faith is a private and serious matter, he argued, not something to be exploited for reality TV. When he first signed up, he explained, he thought the show was going to be much more respectful and deferential toward these sensitive religious matters. Now, he feared, the show would inflame religious passions and exploit the worst in human nature by pitting one faith against another. His people had suffered too much as a result of such passions for him to be a part of this production.

He concluded by noting that many other religious leaders agreed with him. He mentioned a few leaders of the Religious Right whose names Nikki had heard a time or two before, though she happened to know that other conservative Christian leaders thought the show was a wonderful idea and were already drumming up support for Finney. Rabbi Demsky concluded by noting that even the father of the executive producer of the show, Pastor Ronald Martin, had sent a letter of protest to the network.

What a strange way to start a reality show, Nikki thought.

The producer himself came on the screen next and said he regretted that Rabbi Demsky had withdrawn but that the show would go forward. "Enough already!" somebody yelled. "Bring back the judge!" shouted somebody else. And soon the entire place was again buzzing with anticipation.

Things picked up as the show featured short highlight pieces on each of the contestants. Though nobody was quite sure what the etiquette was for an event like this, a show involving serious matters of faith, they started booing the other contestants anyway, as if it were a college football game.

By the time the network cut to a commercial, right after the first few lines of Finney's powerful opening statement, the crowd was totally into the show, chanting, "Fin-ney! Fin-ney!" It made Nikki proud to be an American.

The same crowd started jeering and hissing a few moments later, not at Finney, but at the juror in the back row whom the camera caught dozing. "Throw her in jail, Judge!" somebody yelled. The camera zoomed back out, and Finney concluded his opening to thunderous barroom applause.

The wisecrackers got going in earnest during the highlights from the Swami's opening, though Nikki thought he was fairly compelling. Nobody that hot should also be that smart. You could barely hear the television as the audience heaped derision on both Kareem Hasaan and Dr. Victoria Kline, the women being especially critical of the atheistic scientist. This sports bar wasn't usually quite so sanctimonious, but Finney was a hometown boy and that ought to count for something.

But the crowd grew unusually quiet, Nikki noticed, during the opening statement by the Buddhist representative, whatever that guy's name was. Even Finney seemed to be moved by it, according to the results of the lie-detector test. The lie-detector guru made a big deal about the fact that Finney's heart rate and breathing increased when he was asked about Ando and Hadji.

Nikki wasn't completely shocked when the judge announced his verdict in favor of Ando, though she thought a small riot might break out at the sports pub. The plaintiffs' lawyers in the crowd—the ones who made their livings accusing big corporations of fraud and negligence and conspiracies—were the first to suggest that the judging on the show might be rigged.

The show ended with dialing instructions and some titillating peeks at what lay ahead. In the next few episodes, temptation and trauma would be coming to Paradise Island, and everyone would see whose faith could hold up to that. Thursday they would reveal the results from the viewers' verdict for round one and another charity would be fifty thousand dollars richer. As soon as the credits rolled, cell phones popped up everywhere, the lawyers drinking with one hand and dialing with the other.

Despite the judge's verdict for Ando, Nikki thought the home team was off to a decent start. But it did worry her when it was easier to get through voting for the judge than it was when she voted for the Swami.

∾

The Patient turned off his television with mixed emotions. There were, on the one hand, a lot of things to like. He was more than pleased with the publicity the show had generated. The opening segment worked brilliantly, and he was sure that millions of people had tuned in just to see what all the fuss was about. The unanswered question, of course, was how many people had changed the channel after Rabbi Demsky's remarks. He doubted that number was high.

The production quality of the show had been superb. This was tricky business—a reality show involving the most volatile and sensitive issue known to the human race. It had to be entertaining (after all, this *was* television), but it also had to be handled with great respect. The show needed to gain credibility week after week, increasing its ratings, garnering positive reviews—basically, doing whatever it took to gain worldwide attention. They were a long way from where they needed to be, he thought, but they were off to a good start.

His mind turned to the final episode; he considered all they would be putting on the line in that one short hour. He wanted to build to a huge audience—not easy to do in the middle of the summer. But still, that final episode deserved nothing less. Truth be known, he wanted it to be the most watched hour in the history of television. He was already sure it would be the most talked about.

So, on the one hand, he was pleased with their progress. But on the other hand, that first show hadn't helped him at all in his own dilemma. The doctors were still all gloom and doom, and they seemed to shorten his already truncated life expectancy every time he saw them. Brain cancer. A cruel twist of fate for a man widely envied for his gray matter.

The opening statements had been sincere and passionate but confusing. Ando had shown nobility in the face of suffering and deserved to win the first round. But being the best advocate and serving the true God were two different things. Finney's profile of Jesus seemed compelling, and the Patient liked Kareem's passion as well as Hadji's acceptance of everything life threw at him. He had listened to every word the advocates had said, but he had no idea who was right.

He knew the answer wouldn't come from analyzing opening statements. Faith was about so much more than that.

CHAPTER 19

By Wednesday morning, Finney noticed that the contestants were getting into a routine. Kareem had started the last two days with prayer rituals outside his condo at sunrise, making sure everyone was awake with his loud chanting. Dr. Kline would be the next out, stretching before she took off on her morning run, doing ten or fifteen laps on the sidewalk around the small resort, making Finney tired just watching.

Finney would then begin his own morning exercise, walking around the same half-mile loop two or three times—something far more reasonable. Even that distance made his lungs ache, but he was determined to keep exercising.

Next, the Swami would find a spot on the beach and practice yoga for the appreciative cameras. Ando apparently meditated somewhere inside or maybe just slept in.

∽

The Assassin took careful mental notes about the habits and capabilities of others on the island. He put nothing in writing. Still, he filed away in the recesses of his mind critical details on each person—background information he had gained before coming to the island, physical strengths and weaknesses, personalities, alliances. He knew which contestants played cards together and which contestants operated alone. He knew that Finney started each day with a cigar, coffee, and twenty-five minutes of Bible reading. He knew that Victoria Kline had averaged three minutes and forty-five seconds per lap on day one and three minutes and thirty-eight seconds per lap on day two.

He had already met every security guard at the resort, filing those names away for possible future reference. He took careful note of the firearms and radios they carried. He scouted out the location of every camera on Paradise Island.

It had been only three days, and he had more than a week left to complete his reconnaissance, but he was already getting into the zone. So far there had been no surprises, nothing that would keep him from carrying out his assignment.

In his mind, with a few brain cells not busy cataloging key facts about his environs, he was already counting the money.

∽

On Wednesday morning Finney decided to have a seat on the lounger a few feet away from the Swami. Finney took his Bible with him—there was nothing he liked better than having his morning devotions while the sun crawled up out of the ocean, throwing off splashes of orange and yellow in spectacular fashion.

He took a seat, kicked off his flip-flops, perched his reading glasses on the end of his nose, and watched Hadji for a few minutes over the top of the glasses. The kid was looking out over the water, deep in meditation, and apparently didn't even notice that Finney had joined him. The Swami was wearing nothing but a pair of baggy plaid shorts and was standing with his feet spread wide, his toes and knees pointed outward, and his arms dangling at his sides. He would squat down while inhaling, keeping his back straight as a board, then would bend his elbows at the waist and emit some kind of "ha" sound. He would inhale again as he extended his arms straight in front of him, then pull his elbows back to his chest with another "ha."

The Swami did this over and over for a few minutes while Finney watched him, the Bible lying unopened in Finney's lap. Then the Swami stood up, turned his toes forward, and hinged down at the waist, keeping his legs straight and placing his palms on the sand. He slowly rolled up to a standing position and turned toward Finney, smiling.

"*Ha kriya,*" he said.

"*Ha kriya,* yourself," said Finney. He took off his reading glasses and began fiddling with them in his right hand.

"No, Judge O, that's the name of the exercise. *Ha* means 'sun' and *kriyas* are ritual actions that unite movements and breath to alter our energetic states. It's a way to draw on solar power, Judge, to get the kind of energy we're going to need in the next few days."

"Yeah," said Finney. "I can feel it too."

The Swami looked at Finney, unsure of whether he was serious. "Why don't you give it a try, Judge O? I'm just about ready to do something to experience the soothing energy of the water."

"Thanks, but I think I'll pass. I draw most of my power from reading this Book."

"That's cool, Judge, but I'm not trying to convert you to Hinduism or anything. I'm just saying that if you want to relax and get ready for the day, this can help you."

Finney shook his head. "I've got cigars for that."

"But, dude, cigars are poison. This stuff is soothing and rejuvenating." Then the Swami shrugged. "But hey, man, it's up to you. I don't want to tell you how to get in touch with your spiritual side. I do know a lot of Christians who like to meditate, though."

"Maybe some other time," said Finney. He put on his reading glasses, opened his Bible, and started where he had left off yesterday. The Swami resumed his yoga.

Finney thought about the Swami's last comment. Meditation was one thing, but yoga was meditation of a different sort, centering your thoughts on a spiritual force at odds with Christianity. But that didn't necessarily mean that Christians had to avoid meditation altogether—to concede the field, so to speak. Finney knew a lot of Christians, including a lot of heroes of the faith, who meditated on God and His goodness. Sure, it was more of a Middle-Ages practice than a modern one—another spiritual discipline that had fallen victim to fast-paced lifestyles. But there was certainly nothing wrong with meditation per se.

Finney had an idea.

"You ever read this Book?" he asked.

The Swami looked over at him, finished a repetition of what looked like a breaststroke on dry land, and then stopped. "The whole thing?"

"Let's just say the New Testament."

"Not really. I've heard a bunch of sermons, though. And I watched *The Passion* once. I think I get the general drift."

"But you've never read it yourself?"

"Not that I remember."

"Tell you what," said Finney. "If you read one of the books in the New Testament that I get to choose, I'll try one of your exercises. But I'm not into all that chanting and meditating, just the exercise."

The Swami shrugged. "Deal."

Finney showed the Swami where the gospel of John started, took off his glasses and put down his Bible, then received his first lesson in yoga exercises. This one was all about water, the Swami said. He had Finney stand with his heels together and toes apart, place his palms together in front of his body, and then reach up over his head and push the air away, rising up on his toes and exhaling, as if he were swimming through water.

"Are you soaking in the water?" asked the Swami.

"Not really," admitted Finney, "but I am getting a little tired."

They stopped the exercise when Victoria Kline wandered their way.

"Want to join us?" asked the Swami.

"No thanks." She snickered. "Judge Finney, you hardly seem the type for yoga."

Finney shrugged. "I'm not. I just thought it might help me to focus better on the scripture I'd been reading."

"Did it?"

Finney looked at the Swami, as if to apologize. "Not really."

"You sure you don't want to try it?" the Swami asked Victoria, undeterred.

"No," said Dr. Kline. "But there is something I've been dying to try." To Finney's surprise, she motioned to the Hobie Cat sitting a few hundred yards down the beach. "I always wanted to learn how to sail. Judge, did you say the other day that you knew how to sail one of those things?"

The question caught Finney off guard. Was Dr. Kline asking him to take her sailing? "I'm better at sailing than I am at yoga."

They talked for a few more minutes and agreed on a time for Victoria Kline's first Hobie Cat lesson. The Swami stared after her as she walked off down the beach.

"Dude," he said to Finney, "I knew you had good karma."

CHAPTER 20

By late morning, Finney was doing the second thing he never thought he would be doing that day—sailing on the Hobie Cat with the enigmatic Dr. Kline. The warm breeze cooperated, blowing hard enough to keep the colorful sail full and propel them across the bay at a respectable speed. Kline quickly learned how to work the tiller, tacking as if she'd been born on the water.

She seemed to relax on the boat, smiling more as they sailed around the bay than she had the three previous days combined. Finney caught himself grinning as well, watching Kline's intense focus as she fiddled with the rope to adjust the sail. She wore blue cotton shorts, a black bathing suit top, sunglasses, and a baseball hat that hung low over her eyes. Finney wore an old bathing suit, a tank top, and his trademark John Deere ball cap, frayed badly around the bill.

"Can you take over for a minute, Judge?"

"Sure." Finney traded sides and took control of the tiller. He could do this in his sleep.

"I'm grateful for the sailing lessons," Dr. Kline said, her smile gone as she looked in the direction of the security guard standing on shore next to the Wave Runners. The guards seemed to be everywhere on the property, making Finney feel strangely claustrophobic, as if he were serving time in a minimum-security prison rather than competing on a game show.

"I've enjoyed it," said Finney.

"But I really didn't haul you out here to give me sailing lessons," Kline continued. "I knew they would let us take off our microphones if we came on the water, and I needed to talk to you about something."

"Okay." Finney focused on the sail, sensing that Dr. Kline was struggling with whether to tell him something. He didn't want to intimidate her with the famous Finney stare.

"I debated all night whether to even say anything. But I decided to talk to you because you seem like someone I can trust." She paused for a beat. "But you've got to promise me that this stays just between us."

Finney adjusted the sail and turned to face her. It was hard to tell what she was thinking behind the dark glasses. "It will."

"Well, I don't know how to explain this without giving you the whole story." She sighed. "You know Bryce McCormack, right?"

"The director."

"Yeah. Well, he started hitting on me before we even got to the island. I didn't do anything to encourage it, but… Well, he's the director, so I didn't exactly discourage it, either. So when we set up here on the island, he said something like I ought to come and visit him some night. Instead of just blowing him off like I should have, I took advantage of the situation in order to get out from under the constant surveillance of these cameras; they drive me nuts."

"Know what you mean."

"I told McCormack that it would be hard to pay him a visit when my every move is being recorded. He asked if it might help if he had the cameras in my condo turned off at night so I could come and go as I pleased. Maybe I shouldn't have, but I said yes."

Kline paused and blew out a breath. Finney pushed the tiller hard away from him and swung the sail around, making it necessary for him and Kline to change sides of the boat.

"Last night I got bored and headed over to his place. Not to do anything—frankly, the man disgusts me. But, to be honest, I knew that the first episode had aired, and I wanted to maybe share a drink with McCormack and see what I could find out."

Now things are starting to feel like a regular reality show, Finney thought. Intrigue, conniving, and illicit relationships. One part of him wanted to lecture Kline on ethics. The other part wanted to know more.

"As I was walking down the sidewalk toward his condo, I heard some voices on his back patio, so I stayed in the shadows on the side of the building and listened for a few minutes. It was McCormack and Murphy, and they were talking about the show. It was one of those things where I knew I shouldn't be listening, but I couldn't really just come bounding around the corner at that moment and be like, 'Hey! How's it going?' or they'd wonder what I heard. So I just stood there."

"And?"

"They were talking about some really weird stuff. It was like they had a piece of serious dirt on each of us, and they were talking about how they could hold it over our heads if we tried to go public or go to the cops or whatever."

"Go to the cops about what?" Finney asked.

"That's what I couldn't figure out. It was like they were planning on doing something to us and then blackmailing us with this secret information."

Finney's head started spinning. This was too weird. Maybe Kline was making it all up, trying to throw him off. Maybe she had some paranoid tendencies. He couldn't imagine what the show's producers could possibly have on him. He was clean. Boringly clean. It was a job requirement— judges couldn't be involved in things that might later subject them to blackmail.

"Did you hear what they said about me?" Finney asked. It seemed like a good way to figure out whether Kline was making something up.

"I couldn't tell for sure," she responded. "But something about the speedy-trial law and some guys you let off."

Stunned, Finney lost focus on the wind for a moment, and the boat slowed considerably. Those cases were ancient history. Or so he had thought. He felt his stomach clench, though he kept a straight face. "What about you? What'd they say about you?"

This brought such a long pause that Finney wasn't sure that Kline was going to answer at all. When she did, she spoke softly, staring at the ocean water whipping by the side of their boat. "Plagiarism. It was a long time ago, but it would still ruin my career if it ever came to light. I have no idea how they found out."

They spent another fifteen minutes on the boat, devising a plan for dealing with this latest development. They would need more information. They reluctantly decided that they should inform the other contestants in the meantime by passing notes at counsel table. Finney would tell Kareem. Kline would tell Ando and Hadji. Also, Kline would make up some emergency reason for needing to communicate with her agent, an attorney in whom Kline had great confidence. Finney had a few ideas about how to contact Nikki as well, though he didn't say anything about that to Dr. Kline.

Hopefully, it was all a big misunderstanding that would be clarified in the next few days. *The speedy-trial statute,* thought Finney. He thought he'd heard the last about those cases.

CHAPTER 21

M urphy had it all going—the back-of-the-neck rub, the terse comments, the inability to sit still, the rapidly narrowing eyes. Bryce had learned the warning signs of an explosion, but unfortunately the PR member of the team didn't seem to notice.

"We've got some damage control to do on Finney," she said. "A lot of Christians are complaining because we've got a cigar smoker representing them. Others have joined with the Anti-Defamation League in denouncing the whole concept. And even the Christians who do like this guy— and there must be a ton of them, because he got over sixty percent of the vote—they all think that the voting system is rigged."

"Are you done?" asked Murphy.

"Yes sir."

"Good. That's a wonderful synopsis." Murphy paused, glaring at the woman. "The only minor critique I have of your presentation is that it lacks this silly little item called solutions."

The two faced off for a moment before Murphy turned his ire toward another attendee. The man tried to paint an optimistic picture of the Nielsen ratings, but Murphy was not buying it. Eventually, Howard Javitts came to the man's defense.

"I don't see anything wrong with our Nielsens," Javitts said. "A six-point-one rating and a thirteen share. Twelve million homes. Other than *Survivor, American Idol,* and *Dancing with the Stars,* what reality show beats that?"

Murphy responded by articulating his words slowly and forcefully, the way teachers reprimand disruptive junior high students. "The Nielsens demonstrate that our decision to let Demsky have his say at the start of the show worked. People tuned in to see what all the controversy was about. But, Larry, how many phone calls did we get last night?"

"Not quite eleven million."

"Not quite eleven million," Murphy repeated. He leaned back in his chair, looked at the ceiling, and cursed, as if everyone around the table was too stupid to understand what he was saying. "*American Idol* hits thirty-four million homes and gets sixty-five million calls—nearly two calls per home. But us? We hit twelve million homes and can't even generate twelve million calls. And most voters call multiple times. So we're talking maybe four or five million total voters. Anybody see a problem here?"

"I see a real problem," volunteered Larry, a young associate producer.

No kidding, moron, thought Bryce.

"We started the night with a lot of homes, but our call volume says we lost half of them during the show. And the reviews stink. Everybody said it was too cerebral. No human drama element. Fell short of expectations."

"What do they want?" asked Javitts. "It's not supposed to be *Fear Factor*."

"I'll tell you what they want," Murphy replied. "They want conflict. They want controversy. They want love triangles and temptation and people losing their tempers. They want something outrageous enough that it gives the Anti-Defamation League and the Catholic Church and the Christian Right a reason to be upset. We promised them *Temptation Island*, and we're giving them *Jeopardy!*"

"I didn't sign up for *Temptation Island*," insisted Javitts.

Bryce braced himself for a serious Cameron Murphy eruption, but the producer surprised him. Murphy thought about the comment for a moment and then exhaled. He took a sip of water, and the whole room seemed to relax a little. "We aren't going to dumb down this show just to get ratings," he said. "But we do need to ratchet up the drama a few notches. Now, what kind of footage do we have in the hopper for our next show…"

∾

The contestants gathered in the Paradise Courthouse on Wednesday afternoon and took their seats at their counsel tables. The production crew performed its mike checks and lighting checks. Makeup assistants dabbed foreheads with powder. Finney's forehead took a little more dabbing than the others. He gave Dr. Kline a knowing nod, but she was back to her old self, ignoring him like the snob he had pegged her to be on day one.

Tammy made a few announcements, and then Javitts took the bench. The court clerk called the court to order, and Finney felt at home. He coughed a little, drawing dirty looks from the audio techs.

"Two days ago, each of you was interrogated in the cross-examination room," said Javitts, his voice authoritative as always. "In addition to being strong advocates for your faith, each of you also has another thing in common." Javitts stopped and surveyed the contestants.

He makes a pretty good television judge, thought Finney. *Even if he hasn't learned how to control belligerent lawyers like Kareem.*

"Each of you, with the exception of Dr. Kline, has been diagnosed with an incurable terminal illness," Javitts said grimly. "In fact, though it may sound morbid, one of the reasons you were chosen is because you are bravely facing your own unique physical challenge. It was not a requirement for the advocate in Dr. Kline's position, for reasons which will become clear momentarily."

As Javitts talked, Finney took the opportunity to scribble a few words on his legal pad. He made it look like he was taking notes. In fact, he was writing one.

"One of the most important tests of any faith, if not *the* most important test of any faith, is how well it prepares you to face death. We will give you a chance to talk to our viewers about that in the days ahead. More important, they will get a chance to observe you as you continue to battle your health conditions."

As Finney finished his note, he found himself wondering what could possibly be wrong with Kareem and Hadji. They both seemed so healthy.

"But the other thing our viewers will want to know is whether your gods have the ability to miraculously deliver you from life-threatening circumstances. Tomorrow night, viewers will see the video footage of each of you being asked about this issue. In particular, they will see Judge Finney and Mr. Hasaan each claim that their God can perform miraculous healings. Viewers will also hear Mr. Hadji claim that when you become absorbed in meditation you realize that self is separate from body, and you will not be affected by disease or death. Dr. Ando did not claim that his faith could deliver him from death, only help him through it."

Judge Javitts paused and sucked in a deep breath, while Finney took advantage of the moment to pass his note to Kareem.

Strange stuff is going on here. Kline thinks she heard some of the producers talking about blackmailing us. Keep it quiet. I'll tell you more as I find out more.

Out of the corner of his eye, Finney watched Kareem slide the note over and casually glance down to read it.

"Next week, each of you will be thoroughly examined by the best physicians available to see if your faith has indeed provided any miraculous healing during your time on this island," Javitts continued. "Needless to say, that would greatly impact your chances of being named as one of the two finalists."

Kareem folded the note while Judge Javitts, like a seasoned pro, held his pose for the cameras. The producers were probably planning on putting some dramatic music in the background as they played this segment on Thursday night. Finney decided to rain on their parade.

"May it please the court," said Finney, rising to his feet. He decided not to wait for permission to proceed. "Of course, the Christian God *can* heal—that has been proven millions of times. But my God also says, 'Do not test the LORD your God,' and it occurs to me that asking God for healing so that I can win a reality show is exactly the kind of thing He must have had in mind in saying that."

Finney took great delight in the alarm he saw on Javitts's face. This was certainly not in the script. "So I just wanted to put the court on notice that I won't be submitting myself to any tests next week, nor will I be asking God to heal me on national TV."

Before Javitts could respond, Kareem stood next to Finney. "Allah is not to be tested either. And accordingly, his servant will not be tested by the producers of this show—not next week, not ever."

Hadji sprang up at the other table to join in the revolt. "You don't schedule the healing that comes through meditation; it occurs as enlightenment occurs," he said. "So don't schedule any tests for me."

"Cut!" yelled Bryce McCormack, shaking his head ruefully.

Cameron Murphy stormed to the front of the courtroom, his face flushed with anger. "This is wonderful. We've got all these hard-core believers in God, but none of their gods is big enough to heal them."

He scowled at the advocates and then cut his eyes back to McCormack. "Let's just get started in the cross-examination room," he said. He took a couple of breaths, turned back to the advocates, and seemed to calm down a little. "And by the way, we're going to want to check your papers before you leave. We've been hearing some nasty rumors about communications with people outside the island."

Finney noticed, under the table, Kareem stuffing a folded piece of paper into the front of his pants.

CHAPTER 22

This time Finney went last. None of the others said a word after coming out of the cross-examination room. They seemed to be operating under an unwritten "don't ask, don't tell" policy. It was late afternoon by the time Finney took his turn.

The room was the same as it had been two days ago—sweltering hot, close to ninety degrees in Finney's estimation—with the harsh spotlight focused on the single black wooden chair in the middle of the room. This time, however, there was no polygraph machine, no Dr. Zirconni. It was just Finney, Judge Javitts, two security guards, and a cameraman.

"Have a seat," said Javitts.

Finney carried bottled water with him, compliments of the well-stocked refrigerator at his condo. Javitts stood in the shadows by the door so that, from where Finney sat, he could hardly see the man's face.

"We're going to be filming a segment now that we have no present intention of using," said Javitts. "But sadly, in the reality-show business, pieces like this have become something of a necessity."

There was something about the way Javitts said the words "present intention" that hung with Finney and made him suspicious. He looked toward the wall of mirrors, thought about making a face, and decided against it.

"This is a worst-case-scenario segment," Javitts continued. "We tape it, in part, because so many reality-show contestants in the past have shown an inability to play by the rules. There are millions of dollars invested in this production. Producers need some assurances that contestants aren't going to improperly receive outside help, divulge results before the final episode airs, or perhaps even file suit after the show is over because they're disgruntled with the results. Ever since the allegations that an *American Idol* judge got involved with one of the contestants, smart producers have been taping segments like this one so that contestants will think twice before they put their credibility on the line by making allegations like that."

"In other words, blackmail," said Finney.

"Judge, you of all people should know better," lectured Javitts, with an edge to his voice. " 'Blackmail' is a legal term with such nasty connotations. What we're about to do, on the contrary, is bend over backward to show you some leniency. We would be well within our rights to air the segment we're about to film immediately. Faith is about forgiveness and overcoming past mistakes, and our viewers are entitled to know if you've experienced that. But we're not going to do that. In fact, there's a good chance this segment will never air—"

The door opened and the voice of Bryce McCormack chimed in. "Let's get this segment taped already. Every other contestant did this, including Mr. Hasaan. Judge Finney, do you want to stay in this game or not?"

Finney shrugged. "I never said I wasn't going to do it. I just wanted to call it what it is."

∾

"Have you ever heard the name Antonio Demarco?"

"It sounds familiar."

"Would it help refresh your memory if I told you that Mr. Demarco's was one of the cases you dismissed approximately five years ago because of the speedy-trial statute?"

"I said the name sounded familiar. I don't need my memory refreshed."

"What is the Virginia speedy-trial statute?"

"It codifies the rights of alleged criminals in Virginia to receive a speedy trial. Under its terms, any case not brought to trial within one year of arrest has to be dismissed, unless the delay was at the request of the defendant."

"Have you ever dismissed cases under the Virginia speedy-trial statute?"

"You obviously know that I have. Several years ago I had to dismiss six cases that weren't prosecuted in a timely manner."

"There was a fair amount of newspaper coverage about that, wasn't there, Judge Finney?"

"Yes."

"Blaming the prosecutors for not having a better case-management system to move those cases forward, right?"

"Yes, and also a particular defense attorney who happened to be a member of the Virginia House of Delegates. Under Virginia law at the time, a member of the House of Delegates can get an automatic continuance if the case is scheduled for trial on the date of one of his committee meetings. This guy would get a couple of continuances and then the prosecutors would let the case slip through the cracks."

"That lawyer did not represent Antonio Demarco, did he?"

"I don't think so."

"Demarco was facing a third felony that would have brought substantial jail time under Virginia's three-strikes law, isn't that right?"

"If you say so; I really don't remember."

Javitts paused for a moment, as if he didn't believe the answer. Finney could tell the man had tried a few cases in his day—he had a methodical way of zeroing in on the damaging information, creating a crescendo as he did so.

"Now, Judge Finney, isn't it true that, although the newspaper never figured this out, the delay in the Demarco case was not really the fault of the prosecutors?"

Finney took a swig of water, wondering how Javitts knew this stuff. Denying it would only make Finney look worse. "I never blamed that case on the prosecutors."

"Did you ever tell the press why that case didn't get tried within one year?"

"I had no obligation to tell the press anything."

"Isn't it true that you had a rule in your courtroom prohibiting cases from being set for trial until all major pretrial motions were resolved?"

"Yes. It was a way to make sure we didn't waste everybody's time."

"And isn't it true that you allowed a motion to suppress filed by the defense attorney in the Demarco case to sit on your desk for three months without a decision, causing the case to go past the speedy-trial deadline?"

Finney felt the intense heat from the spotlight as his mind flashed back to that dark period of his life. Eighteen months after losing his wife to a heart attack, his only child, twenty-four-year-old Tyler, had died when he lost control of his motorcycle. Demarco's wasn't the only case that got neglected.

"Judge Finney, is it true?"

"Yes."

"Did you know that eight months ago, just outside Youngstown, Ohio, Mr. Demarco was arrested again?"

"No."

"Would it surprise you to learn that Demarco was selling crack and meth to fourteen- and fifteen-year-old kids?"

The dark shroud of that news seemed to cover the room. But did it surprise Finney? "No," he said. "Unfortunately, I would be surprised if Demarco ended up being one of the rare dealers who actually turned things around after getting a break like he did."

"A break," Javitts repeated sardonically. "Is that what you call it?" He walked toward Finney and handed the judge a picture. It showed an attractive young woman with a broad smile.

"Would it surprise you to learn that Demarco shot and killed this young woman in a convenience-store robbery?" Javitts asked.

Guilt stabbed Finney, ripping at his gut. He stared silently at the picture in his hand. A judge's worst nightmare. An innocent woman killed because Finney hadn't done his job. The one thing he had always prided himself on—being a fair and conscientious judge—was blown away in the time it took for the devastating implications to sink in.

"Somebody's daughter," said Javitts. "Somebody's friend."

"I'm sorry," said Judge Finney softly. "I had no idea."

He was hardly coherent for the rest of the interrogation—a series of questions about how his faith would help him deal with this kind of failure. Javitts asked about forgiveness and confession and absolution, and Finney answered like a zombie, all the while thinking about the young woman in the picture. She looked to be about the same age as Tyler had been at the time of the accident.

∽

Bryce McCormack listened intently on the other side of the two-way mirror, flanked on one side by Cameron Murphy and on the other by a small string of a man who served as the lead postproduction editor.

"When you edit Finney's cross-examination, make sure you cut the part where Javitts shows him that picture," Bryce said as soon as Finney had answered his last question.

The editor mulled this over for a minute. "What are you saying? Demarco didn't commit that murder?"

Bryce continued staring through the glass, watching Finney leave the room. "Javitts never said he did," Bryce replied. "He just asked a carefully worded hypothetical question."

"Yeah, but the way he said it—"

"Look," interjected Bryce, "we all know that these guys Finney put back on the street have been doing some pretty nasty stuff. We know Demarco was still selling. Did he commit murder? Maybe not with a gun, but the drugs do the same thing; it's just slower. Javitts showed him that picture as an example of the kind of damage his actions have caused. Now Finney will wrestle with the issue of forgiveness, a point driven home by a memorable face, and we'll have the leverage this session was intended to create."

The editor's silence signaled that he still wasn't convinced.

"Just edit the tape," said Cameron Murphy.

∾

Finney left Paradise Courthouse under an overcast sky without saying a word to the other contestants. He flung his suit coat over his shoulder and walked around the resort property two or three times, praying as he shuffled along. He didn't really care if the information became public—it would probably serve him right. But he was sick to his stomach about what had happened.

As a judge, Finney was used to making tough rulings that sometimes upheld constitutional rights by setting felons free. And he had made his peace with the consequences of that. But he was tortured by the thought that his own negligence, not the Constitution, had turned Demarco loose so he could kill this woman. "Somebody's daughter," as Javitts had said. "Somebody's friend."

Finney's grief was doubled by thoughts of his own son—all the words left unspoken, the relationship that had never been what Finney hoped for. Tyler had always been closer to his mother, and her death seemed to drive Finney and Tyler further apart. The son was as stubborn as the father. Tyler, a law-and-order type who had joined the police force right after college, could never understand how Finney could release felons based on things Tyler called technicalities.

But it was so much more than that. For all practical purposes, while Tyler was growing up, Finney had been an absentee father, serving the jealous mistress of the law day and night. When Finney discovered a vital faith late in life and reordered his priorities, he and Tyler had already drifted too far apart. It was the "Cat's in the Cradle" phenomenon—the busy son no longer had time for a prodigal father doing his best to reunite.

Tyler's death had shaken Finney to the core.

He wondered now about the young woman in the picture. Was she an only child? Was she close to her parents? What had been her hopes and dreams?

When he got off this island, he would find out her name. He would pay her parents a visit and ask forgiveness. It was one more thing to put right while he still had time.

Suddenly, he didn't really care whether he won this game show or not. In the real world, five years ago, he had performed like a loser. Nothing on Paradise Island would change the results of that.

CHAPTER 23

The contestants were a somber bunch at dinner. Under the watchful eyes of the cameras, nobody talked about their afternoon sessions in the cross-examination room. From the looks on their faces, the others had endured interrogations every bit as tough as Finney's. Even the Swami wasn't his normal vivacious self as he and Finney shared a table with Kareem.

As the food was served—custom orders the men had submitted earlier—the discussion turned to their medical challenges. It shocked Finney to learn that the Swami suffered from acute Hodgkin's lymphoma, a disease that attacked the lymph nodes and, in the Swami's case, other nearby organs. He was in stage IVA, meaning that the disease had led to widespread tumors in the lungs, liver, and bones. But the Swami hadn't experienced the fever, exaggerated sweating, and weight loss that afflicted some patients.

Finney was having a hard time wrapping his mind around the fact that a guy with as much energy as the Swami could have a terminal illness. "You seem so healthy," said Finney.

"That's because I'm using a holistic approach to treatment," said the Swami. "I'm not injecting chemo poisons into my body. Plus, I'm only eating natural foods, no preservatives, and I'm on an herbal regimen."

Finney had noticed that the Swami ate some weird stuff. Now he knew why. He suddenly felt self-conscious about his own burger-and-fries selection.

"What parts of your body did you say were affected?" asked Kareem, making the not-so-subtle point that he was unimpressed with the Swami's regimen.

"Basically everywhere," said the Swami, not even trying to put a good face on it.

"I'm not doing chemo anymore, either," said Finney. "Once the liver's involved, it's just a matter of time. Might as well feel good."

They took a few bites in silence before Kareem broke in. "That's not necessarily true," he said.

"What isn't?" asked Finney.

"That when the liver's involved it's just a matter of time."

"Could have fooled me," said Finney.

Kareem set down his fork. This subject didn't do much for a guy's appetite. "I took an antidepressant drug named Serzone," Kareem said. "I didn't notice at the time, but it had a black-box warning on the side listing several potential side effects, including liver failure. About a month ago, I got a call from some big plaintiffs firm that is filing a class-action lawsuit, and I went in to get tested."

Kareem frowned at the table, recalling the moment. "Because I'm otherwise pretty healthy, I'm now on a list of possible transplant recipients, though younger patients have priority."

Finney just shook his head—what do you say? "I hope you get one," he managed. "I'll trade you mine if you're interested."

"I'll pass, Judge."

"You need to change your diet," suggested the Swami, looking at the slab of meat on Kareem's plate. "I could hook you up."

"Right," said Kareem. "That way it can spread to my bones and lungs as well."

"Did you know you had anything wrong before you got tested?" asked Finney.

"Not really. I didn't have much of an appetite and got a little jaundiced, but that's about it. Since then, I've noticed some yellowing in my eyes."

Finney looked but couldn't see anything like that.

"You ever try green-tea extracts?" asked the Swami.

CHAPTER 24

Finney wasn't sure who was in charge of enforcing the rules for the island, but he figured that he might as well go straight to the top. After dinner, he knocked on the door to Cameron Murphy's condo.

A cameraman had followed Finney and was shooting over his shoulder. As usual, Finney had a small mike attached to his golf shirt with the ever-present battery pack snuggled in the small of his back.

Murphy answered the door shirtless, wearing a pair of baggy khaki shorts that sagged low enough to expose a two-inch band of boxers. The skin underneath the hair on his bony chest was at least two shades lighter than his tanned neck, face, and arms. He was holding a beer in his right hand.

"You got a second?" asked Finney.

Murphy shrugged. "What's up?"

Finney motioned to the camera over his shoulder. "Can I ask you something in private?"

Murphy thought about this and frowned. "Okay," he said. Then, to the cameraman, "Take a break. Come back in five minutes."

Murphy turned around and walked toward the wicker furniture in the TV room. "I'd offer you a beer," he said over his shoulder, "but that would violate our no-fraternization policy."

Finney unhooked his mike and the attached battery pack, dropping it all on the kitchen counter. "I don't drink anyway."

"I knew that," said Murphy as he sank into the couch. "We know a fair amount about you."

It was a subtle reference to the speedy-trial cases, an interrogation that Finney was certain Cameron Murphy had watched. And enjoyed.

"Actually," said Finney, "that's what I wanted to talk to you about."

Finney took a seat, coughed for a minute, and explained his dilemma. The interrogation earlier today had reminded him of another case he had left sitting on his desk. Finney told Murphy about the Terrel Stokes matter, knowing that Murphy's goons could look it up if they wanted. Finney explained how Stokes had sent a letter to a gang member outside the prison, ultimately resulting in the bloody execution of a critical government informant. He explained how prosecutors had filed a motion to use the out-of-court confession of the witness at trial based on their theory that Stokes had ordered the killing.

Finney failed to mention that he had ruled from the bench on the same day as the hearing.

"My recollection is that Stokes has been in jail for nine or ten months already. If that motion filed by the prosecutors is not resolved in a timely manner, I may be looking at another speedy-trial problem. And, Cameron, I'd rather quit this show right now than allow a man like Stokes to go free."

Finney waited in silence for an answer, looking Murphy dead in the eye.

Murphy took a healthy pull on his beer and studied the judge. "Two weeks is going to make a difference?"

"I'm not sure exactly how long he's already served," Finney responded. "But after today, I'm not willing to take any chances. You can't just arbitrarily set a trial date without giving the defendant a few weeks' notice so his attorneys can subpoena witnesses and get prepared. And, as you undoubtedly know, I don't set trials until motions like this one are resolved. Two weeks at this stage could make all the difference."

"Okay," Murphy said with an exaggerated sigh. "What are you proposing?"

"I've written a brief opinion resolving the motion. Can you just see that it gets sent to my law clerk, Nikki Moreno?" Finney pulled a piece of paper from his pocket. "Here's the opinion and her e-mail address."

Murphy read the opinion while Finney watched in pained silence.

Murphy looked up when he finished, studying Finney again with suspicious eyes.

"I really shouldn't do this," Murphy said, and Finney knew he had him. "Don't tell the others."

"Thank you."

"And don't even think about asking again."

"I understand." Finney stood and reached out his hand.

Murphy rose and shook it awkwardly. "You ought to be a little more diligent with your cases, Judge Finney."

∽

Though he wasn't in the mood, Finney hosted a poker party on his patio that night. It was part of the plan that he and Dr. Kline had cobbled together earlier on the Hobie Cat. Finney would yuk it up with the Swami and the two cameramen who had joined their poker game on the plane. Meanwhile, Kline would pay a visit to Bryce McCormack.

Finney chomped through two cigars and lost nearly a hundred dollars—no small feat in a dollar-ante game. The Swami was the big winner, but he was probably cheating again. Finney didn't care. His body was on the patio, but his mind was elsewhere.

One of his concerns was whether Nikki would catch on to the code he had used. His first thought had been to employ the same code used by Terrel Stokes, but he soon realized that code wouldn't work. Stokes's code would have required Nikki to locate any dates, then count down the number of lines that corresponded with the month and then count to the word in that line that corresponded with the day part of the date. But that approach required that the message transmitted to Nikki would stay in exactly the same format as the handwritten message drafted by Finney. There was no way to guarantee that would happen. For example, the eleventh word on the fourth line after the date 4/11 in Finney's handwritten message wouldn't necessarily be the same as the eleventh word in the fourth line in whatever typed e-mail Nikki received.

Finney thought about possible ways to use the computer in his condo to overcome this problem, but he came up empty there as well. The game-show's producers had been explicit in their instructions about computer use. They had shown the contestants the computer center where a bank of screens in front of production assistants showed them everything that appeared on the screens of the contestants' computers. These assistants monitored every keystroke made by the contestants and had the power, using the keyboards in front of them, to take control of the contestants' computers and override the contestants' keystrokes. Any e-mails, instant messages, or other attempts by the contestants to communicate with the outside world were strictly prohibited. In addition, any attempts to access Internet sites with reports or news about the reality show would be blocked. If a contestant abused his or her limited Internet privileges, the computer would be taken away.

Finney's other problem was the inability to print documents from his computer. Otherwise, he would have just printed out the document and asked the producers to fax it to Nikki. Any request by Finney to personally type and send the e-mail would have made Murphy and his staff suspicious.

In the end Finney decided to modify the code slightly from the version used by Stokes. To compensate, he dropped obvious hints to Nikki. He was pretty sure that anybody who could pass the LSAT puzzles-and-games section would have no problem with this.

Which is what worried him so much about Nikki. He said a prayer for her as he lost another poker hand and chomped harder on his cigar. The key would be the name of Wellington Farnsworth. If she just picked up on that, she would be fine.

But as much as he hoped Nikki would figure it out, she was not the main focus of his thoughts as the cool ocean air blew through the back patio of Finney's condo.

"You aren't very talkative tonight, Judge O," the Swami said.

"Just thinking," replied Finney.

"About what?"

"A bunch of stuff."

It was a lie. He was really only thinking about two things. The code-breaking capacity of Nikki Moreno was a passing concern. But what really weighed him down was the family of a young woman in Youngstown, Ohio, on whom he had inflicted inconsolable grief.

What kind of judge am I?

CHAPTER 25

The e-mail arrived at approximately 10:35 p.m., and Nikki just happened to be online. She read the message immediately, her brow knit with confusion. Finney had ruled from the bench the day of the Stokes hearing. The drug case was already scheduled for trial, and as Nikki happened to know from bumping into Mitchell Taylor recently, Stokes was about to be indicted by a grand jury for conspiracy to commit murder as well.

So what was Finney doing? Why send a written opinion on the Stokes case out of the blue, especially when it was unnecessary? It obviously had something to do with the game show. And knowing Finney's love of puzzles and codes, it probably contained a hidden message. She read the opinion a second time and tried to remember how the Stokes code worked. It had something to do with the dates—she was sure of that much.

Opinion in the Matter of Terrel Stokes

(Revised 6/7)

In our criminal justice system, things are seldom as clear as this case. A hearing was held in my courtroom on 5/9 with arguments becoming unusually tense. After hearing arguments, I took under advisement the issue of whether an out-of-court confession from an informant who was prepared to testify against Stokes but died on 4/11 under suspicious circumstances may be used at trial if prosecutors need it to prove their case.

The court is now prepared to rule on that issue.

Defendant Stokes, an alleged leader in a gang called the Black Gangster Disciples, told other gang members that a man named Antoine Carter was a confidential informant on the government's witness list. (Stokes passed along this information, which he had received from his attorney, in a letter Stokes wrote from jail dated 4/5.) Did the letter help enlist gang members in an assassination attempt? This court thinks so.

The 4/5 letter, addressed to Wellington Farnsworth by the defendant, contained coded language presumably understood by Farnsworth to authorize the 4/11 hit. Wellington Farnsworth and others made sure they would have no trouble in the future with gang members turning state's evidence. They cut out Carter's tongue and allowed him to choke to death on his own blood.

In a reply letter to Stokes dated 4/12, Farnsworth and the others confirmed the hit. Farnsworth decided he would use the same code in his letter as the one Stokes had originally used to authorize the hit.

In the last 4 weeks, through various Westlaw searches and a review of the cases cited by the parties, the court has examined the relevant case law on this issue. It is clear that defendant Stokes procured the absence of a key witness at his trial by ordering a coded hit on the potential informant. Stokes will not be allowed to benefit from his own misconduct.

Accordingly, this court hereby rules that the out-of-court statement of the informant may be used at trial as well as the 4/5 letter that may account for the death of the informant. The fact that the 4/5 letter is a coded communication does not make it any less culpable. Since all pretrial matters are now resolved, the clerk of the court is ORDERED to set this case for trial on an expedited basis.

Judge Oliver G. Finney

Nikki pulled out a sheet of computer paper and her pen. She was pretty sure she remembered how that Stokes thing went. She would look at the month and count down that number of lines. Then she would look at the day of the month and count over that many words within the line. When she had finished her decoding, Nikki was left with the following message:

rule called was made death others law _____ _____

She stared at her solution. The first blank represented a line that didn't even have enough words to fit the pattern, and the second blank indicated that the message didn't seem to have enough lines. She was obviously doing something wrong.

Maybe the days represented how many lines down she needed to go and the months represented how many words in. She checked that method. More nonsense.

She tried going up the specified numbers of lines instead of down. Argh! Why did Finney have to make things so difficult?

She read the opinion again. It said *revised* on 6/7—today's date. Was that a hint that Finney had revised the code used by Stokes? If so, she'd never figure it out.

But there was another hint. Wellington Farnsworth. The name rang a bell. She knew it wasn't somebody involved in the Stokes case, but she couldn't quite place the name. She stood up and started pacing around her apartment. She grabbed some celery sticks from the refrigerator. Maybe they would help.

Wellington Farnsworth. Wellington Farnsworth. His name might be in Finney's contact list. She could access the judge's computer tomorrow. In the meantime, she decided to read through the message one more time.

∾

When the card game ended, Finney slipped inside his condo and, under the watchful eyes of wall-mounted cameras, lit a cigar, stripped off his shirt, and sat down at his computer. He knew that everything he pulled up on his computer screen, every keystroke he entered, was being mirrored on another screen monitored by one of the show's assistants. These next few hours would be critical.

On the one hand, he was probably overreacting. Dr. Kline thought she heard the show's producer and director talk about having some dirt on the contestants that could be used for blackmail, that could keep the contestants from going to the cops. This afternoon Finney and all the others had found out exactly what the show's producers had on them. And Javitts had given a plausible explanation for why they were taping those segments—in case any of the contestants didn't play by the rules.

But on the other hand, some things still didn't add up. And besides, Finney loved a good intellectual challenge. If the producers wanted to play "gotcha," it was a game two could play.

First, he logged on to Westlaw—a password-protected Internet search engine that Finney had been using for the past ten years. Like thousands of other lawyers, Finney paid a monthly subscription fee that gave him access to every reported case in the country, categorized by jurisdiction and subject matter. Big law libraries with impressive-looking books were a thing of the past. Westlaw now provided all the information formerly housed in thousands of bound case volumes and more—real estate records, periodicals, newspapers, scientific treatises, regulatory rulings, company information databases, people-finding databases, just about anything a lawyer would need to do his or her job.

Finney had already used Westlaw a few times yesterday when he had been performing research for his cross-examination of Dr. Ando. Whoever was monitoring Finney's research would not be surprised if he used it again tonight for more research about Buddhism.

Finney's idea to use Westlaw as a pipeline for messages hit Finney right after dinner, just before he drafted the encoded message to Nikki. It would be ideal for several reasons. Nikki used his Westlaw account when she conducted research, so she knew his password. Also, Westlaw stored the history of past search requests in sequence under a tab labeled Research Trail, so Nikki would be able to log on and see what Finney had typed in earlier. Plus, the cumbersome search engine worked better if you entered a date to serve as a cutoff for information. So, for example, typing in "da (after 1/1/05)" in the magazine database meant you were looking for all articles dated after January 1, 2005. Quotes were used to designate an entire phrase to be searched as opposed to individual words. The use of the word "and" to connect two words or phrases meant that the article had to contain both words or phrases. The use of "or" meant an article had to contain at least one.

For tonight's message, the dates would be critical.

Finney opened the database for "allnews" and plugged in his first search request:

da (after 1/1/05) Change and Buddhist and "codes of conduct"

Westlaw generated one article from the *Journal of Sex Research,* and Finney decided not to spend much time reviewing that one. A few seconds later, he was typing in his second request:

da (after 1/1/01) "Frequently quoted" and Buddha

This search generated six results, and a few of the articles were actually helpful. As Finney scrolled through synopses of the articles, he realized that this would take a lot longer than he had anticipated. Altogether, he would have to plug in around twenty different search requests. And, to make it look good, he would have to scroll through several of the magazine articles produced by each request.

But he was having fun trying to think up legitimate search requests that would get his message across. Once Nikki figured it out—*if* Nikki figured it out—they would have a much faster system in place. Plus, they would have dealt with the two greatest weaknesses of any encryption system: the vulnerability of the key and the issue of predictability.

The history of codes was also the history of stolen or intercepted keys. It was the lesson the Nazis learned with their World War II encryption system named Enigma. They thought it was unbreakable. And it might have been if the Allies hadn't constantly been stealing the code books that contained the keys to Enigma.

But a second problem could be equally fatal. If the same encryption system was used over and over, it became predictable and easy to crack. It was an inviolate rule acknowledged by every cipher expert—the ease of cracking a code increases in direct proportion to the number of messages that use the same method. Sooner or later, your adversary figures out one small piece of the puzzle and then the rest fits into place.

Finney was too smart for all that. In just a few short hours, he had concocted a system in which it would be impossible for his adversaries to steal the key and, even better, in which the code itself would change every day. There was only one serious flaw in Finney's otherwise brilliant plan.

Nikki Moreno. Code-challenged Nikki Moreno. If she didn't understand enough about the first message to get Wellington Farnsworth involved, then the plan would be a nonstarter.

Which triggered one other ironclad rule recognized by every cipher expert, and even a man as smart as Finney couldn't figure a way around this one. Your ability to communicate in code is only as strong as your weakest link.

He tried to ignore that thought as he typed in his third Westlaw search for the night:

da (after 1/1/03) "Use of capital assets" or "financial resources" and Buddhists

This time he got a message that said, "No documents satisfy your query." But that was okay. The search request looked legitimate. The rest would be in Nikki Moreno's hands.

Chapter 26

On Thursday morning, Finney and the Swami did their earth, wind, fire, and water exercises and discussed the first few chapters of the book of John. The Swami was fascinated with the imagery of Jesus as the light of the world—he'd somehow missed that in the handful of television sermons he'd heard and his thorough watching of *The Passion of the Christ*. After Dr. Kline finished her run and cooled down, Finney excused himself and headed over for day two of sailing lessons.

Finney knew he wasn't yet ready for the afternoon's courtroom festivities, but sailing with Dr. Kline had to take priority. They decided to make this one as short as possible without tipping off the ever-watchful cameramen and security guards.

Due to time constraints, Victoria didn't bother to head back to her condo and change from her running clothes into her bathing suit. Instead, she just took off her shoes and socks, rolled up the sleeves of her T-shirt, repositioned the elastic holding her ponytail, and pronounced herself ready. Finney liked this woman better every day. Not in a romantic sense, of course—she could have been his daughter. But the pretenses he had seen earlier seemed to be melting away under the heat of the tropical sun. The woman Finney found underneath that hard exterior was much more to his liking.

"Good run?" Finney asked as he shoved the boat into the water.

"Not quite as fast as yesterday," said Victoria. "Hard to focus with so much going on."

They chatted like old friends as Finney hoisted the sail and got them underway. After a few minutes, he asked Victoria to take the tiller. It seemed to be a signal to get down to business.

"I paid a visit to McCormack last night," she said.

Finney expected her to continue, but she apparently needed some prompting. "And?"

"And it was awful. The man is disgusting." Another thing the two of them had in common. Finney thought McCormack's sleaze factor was off the charts. The long gray ponytail, tattoos on both skinny arms and who knew where else, the small gut that overhung his jeans—it all gave Finney the impression of a man going through a serious midlife crisis.

"I took a shower as soon as I got home," Victoria continued. "It must have been an hour long."

"He didn't try anything, did he?"

Victoria laughed. "Not unless you count frat-boy pickup lines. I would have broken his arm if he made any real moves."

Finney watched her jimmy the tiller a little, her lean arms working effortlessly. His money would definitely be on Victoria in an even fight.

"Learn anything?"

"He's divorced. Must have said that three times. He said that he thought I could have a career in acting." She chuckled at the thought. Finney kept quiet, since he thought maybe McCormack had a point on that one. "I think he mentioned at least twice that directors make or break acting careers."

"Wonder if he had any particular directors in mind?" mused Finney.

"I wonder."

Kline made a small course adjustment, resulting in a fuller sail. It occurred to Finney that she'd better quit doing so well or the need for lessons would soon be over. He threw his legs over the side and let them trail in the water.

"I didn't bother to tell him that I'm a thirty-six-year-old university professor who considers acting to be a step down," said Victoria.

"Yeah," said Finney. "That's why I'm not going to pursue any acting offers after the show either. I'd much rather resolve nasty marriage disputes in Norfolk Circuit Court."

This actually made Victoria smile—something that accentuated her made-for-the-big-screen features. "He did let me use his cell phone," she said. "I told him I hired an agent when I was selected for this show and wanted my agent to talk with him about future projects."

Finney loved it. How many times had he seen this happen in the hundreds of cases he'd handled—men getting suckered by beautiful women? "Did you get in touch with your agent?"

"No, but I didn't want to. I called his direct line at work, knowing he wouldn't be in. That way I could leave a message, and he would have an excuse to call me back."

"Remind me never to tangle with you in court," said Finney.

"Too late for that," Victoria replied. "Anyway, I told McCormack I needed some privacy, so I slipped outside his condo to call. I left a voice mail telling my agent what I suspected. I asked him to investigate and then call me back on McCormack's cell phone. After I left the message, I stepped back inside and told McCormack that I had to leave a message and that my agent usually took a day or two to return my calls. McCormack told me to get a new agent, but he promised he'd talk to the guy and let me talk to him as well when he returned my call."

"Who's your agent?" Finney asked. Then he pointed toward the barely visible shore of a distant island. "If you head in that direction, you'll get a little more wind."

Victoria pulled on the tiller and corrected course. "A Washington attorney named Preston Randolph—ever hear of him?"

"The guy who handles mass tort cases?" Finney knew Randolph. Who didn't? But Finney had no idea that Randolph was in the agency business. Especially for someone as low on the food chain as Kline.

"Yeah. I've served as an expert witness for him a few times. He said his firm would handle any offers that came out of this show for free."

Now it made sense. A little quid pro quo for a professor who helped Randolph fleece millions from corporate America. Kline might have a soft smile, but Finney bet she could be hard as onyx.

"At least we've got a line of communication open to the outside world," said Finney. He said it with no guilt about keeping his messages to Nikki quiet. Every code maker knows that you never broaden the circle of knowledge any further than absolutely necessary. But the way Victoria looked at him—it was almost like she knew.

"Let's head back in," suggested Finney. He had the information he needed. "On the way, I'll teach you a foolproof method for passing coded messages to our colleagues in court right under the noses of the cameras."

"You should have worked for the CIA," said Victoria.

∽

"I've got it!" Nikki Moreno blurted out, pumping her fist. She laughed out loud. "I'm a genius!"

Heads swiveled all over the courtroom. The judge, the ancient female deputy sheriff who provided security, the lawyers seated at their counsel tables arguing the motions—all turned toward Nikki in unison.

The judge filling in for Finney was a thirty-five-year-old divorce attorney named Miranda Fitzsimmons. In Nikki's humble but correct opinion, Fitzsimmons tried too hard to show everybody how tough she was, and the chip on her shoulder sometimes interfered with her better judgment. Plus, she was too young to be a judge—unlike Finney, who was the perfect age.

Right now Fitzsimmons was doing her best imitation of an Oliver Finney glare.

"Sorry," said Nikki.

"Anything you want to share?" asked Fitzsimmons.

Just that I'm the baddest, coolest, and most gorgeous code buster in the history of private-eyedom. "No, Your Honor."

Fitzsimmons looked displeased but soon turned back to the mundane business at hand, leaving Nikki free to gloat over her accomplishment. Nikki had arrived at court a few minutes late (shocker) and therefore had to slip into court without looking at Judge Finney's contact list. But an hour into the hearing it hit her—*Wellington Farnsworth.* He was a local college geek whom Finney used as a guinea pig for Finney's proposed LSAT questions. If Wellington couldn't figure out the answers, Finney would know they were too hard. In other words, Wellington was the anti-Nikki. Though Nikki had never met him, she had heard Finney talk about Wellington on more than one occasion—the same way proud parents talk about their honor-roll son or daughter.

But did Nikki even need his help anymore? Like James Bond or, more precisely, one of the sizzling Bond girls, she had cracked the impossible code.

Once she remembered who Farnsworth was, Nikki realized that his name must be a part of the message generated by the code. She stared for nearly five minutes at the first sentence in the code that contained his name: "The 4/5 letter, addressed to Wellington Farnsworth by the defendant, contained coded language presumably understood by Farnsworth to authorize the 4/11 hit." When the light bulb finally turned on, Nikki felt like an idiot for not having seen it sooner. Instead of the month and day working together to designate a single word, like they had in the code created by Stokes, they worked independently so that each number generated its own word. The words "Wellington Farnsworth," for example, were the fourth and fifth words after the date 4/5. *Duh,* thought Nikki. Could it be any simpler?

Smiling, she counted words and carefully generated the rest of the message. She wanted to announce to the world what she had done, but the message itself cautioned against it. Judge Finney apparently knew her too well.

> things are tense I may need help enlist Wellington Farnsworth and no others use Westlaw account for coded communication

Now she was pumped! Judge Finney was obviously more focused on winning this reality game than Nikki had originally thought. It seemed out of character for the judge to bend the rules so much, but then again, there was a lot on the line.

Nikki could hardly wait to check Judge Finney's Westlaw account. But after the initial high of solving the code dissolved, Nikki started to get worried. "Things are tense," the judge had written. Yet she had seen Finney defuse the most nerve-racking situations in court without batting an eye. If Judge Finney said things were tense, there had to be some pretty serious stuff going down.

Nikki couldn't sit still a minute longer. She weighed her options and decided that a wet skirt was a small price to pay. She took a deep breath and knocked over her bottled water, grateful for once that Fitzsimmons didn't allow soft drinks in court.

She emitted a small curse word for authenticity and looked at her judge in embarrassment. "Sorry, Your Honor," she said as she wiped off her papers. She frowned at the water that had spilled on her lap. "I'll be right back."

She walked through the wooden courtroom door and turned left, as if she were headed to the rest room. Once the door swung shut, Nikki did an about-face and headed back to Finney's chambers.

CHAPTER 27

D r. Ando limped to the witness box and sat rigidly in the large wooden chair. It seemed to dwarf him, reminding Finney of the way Yoda looked when he took his seat among the council of Jedi knights in the *Star Wars* movies.

Finney stood to examine his dangerous little foe. "You want to trade?" he whispered to Kareem.

"Why should I?" responded Kareem, his gruff voice a little louder than a whisper. "I've got the easiest witness of all."

Finney snorted. Kareem would be tomorrow's problem. Today's was sitting there waiting to get started, his bright eyes following Finney's every move. Finney knew he would have to keep the questions focused on religious differences. Attacking this sympathetic man, who obviously lived what he believed, would gain Finney no points.

"Are you a Mahayana Buddhist or a Theravada Buddhist?"

Ando smiled. "Very good, Judge Finney. You even managed to get the pronunciations correct. I follow the original form of Buddhism."

"Theravada?"

"Yes."

"As a Theravada Buddhist, you take quite literally the teachings of Siddhartha Gautama, also known as the Buddha—true?"

"Yes. He was the enlightened one."

"When did he live?"

"The fifth century BC—near the border of present-day India and Nepal."

"When were his words written down?"

"Sometime later."

Finney made a mental note. Ando acted like the perfect gentleman, but he was not going to make this easy. "How much later?"

"Perhaps two hundred and fifty years or so."

Finney wanted to make sure the good folks at home nestled in front of the TV caught the significance of this. "How do you know Buddha actually said these things? Two hundred and fifty years is a lot of time."

Ando smiled thinly. He actually seemed to be enjoying this. "The Buddha's culture was an oral culture. It was not unusual for people to memorize and accurately preserve massive amounts of information without the benefit of written documents. It is no different from the teachings of your Jesus, which were not written down for many years either."

"About thirty years, to be precise," Finney responded. "When thousands of people were still alive who had heard Jesus teach and could verify the written Scriptures. How many people who actually heard the Buddha teach were still alive when his teachings were written down?"

"That sounds more like a speech than a question," said Ando evenly. "But as you know, the answer is none."

"And your scriptures are about ten or eleven times longer than the Bible, isn't that right?"

"That is correct, Judge Finney. You should read them sometime." Though the comment was biting, Ando said it with no apparent guile. Finney realized how difficult it would be to fluster this witness. He decided to change the subject.

"As I understand your faith, we are all involved in a cycle of transmigration called samsara, or the 'endless wandering.' When we die, we are reborn into one of six possible realms—gods, titans, humans, ghosts, animals, and hell—and the cycle continues without end until we reach Nirvana. Is that a fair synopsis?"

"There is much more, Judge Finney. But you are correct in what you have said."

"And we reach Nirvana, in part, through the principle of nonattachment—that is, freeing ourselves from involvement with the things of this world?"

"Yes. The Four Noble Truths teach us that life is suffering and that this suffering is caused by attachment to the world and the people around us. We end our suffering by dropping all worldly attachments and through extensive meditation, austere living, and strenuous exercises."

"I see," said Finney. "Now, I notice that you said the Four Noble Truths require detachment from the world *and the people* around us. Does that include family?"

"It includes all people, Judge Finney."

"And, in fact, the Buddha, who is your model, abandoned his family to become a wandering monk. Is that true?"

"At great sacrifice, the Buddha renounced his wife, his infant son, his wealth, and his power when he fled to the mountains to meditate upon the way of truth."

"He named his son Rahula, Dr. Ando. What does that mean?"

"It means 'obstacle.' But Judge Finney, again, this is not so much different from your own religion. Did not your Jesus say that a man should hate his own mother and father, his own wife and children, for the sake of the kingdom—or words to that effect?"

Finney wanted to remind the witness about who was supposed to be asking the questions here. But he knew the folks at home wouldn't appreciate that. "But Jesus said it in the context of comparing our love for family with our love for Him. In a broader sense, Jesus taught us to love everyone—our enemies, our neighbors, certainly our family. Our Scriptures teach husbands to love and honor their wives as Jesus loved the church, Dr. Ando. What do your sutras teach about loving family members?"

"Another interesting speech," said Ando calmly, offering a subtle chastisement of Finney's approach to cross-examination.

"Yes," agreed Judge Javitts. "I'm giving you a lot of leeway here, Mr. Finney, but you need to stick to asking questions. You'll have your turn to testify later."

"My question is," said Finney, "what do your sutras teach about loving family members?"

"Love is an emotion," replied Ando. "We must lose every emotion." Finney had to hand it to the man—he didn't blink when it came to defending traditional Buddhism. "Attachment to other individuals means embracing a lie. We end up showering our family with material expressions of our attachments and we 'spoil' our children, as you would say in the West. But the Buddha said, 'I have killed all of you before. I have been chopped up by all of you in previous lives. We have all killed each other as enemies. So why should we be attached to each other?' "

Finney smiled. "So you may have chopped me up in a prior life, Dr. Ando?"

"The more surprising thing," said the witness, without returning the smile, "is that we may have been friends. Perhaps family members. Perhaps I was your family pet."

Finney didn't miss the implication. Perhaps Ando had been reincarnated into a higher form, whereas Finney was stuck or regressing on his march toward Nirvana. Oh well, if Buddhism was true, Finney would probably be a cockroach in the next life after this cross-examination.

"Sounds a little like the story about the monk named Katayana," said Finney. He thought he detected a brief flicker of surprise shoot across Ando's face. Finney had done his homework.

"Yes. That story illustrates my point."

"Please share it with us, Dr. Ando."

"The short form goes something like this. A monk named Katayana walked through a forest and saw a man, a woman, and a baby eating lunch. Katayana laughed at the scene before him, and when his disciples asked why, he told them. 'They're eating a fish they caught from the lake,'

Katayana said. 'In a former life, that fish was the grandfather. The dog who is now barking for the fish was the grandmother. The nursing baby in a former life was an enemy of the husband, a man the husband killed for attacking his wife.' "

Ando paused and took a drink of water. "That may sound foolish to you, Judge Finney, but that is because you have a Western mind-set. We look at reality differently. You grew up in the most prosperous country on earth—you have never been truly hungry or seen a family member murdered. But in other parts of the world, people suffer greatly. My religion helps them detach from the things of this world and overcome that suffering."

Now who's giving the speeches? thought Finney. "I appreciate the explanation, Dr. Ando, but I think the story speaks for itself."

"That it does."

Finney and the witness sparred for another half hour, with Finney spending most of his time on the concept of Nirvana—the extinction of all personality. Javitts eventually interrupted, telling Finney he had one more minute.

"So you're saying that real enlightenment comes from realizing that our situation on earth is hopeless and we just need to detach from it?" asked Finney.

Ando thought about the question for a moment and gave Finney a patient smile. It was almost as if the witness was waiting just long enough before starting his response so that Finney wouldn't have time for a follow-up.

"You ask excellent questions, Judge Finney, and as long as we keep asking these questions, we will find the truth. Your own King Solomon, one of the smartest men in the Jewish and Christian tradition, asked a lot of the same questions. He searched for the purpose of life. He tried everything—wealth, labor, women. In the end, what did he conclude?" Ando did not wait for Finney to answer. " 'Vanity of vanities. All is vanity.'

Material things did not satisfy. That's why Buddha teaches nonattachment. Perhaps your Solomon was not so far from Buddha?"

"Time is up," said Javitts.

"Didn't Solomon conclude that book by saying we should fear God and keep his commandments?" asked Finney.

"Time is up," repeated Javitts.

Finney frowned and reluctantly returned to the counsel table. When he did, Kareem leaned over and provided his assessment: "Not bad for an infidel."

"Not bad for which infidel?" asked Finney. "Me or him?"

CHAPTER 28

Nikki double-checked the address and pulled her bright red Sebring convertible into the drive. She expected a college dorm, maybe a frat house, or at least some college apartment. Instead, she got middle-class suburbia—a two-story vinyl-sided house at the end of a cul-de-sac in Chesapeake, Virginia.

Nikki walked up to the front porch, smoothed her short leather skirt, and rang the bell.

A middle-aged woman in knee-length shorts and a T-shirt cracked the door. She was tall and thin with curly brown hair and a forgettable face. She blocked a brown-and-white corgi with her foot. The dog looked like a fox that somebody had mistakenly fitted with Chihuahua legs.

"Hi. I'm Nikki Moreno, law clerk for Judge Oliver Finney. I'm looking for Wellington Farnsworth."

"Corky!" the woman said, but it was too late. He was already jumping up on Nikki's bare leg and licking. Nikki wanted to drop kick the runt. Dogs were not her thing.

"It's okay," she found herself saying. She squatted down, bending at the knees in a ladylike fashion, and reached out to pet him ever so gingerly with her left hand. This made the dog slobber more, his potent bursts of dog breath almost knocking Nikki over. She scratched his back for a few seconds, in order to pass herself off as a dog lover, and then stood up.

"I'm sorry," the woman said. "He loves people." She reached down and dragged the dog by its collar back into the foyer. He ran into another room to grab a ball.

"Wellington!" the woman yelled.

"Who is it?" came a shout from upstairs.

"Someone from Judge Finney's office."

The corgi was back with a slimy plastic ball in his mouth. He dropped it at Nikki's feet. *Fat chance.*

The woman picked it up and threw it, sending the dog scampering. A few seconds later, Wellington came clumping down the stairs.

Nikki's first thought was that she must be getting old. This kid looked way too young for college. If it hadn't been for a trace of acne, he could have passed for an oversized middle schooler.

Wellington was big—about six feet two inches or so, Nikki would guess—and chunky, with a round baby face and curly brown hair he must have gotten from his mom. It didn't look like a razor had ever grazed the boy's skin. He wore dress shorts that were a size too small—halfway up the thighs and tight—together with a tucked-in button-down shirt and white socks that covered his calves.

Nikki had been expecting a Pierce Brosnan–style James Bond. Instead, she got Napoleon Dynamite with a Twinkies fetish.

There were now four of them in the foyer since Corky had returned with his disgusting ball. It looked like Mom planned to stick around too.

Nikki stuck out her hand. "I'm Nikki Moreno, law clerk to Judge Finney," she said. "He asked me to talk with you *in private* about a matter where he needs your help." She knew she must have been overwhelming for the kid. This was Nikki Moreno dressed for the second Oliver Finney party—a tight knit aqua top, appropriately low cut, a black leather miniskirt, and color-coordinated sequined sandals with straps that wound provocatively up the ankles. No sense spending money on a pedicure if you weren't going to draw a little attention to it.

Wellington swallowed hard and shook Nikki's hand. "More LSAT questions?"

"Something like that."

Corky dropped the ball at Nikki's feet and started pawing at her. Nikki waited a second, giving her hosts time to call this mutt off. Then she bent over and picked up the ball, using only the tips of her thumb and forefinger, and tossed it down the hallway. She wiped her fingers on her skirt.

"Why don't you use the dining-room table?" suggested Wellington's mom.

After Nikki and Wellington settled in at the table, Nikki started asking questions right away. Though she had to pry it out of her painfully shy new partner, Nikki learned that Wellington was a seventeen-year-old whiz kid in his second year at Old Dominion University. He had been homeschooled and had graduated from high school at sixteen. He was now pursuing a math major with an emphasis in differential equations and approximations theory. *Whatever,* thought Nikki.

As they talked, Wellington's mom and the dog competed for the prize of most annoying. Mrs. Farnsworth was a hoverer. She brought in iced tea. She checked to see if they needed anything. She busied herself in the kitchen, puttering around at a counter just on the other side of the dining-room door.

Meanwhile, the bothersome little Corky kept bringing his slimy plastic ball and placing it at Nikki's feet. Wellington would reach down and throw it, but the dog would bring it back to Nikki. She ignored him until he started chewing on her sandal. She slyly slid her feet under the table… and gave him a swift kick.

Above the table, she swore Wellington to secrecy and told him about Finney's clandestine contact with her. She showed him a printout of Finney's e-mail and noticed his eyes go wide as he read his own name. "There's a code in there," Nikki said proudly.

"I know," said Wellington. "The dates are a dead giveaway. I can't believe Judge Finney used something this easy."

"Yeah," said Nikki, clucking in agreement. *Easy?*

"I can't believe the show's producers didn't catch this one," said Wellington.

"Me, either," said Nikki, though she felt out of her league with a guy who studied different kinds of equations and approximated theories.

"Did you check Westlaw?" Wellington asked.

"Yeah," said Nikki, just as Mrs. Farnsworth reappeared to fill their tea glasses.

"You sure you don't want anything to munch on?" she asked, sneaking a peak at the message on the table.

"Nope," said Nikki. She let silence fill the air until Mrs. Farnsworth took the hint and left. Nikki leaned forward.

"Even your mom can't know about this, Wellington. The judge said nobody but you."

"Okay."

Nikki brought out her second prized document. It was a printout of the words she had deciphered by applying the same code to the Westlaw search requests. She had double-checked her work and now watched as her new prized pupil studied it.

change codes frequently use capital letters in search requests then solve using keys from my book each new search session use new key from next chapter starting with introduction for next message and so on

"What book?" asked Wellington.

Nikki lowered her voice so the eavesdropping ears of Mama Farnsworth wouldn't hear. She gave Corky another not-so-gentle kick. "Finney wrote a book under a pen name. It's called *The Cross Examination of Jesus Christ*. I don't think anybody else knows about it. He told me once that he hid secret messages in that book."

Wellington smiled, his shyness dissolving as the task became clear. "Brilliant," he said. "Judge Finney wants to send secure encrypted messages, so he references a key source that only you will know. The key never changes hands and therefore can't be compromised. The encryption method changes with every message and therefore can't be deciphered—even if they figure out that encrypted messages are being sent." Wellington shook his head in amazement and approval. "That's ridiculous," he said.

What?

He must have noticed the look on Nikki's face. "I mean a good kind of ridiculous."

"Yeah," said Nikki. "It is ridiculous."

Nikki had to get going; she was already late for her own Judge Finney party. She had mixed emotions about dragging Wellington along. On the one hand, he would severely cramp her style—it wasn't exactly like appearing on the arm of Brad Pitt. On the other hand, she needed to get him away from Mama Farnsworth so they could talk more freely. Also, she wanted him around if Finney sent another set of Westlaw messages tonight.

Against her better judgment, she ended up inviting Wellington to the party, confident she could sneak him into the bar despite his youthful looks. She needed him to explain the keys in Finney's book, and then they could check Westlaw afterward to see if there were any new messages. When she asked him, Wellington looked like he had mixed emotions— perhaps torn between this intriguing new mission and his fear of meeting people he didn't know. To help the kid make up his mind, Nikki pulled her legs out from under the table and strategically crossed them. "I could really use your help."

"Mom," called out Wellington, "I've got to help Ms. Moreno on some things for Judge Finney. It's kind of confidential, but we've got to get started tonight."

Ms. Moreno? She'd have to break the kid of that habit.

Mrs. Farnsworth immediately appeared at the doorway, shooting a disapproving look toward the Moreno legs. "Can't you do it here?" she asked.

"No, we really can't," said Nikki.

Wellington ended up promising his mom he'd be back by midnight.

Mrs. Farnsworth let him borrow the keys to the minivan. He and Nikki exchanged cell numbers in case they got separated.

"I'll wait here while you throw on some jeans," said Nikki. If this guy was such a code expert, he could certainly catch that hint. She would have to work on the shirt next time.

"Okay," said Wellington, heading upstairs to change.

When he came back down, he had his laptop tucked under his arm. Nikki didn't have the heart to tell him that it wasn't that kind of party.

CHAPTER 29

Right after dinner, Finney slipped back to his condo and sat down at the keyboard. He logged on to Westlaw and stared at the screen. This would be so much easier if he could write a few things down. But the camera recorded every move and he couldn't take that chance.

He racked his brain to think of search requests that would fit the encryption pattern for the code contained in the introduction to *The Cross Examination of Jesus Christ*. Everything that crossed his mind was too obvious. Today he had cross-examined Ando. Tomorrow it would be Finney's turn to be grilled by Kareem. Finney needed to think of search requests that made it look like he was getting ready for Kareem's questions.

He finally settled on a few simple searches, though he knew Nikki Moreno would not be happy.

da (after 1/1/03) Hearsay and "Proof of Resurrection" and "first-hand Knowledge"

He received a response from Westlaw that said no documents satisfied his request, but he thought it at least looked legitimate. His next request read:

da (after 1/1/02) Resurrection and Muslim and "Generally held beliefs"

This search generated a whole slew of documents, and Finney took his time reviewing them. Then he typed in one final search:

da (after 1/1/00) Islam and "Lebanese sects"

He reviewed the one newspaper article that surfaced and shook his head. He should have thought of this earlier. He could hear Nikki now.

❧

Nikki arrived at the Waterside parking lot after a painfully slow trip from the Chesapeake suburbs. Wellington Farnsworth might be the world's greatest code geek, but he clearly had a thing or two to learn about driving if he intended to keep up with Nikki Moreno. Twice she had to pull the Sebring over and wait after sneaking through a yellowish-reddish light that Wellington refused to run through. She tried to reach him on his cell phone so she could tell him to pick it up a little, but she ended up in his voice mail. On the interstate she finally gave up and putted along in the right lane with the grandmas and accountants so Wellington wouldn't disappear from her rearview mirror.

By the time they hit the parking deck, it was nearly 9:00 p.m. Nikki had been working her cell phone furiously, making sure the collection buckets would be sitting at the door of Norfolk's Finest Sports Bar.

Nikki squeezed into a spot with her Sebring and watched Wellington take forever to park the minivan. Forward and back three times before he finally got it straightened out. He emerged from the vehicle with his trusty laptop under his arm.

"You won't need that until later," said Nikki. "We'll check for messages after the show."

Wellington put the laptop back in the van and pushed the automatic lock on the key chain twice. Each time, the van responded with an obedient beep.

Nikki gave Wellington the dog-eared copy of *The Cross Examination of Jesus Christ* she had lifted from Finney's office. "Don't lose this," she said. "I ordered another book online, but right now it's the only copy we've got."

Wellington took the book gingerly, his round eyes wide, as if he were holding some ancient Egyptian treasure. He opened it to the introduction.

"Not now," said Nikki as she started toward the elevator in the parking garage. "We're already running late."

In the elevator Nikki handed Wellington the second piece of the puzzle: a folded sheet of paper with a series of random letters written on it.

"I pulled these from the first page of the introduction," Nikki explained. "Finney tried to hide them in the interior design of the book—you'll see what I mean. They're somewhat obscure, but I found them." She took a second to bask in her accomplishment before having to admit her failure. "But I couldn't find the key anywhere in the introduction. Seems like we're missing the secret decoder ring."

Wellington took the paper and stared at it. The bell rang and they disembarked from the elevator. Wellington walked slowly, his eyes glued to the letters Nikki had recorded:

YOVHHVWZIVGSVXLWVYIVZPVIHULIGSVBHSZOOFMWVIHGZMWGSVNBHGVIRVH

"C'mon," Nikki said, picking up the pace. "You'll have time to analyze that inside." She watched Wellington tuck the paper inside the book as they crossed the street.

"I can probably solve it without a key," Wellington said matter-of-factly. "I think that's the whole point."

"Yeah," said Nikki. "I tried that too." She tried not to sound defensive. But how could anyone solve that list of garbled letters without a key?

"By the way," she said, "you might want to make sure your cell phone is on. I tried to call a couple times but kept getting your message."

"I know," said Wellington. "Sorry about that, but I don't use my cell phone while I'm driving, and I didn't want to pull over and lose you."

That's a dumb rule, thought Nikki, but for once in her life she chose not to verbalize her every thought. Still, her silence must have conveyed the message because Wellington felt compelled to respond.

"Drivers who talk on their cell phones are four times as likely to have accidents injuring themselves," said Wellington. "It's why New York State made it illegal to talk on a cell phone and drive at the same time."

"What do the studies say about talking on the cell phone while putting on makeup?" Nikki asked.

"While driving?" asked Wellington, as if the feat Nikki described were humanly impossible.

But Nikki didn't have time to answer. They were walking through the door of Norfolk's Finest Sports Bar, and Wellington was about to get carded.

"He's my designated driver," said Nikki, pulling Wellington past the bouncer. "He won't be drinking tonight."

The bouncer nodded. He knew whose party this was.

❧

Thursday night's show started slowly, in Nikki's opinion. The first half hour seemed more like a documentary than a reality show. She had distanced herself from Wellington quickly so the eligible bachelors wouldn't get the wrong impression, though they would probably think he was a little brother or cousin rather than a date. She did walk over to check on Wellington a few times. He was sitting alone in a booth, sipping a soft drink while he watched the show with one eye and studied Finney's book with the other. He would check something on a page in the book and then make a note inside the front cover, check the page again, and make another note.

"You having fun?" Nikki asked.

"Sure."

"Making any progress?"

"I think so. But I need to slip outside and make a call. It's a little loud in here."

"Okay," said Nikki, talking above the noise. She felt a strong arm drape around her shoulder. It was attached to a killer body. Byron had finally noticed the vibes she had been throwing off. "There's someone I want you to meet," he said.

She tried not to act excited, but it wasn't easy. Byron was an investigative reporter for a local television network—the consumer advocate for Hampton Roads. Nikki had always swooned at Byron's hidden camera pieces. "He can hide a camera on me anytime," she told her friends.

"I'll check back a little later," she told Wellington.

Byron introduced Nikki to a few of his cohorts, and she threw out some hints about dancing later. Though Byron worked for a different network than the one airing *Faith on Trial*, he seemed to be enjoying himself. He bought another round of drinks and critiqued the production values of the show for anybody who cared to listen. Most turned their attention back to the television as the commercials yielded to another segment of the show.

The producers had zeroed in on the relationship between faith and health. They raised the question of whether miracles of healing ever occurred, and they interviewed various experts. They did profiles on the terminal diseases attacking the contestants—all except Dr. Kline, who apparently didn't need a terminal disease to be healed from since she didn't believe in God anyway. They showed the interviews of the contestants from the cross-examination room, with Finney affirming his belief in a God who heals.

They concluded the segment by showing Judge Javitts's challenge to the contestants, telling them that they would be examined by medical experts near the conclusion of their two weeks on the island, just to see if God had chosen a favorite in the reality show and had healed one of the contestants. They didn't show the reactions of the contestants to Javitts's challenge.

Nikki seriously doubted whether God was going to heal a man who had been a smoker his entire life. Especially one who refused to give up cigars even now. She was saddened, however, as she learned the full extent of her judge's cancer. She knew he had been treated in the past, but she didn't realize how much the cancer had spread. Finney had always been private about it. Now the whole nation knew.

She found herself with conflicting emotions. There was the spine-tingling thrill of sitting next to Byron, who was chock-full of insider tips about how to improve the show. Nikki was imagining herself later that night, cavorting around the Virginia Beach dance floors with God's gift to women, a local celebrity desired by every red-blooded young lady in Tidewater. But then there was the judge, his face plastered all over the television screens in Norfolk's Finest Sports Bar, talking about his inoperable and spreading cancer.

The morbid subject seemed to cast a pall over everyone. It didn't stop the flow of beer; in fact, it probably increased it as the patrons thought about their own mortality. But there was none of the bawdy cheering and hollering that had characterized the place on Tuesday night.

Until the show entered the last twenty minutes.

On Tuesday the producers had promised temptation, and on Thursday they delivered. They focused first on Dr. Kline and the Swami, with hints that the others would have their day later.

Surprisingly, Dr. Kline's temptation had been orchestrated even before she arrived on Paradise Island. Through clever use of hidden cameras, and the cooperation of some of Dr. Kline's colleagues at the university, the show's producers had set up a scenario tempting Kline to exaggerate some test results on a government grant proposal. Though the shading of the results would have virtually guaranteed the grant, Kline steadfastly refused to go along with her colleagues.

Boring, thought Nikki. She was much more interested in the temptation of the next contestant. The Swami, it seemed, had been falling under the spell of the ex-reality-show bachelorette, Tammy Dietz. Though the girl made a lousy host, she knew all the right signals to send to the eager Swami, enticing him to stop by her condo late one night. She shooed away the cameraman who had followed him and apparently neglected to inform the Swami that her condo had cameras hidden in the walls.

"Are you sure we should be doing this?" she asked, coming up for breath after a particularly long kiss. "I signed something saying I wouldn't get involved with any contestants. I don't want to lose my job."

"Nobody will ever know," said the Swami as he pulled her close for more.

It turned out to be quite a night for the Swami. He not only got the girl, but when the results from Tuesday's audience verdict was announced, the Swami came out the winner. "Remember," said Judge Javitts, "the results are based not on the total number of votes but on the number of converts, determined by the extent to which the contestants exceeded their baseline percentages."

The verdict brought Norfolk's Finest Sports Bar to life, with a hearty round of boos and widespread heckling of the television screen. Byron had a few choice words about the Swami that Nikki chalked up to jealous male testosterone. The lawyers at the bar tossed around talk of lawsuits and corrupt Hollywood producers. On the screen, Javitts was explaining that next Tuesday's show would feature excerpts from the contestants' cross-examinations of one another. Viewers could submit their own questions by e-mail. Javitts would pick the most interesting ones and ask them in the cross-examination room.

Things quieted down again for the stunning conclusion. There were pictures of Kline and Finney sailing, with hints of a May-December romance. A question was left hanging in the air: "Will other contestants fall to the temptations of Paradise Island?"

And then the credits rolled.

CHAPTER 30

Nikki pried herself away from Byron half an hour after the show ended. She promised to return in a few minutes so they could head out to the Virginia Beach dance floors.

She found Wellington still toiling away in the booth and slid in next to him. She felt guilty for ignoring him most of the night. "How's my partner in crime?" she asked.

He was staring at a chart of block letters in front of him. "I think I've just about got it figured out."

"You found the key?" Nikki scooted closer and glanced at Wellington's writing. It looked like hieroglyphics to her. Neat hieroglyphics, with letters encased in perfectly formed boxes. "Where?"

"I didn't exactly find the key," said Wellington. He seemed to be blushing. "But I'm using techniques of cryptanalysis to unscramble the message without the key."

"Oh," said Nikki. *Cryptawhat?*

She stared at the letters but didn't know where to begin. "You gonna show me?"

"Sure." Wellington actually slid a little *away* from Nikki, to give himself room to think, apparently. *When is the last time a guy did that?* He placed the book between them and turned from the page where he had been writing to the first page of the introduction—the page where the random code letters were hidden.

"I think this is a simple monoalphabetic substitution cipher," he began.

"I see," said Nikki.

"You know what that is?" Wellington looked surprised.

"Some kind of code?"

Wellington's face fell, as if Nikki had guessed wrong. "Yes. Well, it's a particular type of code where one letter is substituted for another."

No kidding, Sherlock, Nikki wanted to say. Instead, she just put her elbow on the table, chin in hand, and nodded.

"For centuries," continued Wellington as if he were a university professor, "this type of code was considered unbreakable without a key. But then Muslim cryptologists were the first to realize that frequency analysis could decipher just about any monoalphabetic substitution cipher."

"Frequency analysis," repeated Nikki, her elbow sliding farther forward on the table.

"Yes. That's why I needed to make a call," said Wellington. "I had my mom check something on the Internet." He turned back to the title page in the front of the book—a mostly blank page he had been using as his scratch pad. "I had her look up the average frequency results for the letters of the English language."

Nikki slid up so she could see the chart.

E = 12.7%
T = 9.1%
A = 8.2%
O = 7.5%
I = 7.0%
N = 6.7%
S = 6.3%
H = 6.1%
R = 6.0%

"Now, these are just averages," continued Wellington, "but they give us a good place to start."

Who thinks of these things? wondered Nikki.

"The next thing I did was to count the various letters in the encoded message and see which ones occurred most frequently." Wellington flipped back to the first page of the introduction and ran his finger along the code.

"You counted every letter in there?" Nikki asked in amazement.

"That's just the start," said Wellington, flipping back to the title page. "Here's what I found." He pointed to a place where he had carefully recorded his results. "I started by focusing on the top three letters. V occurred twelve times; H occurred seven; and I occurred six."

"I'll take your word for it," said Nikki, sounding unimpressed. But she actually thought it was clever.

"So if everything followed the law of averages exactly, which it never does, then V would be the substitution for E; H would be the substitution for T; and I would be the substitution for A. Do you follow me?" Wellington astounded Nikki with how much he was into this stuff, coming out of his shell when he talked about code breaking.

"You sure you haven't been drinking?" mumbled Nikki.

"No. I haven't."

"I was just kidding, Wellington. I follow you."

"Good. Next, I decided to test my assumption about V being the code text for the letter E. I did this by performing a before-and-after analysis. This is based on the well-known fact that vowels like E can be found adjacent to just about any letter of the alphabet, but consonants like the letter T—the second most frequent letter in the English language—tend to avoid certain other letters. For example, how many words do you know where T is next to the letters B or D or G or J or K or M or Q or V?"

Nikki let her head slump a little lower. "None. But then it's not something I spend a lot of time thinking about."

"Hey, Nikki, great party." A few guys stopped by the booth and Nikki perked up. She noticed Wellington discreetly close the book and slide it under his forearm. She talked to the intruders for a few minutes and then they left. She thought about Byron and the Virginia Beach bands in full swing.

Wellington reopened the book, and Nikki returned her chin to her hand. "So anyway, I found that the letter V acted like a vowel," Wellington said. "It was next to a lot of other letters—thirteen to be exact. Pretty good confirmation that V probably does represent E, just like we thought."

One letter down, twenty-five to go. Nikki made a conspicuous show of checking her watch.

"And it gets better. If V is truly E, then it usually doesn't take long to figure out which letter represents the letter H. Do you know why?"

"Look, Wellington, to be honest, I don't have the foggiest idea. This stuff is all fascinating, but it would probably go quicker if you just explained it rather than asking me questions." Wellington looked deflated, and Nikki immediately felt like a jerk.

"Don't take it personally," Nikki continued. "You're doing great. It's just that I'm more of a lecture-at-me student than a question-and-answer student."

"Okay." He took a sip of soda. "No problem. Anyway, the answer is found in this quirky little personality trait of the letter H—it almost always comes before the letter E but never behind the letter E. Can you think of a word where H comes behind E... Oops, sorry. Like I was saying, there are very few words where that happens."

"Exactly," said Nikki, sensing the kid's need for encouragement. She glanced over her shoulder. Byron was still where she had left him, but it looked like another woman had elbowed into his group.

"Here are the results of my before-and-after analysis," said Wellington, pointing to another chart on the front page. "The one letter that occurred before V three times but never occurred after V is the letter S. So I was thinking that S in the code letters probably represents H in real life, or what we call plaintext. And I also noticed that S appears in this coded message four times, which would also be consistent with S representing H, because H is a frequently used letter." Wellington paused and looked pleased. "That's where I was when you sat down."

Nikki looked down at his chart.

Y	O	V	H	H	V	W	Z	I	V	G	S	V	X	L	W	V	Y	I	V	Z	P	V	I	H	U	L	I
		E			E				E		H	E				E			E			E					

G	S	V	B	H	S	Z	O	O	F	M	W	V	I	H	G	Z	M	W	G	S	V	N	B	H	G	V	I	R	V	H
	H	E			H							E								H	E					E			E	

That's it? she wanted to ask. *All that for two lousy letters?*

But Wellington slid forward on his seat, and Nikki had to admit that his enthusiasm was contagious. She took her chin out of her hand and sat up straighter. Was it possible they could solve this entire hodgepodge of letters without a key?

"What do you notice?" Wellington asked, forgetting the rule about questions.

"Can we buy another vowel?" asked Nikki.

"Don't need to," said the young genius. "We just need to look for repeating patterns. What is the most common three-letter word in the English language?"

"Sex?"

Wellington turned red, which Nikki thought served him right for asking another question. "Actually, it's 'the.' And if you look at our chart, you'll see that the code letters G-S-V repeat themselves three times. Because we already think that S is a symbol for H and V is a symbol for E, it would make sense that G would be a symbol for T, thus spelling the word 'the' several times."

"Plus," said Nikki, looking at one of Wellington's charts, "G is one of our frequently occurring letters in the code message. You would expect it to be if it stood for the letter T, which is the second most popular letter in the English language."

Nikki smiled at herself. Not quite Mensa material, but she had her moments.

"You're a natural," said Wellington. He handed his pencil to Nikki to fill in the chart with their new discovery. She did so, resisting the urge to ask him why he was carrying a pencil around with him in the first place.

"Now we look for pairs where the same letter is repeated," said Wellington.

"I see two," said Nikki. "What does that tell us?"

"Since we don't have spaces between the words, it's a little hard to tell. It could just be coincidence—one word ending in the same letter that the next word starts with. But more likely, it's one of the letters in the English language that we sometimes see as a pair—S-S, E-E, T-T, L-L, M-M, or O-O. So let's take an educated guess at what plaintext the code letters HH stand for."

Wellington pointed to the appropriate spot on his diagram. "We know it can't be either E-E or T-T, because those letters are already taken. And since the code letters H-H are surrounded with a code letter that represents E on one side and another E on the other side, we know they can't stand for O-O either. I can't think of any words that have the sequence of letters E-O-O-E. So that pretty much leaves L-L or M-M or S-S. And, since the letter H occurs seven times in the code letters, it must be a popular letter."

Nikki nodded her head, pencil in hand.

"Let's therefore assume that H represents S," said Wellington.

The chart was getting better:

Y	O	V	H	H	V	W	Z	I	V	G	S	V	X	L	W	V	Y	I	V	Z	P	V	I	H	U	L	I
		E	S	S	E				E	T	H	E				E			E			E		S			

G	S	V	B	H	S	Z	O	O	F	M	W	V	I	H	G	Z	M	W	G	S	V	N	B	H	G	V	I	R	V	H
T	H	E		S	H							E		S	T				T	H	E			S	T	E			E	S

"Now, focus on parts of the chart where we have a lot of letters filled in," instructed Wellington. "Like right here." He pointed out a section that had drawn Nikki's eye as well. "Take a guess at the missing letters."

G	S	V	B	H	S	Z	O	O
T	H	E		S	H			

Nikki stared for a minute, feeling like a contestant on *Wheel of Fortune*. "Do you know?" she asked Wellington.

"I think so."

"Don't tell me."

Another minute passed... "I've got it!" She picked up the pencil and wrote in the letters.

G	S	V	B	H	S	Z	O	O
T	H	E	Y	S	H	A	L	L

"Now fill in those same letters on the rest of the chart," instructed Wellington.

When Nikki did so, she realized they were almost there.

Y	O	V	H	H	V	W	Z	I	V	G	S	V	X	L	W	V	Y	I	V	Z	P	V	I	H	U	L	I
	L	E	S	S	E		A		E	T	H	E				E			E	A		E		S			

G	S	V	B	H	S	Z	O	O	F	M	W	V	I	H	G	Z	M	W	G	S	V	N	B	H	G	V	I	R	V	H
T	H	E	Y	S	H	A	L	L				E		S	T	A			T	H	E		Y	S	T	E			E	S

She was so enthralled with the chart that she hadn't noticed Byron standing beside the booth. "Must be a fascinating read," he said.

Wellington abruptly closed the book as if it were a *Playboy* magazine and Byron were his mother. *Can we call any more attention to it?* Nikki wondered.

"You know me and books," said Nikki.

"How much longer do you think you'll be?" Byron asked.

This is, thought Nikki, *what some would call a moment of truth.* She and Wellington were so close to solving this code. Afterward, they would need to check the Internet to see whether Finney had left a message. Her boss might be in some kind of trouble.

But then again, he sure didn't look like he was in any trouble at the end of the night's show. And if he were *here,* Finney would probably just tell Nikki to go out and have a good time.

She ultimately decided to do what Nikki Moreno always did—have it both ways. She turned and faced Byron. First, she had to establish that she didn't like competition.

"I've got to finish tutoring Wellington here, and he's got a big test tomorrow." She didn't dare check behind her to see how badly Wellington's face was giving away the lie. "Looks like you've got someone else over there waiting for you anyway."

"Kaitlin?" Byron said, looking genuinely surprised. "Not exactly my type, Nikki. If you don't come, I won't be able to ditch her all night."

Next came Nikki's quick but effective deep-in-thought look. "Tell you what," she said. "Why don't you guys go on ahead to someplace at the beach and let me finish up a few things with Wellington. I'll call you in about an hour, and we can rendezvous at a different bar, away from the gang over there, including Kaitlin."

Byron gave her a sly "I catch your drift" nod. "Sounds great," he said. "You need my number?"

Nikki plugged his number into her cell phone and watched him walk back to his table. "That," she said more to herself than to Wellington, "is how you solve a real code."

She turned back to her instructor—or her pupil or whatever Wellington was. "Where were we?" she asked.

He already had the book open to his chart. "What do you think this first word is?" he asked.

"I see it now," she said. "Y must be B because that first word is 'blessed.' Which also means that W must represent D."

Wellington filled in the blanks below Y and W and then another match occurred to Nikki. "Z must be the letter A because it's going to say 'Blessed are the…something.'" And so it went, Nikki filling in blanks as Wellington watched like a proud seventeen-year-old father.

Eventually Nikki filled in the last letter and leaned back to read her creation: "Blessed are the code breakers, for they shall understand the mysteries."

She held her hand up for Wellington, who managed a clumsy high-five.

"It's a centuries-old cipher," he explained, his demeanor all businesslike again. "You just reverse the alphabet. A stands for Z and vice versa. Even Old Testament scribes used it occasionally."

"Oh yeah," said Nikki. "The *atbash* cipher."

She thought the poor boy's jaw would drop on the table.

CHAPTER 31

Twenty minutes later, Wellington and Nikki arrived at a Starbucks with wireless Internet access that just happened to be on the way to Virginia Beach. Nikki ordered a cinnamon spice mocha with a double shot of espresso. Wellington wanted water. Nikki checked her purse but was low on cash, though she had a few donation buckets full of it in the backseat of the Sebring. "Guess I'll have to use a credit card," she said, waiting for Wellington to take the hint.

Sure enough, her sidekick reached into his pocket just as she handed the card to the cashier. "Here," he said, handing Nikki his pen.

She frowned, took the pen, and signed the receipt. "Thanks," Nikki said, with a healthy dose of sarcasm as she handed the pen back.

"You're welcome," said Wellington.

Back at the table, Wellington lectured Nikki as he fired up his laptop. "They've done extensive germ studies, you know. Guess what surface consistently has the most germs?"

"The toilet handle," said Nikki. "That's why I use my foot."

"Nope. It's the pens at stores and restaurants that you sign credit-card receipts with. You know how many people have left their germs on that pen? You know where their hands have been?"

"It's a dangerous world," Nikki said.

At Nikki's request, Wellington turned his laptop toward her so she could log on to the Westlaw site. She suspected that a guy as tech savvy as Wellington would be able to retrieve the password later even if he didn't see her enter it. Still, she didn't have to make it easy for him.

Nikki checked under the tab marked Research Trail and took a sip of her drink. She sat forward. Finney had left a fresh research trail, complete with a number of words capitalized. Now that they knew the key for the introduction, deciphering this message using that key would be a piece of cake.

"Here it is," she said, feeling like a CIA agent. "Write these capital letters down."

Wellington took out his pencil and a pad of paper he had brought from the car while Nikki looked at the first search Finney conducted in this recent series:

da (after 1/1/03) Hearsay and "Proof of Resurrection" and "first-hand Knowledge"

"H-P-R-K from the first search," said Nikki. "And here's the second one: R-M-G. And the third is just I-L. Three searches. Must be a short message."

Nikki sat back and took another sip of her coffee as Wellington decoded the letters using the *atbash* key they had discovered. She noticed the edges of his mouth turn down in worry. "What?" she asked.

Wellington looked at his paper as he spoke. "It says, 'Skip intro.'" He began double-checking the letters.

It took a second for the implications to sink in. "You have *got* to be kidding," Nikki sputtered. "'Skip intro'? What kind of message is that?"

She leaned forward and Wellington turned his paper toward her. *Skip intro?* she thought. *Now's a fine time to tell us!*

"I was afraid of that," said Wellington calmly. He hadn't even opened his bottled water yet. "The problem is that the *atbash* cipher ends up replacing all the popular letters of the alphabet with letters that are hardly ever used. A becomes Z. C becomes X. E becomes V. It's very difficult to use letters like Z, X, and V in a Westlaw search request without looking suspicious. Judge Finney probably thought he would be ill advised to use this cipher to send us a long message."

"He's the one who told us to start with the intro!" Nikki said, her voice rising. She loved Finney, but this was ridiculous.

"I know," Wellington said softly.

Nikki needed to vent, but it was hard to argue with a guy who didn't fight back. And even harder to argue with a judge who was thousands of miles away. "All that work we did," Nikki complained. Wellington looked at her like maybe she had used the word "we" a little loosely.

"What?" she shot back, though Wellington hadn't actually said anything. "I deciphered the first message and helped with this one."

"I didn't say you didn't."

Nikki sighed and slumped in her chair. What was the use of getting upset if nobody was going to put up a fight?

"Well," she said, "at least we know it's not a huge crisis, or Finney would have had the next message waiting for us."

"Can't argue with that," said Wellington. But Nikki wished he would argue with *something*. Anything. Right now she just needed a good argument so she could get rid of her frustrations.

Instead, Wellington was still focused on the details of the code. "We need to put some Westlaw searches in as a reply," he told Nikki. "That way Finney will at least know we're with him." Nikki found it hard to disagree with that logic, though she tried to think of a reason to do so anyway. It took Wellington about fifteen minutes to construct and send two simple Westlaw searches that conveyed to Finney their own message: "OK."

That done, Nikki was ready to head to a certain Virginia Beach dance floor.

"Do you mind if I take the book home so I can work on the next cipher?" asked Wellington.

Nikki eyed Finney's book and suddenly felt territorial. In her opinion, she was in charge of this espionage outfit. Wellington was just a decipherment specialist. "Tell you what," she said. "Let me write down the code letters for chapter one, and you can take those with you. I'll call if we get another message on Westlaw."

Nikki opened the book to chapter one and began writing. This batch looked every bit as jumbled as the one before, but she had no doubt they would solve it. It read:

SANHOVVORYBUNKSAQLTYAJLRNRGTSYQOFNOKISQTSAFOJNSAQLTYACNRTRFAQBRS

Nikki suddenly had an idea, one inspired by her memory of Farnsworth's corgi. "How far is this Starbucks from your house?" she asked.

"Twenty-five minutes."

"Good—about halfway. This will be our rendezvous. If I call and we decide to meet at a certain time, we'll both know without saying it that this will be the spot."

"Is that really necessary?" asked Wellington.

Nikki looked around as if national security were at stake. "You can never be too sure," she whispered.

CHAPTER 32

L arge thunderhead clouds filled the sky. The winds buffeted the sail and kicked up small waves that clawed at the Hobie Cat as it skimmed across the water. Finney had his hand on the tiller, the full sail tilting the boat. They leaned back over the port side of the boat to provide counterbalance, the spray from the rough surf soaking them both.

"You really love this, don't you?" Victoria called out.

Finney had his eye on the rolling waves, catching them at just the right angle. "Believe it or not, it helps me relax," he said. "Even when the water's rough."

Victoria leaned back even farther, holding on tight and allowing the wind to rush across her face. She shook some hair out of her eyes and glanced back toward the shore where Hadji was still doing yoga.

"Is that stuff working for you?" Victoria asked.

"What?"

"Yoga. You know, connecting with your inner self and all."

"I don't do yoga," responded Finney. "For me, it's just exercise."

Kline regarded Finney, her blue eyes full of skepticism. "Running is exercise. What you do with the Swami—that's yoga."

Finney considered this for a moment. He wanted to argue the point but knew that he wasn't going to influence the other contestants by sounding defensive. He had joined the Swami to strengthen a relationship and share the essential elements of the Christian faith. He hadn't worried too much about how it might be perceived by the other contestants—or a national television audience for that matter.

"Maybe you can get a little exercise tomorrow by joining Kareem on his prayer mat," Victoria teased.

"Okay," said Finney. "You win. I'm a closet sun worshiper. It's why I'm in such a bad mood today." As if to emphasize the point, the hull slapped down on the backside of a wave, soaking them both with ocean spray.

"I didn't say there's anything wrong with it," said Victoria, but Finney had already made up his mind about discontinuing the exercises. Why run the risk that viewers and other contestants might think he was combining Christianity with Hadji's pantheistic religion?

He trimmed the sail so that it caught less wind, reducing their speed. He and Victoria both leaned forward as she shook her hair out of her face.

"This has been fun," she said.

Finney took advantage of the relative calm to ask her about the cross-examination room.

"I survived it," she said. Her eyes gave nothing away. "How about you?"

Finney told her about the speedy-trial cases and the death of the store clerk in Ohio. "I don't want it to go public," he said, "but I'm not going to let them blackmail me with it."

"You didn't know about that already?" she asked.

"Not about the Ohio case. Not until Javitts told me."

As they sailed, the sky darkened further, and Finney turned downwind. They ducked as the sail swung overhead, and then they slid to the other side of the boat. They sailed without talking now, comfortable enough so that they didn't have to fill the air with words.

They were more than halfway to shore, cutting swiftly through the waves, when Victoria broke the silence. "My agent called McCormack yesterday, but McCormack didn't let me talk with him. Instead, McCormack told Preston that they needed to talk again as soon as the show was over about some television opportunities but that he really couldn't talk during the show. McCormack said he had second thoughts about me talking to Randolph while I'm on the island, since it violates the rules for the show."

"When did McCormack tell you this?"

"I went to his place again last night," Victoria said. She was staring at the shore, beautiful in silhouette, her full lips mesmerizing as she spoke. Finney kept one eye on the hull cutting through the water and the other on his crew.

"Toward the end of the night, McCormack moved close enough to make me uncomfortable and then told me under his breath to follow him out to the patio," Victoria said.

She brushed some stray strands of hair behind an ear. "I was uneasy but figured I was probably safer outside than inside. We were standing side by side on his patio, facing the ocean, and he mumbled a few more things. 'Grab my hand for a minute,' he said. 'And then we're going to hug. It doesn't mean anything, but I don't want to risk being overheard.'"

Victoria paused as she recalled the moment, breathing in the moist ocean air. "To be honest, it sounded pretty stupid, but he seemed so serious. He reached out and took my hand and then turned and gave me a hug. He whispered that he didn't think his condo was wired, but he didn't want to take any chances. Then he said something that really freaked me out: 'Don't make the cut for the final two. I don't want anything to happen to you.'

"I asked him what he meant, but he just said I needed to trust him and that there was a lot going on that the contestants didn't know about. Then he said to act normal and said it might help if we kissed, just in case anybody was watching."

She turned to Finney with a wry smile. "I told him that was the worst pickup line I'd ever heard but I appreciated the tip."

"He was serious?" asked Finney. He guided the boat down the crest of a wave as they closed in on the shore.

"About the kiss?"

"About not making the final two."

"I guess so. He said he didn't want anything to happen to me."

"Do you believe him, or is this just a reality-show twist?"

"I'm not sure what to believe. I debated whether I should even tell you."

"I'm glad you did," said Finney. He ran the Hobie up on the sand and glanced over his shoulder. The dark clouds seemed closer, spreading across the sky like a curtain. "Looks like we made it just in time."

∽

When Finney returned to his condo and logged on to Westlaw, he breathed a sigh of relief at the two new searches that showed up in his research trail. Translating the capital letters using the *atbash* cipher, Finney decoded the message: "OK."

Nikki and Wellington are in the game!

With renewed focus, he began a few new Westlaw searches of his own.

Chapter 33

Nikki hadn't been at the courthouse for more than fifteen minutes when the phone call came.

"Nikki Moreno, please."

"This is she."

The female voice on the other end was all business. "Are you the law clerk for Judge Oliver Finney?"

"Yes."

"Please hold for Mr. Randolph."

Who?

"Nikki Moreno?" This time it was a silky-smooth man's voice.

"I think we've established that," Nikki said.

"Good. I'm Preston Randolph, attorney for Victoria Kline. Did you watch the show last night?"

That was the part of the night that Nikki remembered. "Sure. Good stuff."

"You must not have watched the same show I did. Can you hang on a second?"

Preston didn't wait for an answer before he started talking to someone in the background. Preston Randolph? Where had she heard that name before?

"I'm back. Thanks. I normally do toxic tort class-action cases," Randolph said. "But Dr. Kline has served a few times as an expert witness for me, so I agreed to act as her agent in matters related to this show. I forget—did you say you watched it?"

"Yes."

"Well, what they did last night was shameful. My client and Finney go sailing together, and the show's producers make all these insinuations. Nothing against your judge, but I know Victoria well enough to know there's nothing more to it than sailing."

"Of course not," said Nikki.

Randolph next asked about the judge's family and how to reach them. Nikki explained that Finney was a widower who had lost his only child in a motorcycle accident. "I'm probably the closest thing to family he's got," Nikki said. She had always taken pride in that relationship, but hearing herself say it out loud made her strangely melancholy.

"Well, then, I'm glad I'm talking to you," said Randolph. For the next several minutes, he talked about his plans to call the network and read them the riot act. He would file suit if they didn't stop casting false aspersions about Kline. He'd be happy to represent Finney, too, and make sure the reality-show producers would start playing fair with the judge, if Randolph only had some way to get in touch with him.

While Nikki was thinking about how she might get that done through the cipher system they had established, Randolph had his own idea. "Finney didn't happen to leave you with a power of attorney, did he? I'm sure he'd want someone looking after his affairs if anything critical came up."

Nikki was starting to like this guy—he knew how to spell things out. "Yeah, I'm pretty sure he did. You need a copy of that?" She had signed the judge's name to a few orders in the past. Her Oliver Finney signature wasn't perfect, but it would do.

"Eventually," said Randolph. "But for this initial phone call with the producers, I'll just take your word for it."

"Great."

Randolph lowered his voice, and Nikki pressed the phone tighter to her ear. "These reality-show people are warped, Nikki. I just want them to know that they'd better think twice before they try to embarrass or defame any of my clients."

Suddenly, Randolph had her undivided attention. She had just pulled up a picture of the man from his firm's Web site. Classic good looks: a square face, curly jet-black hair, a blinding white smile. He looked to be about thirty-five or forty—a few years older than Nikki, but then again, she was pretty mature for her age.

Besides, she just happened to be on the prowl again today. Byron had been pitiful at dancing and even worse at casual conversation. When he leaned in to kiss her at the end of the night, the onions arrived a few seconds before his lips.

"Maybe we should meet in person," suggested Nikki.

"Sure," said Preston. "But let me see what I can do through a couple of phone calls first. I've already talked to the show's director, who seems to be a reasonable guy. Now I'll put some heat on the network execs in New York. I think as long as they know I'm watching them, they'll quit jerking us around."

Us? That didn't take long. "Right," said Nikki. She had Googled Preston and discovered that the man was closing in on the billionaire club. A quick skim revealed no mention of a wife.

"I may be in DC in the next few days," claimed Nikki. "Maybe I could stop by for a few minutes to compare notes." If she could only get a foot in the door, a job offer—and maybe more—would soon follow.

"That'd be great," said Preston. "Just make sure you give me a call first. I'm not in the office much—between trials and traveling and golf. In the meantime, if you hear anything about the island that worries you, give me a call."

She promised she would, and Preston Randolph moved on to the next pressing phone call. Nikki loved Virginia Beach, but she could see herself living in DC for the right kind of money.

Before logging off, she decided to check Westlaw and see if Finney had left any new breadcrumbs. "Yes!" she whispered when she saw the new searches. Time for some more spy games.

She called Wellington and told him to meet her at noon. The usual place, Nikki said, like a real gumshoe.

"Okay," said Wellington. "Hang on for a second while I ask my mom if I can borrow the minivan."

CHAPTER 34

inney's cross-examination was the last session before lunch. It felt strange being on the receiving end, with Kareem stalking the courtroom and launching caustic questions at him as fast as Finney could answer. Javitts assumed Finney's traditional role, rocking back in the judge's chair, his face a mixture of curiosity and boredom.

"Three gods or one?" asked Kareem.

"One God," responded Finney, "in three persons—the Father, the Son, and the Holy Spirit."

"Like our friend Hadji." Kareem pointed in the Hindu's direction. "You just have a few million gods less. But that's what he said: one god in different manifestations."

"No, that's totally different. Hadji believes that God is some kind of impersonal ultimate reality with millions of manifestations. The Christian God is personal and relational—One who loves people, One who created people in His own image."

"Thomas Jefferson believed in a Creator God, did he not?"

Where is this going? Finney wondered. He respected Jefferson as a political thinker but not as a theologian. "Jefferson was a deist. But in answer to your question—yes, he believed we were endowed by our Creator with certain inalienable rights."

Kareem headed back to his counsel table and picked up his legal pad. "Let me read you a quote from Jefferson, Judge Finney, and ask you to explain it: 'When we shall have done away with the incomprehensible jargon of the Trinitarian arithmetic, that three are one, and one is three... when in short, we shall have unlearned everything which has been taught since Jesus's day, we shall then be truly and worthily His disciples.'"

Kareem finished and looked up at Finney.

"And your question is what?" asked Finney.

"Just how do you explain this incomprehensible jargon of one plus one plus one equaling one?"

Finney took a deep and labored breath. Then a quick cough. Though he knew he couldn't convince Hasaan, maybe Finney could reach a few viewers who still had an open mind. "It's more like one times one times one equals one, Mr. Hasaan. It should not surprise you that we don't understand everything about the attributes of God. In fact, if we did understand everything about God's nature, it would be a signal to me that we had created God, rather than the other way around."

Finney shifted in his seat, trying to figure out a way to explain this that wouldn't sound clichéd. He had known Kareem would ask this type of question, highlighting a quintessential difference between Islam and Christianity. The best explanation Finney had seen came from C. S. Lewis. And he had borrowed a small box from the dining-room crew for just this reason. "May I use the easel to explain, Mr. Hasaan?"

"Be my guest," said Kareem with the confidence of a seasoned trial lawyer. He stepped out of Finney's way as Finney moved to the easel in the courtroom and picked up a black Sharpie.

Finney drew a square on the board. "One square or more than one, Mr. Hasaan?" Finney asked.

Kareem shook his head. "I said you may explain, Judge Finney. I did not relinquish my role as interrogator."

"Sorry," said Finney. "This is one square. Now, this easel operates in only two dimensions—representative of the limited capacity of humans to think and understand things supernatural. And so, if I draw another parallelogram"—Finney did his best to draw the second side of a cube—"to a person thinking in two-dimensional terms, we just have two four-sided figures. Actually, a square and a parallelogram. Then I draw a third"—this time Finney drew what looked to be the top of the box—"and to a two-

dimensional thinker, it still just looks like three connected parallelograms."
He then walked back to his counsel table and picked up the small box he
had placed behind his seat. "But to a three-dimensional thinker, it is actually one single cube. Six separate squares but all part of one box. God operates in a different dimension, where He is three persons but still one Being."

Finney left the box on his counsel table and returned to his seat.

"Very clever," remarked Kareem. "And totally incomprehensible. So
let's turn from the issue of Christianity's many gods to the issue of the
Bible's many authors. How many authors participated in the writing of
your Bible?"

Finney was embarrassed not to know the answer. He knew that the
Muslims claimed the Koran came from one source—the angel Gabriel's
revelations during the course of twenty-three years to the prophet Muhammad—and was therefore superior to the Bible in terms of consistency and
reliability. But it never occurred to Finney to memorize how many authors
the Bible had. "More than twenty," he said, which seemed safe.

"In other words, you don't know?"

"That's correct."

"Would it surprise you to learn that there were more than forty?"

"That sounds about right."

"And we have no original copies of even the New Testament part of
your Bible. All we have are copies of copies of copies. Would you agree?"

Finney had prepared for this point. "There are twenty-four thousand
ancient manuscripts verifying parts or all of the New Testament, with the
earliest ones dated less than fifty years from the originals. By comparing
these ancient copies to each other, we find that there are no variations that
affect any doctrine of the Christian faith."

Kareem turned to Javitts with his arms spread. "Judge, could you
instruct the witness to just answer the question asked."

Javitts's eyes turned hard as he looked at Finney. "You'll have your
chance to give a closing argument later," he lectured. "Just answer yes or no."

Kareem looked smug. "We have no originals of the New Testament, Judge Finney. Would you agree?"

"Yes."

"All we have are copies of copies of copies—right?"

"Yes. And lots of them. With no inconsistencies."

"Is that a yes or no, Judge?"

"A yes," Finney admitted.

"We'll deal with contradictions in your Scriptures in just a minute. But first let's establish one other point." Kareem took a step toward Finney and studied him with an unyielding stare. "You understand that Muslims do not believe that Jesus died by means of crucifixion or that He was resurrected from the dead?"

"Yes, I understand that."

"And other than the copies of copies of copies of the various books of your New Testament, which also happen to be internally contradictory, there is no other written evidence to support your claim of the Resurrection, is there?"

Finney shook his head and smiled. "That question's so bad, I don't know where to start."

Kareem flushed and moved in closer, his face tight. "Why don't you just start by answering the question?"

"All right. First, the New Testament is not internally contradictory. Second, there is plenty of evidence for the Resurrection outside the pages of Scripture. For example, the disciples all died as martyrs, clinging to the truth of a resurrection that they had witnessed with their own eyes. Their deaths are documented outside the pages of Scripture. Do you really think they made it all up so they could be crucified, stoned, and beaten?"

"I'll ask the questions, Judge Finney. And since you claim there are no inconsistencies, let's start with a few pertaining to the Resurrection itself. Did Jesus allegedly prophesy about the Resurrection to your supposedly infallible gospel writers?"

"Yes."

"And how many days did he predict He would be in the ground before He rose again?"

"He said that the Son of Man—that's what He called Himself—would spend three days and three nights in the ground, just like Jonah spent three days and three nights in the belly of the fish. Then He predicted He would rise again."

"And do your gospel writers record the day on which He was allegedly crucified?"

"Yes. They said it was the day before the Sabbath."

"And do they record the day on which He allegedly rose again?"

"Yes. They said it was early in the morning, before the sun came up on the day after the Sabbath."

"Now, Judge Finney. Jesus supposedly died the day before the Sabbath and rose the day after. Is that more Trinitarian math—two days become three? Or maybe you're saying Jesus miscalculated the timing for the most important event in His ministry. Or maybe, just maybe, the gospel accounts have been corrupted."

"Is that a question or a speech?" asked Finney.

"I'm waiting," challenged Kareem.

"All right," said Finney. He had done a lot of research on the Resurrection when he wrote his book. He tried to remember exactly how this worked. "First, understand that in the first century the Jewish day was sunup to sundown. Also, when the gospel writers say that Jesus was crucified on the day before the Sabbath, Mr. Hasaan, they literally said that He was crucified the day before a *High Sabbath*. That's the way they described certain holy feasts, like the Passover. The date of that feast was tied to a certain day of the month and did not necessarily fall on a Saturday. Thus, Jesus was crucified the day before the Passover Sabbath. The next day was a regular Sabbath—the last day of the week. Then He rose early in the morning on the next day. Three days and three nights, just like He claimed."

Finney could tell that the answer surprised Kareem. The Muslim seemed to be pondering a response. "Then you're saying that Jesus died on a Thursday?" he eventually asked.

"That's what I believe."

"And the entire church has gotten it wrong for two thousand years, thinking it happened on a Friday?"

"A heartfelt remembrance of the Crucifixion and Resurrection is what matters, not the day of the week we choose to do it on. You'll find a similar issue with regard to the timing of our Christmas holiday."

"Judge Finney, I find similar contradictions everywhere I look."

"It's not a contradiction, Mr. Hasaan. I already explained that."

Undeterred, Kareem zeroed in on some other alleged inconsistencies. Then he moved to the Crusades and a few other examples of notorious conduct in the name of Christ. He and Finney traded verbal punches and counterpunches for the rest of the examination, neither of the advocates willing to concede even the smallest point. Finney tried to keep his emotions in check but found himself getting frustrated at his Muslim counterpart.

"One minute," said Javitts finally.

"Let me read one last verse from your own Scriptures, Judge Finney, and ask you to explain it," said Kareem. He walked over to the counsel table and picked up a copy of the Bible he had brought to court with him.

"This is from the New Testament book of Hebrews," Kareem said. "By the way, who wrote that book?"

"I don't know," admitted Finney.

"You don't know or nobody knows?"

Finney hesitated, then remembered that doing so only made things look worse. "Nobody knows."

"And yet it's part of your Scripture?"

"Yes. It's been accepted from the earliest church councils as part of the inspired Word of God."

"Given that fact, let me ask you to explain chapter five, verse seven.

'During His earthly life'—and the writer of Hebrews, whoever that might be, is apparently referring to your Messiah—'He offered prayers and appeals, with loud cries and tears, to the One who was able to save Him from death, and He was heard because of His reverence.'" Kareem walked toward Finney, crowding his victim as much as possible. "How can you claim Jesus died on a cross when your own Scripture says Jesus was saved from death?"

To be honest, Finney didn't have the foggiest idea. He'd never noticed that verse before. But he also knew that an effective witness must sound confident and not hesitate.

"I'm not sure exactly what that verse means, Mr. Hasaan. But I would look at it one of two ways. First, it doesn't say Jesus was saved from death. It says that He prayed to the One who was able to save Him from death and that His prayers were heard. The gospel writers record just such a prayer of Jesus prior to His death, pleading to be delivered from the bitter cup of the Crucifixion. However, He ends that prayer by submitting to the will of God the Father. And second, I would say that rising again on the third day qualifies as being saved from death, because with Christ, death wasn't final."

Kareem's lips curled into a wry smile. "That's the best you can do?"

"Time is up," said Judge Javitts. And Oliver Gradison Finney was glad.

CHAPTER 35

To combat the heat, Nikki decided to go with a mocha lite frappuccino. Before getting in line, she checked with Wellington. "Water?" she asked.

Wellington glanced up from his notes. He had a spiral notebook with several pages of penciled charts. "Yeah, thanks. You need a pen?"

"I've got cash today, Wellington."

When Nikki returned to the table with their drinks, she dug deep into her latest wardrobe addition—a Fendi Spy bag necessitated by the dictates of style and the recent Judge Finney escapades. Given the circumstances, she couldn't even wait for the designer bag to go on sale as she normally would. It was an oversized black leather slouchy version with a hidden storage compartment inside, from which she retrieved a folded piece of paper and her trusty copy of the *Cross Examination* book. "Here's the message from Finney," she said, handing the paper to Wellington. "I wrote down all the capital letters."

Nikki nursed her drink while Wellington studied the hodgepodge of letters in front of him. Nikki waited for him to pull out the key and translate.

"Well?" she asked after giving him five or six full seconds.

"I don't know," said Wellington. "I haven't figured out the code yet."

Nikki leaned back. *What have you been doing all morning?* she wanted to ask. But she knew she had to keep her cryptoanalyzer guy motivated. "It's harder than the first one, isn't it?" Nikki asked like an old code veteran. She opened the *Cross Examination* book to the page where the letters were embedded, turning it so that Wellington could see. "But I've got a few ideas."

She tried to check her watch without being too obvious. She had told Judge Fitzsimmons that she might be a little late getting back from lunch. But she hadn't planned on a full-fledged code-breaking session.

"Here are my preliminary results," Nikki said, pointing to the page. She had used a red pen to scribble in her guesses on the first page of chapter one. In a few cases, she had crossed out her first guesses and replaced them with others. Wellington frowned at the ink-covered page as if Nikki had drawn a moustache on the *Mona Lisa*.

"I didn't really have time to do that whole frequency analysis thing," admitted Nikki. "But I did notice that these three letters, S-A-Q, repeated a couple of times, so I assumed they stood for 'the.'"

Wellington frowned. "That won't work," he said.

"I know," Nikki said. "So then I figured that maybe they stood for 'and.' That's my second set of marks."

"I don't think so," Wellington replied. "I tried that too. I've got two summer-school classes that pretty much took up the whole morning, but I did take a quick run at some of the more obvious possibilities." He turned to the second page of his notebook. "The most common trigraphs in the English language—" He must have noticed the look on Nikki's face. "The three letters that appear together most frequently, in descending order, are 'the, and, tha, ent,' and 'ion.'" He shook his head. "None of those work."

"Don't look at me," said Nikki. "I don't know a trigraph from an *atbash*."

Wellington thought about this for a minute. "How did you know about the *atbash* cipher in the first place?"

Nikki explained, as briefly as possible, about her conversation with the judge after the Stokes hearing. This put Wellington even deeper in thought, as if Nikki had simply ceased to exist.

"Well?" she asked at last. Being invisible was not one of her strong suits.

"I think reading the book might act as kind of a shortcut for deciphering the code," said Wellington. "It might help me know what Judge Finney was thinking when he wrote the chapter in question."

Nikki could see where this was headed and wasn't excited about the idea of parting with her one copy of the book. "I don't know..."

"Think about it, Ms. Moreno."

She withered him with a look.

"Nikki, I mean. The *atbash* cipher was a religious cipher used by Old Testament scribes. Have you ever read the introduction to the book?"

Nikki shrugged. "Sort of skimmed it."

"Well, I read the introduction last night during the party. The book is about how the lawyers and scribes cross-examined Jesus and, of course, His ultimate cross-examination by Pilate as well. It shows how Jesus turned their hostile questions into opportunities to teach or minister."

"I figured that much from the title."

"The point Finney made in the introduction is that he discovered a lot of himself in the Pharisees, particularly in the questioning and cynicism that characterized them. He said, 'To become more like Christ, I first had to understand how much I was already like the scribes and Pharisees.' Or something like that. In other words, this concept that Finney is unpacking in the introduction is counterintuitive, exactly the opposite of what you might expect."

"Like A being Z and Z being A," Nikki interrupted, finishing the thought.

"Exactly. And it seems to me that the key to understanding some of these codes might just be to read the book." He glanced furtively at the book on the table. "I can run my frequency analysis techniques, but that might take a few hours. It might save us time if I just read chapter one."

Nikki found it hard to argue with Wellington's logic—no surprise there—so she reluctantly left the book with him and told him she would call in a couple of hours. By tomorrow, her new *Cross Examination* book would probably arrive. She had already called several local bookstores, but they no longer stocked it.

Somehow, though, she would have to teach Wellington a thing or two about priorities. What was he doing going to class when there were codes to be solved?

∾

Two hours later Nikki received the phone call while sitting in her small office adjacent to Judge Finney's chambers. Wellington's name showed up on caller ID, so Nikki answered in an appropriately secretive tone—not quite a whisper, but almost. "Wellington?"

"I solved the code, Ms. Moreno." Nikki ground her teeth. For a genius, this guy sure was slow at certain things.

"Great," she said. "But it's Nikki, remember?"

"Oh yeah, sorry. Do you want to meet?"

Nikki thought about the prospects of driving a half hour to Starbucks. What if it was another one of those "Skip chapter one"–type messages? And what was the likelihood of someone's tapping her cell phone, anyway?

"I don't think we need to, Wellington," Nikki said. "Nobody's listen-ing to this phone. You can just give me the message."

"Are you sure?"

Just a few seconds ago, Nikki had plugged her credit-card number into some Internet site, and for all she knew, some hacker might be access-ing it right now. She was getting ready to do it again. Life was full of risks. "Yes, Wellington, I'm sure."

"All right." She could hear the sigh coming through the phone line. These cipher guys sure were paranoid. "But don't you want to hear how I solved chapter one?"

Not really, thought Nikki, but she knew she couldn't tell Wellington that. "Of course."

"Well, I assumed maybe it was another substitution cipher, so I started with a standard frequency analysis—checking out individual letters, digraphs, and trigraphs." His tone conveyed the excitement of a morning deejay. "One thing that stood out was the letter combination S-A, which was used four times. Well, I naturally suspected that those letters represented T-H, since that combination is by far the most commonly occurring digraph in the English language."

"Naturally."

"Since the code started with the letters S-A-N, and I knew that S-A stood for T-H, I followed a hunch that N represented E, since a lot of sentences start with 'the.' Another reason this made sense is because the code letter N also happened to be adjacent to more letters than any other code letter—behavior absolutely consistent with the most popular and sociable vowel."

"Mmm," grunted Nikki, showing her enthusiasm. She was distracted by the jean styles she was now checking out on the Internet.

"After I had those three letters, I used what's called a crib. Since the first chapter is all about the cross-examination of Jesus before Pontius Pilate, I guessed that the message might have the name of Jesus in it. I already knew that N stood for the E in Jesus. And, of course, the word 'Jesus' uses the letter S twice—immediately following the E and again three spaces after the E. So I looked in the code text for a place where the same letter immediately followed the N and occurred again three letters after the N."

"I see." She had her eye on the low-cut Duchesse stretch denim jeans with a cool pink pocket embroidery and a light-blue vintage wash that made them look old as dirt.

"Sure enough, I found the word 'Jesus.' And so now I knew all the letters in that word as well as T and H. From there, it was just a matter of time and a few educated guesses."

"Mmm hmm." *Sixty-eight bucks.* She ought to be able to do better than that.

"Chapter one of Finney's book is all about how Jesus maintained incredible dignity and grace in front of Pilate and how He answered through His actions the ultimate question that troubled Pilate: What is truth? So, when you solve the code, the hidden message in chapter one of Finney's book says this: 'The law was given through Moses, but grace and truth came through Jesus Christ.'"

Nikki clicked to add the jeans to her cart. *You can't stress out over price when you find exactly the jeans you're looking for.*

"Still there?" asked Wellington.

"Yeah, sure. Good work, Sherlock. Listen, I've got about a million things going on this afternoon, so why don't you just go ahead and give me Finney's new message so we can figure out what to do next."

"Okay," said Wellington. "But one more thing first…and this is the coolest part of all."

Nikki bit her tongue. Hard.

"A lot of cryptologists use a key phrase when they're doing a substitution cipher so they can remember how they did the substitution without having to write it down. That way, the cipher alphabet is the key phrase first and then the remaining letters of the alphabet in their correct order, starting where the key phrase ends. Are you on your computer?"

How does he know? "Um, sure."

"Good, check your e-mail."

Nikki pulled up an e-mail from Wellington.

"I figured even if they happened to be listening, they wouldn't have access to your e-mail as well," Wellington continued. "Check out the key phrase our friend used at the start of the cipher alphabet."

Nikki glanced at the simple table in the message Wellington had sent. "Very clever," she said.

Plain Alphabet	a	b	c	d	e	f	g	h	i	j	k	l	m	n	o	p	q	r	s	t	u	v	w	x	y	z
Cipher Alphabet	O	G	F	I	N	E	Y	A	B	C	D	H	J	K	L	M	P	Q	R	S	T	U	V	W	X	Z

"Just in case you had any doubt who wrote the book," said Wellington.

"Sounds like the judge had too much time on his hands," replied Nikki, "which is certainly not true of me right now. So, what's the message in Finney's Westlaw searches using this key?"

"You want me to say it over the phone?" asked Wellington. "That's why I sent you the key, so you could figure it out."

"Okay," Nikki started working through the letters one at a time. "Hold on." *Let's see. F is the first capital letter in Finney's Westlaw search, so that would actually be C. A is the second letter, so that would actually be H. Or is it the other way around?*

"This is insane," Nikki concluded after a few minutes. "Why don't you just tell me Finney's message?"

"Are you sure?"

Nikki grunted. "Do the words 'Black Gangster Disciples' and 'cat's got my tongue' mean anything to you?"

"Huh?"

"Never mind, Wellington. Just read me the message."

"Okay. Here's what Finney's message says: 'Check ties between Murphy, McCormack, and Javitts and my speedy-trial cases.'"

"That's it?"

"That's it. Do you know what he's talking about when he says 'speedy-trial cases'?"

"Not yet," said Nikki. "But I've got ways of finding out."

CHAPTER 36

The two cameramen who joined the nightly card game with Finney and the Swami were a regular Mutt-and-Jeff combination. Finney thought the taller of the two, a hairy European named Augustus, was the more dangerous card player. Gus had that deadly quiet thing going, along with a dry wit that always made you wonder whether he was serious or kidding. During off-hours, he was fond of displaying his hairy and wiry body at the beach in his classic-cut European Speedo. He competed with the Swami for having the island's darkest tan, with his hairy back and chest giving him a natural advantage.

His cohort, all five feet eight inches and two hundred ten pounds of him, was a talkative guy named Horace, who smeared on SPF 30 sunblock and managed to stay pasty white even on Paradise Island. Horace sported a thick moustache and rounded shoulders that came in handy for shielding his cards from the prying eyes of the other players, though nobody had to peek at Horace's cards to take his money. Every time he bluffed, Horace's balding head would turn a shade of red, the exact hue depending on how much was at stake. He hadn't won a big pot in two days.

The first night they played—Wednesday night—the men had painstakingly avoided any talk about the show or the challenges facing the contestants. Last night, Mutt and Jeff had brought their own drinks, chips, and dip. The conversation flowed as freely as the beer being consumed by the cameramen. Halfway through the night, they were making fun of all the contestants except Finney and the Swami. By the end of the night, there were no exceptions.

On this night, the third straight poker night, the conversation centered on women and the upcoming challenges for the contestants. With regard to women, the Swami was the only player who rated Tammy Dietz ahead of Dr. Kline for looks. In fact, he seemed so adamant about it that Finney took special note. Regarding challenges, they talked a little about the next two courtroom challenges and a lot about the upcoming psychological challenge.

"No offense, Judge O," said the Swami, "but that one will come down to me or the mini-Buddha. Eastern religions know how to meditate and transcend."

On camera, Tammy had described the particulars of the upcoming Chinese water torture. Next Wednesday morning, the contestants would be shackled into a reclining chair, then water would de dripped onto each contestant's forehead until he or she called it quits. A clinical psychologist would be on hand to continuously evaluate the contestants. Blood pressure and heart rate would be monitored. The last holdout would win one of the fifty-thousand-dollar verdicts for their charities. If more than one contestant was still in his or her chair after twenty-four hours, then the one with the fewest physiological signs of stress would win.

"It's basically what I go through every day in court," said Finney. "I'll be ready."

He coughed and grimaced, his chest aching as he hacked away. By now, his card buddies were used to it, hardly noticing as Finney coughed phlegm into a paper cup he kept by his side during the game. Lately, Finney had felt like he was coughing under water, drowning by small increments with every breath he took. It was the beginning of fluid on the lungs, he realized—the final stages of his cancer.

"Don't they have allergy medicine for that?" asked Gus.

When they decided to call it quits, Horace withdrew a folded piece of paper from his pocket and wrote each of their names on it. No money had actually changed hands in the last few nights; they merely kept a running total so they could settle up at week's end.

"Don't we already have a tally sheet someplace?" asked the Swami.

"Yeah, it's on the kitchen counter, I think," said Finney.

Horace quickly wrote the night's results on the folded paper he had in his hand. "Here," he said as he handed it to Finney. "Add it to the other totals."

On the way out, Horace leaned over and whispered in Finney's ear. "Check the other side of the score sheet."

A few minutes later, Finney took the paper into the bathroom with him, away from the prying cameras. He unfolded the paper and looked at the opposite side. It contained a photograph of Bryce McCormack and Dr. Kline holding each other close in the dark on McCormack's patio.

My new friend wants me to know, Finney thought. Finney might have lost money tonight, but the card games were paying off. Alliances were being forged on Paradise Island.

aturday morning started with the religious rituals of the contestants: Kareem with his loud prayers. The Swami practicing yoga while Finney sat reading Scripture in a beach chair near him. Dr. Ando meditating inside someplace. The Swami had responded with a signature shrug to Finney's decision to suspend his yoga exercises. "Whatever works for you, Judge O. But you've got to give it more than a few days to get any benefit."

When Victoria Kline finished her run, she and Finney enjoyed a relaxing sail around the bay. Today the sun burned bright in a cloudless eastern sky, yesterday's thunderstorms a distant memory. After sailing, Finney decided to add a couple of laps of walking around the premises to clear his head. After one, he decided his head would clear just fine in a lounge chair next to the ocean.

He still had more than an hour before he had to be in court. He took off his shirt and lay back on the lounger, pulling his hat down over his eyes. He listened to the gentle rhythm of the ocean, smelled the salt water, and tried to sort things out.

Finney was a visual guy. He needed a yellow legal pad with a line down the middle and little boxes drawn on the page around important facts. But here, on Paradise Island, the cameras recorded everything except the thoughts in your head. So Finney had to sort this all out in the catacombs of his mind, building block by building block, solving this reality show like a complex encryption.

What did he know for sure? Whom could he trust? Were some seriously bad things going to happen, or was this all just part of the reality-show hype?

One thing he knew for certain: this was not the reality show he had signed up for.

The producers seemed to push everything to the edge and beyond—the lie-detector test, the cross-examination about his speedy-trial cases, the upcoming Chinese water torture, and the way they exploited the terminal diseases of the contestants. The one thing that Tammy had promised on camera, but that Finney had not yet faced, was temptation. What did the show's producers have in mind? What could they possibly tempt Finney with, especially knowing he would be on his guard against it?

And then a thought hit him. Maybe they weren't going to tempt him while his guard was up. Maybe they had already done it. They had already demonstrated that they knew a lot about Finney's past. Who could say that they had limited the show to the confines of Paradise Island?

Finney thought about one rather bizarre temptation that came his way shortly before he left for the show. William Lassiter, a representative from the governor's office, had presented Finney with a once-in-a-lifetime offer. Could it have all been staged? There was one way to find out. Nikki. Finney's own "windtalker."

It was becoming clear to Finney that this show would not be won or lost in the courtroom. He could only guess at some of the other stunts the producers would throw his way in the days ahead.

But it was quite a leap from staging those kinds of reality-show gimmicks to physically harming one of the participants. Could Dr. Kline be playing mind games with him, trying to keep him from pushing for the finals?

His instincts told him otherwise. Just this morning she had agreed to go back to Bryce McCormack's condo one more time to troll for more information. Finney could tell from her body language that she didn't relish the task. Plus, the picture Horace gave him seemed to confirm Kline's story. Maybe, on the other hand, McCormack was playing mind games with Kline. It seemed unlikely, given the fact that the first piece of information gained by Victoria came when she overheard a conversation and McCormack didn't know she was listening, but Finney supposed it was a possibility.

Why would the producers seriously hurt or even kill one of the finalists? Finney knew that television shows lived and died with buzz. And what could generate more buzz than a freak accident—an "act of God"— happening to one of the contestants? Or maybe even a finalist dying an accelerated death from his or her terminal disease?

Yet Finney had tried enough cases to know a thing or two about motive. And it didn't seem as if a whole group of television executives would agree to kill somebody just for the sake of ratings. It could be that one or two executives hatched a plot, and McCormack found out about it surreptitiously. Still, murder for ratings didn't seem plausible.

Religion was another possible motive. Maybe Murphy or McCormack or one of the other higher-ups was sympathetic to a certain religion, and the fix was in. Game-show rigging had happened before when a lot less was at stake. But it didn't seem to Finney as if any of the bigwigs involved in filming this show were particularly religious people. And even if they were, they didn't have to kill somebody in order for their religion to win.

That's why he kept coming back to the speedy-trial cases. A young woman dead—perhaps even a daughter or sister of somebody involved with the show. That would be a powerful motive to go after the judge whose negligence had allowed it to happen. Maybe one of the other speedy-trial defendants had done something equally reprehensible, and they purposefully didn't show Finney a picture of that victim. There wouldn't have to be a lot of people involved. It could be that just one person was targeting Finney, and somehow McCormack found out.

But if they were after Finney, why would McCormack have warned Dr. Kline not to make the finals? Maybe McCormack knew only part of the story. Maybe he overheard some plans about something bad happening to a finalist but didn't realize they were talking about Finney. It was the only thing that made sense from a motive perspective.

But then again, things hadn't been making sense on Paradise Island from day one. Why should Finney assume they would start doing so now?

∾

Later that morning, as Javitts spelled out the contestants' assignments for the next few days, Finney passed on a critical message to Kareem Hasaan. Finney assumed that Dr. Kline was doing the same for both Hadji and Ando.

"Tomorrow," said Javitts, "each of you will be conducting a cross-examination by satellite uplink of an esteemed scientist whose name will not be revealed until he or she takes the stand. You will each be allowed ten minutes of cross-examination to see how well your faith coincides with the best-known scientific evidence. Dr. Kline, since you advocate a scientific worldview that is devoid of any particular religious belief, we'll let you go first."

Finney looked over as Victoria nodded. He watched her write a few notes, which Hadji appeared to be studying.

"Since tomorrow's theme is Faith and Science, we will also be conducting a series of medical tests on each of the faith advocates," announced Javitts. "This will allow a few days for any necessary biopsy results to be returned prior to next Thursday."

Kareem Hasaan stiffened but held his tongue. Finney made a few more marks on his notes.

They were communicating using the pinprick cipher that Finney had explained to Dr. Kline while sailing. It was a centuries-old trick and one they could use even though their papers were being searched every day.

The key was to place a tiny dot under each letter that formed part of the message. The uninitiated eye would not even notice. If it did, the dots would look like stray pen marks scattered around the page. But to somebody who knew the secret, the pinprick cipher could create an effective trail of breadcrumbs for most any message.

"In addition to the upcoming faith-and-science emphasis, we will also be trying to determine how well your faith holds up under pressure. Does it allow you to endure things that life throws at you without stressing out?"

Javitts glanced down at some notes and then back to the contestants. "As we all know, we tend to stress out more when pushing our bodies to the limit—when we're tired and hungry. Yet all of your religions seem to suggest that self-denial, though it may be tough on the body, is good for the soul. Jesus fasted forty days and forty nights. Muslims are called to fast during Ramadan. Buddha almost starved himself over the course of six years, claiming that the skin of his belly came to be cleaving to his backbone. And the Hindu religion teaches an ascetic lifestyle, which, for many adherents, translates to extended periods of fasting."

Finney casually placed some more dots and waited until Kareem nodded. Then he turned to a new page of notes and placed dots there as well.

meet us in the ocean after prayer tomorrow morning all contestants are going snorkeling so we can ditch our microphones and talk

"Therefore," said Javitts, "during our second week on Paradise Island, each of you will be asked to engage in a fluids-only fast. Food will no longer be provided, only beverages. You are not necessarily required to fast. But if you want to eat, you will be responsible for catching and preparing your own food. Are there any questions about that?"

"Is this *Faith on Trial* or a POW survival camp?" asked Kareem.

Javitts hesitated before responding. Finney could sense that Javitts didn't want a widespread revolt. "You knew up front that this show was going to push you to your physical limits, Mr. Hasaan. You signed a release that stated as much."

Kareem just stared back.

"I'm assuming this doesn't include me, since I don't have any religious beliefs that require fasting," said Kline.

"No, that's not correct," replied Javitts. "The whole purpose is to see if religious faith somehow allows individuals to handle these kinds of things better. You're our control group, so to speak."

"Maybe we ought to broaden the control group," suggested Finney. "Include the judge and the set director."

"Very funny, Judge Finney. Are there any other serious questions?"

Kareem frowned, then started placing a few stray dots on his page of notes. Finney shifted in his seat so he could see without being conspicuous.

"Tuesday should be a very interesting day in court," said Javitts, thankful to be changing subjects. "Each of you will be conducting an examination by satellite uplink with an expert member of your own faith group. Dr. Kline, of course, will not participate in this exercise."

Finney pieced together Kareem's message thus far: "I do not..."

"The only catch is that this expert from your own faith is somebody who sees things differently than you. It may be somebody from a different sect or different denomination or someone who doesn't believe that your holy books should be taken literally..."

"I do not swim," Hasaan's message said. Finney had to smile. His big, strapping, tough adversary couldn't swim. Finney now knew why he had never seen Kareem in the water.

"You will not know who it is until you begin your examination on Tuesday," continued Javitts. "And just so you'll know exactly where they're coming from, we've given them ten minutes to share their views before you begin your cross-examination."

Wonderful, thought Finney. *I'll probably get some liberal scholar from the Jesus Seminar.*

But he wasn't too worried about that right now. He was having too much fun dotting out his next message to Kareem.

Don't worry if you start drowning I'll save you

It didn't take Kareem long to reply.

Will not be necessary I am only going in waist deep

CHAPTER 38

Nikki, this is Preston Randolph." Apparently the man made his own calls on Saturdays. "I talked to a few executives at the network who put me in touch with the producer of *Faith on Trial*. I had concerns before, but I've got serious issues now."

"What happened?"

"I told this guy Murphy that I didn't like the way they were portraying my client. Even the show's director thinks that Dr. Kline's got serious potential for television, but they're killing her with this May-December romance thing."

Nikki stiffened. She had an urge to defend her judge—it wasn't like he was a total loser for Kline to be hanging out with. But Nikki also had plans. It would be hard to use Preston if she didn't keep it civil.

"Plus, the way they set my client up for that ethical temptation at work, even before she got to the island—it was totally underhanded. She passed their little test, but still...I told him I wouldn't hesitate to file a lawsuit even while the show was running in order to get Dr. Kline's story out there. That's when he dropped the bombshell."

Preston waited, apparently to let Nikki prompt the next response. Trial lawyers like Preston did that instinctively—everything is drama. "What bombshell?"

"He said he had some confessions on camera from Dr. Kline that could be career threatening if they came out. I challenged him, and he gave me the specifics. He mentioned that he had the same types of career-ending stuff on other contestants. You know anything like that with regard to Judge Finney?"

Twenty-four hours ago the answer would have been no. But Nikki had asked around at the courthouse yesterday after getting Finney's message about the speedy-trial cases. She had read the old newspaper articles that blamed it on the prosecutors, but she also had a confidential talk with the clerk who worked for Finney at the time.

"Judge Finney?" Nikki asked, as if it were the most preposterous question she had ever heard. "It's hard to imagine anybody having dirt on him."

"Yeah. Well, I thought the same thing about Dr. Kline."

There was silence for a moment as Preston apparently tried to figure out the next step. "Did you say you'd be in Washington next week?"

Nikki had almost forgotten. "Uh...yes. Monday."

"Can you stop by the office? I've talked to a few family members of the other contestants—Hadji's parents and Hasaan's wife. We might be able to hook them up by videoconference and get a plan together."

They settled on a time, and Nikki saw her opening. "Have you got any private investigators working for you?" She already knew the answer.

"Sure."

"Do you think they could do background checks on Cameron Murphy, Bryce McCormack, and Howard Javitts by Monday?"

"I think so. Maybe we can get some dirt on them to use as bargaining chips—is that what you're thinking?"

"More or less. And I've got a few names for your investigators to keep an eye on—see if there's any connection between these guys and the men they're investigating or their families." Nikki spelled out a list of defendants who had been freed in the speedy-trial cases, including Antonio Demarco. "I'll tell you on Monday why I'm asking about these men."

"Okay," said Preston.

Nikki tried to keep the conversation going for the next minute or so—"Got any big plans for the weekend?"—but it became obvious that Preston was ready to get off the phone. She let him go without much of a fight and with no resentment. The Moreno charm always worked best in person. That way, the legs could do part of the talking.

Kicking back in a comfortable pedestal chair in her television room, Nikki continued her Internet research on Javitts, McCormack, and Murphy. The men were hard on wives. Combined, they had gone through seven, and Javitts was the only one still married. Nikki was putting together family trees, complete with alimony and support obligations, as well as criminal records for the men. To do this right, she would have to interview all the living ex-wives—always a ready source of dirt. Complicating matters was a name change by Murphy, formerly a small-time actor named Jason Martin. She hadn't yet pulled up any dirt on Murphy under his prior name, but you don't go through a name change for no reason.

But now that Nikki had scammed some help from Randolph's top-notch investigators, she found it hard to garner much enthusiasm for her own research. The pros would have a report prepared for her on Monday. She would use their work as a springboard for any further investigation. Obviously, Finney thought one of these men was out to get him because of something associated with the speedy-trial cases. But Nikki had found no obvious links, and she had been working on it for hours.

She needed a break. She took another glance at the small book that had arrived that morning. Her brand-new copy of Finney's *Cross Examination*. She didn't doubt that another message would be arriving from Finney soon and that Nikki would have to know the cipher system used in chapter two of the book to understand it. Sure, Wellington would be able to solve it. He probably already had. But still, if Nikki could solve it as well, then she would be firmly back in the driver's seat. She wouldn't even have to tell Wellington about the message.

She glanced at her watch. Not quite noon. She would take no more than two hours to work on the cipher before she got back to her research. Time might be of the essence for Finney, but everyone needed a break.

She started by making a chart of the code letters contained at the beginning of chapter two, just as she had seen Wellington do. She would need to find a pencil with a good-sized eraser for her guesses at what the code letters stood for.

A	D	E	A	D	O	E	Y	R	C	I	S	F	I	I	N	F	R	O	F	R	Y	T	E	G	H	S	A

E	E	F	C	I	W	A	N	S	N	H	S	I	T	M	M	G	A	E	S	U	F	C	E	T	O	Y

U	O	M	S	R	N	T	I	M	D	P	R	E	T	N	E	K	E	S

The next step would be tedious, but there was no way around it. She would have to count up the total number of times each letter was used in the code message and compare the result to the average frequencies of letters in the English language. Cruising around the Internet for a chart showing letter frequencies, she struck gold.

Nikki landed on a site that hailed itself as the Black Chamber and included a substitution cipher–cracking tool that was, in her opinion, about the coolest site ever invented by humankind. It looked to Nikki like it had computerized the work of cracking codes. She wondered why Wellington hadn't already seen this site…or maybe he had. She remembered how he stepped outside the noisy sports bar to call his mom that first night, allegedly to get information about letter frequencies. Either way, she couldn't wait to see the look on Wellington's face when he found out she had cracked this cipher all by herself. Well, sort of.

For starters, all she had to do was plug her ciphertext into a blank box on the site. She carefully transcribed every letter. Now there were several buttons that would kick out an analysis of the ciphertext. The button that looked like it had the most promise was Show Solution. She almost cheered as she clicked it. But her spirits soon plummeted when the solution came back "undefined." Did that mean she had to be smarter than the computer to solve this code?

Not yet. There were still a few more tricks the Black Chamber had up its sleeve.

The next button she clicked was entitled Frequency of Individual Letters. It automatically, in less than a second, produced the following chart—a thing of absolute beauty in Nikki's opinion, saving her a half hour of counting.

	A	B	C	D	E	F	G	H	I	J	K	L	M	N	O	P	Q	R	S	T	U	V	W	X	Y	Z
% in Cipher-Text	7	0	4	4	14	7	3	3	8	0	1	0	5	7	5	1	0	7	9	7	3	0	1	0	4	0
% in English	8	2	3	4	13	2	2	6	7	0	1	4	2	7	8	2	0	6	6	9	3	1	2	0	2	0

Nikki jotted a few notes. She assumed that either the letter E or the letter S in the ciphertext, the two most popular letters, represented the letter E in the English language. The other probably represented the letter T. And since it didn't make sense for a letter in the ciphertext to be the same letter in the regular text, she assumed that E in the ciphertext stood for T and that S in the ciphertext stood for E.

But she wasn't done with her shortcuts yet. The Internet site had another useful tool. This one was called Vowel Trowel. The description explained, just as Wellington had a few days ago, that vowels were more "sociable" than consonants and tended to border lots of different letters. Consonants, the site said, were "snobs," bordering only certain other letters. *I'm liking consonants better all the time,* thought Nikki. When she clicked on the button, it showed her how many different letters each letter in the ciphertext was adjacent to. From this, she learned that both E and S were probably vowels.

If they were both vowels, then the ciphertext E probably stood for A and the ciphertext S probably stood for E. She started filling out her graph. She placed E in for the plaintext everywhere the ciphertext showed S. Then she put an A for the plaintext where the ciphertext showed E.

The next button she clicked was something called Common Digraphs. It showed how often certain pairs of letters were together in the ciphertext and the most common letters found together in pairs in the English language. Things were starting to get confusing. Another tool, called Frequency of Pairs of Letters, didn't help much either. She tried looking for a repeating pattern of three letters together, like Wellington had done, but this was a dead end too.

Nikki looked at her data, substituted some letters in her chart, then frowned at the nonsensical message being generated. It all seemed so logical and easy when Wellington explained it. But after nearly two hours, all Nikki had was a lot of scribbling and erasure marks on her chart.

She set down her pencil. The eraser was black around the edges and well worn. Who cared? She could probably solve it if she really wanted to. But why waste more time? The important thing was investigating the backgrounds of Javitts, McCormack, and Murphy. She would leave the menial task of deciphering to a specialist like Wellington Farnsworth.

Maybe *he* was smarter than the computer.

CHAPTER 39

Finney was no scientist. Math he loved. The law he had mastered. But science? People who understand science go to med school, not law school. The only thing lawyers needed to know about science was that doctors carry big insurance policies. And if something goes wrong, then somebody must have been negligent.

But tomorrow Finney would be expected to cross-examine some scientific expert in front of a national television audience, exposing Finney's scientific ignorance for all the world to see. He didn't even know what kind of scientist might take the stand.

He assumed it would have something to do with the showdown between science and religion on matters of origin. The scientist would probably be a distinguished molecular biologist or biochemist or another expert in some other specialty that Finney didn't know a thing about.

Finney started by reviewing the basics of Darwinian evolution. He cruised the Internet until he located a synopsis of *The Origin of Species*. He took some notes and jotted down a few questions that immediately sprang to mind. Maybe this wouldn't be so bad after all. Like a good lawyer, he traced Darwin's research back to the original source and read a few sections of Darwin's journal—*The Voyage of the Beagle*. The entire book was reproduced on the Internet. Intrigued, Finney turned to the chapter on the Galápagos Islands:

Considering that these islands are placed directly under the equator, the climate is far from being excessively hot; this seems chiefly caused by the singularly low temperature of the surrounding water, brought here by the great southern Polar current. Excepting during one short season, very little rain falls, and even then it is irregular; but the clouds generally hang low.

Finney read with interest Darwin's description of the volcanic geology of the islands, the lava streams, the black sand, and the zoology. Darwin described the unique habitat and incredible variety of wildlife with zeal, reveling in his interaction with the indigenous creatures.

In Darwin's concluding thoughts on the Galápagos, he speculated as to why each island had such distinct wildlife. The paragraph triggered a number of additional questions for Finney, and he scribbled more notes.

The only light which I can throw on this remarkable difference in the inhabitants of the different islands, is, that the very strong currents of the sea running in a westerly and W.N.W. direction must separate, as far as transportal by the sea is concerned, the southern islands from the northern ones; and between these northern islands a strong N.W. current was observed.... As the archipelago is free to a most remarkable degree from gales of wind, neither the birds, insects, nor lighter seeds, would be blown from island to island.... Reviewing the facts here given, one is astonished at the amount of creative force, if such an expression may be used, displayed on these small, barren and rocky islands; and still more so, at its diverse yet analogous action on points so near to each other.

Creative force, thought Finney. He now had a theme. Every good cross-examination needed a theme. He began scouring the Internet with increased enthusiasm. Darwin had been more help than Finney had anticipated.

∾

At 8:00 p.m. Nikki called Wellington to find out whether he had solved chapter two. Finney had posted a new series of Westlaw searches, and Nikki didn't have a clue what they meant.

"The normal spot?" asked Wellington.

Nikki checked her watch. The night life wouldn't really get started for a few more hours. She could do it over the phone, but the kid probably needed some encouragement.

"Sure," said Nikki.

∽

Wellington arrived later than Nikki, probably due to the fact that the Starbucks was actually about ten minutes closer to her place than to his. He wore a pair of khaki cargo shorts that thankfully weren't as tight as the last pair, a button-down Hawaiian shirt that he had tucked in (contrary to every fashion dictate known to Nikki), and a pair of white boat shoes with no socks. He had his backpack slung over his shoulder and undoubtedly had a fresh supply of sharpened number-two lead pencils as well as his computer and Judge Finney's little book.

" 'S up?" he said.

Nikki just shook her head. Some kids were better off not even trying to be cool.

"You need to untuck that shirt," Nikki said. "That's what's up."

Wellington looked mortified. "Why?"

Because I don't want to be seen with the world's biggest nerd. Because tucking your shirt in went out of fashion with the Backstreet Boys. "Because if this mission gets any more intense, you may have to carry. And you've got nowhere to hide your piece when your shirt's tucked in. Plus, you don't want to suddenly change styles as soon as you start packing, or people will notice."

Wellington went white. "You're kidding, right? I, um...I don't even know how to use a gun."

"I'm kidding," said Nikki, "about everything but the shirt. If you untuck it, at least people might wonder if you have a weapon. That alone could come in handy someday."

Wellington considered this as Nikki imagined that big cranium of his cranking through all the pros and cons. "Okay," he said after a few seconds. He pulled his shirt out, the wrinkled tail hanging conspicuously exposed.

"You look dangerous," said Nikki.

Since every table inside Starbucks was occupied, they took their drinks and Wellington's pound cake into the Farnsworths' minivan and cranked up the air conditioning. The van had a wet-dog odor to it, though Nikki pretended not to notice. *How does a guy worried about a few germs on a pen ignore the legions of deadly microbes generated by a slimy corgi?*

"Did you work on this cipher?" asked Wellington between bites of pound cake and sips of Pellegrino water.

"I looked at it," said Nikki, "but I was pretty busy investigating the speedy-trial cases."

Wellington mumbled something that was hard to understand since he had a mouth full of cake. He pulled out some charts as Nikki took a sip of her iced mocha.

"Here's the frequency analysis chart," said Wellington after he swallowed. It looked exactly like the one Nikki had created on the Internet. "Notice anything?"

Other than the smell of a corgi and the fact that you can't remember not to ask questions? Nikki shook her head. "Not really."

"The percentages for the ciphertext match up almost exactly with the averages for the English language," Wellington announced. He ran his finger along the chart. "There are a few exceptions, as you might expect, but look at some of these. A—seven percent in the ciphertext, eight percent in the English language. D—four percent in the ciphertext, four percent in the English language. E—fourteen percent in the ciphertext, thirteen percent in the English language. I—eight percent in the ciphertext, seven percent in the English language. See the pattern? The percentages are almost the same."

It was hard to argue with Wellington on encryption, so Nikki just gave him an "Mmm hmm" and took another shot of mocha. She felt stupid for not seeing it herself.

"Which means that we're not dealing with a substitution cipher in this chapter. We're most likely dealing with a transposition cipher." Wellington turned to Nikki, his eyes expectant.

"Amazing," Nikki said, though her inflection said, "Boring." She didn't bother asking what a transposition cipher was. She knew that would be point number two in Professor Wellington's lecture.

"A transposition cipher is when the letters actually represent themselves but the order of the letters has been scrambled. Our job is to detect the pattern and unscramble them." There was a pause in the seminar as Wellington took his last bite of pound cake, chased it with a gulp of Pellegrino, and then set the empty Starbucks bag he had used for a plate on the floor of the vehicle.

"Most people use a matrix to encrypt a transposition cipher." Wellington pulled his small spiral notebook and pencil out of his backpack. He opened the notebook to a blank page. "Let's say we want to write a message that says, 'Meet me at Starbucks for coffee.' I'll use a matrix that is five letters wide and six letters long to encode it."

Nikki watched as Wellington arranged the letters.

M	E	F	T	M
E	A	T	S	T
A	R	B	U	C
K	S	F	O	R
C	O	F	F	E
E	X	V	Y	Z

"Notice that I added some letters at the end as filler." Wellington looked at Nikki, who nodded her head. "Now, instead of writing the letters in the code from left to right across the rows, we can write them from top to bottom along the columns," continued Wellington. "This will scramble them so that our message would read M-E-A-K-C-E-E-A-R-S-O-X and so on."

"I see," said Nikki, hoping the comment might speed things along.

"That's just one form of transposition cipher, so I thought I would start there."

Wellington flipped the pages in his notebook, showing Nikki a lot of different matrixes. "None of those worked," said Wellington. "So I tried some mathematical formulas to see if I could detect a pattern."

He turned the page again. "Voilà! It was right under my nose the entire time."

Nikki noticed the new pattern Wellington used on the page. "This is called the rail-fence cipher," Wellington explained. "It's so basic that I couldn't believe I didn't see it earlier. You just write the entire message on two different lines, alternating between them, and then you write the encoded message by copying the entire first line and then following it with the entire second line."

Wellington turned toward Nikki. "Did you read chapter two in Finney's book?"

"I skimmed it."

"Good. Then you know it's about the paralyzed man that some friends brought to Jesus for healing in a house so crowded that they had to drop the man in through the ceiling. Jesus pronounced forgiveness of the man's sins, but the Pharisees were thinking that He had committed blasphemy. So, to prove He had power to forgive sins, Jesus healed the man as well."

"Which, of course, would lead any reasonable person to suspect a rail-fence cipher," said Nikki sarcastically.

"Exactly," said Wellington, proving once again that cipher experts don't do sarcasm. "Finney's point was that too often we just operate on the physical plane, whether it's our health or finances or whatever. But Jesus first dealt with the man's spiritual condition and maybe wouldn't have healed him at all if the Pharisees hadn't been so critical. So Finney is saying we need to be cognizant of both dimensions—the spiritual and the physical—and the rail-fence cipher is a perfect picture of that because it only makes sense if you integrate the two planes together."

"Did you solve the code?" Nikki asked. She avoided church so she wouldn't get preached at. She didn't need the Right Reverend Wellington Farnsworth making up for lost time in the minivan.

"Sorry. I just get into this stuff. It's a verse from the apostle Paul after he had prayed without success for God to remove a thorn in his flesh." He slid the paper over toward Nikki. "As you read, alternate from the top line to the bottom, and you'll see what I mean."

```
A D E A D O E Y R C I S F I I N F R O F R Y
N H S I T M M G A E S U F C E T O Y U O M


T E G H S A E E F C I W A N S
S R N T I M D P R E T N E K E S
```

Nikki read the message, and like magic, it all made sense. She raised an eyebrow at Wellington. "Not bad," she said.

Next, Nikki reached into the secret compartment of her black leather Fendi Spy bag. "Here are the letters from Finney's latest Westlaw searches," she said. She rattled them off to Wellington, who wrote them down using the rail-fence cipher.

He studied it for a minute before announcing the solution. "Need to know the location of Paradise Island. Is William Lassiter from governor's office involved with show?"

"That's it?" Nikki asked. It seemed like they were working awfully hard for some pretty meager messages.

"At least it didn't say to skip chapter two," noted Wellington.

CHAPTER 40

Finney woke just before sunrise to the familiar sound of Kareem Hasaan's prayers. Groggy, the judge managed to sit on the edge of the bed, coughing as the monotone chants floated through the patio door.

"*Allah u akbar,*" Finney heard Kareem say. "*Subhana rabbiya al azeem.*"

Finney stumbled into the bathroom and brushed his teeth. He threw on a pair of baggy swim trunks, a T-shirt with cut-off sleeves featuring a Virginia Beach logo, and his frazzled John Deere ball cap. He put on some deodorant and padded out to the kitchen to start the coffee.

"*Allah u akbar,*" he heard Kareem say again. Finney knew that this roughly meant, "Allah is the greatest." "*Subhana rabbiya A'ala…*" Finney listened absent-mindedly as he threw away last night's coffee grounds and picked up the mess in his kitchen. The card game had been a doozie, going until nearly 1:00 a.m. For an old man like Finney, it might as well have been all night.

He stepped onto the patio and watched Kareem while the coffee slowly brewed. Every morning, the same routine. The same prayers—praising Allah, seeking forgiveness, reciting the Koran. The same prayer positions—standing upright, bowing down, kneeling, and then prostrating himself.

Finney thought the monotony of it must surely make the prayer time lose its zeal. But when Finney had raised the issue at dinner last night—a drawn-out affair as all the contestants stuffed themselves in preparation for the time of fasting—Kareem said that just the opposite occurred. The very discipline of the salah five times a day kept him in close relationship with Allah. When he finished his prayer, his heart would be filled with remembrance of Allah. A proper prayer time, said Kareem, would help him strive successfully against all kinds of evils and temptations and remain steadfast in times of trial and adversity.

Finney poured a cup of coffee, then placed it on the counter and coughed until he bent over. The last few days, his lungs had been hurting more when he coughed. More phlegm came up in the process, he wheezed a fair amount afterward, and he had no appetite. He found it harder to catch his breath after even moderate amounts of exercise. Absent a miracle, thought Finney, I probably won't make it to the end of the year.

This is my last summer.

The thought steeled him for the next few days. How many men have a chance to reach an entire generation during the last year of their lives? Maybe his whole life had been preparing him for this.

He took his coffee to the patio and watched Kareem finish his prayers as the sun peeked over the ocean. Finney himself prayed—silently, with his eyes wide open. He thanked God for the promise that one day he would be perfectly healed. He asked for strength to finish strong. He prayed for wisdom and courage in the next few days. The plan he was contemplating would require more than he had to give.

And he prayed for Kareem. So much passion, but he was missing God's grace. *Lord, please show him the way.*

∽

By 7:30 local time, the sun dominated the eastern sky while a few wispy clouds inched their way from south to north. The prevailing winds this morning were virtually nonexistent, providing a good excuse to skip the sailing but also sending a bad omen for tomorrow night. It was the first day that the winds hadn't been in at least a ten- to fifteen-knot range since they had arrived on the island.

Finney walked down to the small shed on the beach that housed the snorkel gear, past a meditating Swami. Five or ten minutes later, Dr. Kline showed up. She and Finney talked about taking a day off from sailing in order to do some snorkeling. They mentioned the schools of fish they had been seeing while sailing and the coral reefs they wanted to investigate. Since God had cooperated with their ruse, Finney also mentioned the lack of wind.

Finney took off his mike and laid it carefully on a lounge chair. He pulled off his T-shirt, feeling exposed in his baggy swim trunks. His bony and pale chest, sporting more gray hair than black, was not going to earn him any points in the beefcake department. He put his snorkel on quickly and did a quick Joe-muscle-beach flex, which brought a hoot from his friend Horace hiding behind the camera.

But Finney quickly lost Horace's attention, as Horace turned his camera to Dr. Kline, who didn't mind stripping down to her small turquoise two-piece swimsuit in front of a camera recording her for all of America. She had a toned body and washboard abs, with an even tan that obviously predated her time on the island. To Horace's credit, he avoided hooting, but he never took the camera off Dr. Kline as she adjusted her ponytail so it wouldn't interfere with the elastic band of the snorkel.

"Over here, Horace," called Finney, waving at the camera, but he might as well have been talking to an island iguana. Horace knew what America expected on its reality shows, and it wasn't a fifty-nine-year-old judge whose chicken legs sprouted out of the bottom of his baggy swim trunks.

"Yeah, over there," said Dr. Kline as she waded out in the knee-deep surf and put on a pair of flippers. Finney followed her in, losing his balance once or twice as he struggled to fit his size ten feet into the flippers. He soon got everything situated and joined Victoria just past the small breaks in the surf. The two began exploring the underwater world of Paradise Island.

The clear water made it seem as if you could reach out and touch schools of small fish swimming several feet below the surface. The colors amazed Finney as he swam with Dr. Kline, pointing and gawking, stopping occasionally so that he could surface and cough.

"Two-thirds of the earth's living organisms are beneath the surface of the ocean," said Victoria when they both came up for a break. They were treading water directly over a colorful coral reef and sponge field. "Let's head back toward Swami."

"Okay," said Finney. They pulled their masks back down and started snorkeling again, meandering in the general direction of the Swami and his yoga exercises. Finney and Kline surfaced again and yelled for the Swami to join them. It didn't take much coaxing, and a few minutes later the Swami had his own snorkel on and swam toward his fellow contestants a hundred feet from shore.

On cue, Kareem walked down to the beach, wearing nothing but his swim shorts. "You coming in?" yelled the Swami.

"No."

"Why not? There's some great stuff out here!" shouted Finney.

"I'll take your word for it."

But the three snorkelers were not to be denied. After some serious cajoling and a confession by Kareem that he didn't swim, he grudgingly agreed to join them if they stayed closer to shore. He took off his microphone and headed for the snorkel masks. A few minutes later, the four contestants were standing in chest-deep water, talking in a small circle. When the small waves crested, Kareem held his arms out to the side as if he couldn't get them wet, while Victoria pointed and lectured about the cool things they were seeing under the surface.

"We don't have long," said Finney, keeping his voice low. "So, Victoria, why don't you bring us up to speed?"

For the next few minutes, Victoria Kline talked about her visits with Bryce McCormack and what she had discovered. She also confirmed, under questioning from Finney, that Ando had declined to join them this morning.

"Is he working with them?" asked the Swami.

"I don't think so," replied Victoria. "But he has this strange way of looking at life. It's pretty much a let-it-be approach. Plus, it's hard to really understand what he's thinking when you can only communicate through that pinprick cipher."

Finney stole a glance toward the camera crews on the beach. Horace and the others weren't even filming, huddled in their own little cluster. "The way I see it," said Finney, "we've got three choices. One: keep playing the game but try to get some more information in the next few days before they select the finalists. Two: leak some information about these threats to the media and let Murphy and McCormack know we've done that. That way, they won't dare try anything. Or three: bring in the authorities right away."

"How can we do number two or three?" asked Victoria. "They've got us cooped up on this island. I can't even get in touch with my agent. If McCormack won't let *me* talk to someone outside the island, I seriously doubt if anybody else can."

"I think I can figure out a way," said Finney. Another glance toward shore told him that a few of the cameramen were getting suspicious. "Tell you what," said Finney. "Everybody put on your snorkels and swim around a little...except you, Kareem. You just walk around. Let's huddle up in a few minutes."

Victoria and the Swami stole a look toward shore. "Sounds good," said Victoria, pulling her snorkel over her face and taking off.

"I'm with her," said the Swami.

After five minutes of snorkeling, the contestants regrouped around Kareem.

"Did you see that turtle?" asked the Swami. "He was huge."

"I saw him," said Dr. Kline.

"And those...like angelfish that are purple and gold—what are they called?"

"Will options two or three involve any risk of the producers going public with the blackmail material they have against us?" Kareem directed his question toward Finney with the same "Take no prisoners" look he wore in court during Finney's cross-examination.

Finney met his gaze. "If we tell McCormack and Murphy that we've leaked information to the press, it will probably keep them from hurting anyone. But I would expect them to retaliate by making the blackmail information, as you call it, public. The same would be true if we go to the authorities, unless we could get the authorities to conduct some kind of surprise raid and shut the rest of the show down."

"On what basis?" asked Kline.

"That's the problem," said Finney, swishing his hands back and forth in the water. "Right now, our evidence is pretty thin."

"I'd rather die than have that blackmail information released," said Kareem. He looked from one contestant to the next, making sure everyone realized how serious he was.

Which didn't stop the Swami. "Dude, what could be that bad?"

"I said I'd rather die than have it revealed," said Kareem. He cut an imposing figure, his sculpted pecs glistening in the sun, his furrowed brow hooding his eyes.

"I get that," said the Swami. "But it just feels like we're playing right into their hands. I don't see how anything could be that bad."

"It is."

Nobody spoke for a beat. "I know the feeling," said Dr. Kline. "I'd survive if my information became public, but my career wouldn't. I'd rather figure out a way to ensure our safety that doesn't compromise that information."

Finney glanced at the camera crew again. A few of them watched the contestants intently. "I've been thinking about a plan," Finney explained softly, "that probably wouldn't risk that information becoming public for anyone but me."

He could tell immediately that he had Kareem's and Victoria's attention. He provided the details as quickly as possible, pointing into the water and out to the horizon as he spoke.

When they all agreed, Victoria swam off toward the shed that housed the snorkel gear. A split second later, the Swami took off in hot pursuit. Finney removed his flippers and walked toward the beach with Kareem.

"There really is some amazing stuff out there," said Finney.

Kareem didn't respond. Instead, he stared toward the shore as if Finney had never spoken.

" 'Course, if you can't swim, it's a little hard to see the best stuff."

Kareem took a few more steps, still ignoring Finney. "It was adultery," he said, his voice so low that Finney wasn't sure he had heard the man right. "Almost ten years ago—a one-weekend deal." They walked a few more steps in silence. "My wife never found out. My kids don't know. What's amazing is that the show's producers somehow found out."

Finney looked straight ahead as well, sensing that for some reason Kareem didn't want to share this face to face.

"They had me hooked up to that lie detector and asked me a few preliminary questions. As a Muslim, how could I defend clients I knew were guilty? That type of thing." Finney thought about his own preliminary questions—the ones about Nikki he had refused to answer. "Then, out of the blue, they showed me a picture of the woman. I denied it, but the lie detector probably bounced off the chart." Kareem paused, still stunned by the ambush. "Ten years," he said. "I thought it was ancient history."

It was uncanny, thought Finney, the amount of preshow investigation these guys had done on each contestant. "I don't know how they found out about my sins either," said Finney. "Because of my negligence, a drug dealer was released. Recently, he killed a woman."

"I dishonored Allah," said Kareem. "I betrayed my wife." They were now getting dangerously close to shore. Kareem stopped. Finney did the same. They stood there for a moment, facing the shore, the water dripping from their bodies.

Finney bent over and washed out his mask. "Why are you telling me this?" he asked.

"Because you're going to stick your neck out for me," said Kareem, "and I want you to know how critical this is to me." But before Finney could get warm and fuzzy, his Muslim friend continued. "And if anybody finds out about my adultery, I'll hold you personally responsible. Whatever you do, don't put them in a position where they need to release that lie-detector information. It would destroy my family." He paused, but Finney sensed he wasn't done. "I'd rather die first. In fact, Allah may require it."

The camera crews on the beach had moved in too close for Finney to risk saying what he really felt. He wanted to talk about forgiveness and about Kareem confessing the matter to his wife, but all that would have to come later, if at all. For now, he could only say something that would be innocuous if overheard.

"I'll take care of it," said Finney.

"Good," said Kareem. He started toward the shore, a half step ahead of Finney, his mask and attached snorkel shoved on top of his head. He took it off and plastered his wet hair back, the water dripping from his broad shoulders. To Finney, he looked like a navy SEAL emerging from a special mission.

Except that Kareem couldn't swim. The Muslim was full of surprises, thought Finney.

CHAPTER 41

r. Henri Fetaya was a diminutive man with short, curly brown hair, and he stayed in perpetual motion. Finney got tired just watching him. Fetaya was beamed into the Paradise Courtroom by the wonders of satellite technology, his larger-than-life face captured on the large screen situated in the jury box. This would be a high-tech cross-examination befitting a scientist of Fetaya's caliber, an Ivy League microbiology professor whose list of peer-reviewed articles ran more than three pages long.

Dr. Kline took her turn with the witness first, comfortably discussing the basics of scientific theories and Darwinian evolution as if she and Fetaya were old friends. Finney found himself scrambling just to keep up with the terminology, struggling to comprehend the scientific code that peppered their language. Next to him, Kareem stared at the large flat-screen monitor as if he could intimidate a witness thousands of miles away.

For most of her ten minutes, Victoria's questions drew out a crisp and forceful critique of creationism and its recently developed first cousin, intelligent design. "It is," scoffed the witness, "just the latest in a series of wild swings by a losing prizefighter hoping for a big knockout punch."

"Has the punch landed?" asked Kline.

Fetaya smiled. "Absolutely not. It's been an impressive roundhouse right, with some credentialed scientists actually signing on, but in the end"—he shook his head—"nothing but air."

After several minutes of kicking around intelligent-design straw men, Kline went for her own knockout punch. "So, what does that tell you about whether some kind of divine being initiated life as we know it?"

Fetaya sat up straighter in his seat, fully engaged. "Many scientists jump on the agnostic bandwagon at this point. But that is not where science leads me." Fetaya looked directly into the camera.

"There is reason and there is faith, and I believe both are necessary for ultimate truth. Science allows us to investigate the natural world through observation, experiment, and theory. Science allows us to understand the world around us, but it does not give our world meaning. As humans, we long to find a purpose in what we observe. And we ultimately learn that this purpose comes from outside science, from a transcendent being who designed a world that actually works and then turned it loose, free from any dictatorial whims."

As Fetaya lectured, Finney watched Kline's face tighten. The response had taken her completely by surprise. Theistic evolution. She had only a few minutes to undo the damage. Finney marveled at the cunning of the show's producers. They had found a scientist who would alienate all the contestants, and Kline had walked right into their trap.

"The self-sufficiency of nature does not mean that God doesn't exist," Fetaya continued, talking rapidly and shifting in his seat as his excitement increased. "It only means that God fashioned a world in which free and independent beings can evolve into ever-higher life forms. It's a world where God loves us enough to give us the ultimate freedom to embrace Him or not, to evolve toward Him or away from Him."

"Are you done?" interjected Kline gruffly as soon as Fetaya paused for breath.

"Not quite," responded Fetaya evenly. His bright blue eyes twinkled as he realized the mischief he was creating in the courtroom. "I didn't get a chance to give you my punch line, a phrase I first heard articulated by a distinguished professor of biology at Brown University." Fetaya paused ever so briefly, just long enough to punctuate his next sentence. "I believe in Darwin's God."

Kline stiffened and launched some rapid-fire questions challenging the logic of Fetaya's conclusions. Was this a God who left everything to chance, including the evolution of humans, or a God who preordained each step of the evolutionary process? If the former, how could Fetaya say that God loved humans if it wasn't even a sure thing that humans would one day exist? And if the latter, how could Fetaya claim to believe in the random mutation and natural-selection process if Darwin's God was secretly guiding the entire process?

As they sparred, Kline didn't hide her contempt for the witness. Finney took some perverse pleasure in her discomfort, though he didn't much care for the happy little biologist either. Finney believed in a God who designed the human race and called humans His masterpiece. Finney's God didn't spin a primitive world into existence and then sit back and watch it evolve. But Fetaya had a quick smile and a winning way. Finney had seen too many cases where a lawyer tried to annihilate an expert as sharp as Dr. Fetaya, only to end up choking on his or her own questions.

Maybe Finney could fake a coughing fit in the middle of his cross-examination.

"Your time is up," Javitts said to Victoria Kline.

"One more question, Judge Javitts."

Javitts banged his gavel and looked stern, just like a real TV judge. "I said your time is up."

"So to sum up, Dr. Fetaya, you acknowledge that the scientific evidence does not support the theory of intelligent design, yet you still claim to believe in an intelligent designer?"

"I said your time is up," said Javitts, raising his voice.

Kline scoffed and returned to her seat. "Pass the witness," she said with contempt.

Kareem took the floor next and used an old trick that Finney had seen many times before—he kept the witness answering questions outside his main area of expertise. Finney sat back and enjoyed the show. Sitting at the counsel table was better than being on the witness stand when the Muslim was on the prowl.

"You have studied enough physics, sir, to know that our universe is incredibly fine tuned so that just the right conditions exist to create and sustain life. Is this true?"

"I am not an expert in physics," replied Fetaya, "but I know the concepts you're referring to."

"Well, you are familiar with the concept of gravity, aren't you?"

Fetaya rose up in indignation. "Yes. Of course."

"And you know that if you alter the ratio of gravity to electromagnetism ever so slightly, our sun could not exist?"

"I'm aware of that."

"Or if the nuclear strong force in the universe is weakened just a little, we would have only hydrogen and no other chemicals?"

"Yes. I understand that to be true."

"Or if we strengthen the nuclear strong force ever so slightly, it would yield a universe without atoms. Correct?'

Fetaya did his best to look bored. "Yes."

Kareem, decked out in another tailored Italian suit (his fourth one so far, by Finney's count), took a step closer to the television monitor. He had no notes for his examination and never took his eyes from the screen in front of him. "In the formation of the universe, the balance of matter to antimatter had to be accurate to one part per ten billion for the universe to arise. And if the expansion rate of the Big Bang had been one billionth of a percent larger or smaller, the universe would be incapable of sustaining life. Am I correct, Dr. Fetaya?"

"I'm not sure about your exact numbers," said the witness, taking a sip of water. Very casual. He gave the camera an "I'm not flustered" look. "But the gist of what you're saying is correct. I'm just not sure it proves what you think it does."

Kareem stared at the monitor for a moment as if trying to decide whether he should chase that thought or not. Eventually, he walked over to an easel and rolled it to the middle of the room. "Can you see this?" he asked Dr. Fetaya.

"Yes."

"Good. I'm going to start by writing the number one on the board." Kareem did this and then turned back to the witness. "Now I'm going to start adding zeros until you tell me to stop. And here's what the zeros represent: there are more than thirty separate physical or cosmological constants that require precise calibration in order to produce a universe that sustains life. You are going to tell me—approximately—what the odds are that all these constants were fine tuned this way by random chance. So one zero would represent a one-out-of-ten chance. Two zeros would be one out of a hundred. Et cetera. Are you ready?"

Fetaya started shaking his head as if it were the most ridiculous idea he had ever heard. "I can't do that, Mr. Hasaan. It makes no sense to do it."

"You can't do it because the number of zeros won't even fit on this board. Am I right?"

"No, Mr. Hasaan. The problem is not the size of the board but the assumption in your question." Fetaya then launched into a long lecture about the multiverse theory—the thought that ours is not the only universe in existence, that there are billions or even an infinite number of other universes, and therefore one universe is bound to have these types of parameters. It just happens to be ours.

An exasperated Kareem finally cut in. "Dr. Fetaya, I have a very limited amount of time. I've asked you about the way our universe appears to be fine tuned for life. Is your response to simply imagine an infinite number of other universes that are not?"

"It's not just my response," replied Fetaya, his frustration starting to show. "It's also the thinking of the best minds in physics today. We cannot assume that we are the only universe in existence."

"Have you or any of these brilliant minds observed any of these other universes?"

"No. Of course not. We are confined in time and space to our own."

"Would you agree that belief in a billion unseen universes requires a certain amount of blind faith?"

"Objection," said Dr. Kline, her face dark. "These questions distort this entire school of thought. And while he's at it, why doesn't Mr. Hasaan ask a few questions about biology—the actual area of expertise for the witness?"

"I'll sustain the objection," replied Javitts. "And Mr. Hasaan, your time has now expired." Javitts then turned to Finney. "Your witness, Judge."

Finney's mind was still reeling with the terms and numbers that Kareem had tossed around for the last ten minutes. He couldn't wait to see the Muslim zero in on the biochemistry aspects. But now it was Finney's turn—Mr. B Minus in general sciences. He felt like Charlie Brown in the cartoon strip where Linus is describing what he sees in the clouds—a map of the British Honduras, the stoning of Stephen with the apostle Paul standing to one side. And Charlie Brown? "I was going to say I saw a ducky and a horsie, but I changed my mind."

Finney stood to his full height and looked at Javitts. He coughed quickly to the side—it seemed to always hit him when he was nervous. "I yield my time to the gentleman from Lebanon," Finney said.

Kline jumped up. "He can't do that."

So much for my sailing buddy. "Judge, I can either have Mr. Hasaan whisper questions in my ear that I will then ask the witness or we can let him ask the witness directly. I suggest that things might go smoother if we just let Mr. Hasaan continue."

"No!" came a voice from the back. "Cut!" Bryce McCormack walked to the front of the courtroom, taking over as self-appointed judge. "This isn't the United States Senate. We don't yield our time to others."

Finney turned to confront him, and McCormack apparently decided to take a more accommodating approach. "Good television isn't necessarily two people discussing terms that the rest of us don't understand. Judge, you may think you're not as qualified as Mr. Hasaan or Dr. Kline, but your approach might be exactly the thing that connects with the viewers."

McCormack turned back to Javitts before Finney could respond. "Let's start with you calling time on Kareem, and we'll take it from there."

"I'll just yield my time again," said Finney.

But McCormack was already walking toward the back of the courtroom. "And Judge Javitts will just overrule that request."

CHAPTER 42

"You ever read Darwin's journal from his time on board the HMS *Beagle*?" asked Finney.

"Many times," said Dr. Fetaya, shifting to get more comfortable. He leaned back in his chair, as if Finney were a lightweight. *Which I am,* thought Finney.

"Do you remember a statement in that journal where Darwin said he was amazed at the amount of 'creative force' displayed on the small, barren, and rocky islands of the Galápagos?" Finney stole a glance at Dr. Kline, who seemed to be enjoying this spectacle way too much. She jotted some notes with her right hand and propped her left elbow on the table, her fist resting against her cheek. The Swami, sitting next to her, gave Finney a thumbs-up.

"I don't recall those exact words, Judge Finney. But in any event, Darwin later realized that the creative force you're referencing was the process of evolution—mutations, natural selection, and survival of the fittest."

"Yes, I'm aware of that. It may surprise you to know that even judges sometimes read books like *The Origin of Species.*"

Fetaya smirked. "Is there a question there?"

"Sometimes I like to warm up a little," said Finney. He walked over to the counsel table for a sip of water. The witness was feisty; Finney liked that. His competitive instincts started chasing away his nervousness. After all, Fetaya might be a scientist, but this was a courtroom. Home turf.

"Let me ask if you recognize this statement from *The Origin of Species,*" said Finney, checking his legal pad. " 'If it could be demonstrated that any complex organ existed, which could not possibly have been formed by numerous, successive, slight modifications, my theory would absolutely break down.' "

"Darwin said that," Fetaya agreed.

"Have you heard of a concept called irreducible complexity?"

"Yes."

"Would you mind explaining it?"

"Sure." Fetaya leaned into the task. "The phrase was popularized by Michael Behe, a biochemist from Lehigh University, who wrote a book in 1996 entitled *Darwin's Black Box*. Behe defines a system or device as being irreducibly complex if it has a number of different components that all work together to accomplish a task, and if you removed any one of the components, then the entire system would no longer function. Moreover, the different components, if they evolved one at a time, would have no value by themselves and therefore no chance of survival. According to Dr. Behe, something that is irreducibly complex is highly unlikely to be formed through evolution, because the odds are against a large number of simultaneous mutations. The illustration Dr. Behe likes to use is the mousetrap."

"So an irreducibly complex structure, according to Darwin's own admission, would cause his theory to absolutely break down?" Finney asked, picking up confidence.

"If one existed," confirmed Fetaya. He gave Finney a quick and phony smile. "Unfortunately for you, none does. They only appear to be that way at first glance."

Finney saw a lecture coming. "Then let me ask you about—"

But the witness appealed to the judge. "May I finish my answer, Your Honor?"

"Yes," said Javitts. "Judge Finney, you know the rules."

Fetaya smiled, and Finney wanted to strangle the little man. "As I was saying, when natural selection acts on chance variations, evolution is capable of scaling peaks that appear impossibly high. In fact, Richard Dawkins wrote a book about this process called *Climbing Mount Improbable*. On the front side a complex biological structure might look like a sheer cliff that cannot be scaled in one big bound, but on the back side there is a gradual slope that permits much easier climbing. Sometimes we've discovered that path; sometimes we have yet to discover it. It might, for example, consist of DNA mutations that we have yet to unveil."

"Are you done?"

"Yes."

Finney checked his notes, ignoring the fact that Kareem was trying to get his attention. There was a certain rhythm to cross-examination. Stopping before questions to consult with a colleague gave the witness too much time to think. "Let's talk about some of those sheer cliffs that Dr. Behe cites in his book," said Finney. "Cliffs where no scientist will ever discover a gradual path up the back side because none exists. They include things like the development of the human eye, complicated microscopic contraptions like cilia and flagella, and the biosynthesis of large amino acids. Even the blood-clotting process—which is the one I would like to focus on, since it's the only one I even begin to understand."

"I don't agree with the premise of your question," said Fetaya, "but I'm happy to talk about blood clotting."

"If your blood clots in the wrong place—like the brain or the lungs—you can die. Correct?"

"Yes."

"If the blood-clotting process takes too long, you can bleed to death."

"Of course."

"And if a blood clot isn't confined to your cut, if your whole system coagulates, then you die that way too. Correct?"

Dr. Fetaya graced Finney with a condescending smile. "Right again."

Finney moved over next to Kareem as he read the following question directly from his notes. "So the system of blood clotting has no margin for error. It involves a highly choreographed cascade of ten steps that use about twenty different molecular components. Without the whole system in place, it doesn't work. Isn't that right, Dr. Fetaya?"

"No. That's not correct."

Finney held up his forefinger and conferred quickly with Kareem. "You were trying to get my attention?" Finney whispered.

"I was."

"Because?"

"I was going to tell you to stay away from the blood-clotting example," Kareem said with a frown.

"Oh." Finney stood back up.

"May I explain, Judge Finney?" asked the witness.

Kareem's eyes darkened into an "I told you so" stare.

"Sure," said Finney.

The witness proceeded to lecture Finney about the blood-clotting cascade in dolphins and porpoises. One of the components cited by Behe— the Hagemann factor, to be precise—was found to be missing in dolphins and porpoises, but the blood still clotted.

This prompted another quick conference with Kareem, after which Finney recovered nicely. So maybe it was ten cascading steps and nineteen different components, as opposed to twenty. But could the witness cite any examples of other mammals that had fewer molecular components than those present in dolphins and porpoises where blood clotting took place? He could not, the witness admitted, but that only meant the precise evolutionary process had yet to be discovered. You couldn't infer that no such process existed.

And so it went, back and forth. Finney held his own with several examples of irreducible complexity, primarily because he sat down next to Kareem and let his Muslim friend whisper each question in his ear.

Except the last few questions. Finney stood back up and handled those on his own. "So even though we haven't discovered any gradual, step-by-step evolutionary paths to these complex organisms, Dr. Fetaya, you still believe that such paths exist?"

"Yes, of course. The evidence of evolution is overwhelming. The fact that we have not yet observed or reproduced the precise process for these molecular organisms does not worry me. History is on our side, Judge Finney. Given enough time, science tends to explain the most baffling things."

"The evidence of things unseen?" asked Finney. "There's a word for that in the Bible, Dr. Fetaya. It's called faith, not science."

"Is that a question?" asked Dr. Fetaya.

∾

Later that afternoon, a medical doctor was flown to the island to conduct biopsies, blood tests, and urine tests on all the contestants except Victoria Kline. For Dr. Ando, the physician used a portable x-ray machine to track the progression of Ando's disease.

At one point during his examination, Finney casually asked the doctor what island they might be on. The man looked directly into the camera and smiled. "I believe that's confidential information," said the doctor.

"I know," said Finney. "I won't tell anyone."

"And neither will I," said the doctor.

CHAPTER 43

Stepping off the elevator on Monday morning, Nikki knew immediately that she could get used to working at a place like Randolph and Associates. Her heels clicked on the marble floor as she walked toward the mahogany reception desk trimmed with polished brass. Expensive impressionist paintings hung from the walls, but the subjects were strangely incongruous with this high-brow law firm. From one painting, the haunting blue eyes of a coal miner, devoid of hope, peered out from a coal-stained face. Another showed the grimy exhaustion of rail yard workers, or at least that's who Nikki thought they were.

But there was no mistaking the picture just behind the bleached-blond receptionist. Big as life, bigger actually, was an impressionist portrait of the man himself—Preston Edgar Randolph—in all his square-jawed glory. They might as well have hung a brass nameplate underneath that said "Friend of the Working Man."

"Can I help you?" asked the receptionist. As Nikki expected, she looked like a model. *Good looks,* thought Nikki, *matter at Randolph and Associates.*

"I'm Nikki Moreno. I'm here to meet with Mr. Randolph."

The receptionist took Nikki's name and called Randolph's assistant. A few minutes later, another candidate for modeling school, this one a brunette, came out to escort Nikki into an equally impressive conference room. Nikki looked the woman over for flaws, but nothing jumped out at her. It was good that looks mattered, but this competition was a little intense.

"Would you like something to drink?" asked the cover girl.

"Water's fine."

The woman took care of Nikki's water and then left her alone. Nikki busied herself by studying the view and making a few cell phone calls. Ten minutes later, she walked down the hall to use the rest room.

Randolph didn't bother to show until fifteen minutes later. He came with an entourage. One thick security guard followed at each shoulder, and an assistant hustled along a few steps behind. Another man, apparently some kind of technical whiz, entered the room and took care of setting up the videoconference. A young woman who claimed to be a lawyer introduced herself, and Nikki secretly wondered what modeling agency she worked for.

Randolph pumped her hand as if Nikki were an old fraternity brother. Up close, he looked ten years older than the picture on the Internet. He was still handsome but more gaunt than she had expected, and his dark eyes turned down at the corners. Though his security guards and associate were dressed to the nines, Randolph himself wore a pair of faded jeans, an untucked polo shirt, and a pair of Birkenstocks with no socks.

As he sat, his assistant poured him a soft drink and then discreetly left the room. Within minutes, the faces of the other conference participants appeared on the big screens—Hadji's mother and father from a FedEx Kinko's in Los Angeles and Kareem Hasaan's wife from Kareem's office in New York City.

Randolph tilted back in his chair and explained the purpose for the conference call. He represented Dr. Victoria Kline, he said, as well as Judge Finney. As he spoke, he stole a quick glance at Nikki, who nodded her approval. She would try to remember to tell the judge about his new lawyer the next time she sent him a message.

The show's producers had not been playing fair with the contestants, Randolph explained, and in particular had probably defamed both Dr. Kline and Judge Finney in last week's show. Not technically, of course, since defamation law required something called actual malice if the people being defamed were limited-purpose public figures. Which, of course, reminded

Randolph of the time he sued one of the major television networks on another defamation case that everybody said was unwinnable. It was a five-minute rabbit trail of a story, but it had a happy ending. Randolph's client obtained nearly two million dollars in settlement.

"Where was I?" wondered Randolph.

"Possible defamation claims," prompted Nikki.

"Oh yeah."

It wasn't just the way the show portrayed the contestants that had Randolph concerned. Based on a phone message from Victoria, he was actually concerned about their psychological and even physical well-being. He didn't want to alarm anyone, but it seemed to him that the show's producers would stop at nothing in their quest for eye-popping ratings. He asked if anybody else had similar concerns.

Hadji's parents took this as a cue to launch into their complaints about the way the show treated their son. For one thing, his girlfriend was in tears after last Thursday's episode. Hadji's mother dabbed at her own eyes as she described the part of the episode where her son's girlfriend left their house in humiliation.

I'm not sure that was exactly the producer's fault, Nikki thought. *It's not like they forced Hadji to hook up with Tammy.* But she kept her thoughts to herself. Moms were entitled to a few blind spots when it came to their children.

"Have you contacted anybody from Dr. Ando's family?" Nikki asked.

"There wasn't anybody," said one of the investigators. "No wife. No kids. Both parents are dead. His siblings haven't talked with him for nearly a year."

"He takes that nonattachment stuff seriously," said Randolph.

After Randolph launched into a few more war stories to impress the potential clients, he made a few things crystal-clear. One: he wasn't afraid to sue anybody. Two: he was about ready to sue the producers of *Faith on Trial* just for sport. And three: he thought the contestants would be in a stronger position if they stuck together. Hadji's parents signed up before the videoconference ended. Kareem's wife wanted to think about it but promised to stay in touch. Finney, by Nikki's earlier commitment, was already in the fold. But she also requested that Randolph not take any actions on behalf of Finney unless she authorized them.

"We'll file an injunction and shut this show down if we have to," promised Randolph.

As soon as the videoconference ended, an assistant reappeared and reminded Randolph of another conference call that had started five minutes earlier. Before leaving, Randolph told his investigators to brief Nikki on their findings about Javitts, McCormack, and Murphy. "Oh, and what's the connection with those other names you wanted us to check?" he asked Nikki.

Nikki didn't think it would be appropriate to lay out Finney's dirty laundry in front of Preston Randolph's entire entourage. "Those are the names of some defendants on a few cases that Finney handled," Nikki said casually. "I just wanted to make sure there wasn't any connection."

"The speedy-trial cases," said Randolph. He smiled and Nikki knew she had just been one-upped. She should have seen it coming—those names were public information.

Randolph rose to leave but then stopped and studied Nikki as if seeing her for the first time. His gaze lingered for a few seconds on the Moreno legs, and Nikki knew that the balance of power had just shifted. "Did you say you clerk in Norfolk Circuit Court right now?"

"Yes. I start my final year of law school this fall."

He nodded, then cocked his head as if something had just occurred to him. "Have you committed to a firm yet?"

"I'm still trying to decide where to work," Nikki said. Despite the opulence of the place, she was having second thoughts about working for an egomaniac like Randolph. Before law school, she had worked as a paralegal for a Virginia Beach lawyer, Brad Carson, and knew she could return there after she graduated. In Nikki's opinion, Brad was twice the lawyer Randolph was, with half the ego. Still, it didn't hurt to keep her options open.

"Excellent. You ought to drop a résumé in here," Randolph responded. He walked over to shake her hand. "Send it directly to my attention."

"I will," she said, standing and giving him a firm businesslike handshake.

His droopy eyes locked on hers for a moment too long, as if Randolph were trying to convey something more than what was being said. "Great. I'll be looking for it."

As soon as Randolph left the room, Nikki noticed that the temperature seemed to plummet. "Don't get your hopes up," said Randolph's pretty young associate.

But Nikki ignored her. "I think you gentlemen were supposed to fill me in on your investigation," she said to the two men who had accompanied Randolph into the room earlier. And then, as an afterthought, she turned back to the associate. "Tell me your name again," Nikki asked politely.

"Kerri."

"Great." She held her empty glass toward the scowling lawyer. "Would you mind getting me a little more water, Kerri?"

CHAPTER 44

Nikki climbed into her Sebring, cranked the engine and the air conditioner, and flicked on the overhead light so she could read in the darkness of the underground garage. She pulled out the confidential files provided by Randolph's investigators and leafed through the information.

Bryce McCormack, age forty-six. Graduated from USC film school in 1981. Married twice, the first time right after college. Two kids—a son just starting an acting career and a daughter who committed suicide at age seventeen. A year after his daughter's suicide, McCormack divorced his first wife. Two years later, he married wife number two. Their divorce was final two days before their second anniversary.

Following college, McCormack worked on B-level movies for about ten years before he hit it big with an independent horror flick titled *Beyond*, the story of demon possession in a small Midwestern town. It landed him a multimovie deal with a big production company, resulting in three straight flops. One newspaper article from that time frame summed it up this way:

> Six years ago, the production companies were saying, "Get me Bryce McCormack for this job." Three years ago: "Get me somebody like Bryce McCormack." Last year: "Get me anybody but Bryce McCormack." And now: "Who is Bryce McCormack, anyway?"

McCormack left Hollywood five years ago and reinvented himself as the director of choice for reality shows, teaming with Cameron Murphy to produce a string of successful programs. Then came *Marriage Under*

Fire, and McCormack started his second fall down the slippery slope of high-profile failure. This time he took a friend along for the ride.

Cameron Murphy, age forty-four, had attended film school at New York University and graduated in 1984. He worked as a deejay for a few years, then tried his hand at acting. Two wives, three drug arrests, and one name change later, he settled down as an associate producer in a large Hollywood production studio. At thirty-seven, he married his third wife and started his own television production company. The marriage lasted nine months, but the production company was still limping along, though the financial records made it clear that *Faith on Trial* would make or break Murphy Productions.

Murphy had three children, all girls, aged twenty, fifteen, and twelve. He paid a small fortune each month in alimony and child support. At least he was supposed to.

Nikki frowned at the reports. This was garbage. She'd found out the same information in a few hours on the Internet, everything except the death of McCormack's daughter. Randolph's goons hadn't personally interviewed anyone. All they did was put nice binding on some reports that contained copies of official public records and a few pictures. Overall, it was worthless.

All those ex-wives, thought Nikki, and not even one phone call by the investigators. What a waste of matrimonial spite.

Javitts was boring with a capital B. A college football star, he had married one of the cheerleaders the summer before his senior year. A few years later, he traded her in for a more sophisticated model he met in law school, a classmate named Katrina Pershing. A month after they graduated, she became Katrina Pershing-Javitts. Five years later, she was Katrina Pershing again. As fate would have it, his college flame was busy dumping her second husband at about the same time, so the two decided to give marriage another try. The second time around turned out to be a charm, and as far as the investigators could tell, Javitts had been happily married for nearly fifteen years.

He had two boys, both teens, and a raging desire to leave the grueling practice of law for the bright lights of a television judgeship. How he hooked up with McCormack and Murphy was unknown.

None of the men or their families had any apparent connection with the defendants from the speedy-trial cases.

Nikki tossed the worthless files on the passenger seat, flicked off the overhead light, and pulled away from her parking space. She started working her phone as soon as she had reception. She called the governor's office first. Nobody there had ever heard of William Lassiter.

Her next call was to Wellington Farnsworth. She gave him a quick synopsis of the information produced by Randolph's investigators and explained that there was no William Lassiter in the governor's office. She asked Wellington to think up some Westlaw search requests that would convey this information to Finney using the same codes that Finney had used. "Oh, and let's tell him we're working with Randolph on this," instructed Nikki. "E-mail those search requests to me, and I'll pull over someplace in Richmond where I can get wi-fi access and transfer them into Westlaw." She could have just given Wellington the Westlaw password, but that would have taken her out of the code-breaking driver's seat.

Wellington said he'd send them right away.

That done, Nikki put on the cruise control as she flew down the interstate and dreamed up some stories that might get the ex-wives talking. For McCormack's and Murphy's ex-wives, Nikki would say she was an attorney advising a new fiancée on whether she should sign a prenuptial agreement. For Katrina Pershing, Nikki would claim to be a casting director for a new judge show, trying to make sure that Javitts, the potential star, didn't have too much personal baggage.

With any luck, Nikki would dig up enough dirt to start a landfill. Hopefully, the boys had been slow with their spousal support payments.

∽

A few minutes after noon on Monday, his stomach growling, Finney logged on to the Internet in his condo and checked out the research trail on Westlaw. Someone had entered a number of searches an hour ago. Finney knew it would be Nikki and Wellington responding to his questions.

He tried to focus on the Westlaw searches rather than his gnawing hunger. Finney had fasted before and knew the routine. The first few days he would feel like he was dying from hunger. Finney would get raging headaches and a thick coating on the tongue. Someone once told him that this was just the body cleansing itself of toxins. Days three and four were generally the worst for hunger pains and fatigue. Then his body would get used to the new routine, and he would actually increase his focus and productivity.

But knowing that didn't make these first few days any easier. Especially when Finney was already weak from cancer.

He squinted through his reading glasses and wrote the capital letters from the searches down on a piece of paper and then slid the paper under a legal pad. After a few more minutes on the computer, he logged off and put the paper into the pocket of his shorts. He headed for the bathroom, moving slowly to avoid the dizziness that sometimes came if he sat for extended periods and rose too quickly. Once in the bathroom, he deciphered the message using the codes from his book.

NO CONNECTION BETWEEN SPEEDY TRIAL SUSPECTS AND NAMES YOU PROVIDED ALSO
NO WILLIAM LASSITER IN GOVERNORS OFFICE WE ARE STILL WORKING ON LOCATION OF
ISLAND HAVE TEAMED WITH PRESTON RANDOLPH WHO REPS KLINE BUT HE DOESNT KNOW
ABOUT CODES

Finney ran his hands through his hair and tried to make sense of the information. The William Lassiter deal had seemed fishy to Finney all along. But the lack of a connection between the show's bigwigs and the speedy-trial cases was a complete surprise. Finney thought for sure he had discovered the motive for the schemes Kline had been warned about. He hoped Nikki had checked *all* of the family members of Javitts, McCormack, and Murphy. She was a good investigator. He would have to trust her.

He found it interesting that Nikki had "teamed" with Randolph and wondered whether that had been her idea or Randolph's. In either event, he was reassured that Nikki was not sharing anything about the codes. The methods of his protégée brought an inward smile. Here Finney was on the island pulling information from Kline without telling her about the codes. And there Nikki was in the real world presumably doing the same thing with Randolph, Kline's agent. *That girl acts more like a daughter of mine every day,* Finney thought.

He considered sending a bunch of clues about the island's location. He had been carefully noting wind patterns, temperature, sunrise, sunset, wildlife, and vegetation. Plus, he knew they had flown in on a Gulfstream IV without refueling. The range of that aircraft would provide a broad starting point.

But putting all this data in a number of search requests would take forever. The people monitoring his computer would probably get suspicious. Besides, Finney had to focus on tonight's plan first. If it worked, the location issue would take care of itself.

CHAPTER 45

Finney called an early end to the card game and ran everyone out of his condo by eleven. He couldn't help glancing up at the cameras a time or two as he got ready for bed. He put on his baggy nylon swim shorts and took off his T-shirt. He grabbed a cigar and padded out to his patio, where he kicked back in a lounger and lit up.

Finney estimated the temperature to be about seventy-five or eighty, with a warm southeasterly wind that was in the ten- to fifteen-knot range. The moon was nearly full, reflecting off the ocean to illuminate the night, along with who knew how many billions of stars. This would be a nearly perfect night for visibility...which could cut both ways.

He tried to keep his mind focused on the plan, but he couldn't help thinking about the broader possibilities. Were the show's producers just messing with the heads of the contestants, using one of the contestants to spread misinformation? If so, they were doing such a good job that they were about to have a full-scale revolt on their hands. Had somebody in the show's production team really decided that a spectacular conclusion would require some type of catastrophe for the show's runner-up—something that would look like divine intervention? If so, was it motivated by a desire to get ratings or a desire to rig the results? And if somebody was trying to rig the show, was it for religious reasons?

As he pondered these issues and blew smoke into the night, Finney thought about his own reasons for being here. At fifty-nine years of age and battling lung cancer, Finney didn't need this. He was here, not because he wanted fame or adventure, but out of a sense of duty. He was willing to put his life on the line for the cause of Christ. The other contestants on the island obviously felt the same about their own religions.

How many wars had been fought over religion? How many men and women had willingly died for their faith? Maybe he had written off a religious motivation too quickly. Though he still thought there might be some connection with the speedy-trial cases that Nikki just hadn't found yet, he couldn't rule out religion entirely. What if somebody involved in the production or financing of the show had recently converted to Islam or Hinduism or Buddhism? Or even Christianity? What if this were some misguided attempt to recreate a modern-day version of Elijah's showdown with the prophets of Baal? The nation worships the winner's god and the losing prophet dies.

Why hadn't he focused more on this angle before?

Finney snuffed out his cigar, checked his Ironman wristwatch, and slipped inside to log on to his computer. He had just enough time to get a message out through Westlaw. But this was chapter three in his book, featuring a cipher so complicated that he couldn't remember the key off the top of his head. He grabbed the copy of *Cross Examination* that he had checked out from the island's library on the first day in order to keep the other contestants from getting their hands on it. He remembered the hidden message conveyed by the code in chapter three—"Man looks at the outward appearance, but God looks at the heart." Using this, he headed into the bathroom, away from the prying eyes of the camera, and worked backward to determine the key for the chapter three code.

Armed with the key, he logged on to Westlaw and entered the searches necessary to convey his message. He logged off at precisely 11:20. He brushed his teeth and threw some dirty clothes on the bed and began folding them. When he was halfway done, he pushed them aside and crawled under the covers.

Five minutes later, with the room completely dark, he began pulling some of the clothes under the covers with him. He piled them in a long line next to where he was lying, then pulled the covers over his head. He was pretty sure that anybody monitoring the cameras wouldn't be able to see anything in the dark, but he didn't want to take any chances.

As quietly as possible, he slid out of bed and onto the floor. He reached up onto the bed and rearranged things a little so that the clothes would look as much like a sleeping body as possible. Then, recalling the camera angles he had been studying for the last few days, he crawled across the bedroom floor, slid along the dining-room wall, and darted across the one spot where the cameras couldn't be avoided.

He slid through his patio door, grabbed the John Deere cap he had left on the lounger, and slid on his docksiders, then climbed over his railing into the bushes. Peering out of the bushes, he allowed his eyes to adjust to the shadows of the moonlit night and scanned the resort property for signs of life. Gus and Horace had told Finney about a few of the fixed security cameras mounted at various spots on the property, and Finney could easily avoid them. He was more concerned with the ever-present security guards who patrolled the property. Finney had met at least six different guards during his time on the island.

Lights shone from the windows of a few other condos, but there didn't seem to be anybody milling around. Finney moved cautiously from bush to bush, staying in the shadows and bending at the waist as he jogged from one spot to the next. A few times he thought he heard a noise and stopped in his tracks. But the only sound was the steady breaking of the small ocean waves and the distant echo of music. He made it unnoticed to a small grove of trees maybe fifty yards from the beach where the Hobie Cat and the Wave Runners were located. Finney took one final look around, crouched over, and ran down to the boats.

He checked the Wave Runners first and confirmed that the ignition keys were missing. That didn't surprise Finney. But the next discovery did. The Wave Runners were secured by a metal chain and padlock. The chain connected them to the Hobie Cat.

He crawled over and took a seat in the sand on the opposite side of the Hobie from the condos, peering over one of the boat's hulls and the canvas trampoline that served as the boat's deck. He detected no movement on the resort premises and started inspecting the metal chain that somebody had woven around the hull of the Hobie, through a canvas strap, and around the shaft of the mainsail. The chain then snaked across the sand and looked like it was anchored to the shed. Another chain connected the Hobie with the Wave Runners.

He had never seen these chains before. Must be the security guards unlocked the boats at sunrise. It seemed like an awful lot of trouble, unless they were worried about the contestants escaping.

Escaping from what? Theoretically, any of the contestants should be free to quit the game at any moment. So why were the people running the show so paranoid about the contestants getting off this island—or at least away from this resort?

He could ponder those questions later. For now, he fingered the padlock securing the first chain around the Hobie and considered his options. If he had a knife, he could slit the canvas strap on the hull, but the boat would still be locked because of the way the chain wound around the hull and mainsail shaft. He tried pulling on the chain anchored to the shed, but it held fast. Even if he could somehow undo that chain, the Hobie would still be chained to the Wave Runners.

He scanned the condos again—still quiet. He remembered the surf kayak they had shown the contestants on the first day, leaning against the shed. Nobody had bothered to use it yet because it was too much work. With the kayak, Finney certainly wouldn't be able to go as far or as fast. But he was running out of options.

He pulled his wristwatch close to his chest and pressed the button illuminating the display: 11:52. Not much time.

Staying low, he moved quickly across the open sand to the shadows of the shed. The surf kayak and paddle were still there, leaning against the shed, unlocked. He felt his heart pounding, his breathing hard and uneven, as he hoisted the kayak over his right shoulder and grabbed the paddle in his left hand.

He walked calmly across the sand toward the water. How could he sneak around carrying a kayak? If he got spotted, he would act like this was the most natural thing in the world. A midnight kayaking expedition. Didn't everybody do that once in a while?

He kicked his docksiders off in the sand and carried the kayak into the breaking surf until the water was thigh deep. He climbed on top of the board, locked his feet into the canvas straps, and took one final glance over his shoulder. The coast was still clear as Finney started paddling. It was approaching midnight, he knew.

He cut diagonally across the small breaking waves, alternating paddle strokes as he distanced himself from the shore. The exertion, or maybe it was the tension, brought on a small coughing fit, but Finney managed to keep it under control. He looked back over his shoulder again at the fading beach area. He was probably one hundred feet away now, hunched over as he paddled, as if that somehow might make him less visible.

He could have gone faster, but he concentrated on making every stroke as quiet as possible, slipping the paddle in and out of the water at just the right angle. Still, each splash of water sounded exaggerated to Finney, and the moon felt like a spotlight shining overhead.

He turned for another furtive glance, nearly losing his balance as he did so. This time, as if they had appeared from nowhere, he saw two figures walking on the path along the beach. They were looking straight ahead and talking, but Finney stopped the boat and braced, using his paddle, then turned the kayak parallel to the shore. They were male and female figures; the silhouettes looked like those of Victoria Kline and Bryce McCormack. They took a few more steps and turned toward the water, directly in line with Finney and his kayak.

Finney saw the female point and knew he had been spotted. He turned the kayak toward the mouth of the bay and started paddling faster. He heard a few shouts from the shore but didn't look back. He forced his arms to act like pistons, pounding out the rhythm of a steady stroke, no longer hunched over but sitting up straight. He angled his kayak to the right so he could make a long swinging turn past the coral reef that separated this cove from the next. His lungs started aching and he coughed as he paddled.

Lactic acid quickly invaded his muscles, tightening his arms. The blood flowing to his forearms made them feel swollen like Popeye's, and now they were binding up. He had to back off the pace, and he risked another glance toward shore.

The figures were more distant now, but there was no mistaking what was happening. Two large males—muscled security guards—were unlocking the Wave Runners and dragging them into the water.

Finney spit some phlegm into the ocean, turned around, and started paddling faster.

Chapter 46

Less than five minutes later, the great escape was over. The Wave Runners cruised to a stop beside an exhausted Finney, their wakes nearly swamping the surf kayak. Finney braced his paddle in the water and leaned into the waves, coughing and wheezing as he feathered the paddle back and forth. After the waves subsided, Finney dropped the paddle across his lap, his shoulders slumping in fatigue.

"Get on the back, Tarzan," said one of the security guards.

Finney could have resisted, but it would only prolong his humiliation. He handed his paddle to one guard and reached out his hand to the other. The guard took it and helped Finney climb onto the back of his Wave Runner. His partner tied the kayak to the back of the other one.

"What were you thinking?" asked the guard.

Finney didn't respond. He sat behind the man, his hands braced on the seat, struggling for breath. The world was spinning.

The guard cranked the throttle, and the Wave Runner lurched forward, nearly throwing Finney off. Finney grabbed the shoulders of the guard and held on. "You on a midnight cruise, Judge?" yelled the guard over his shoulder.

"You going to read me my Miranda rights?" Finney asked.

"You're not under arrest, Judge. I'm just trying to keep you from being shark food." They bounced across the bay at speeds designed to impress the onlookers.

"Good," said Finney, sucking in air. "Then you can save your questions."

They rode the rest of the distance in silence. By the time the Wave Runner swung next to the shore, the camera, lighting, and sound crews were fully deployed. They captured a shirtless Finney stumbling off the Wave Runner and into the surf, followed by the burly security guards who dragged the Wave Runners to shore. Murphy, McCormack, Javitts, and a host of others stood watching. Kline stood on the fringes of the small crowd, and Finney shot her a knowing look.

He put on his docksiders, dried off with a towel somebody handed him, and followed the show's executives into the Paradise Island library. They told Finney to take a seat at the end of the table, which he did, putting his folded towel on the seat first so he wouldn't stain the wood. They provided him with water and then waited for the camera and lighting crews to complete their work.

"All set?" asked McCormack.

Wearing his John Deere cap but no shirt, Finney appreciated the warm heat from the bright klieg lights. The audio and lighting crews gave McCormack a thumbs-up.

"Do you want off the show?" asked Javitts.

Finney smirked at the question—at the way this whole episode was being handled. Another made-for-TV moment. It's why they were having Javitts ask the questions. They had captured the attempted escape on camera and now wanted to stage a postcapture interview with the crazy judge himself.

It's also why they started with this type of dramatic question, one that Finney knew they would ask. He had thought this through carefully in the past twenty-four hours. If he left now (assuming they would let him), he wouldn't have enough evidence to get the authorities involved. What would he tell them—that one of the other contestants told him that the show's director told her that she shouldn't try to make the finals? Hearsay on top of hearsay. Certainly not enough for a warrant.

If he left now, he could probably protect the other participants just by going public with his suspicions. But then the show's producers would play it by the book, Finney (and Christianity along with him) would look foolish, and whoever had plotted harm to the show's contestants would get off scot-free.

And that analysis assumed the best case—that they would actually let him return to his home unharmed. If he quit, Finney would be transported back to the United States by himself. An entire helicopter ride and plane ride for whoever wanted him dead to get at him. How hard would it be to make it look like a crazy lung cancer patient passed away during the flight?

Busting the bad guys would require Finney to stay on the island. But still, he needed to know if leaving really was a possibility. "Am I free to go?" he asked.

"You know the agreement you signed with the show," replied Javitts.

The agreement, of course, required Finney to stay until the end of filming. "I didn't ask about the agreement," said Finney. "I asked if I am free to leave."

"If you can't handle the pressure, you can quit." Javitts leaned forward on the table—a good posture for the whirring cameras. "You need to tell us why you want to quit, and then you will need to stay on the island until the filming is complete. We can only send people back to the States if necessary for medical reasons."

Finney coughed. The timing seemed a little too convenient, but it wasn't anything he could control. He removed his cap and wiped his forehead with his arm.

"I want to finish the show," said Finney calmly. "I just thought a little midnight paddle would be some good exercise, and next I thing I know, you've got the CIA after me."

Javitts snorted. Murphy mumbled something that Finney couldn't quite pick up.

"Are you saying you weren't trying to escape from Paradise Island?" asked Javitts with as much incredulity in his voice as possible. Later,

Finney would have to give the man some pointers on how better to intimidate a witness.

"Why would anyone want to escape from a beautiful place like this?" asked Finney, surveying the skeptical faces in the room.

After a few more questions, followed by a stern off-camera lecture about how disruptive his behavior had been, the cameras started rolling again, and they informed Finney that staying on the show would require that he pass two medical exams, one conducted by the island medical doctor and a second by a clinical psychologist the show had brought to the island for this final stressful week.

"Nobody told me that being sane was a prerequisite," quipped Finney. He was starting to regain a little strength and was having fun at the expense of the worried and tired faces around him.

Nobody laughed. Nobody even cracked a smile.

PART 4

REBUTTAL

*Get the facts first. You can
distort them later.*
—MARK TWAIN

*If you want to take revenge on somebody,
you'd better dig two graves.*
—CHINESE PROVERB

CHAPTER 47

Early Tuesday morning, the Paradise Island Snorkel Club convened about fifty feet from shore, but this time Dr. Hokoji Ando joined them. They were chest deep in the water—nearly neck deep for Ando, who wore baggy swim trunks and a long white T-shirt hanging so low that it nearly covered the shorts.

Though they all had snorkel masks propped on their heads and most wore fins, they knew they weren't fooling anyone. Gus, Horace, and a few other cameramen filmed the entire event from shore, no doubt zooming in on the participants' faces.

Finney coughed, then said, "Cover your mouths when you're talking about last night or do so with your backs to the shore. We don't need any lipreaders."

The others nodded, though Hadji couldn't resist glancing over his shoulder at the camera crews.

"Why don't you just wave and tell them what we're doing?" Kareem sneered.

"Somebody needs a nap," said the Swami.

"Boys," said Kline, "this is not the time."

"First of all, Victoria, great job spotting the kayak," Finney said, bringing a thin smile of appreciation from Dr. Kline. The plan had been for Finney to make his "escape" in the Hobie—much easier to spot.

Knowing that the only cameras on them while they slept were the stationary cameras in the walls of their condos, Finney was to make his escape attempt precisely at midnight. Victoria was to be walking on the beach with McCormack, making sure that his back patio door had been left unlocked. Hadji, who was the most computer savvy of the group, had been assigned to check out McCormack's computer.

Finney turned to Hadji. "What'd you find?"

"Not much," said the Swami. "I was able to log on to his laptop, but his e-mail account is password protected. I checked his documents file and didn't find anything unusual. I did learn that I won the first viewer's verdict, which more or less restores your faith in the system."

Kareem frowned, but Hadji pretended not to notice. "I searched around the condo a while but really didn't come up with anything. In fact, it was weird because I didn't even find the kind of stuff you might expect—concepts for the upcoming shows, files on the contestants, surprises they were going to spring on us, that type of stuff."

Ando stood impassively while Victoria splashed water in her mask. Kareem shot her a hard look.

"I find that strange too," said Kareem. "Especially after what I found."

"You got in?" Finney asked.

"Murphy must have been on his back patio when the commotion started," said Kareem. "When I sprinted over to his condo, the back patio door was unlocked. His laptop, just inside the screen door, had been left on hibernate."

This was a bonus that nobody had counted on. When they put the plan together, Kareem, almost as an afterthought, had volunteered to check out Murphy's condo, just in case he left it unlocked in his haste to arrive at Finney's escape scene.

"What'd you find out?" The question came from Victoria.

"Plenty." The contestants huddled closer as Kareem filled them in. "There were e-mail exchanges with an AOL account user named Seeker discussing possible alternatives for the last two episodes, all of which assumed that one of the finalists on the island would be dead."

Finney watched the group suck in a collective breath. This was a poker-faced bunch, but he could read the shock on every face but Ando's.

"Murphy and this guy were discussing various scenarios for handling this 'tragedy.' They talked about having a tribute show to the dead contestant or just canceling the last two episodes and issuing a press release.

"They even discussed method of death," Kareem continued. "How to make it look natural but still contain religious symbolism. And in one e-mail, where Murphy mentioned that all the contestants might be getting suspicious, they talked about staging a tragedy that would eliminate everyone but the eventual winner."

" 'Eliminate'—is that the word they used?" asked Kline.

Kareem nodded, while Hadji cast a wary glance toward shore. Finney could see the reality of the threat settle on the faces around him. Yesterday they were trying to win a reality show. Now they were trying to figure out if their lives were in danger. Everyone was on edge.

"If Kareem's right," said Victoria, "then meeting like this only arouses suspicions and puts us all in more danger."

Hadji spoke next. "Amazing how I didn't find anything like that on McCormack's computer."

Kareem's expression was one of guarded distrust. "And your point is?"

Hadji threw his hands in the air. "I'm just saying it's pretty convenient that the threat doesn't materialize until the finalists are selected. What a great incentive for the rest of us to back off over the next three days and make sure we *don't* make the finals."

Kareem bristled at this assault on his integrity. For a second, Finney thought he might have to step in front of the big man in order to give Hadji a head start toward deeper waters.

"But it's consistent with what McCormack's been saying to me," Victoria Kline interjected. The comment seemed to relax Kareem a little, and Finney saw a chance to call the Muslim's bluff.

"Are you prepared to testify about what you found?" Finney asked.

"Of course," said Kareem without hesitation.

"Then before Saturday arrives," said Finney, "I'll have this show shut down."

"How?" asked Victoria Kline.

"Leave that to me."

∾

After the other contestants returned to the shore, Finney and the Swami stood in knee-deep water doing some stretching exercises that the Swami had conjured up. He assured Finney and the others the exercises included no religious components of yoga, but the other contestants declined anyway.

Just like Finney knew they would.

The two men faced the ocean as they stretched and slowly went through the motions of the Swami's routine. Their mikes were still on-shore, and they were out of earshot of the others.

"Do you believe him?" asked Hadji.

"I don't know," said Finney. "He didn't blink when I claimed I would shut down the show."

"C'mon," replied Hadji. "Murphy *just happens* to leave his patio door open. And *just happens* to leave the computer on hibernate. And *just happens* not to delete incriminating e-mails?"

"It's a stretch," admitted Finney. He wanted to mull it over some more but knew they didn't have much time. "What'd you find?"

"Nothing unusual on Kline, Ando, or Javitts," the Swami said, describing what his Internet search had uncovered. Unknown to the other contestants, the Swami had used his time on McCormack's computer to freely search the Internet, using Westlaw and other databases as instructed by Finney to obtain personal information on "persons of interest." Finney was implementing the principle of redundancy: get some of the same information from two different sources—in this case, the Swami and Nikki—and then cross-check.

"Kareem?" asked Finney.

"Two things that made me suspicious of him even before he gave us that line about Murphy. First, the city where he grew up in Lebanon is right in the middle of Hezbollah country."

"The Party of God," said Finney.

"Exactly. And second, he's served as a consultant to some of the defense lawyers representing the Guantánamo Bay detainees."

Finney started processing the implications, but the Swami had quickly moved on.

"McCormack had a daughter who committed suicide. He sued the psychiatrist who was treating her at the time for posttraumatic stress disorder. Some kind of rape or sexual assault the prior year. Suit got thrown out before it went to court."

One of the pushier associate producers called to the two men from shore. They needed to put their mikes back on, she said.

"How long ago?" Finney asked, thinking of the speedy-trial defendants whom Finney had released five years earlier.

"About six or seven years," said the Swami.

Finney filed it away, realizing that the speedy-trial defendants were in jail at the time. "Murphy and Randolph?" he asked.

The associate producer shouted again. Finney and the Swami turned around and started walking slowly toward shore. "Murphy's got lots of stuff. Abused an ex-wife. A fundamentalist Christian father who's boycotting this show. Daughters who would probably be about the same age as that store clerk you described, though there's no indication any of them died recently."

The Swami lowered his voice as they approached shore. "As for Mr.

Preston Edgar Randolph, just like you suspected, he hasn't done much agency work; he's too busy suing everybody in sight. He's been up to his eyeballs recently in cases against the Catholic Church for abusive priests. I ran out of time researching the ages of his daughters."

"Thanks," said Finney, his mind already rapidly processing the new data. He was envisioning his trusted yellow legal pad, with a straight line drawn down the middle separating the incriminating and exculpating information for each person of interest.

"I could have just sent an e-mail to the feds last night if I really thought we were in danger," said the Swami.

"I know."

"Are you really going to try and shut down the show?"

"I don't want to," replied Finney. "But I'm not sure we've got much choice. What if Kareem *is* telling the truth?"

The Swami's twisted face registered his doubt. But he'd already made his case and apparently decided to just change the subject. "Just so you'll know, Judge O, I took a peek at the results last night. You're getting a lot of votes from viewers, but you're not helping yourself with those cigars."

"I'll keep that in mind."

∾

Before heading to work on Tuesday morning, Nikki logged on to Westlaw and discovered the new search requests. She called Wellington immediately. "We need the key for chapter three," she said. "Finney sent a new message."

"I already solved chapter three," boasted Wellington. "I was up until one in the morning working on it."

Nikki knew the drill, though she really didn't have the patience for this. Wellington wanted to feel appreciated. She would have to listen to all the details of his brilliant deciphering of the code. Nikki had given up working on the codes herself. Some people had a gift for cracking codes; she had other assets.

"What kind of code is it?" Nikki asked. She found herself yawning, though she'd had plenty of sleep last night.

"Over the phone again?"

"Yeah. I think it's safe."

"Okay. Well, did you know that Edgar Allan Poe was a code freak?" asked Wellington.

"That's a question, Wellington. You know I don't do questions."

"I forgot. Anyway, Poe was into cryptanalysis big time. One of his most famous stories, 'The Gold-Bug,' revolved around the solution to a cipher. Plus, he concealed anagrams and hidden messages in many of his poems."

"Fascinating."

"He even conducted his own cryptographic challenge, boasting to readers in a magazine article that he could solve any substitution ciphers they sent to him. For the next six months, he solved every cipher but two. He ended the contest because he said that solving ciphers was consuming too much of his time."

"I know the feeling," Nikki said absent-mindedly. She was sure this story had a point and equally sure that Wellington wasn't coming to it anytime soon. Still, she had learned that rushing Wellington only seemed to prolong the process.

"He told readers that the two ciphers he couldn't solve came from a gentleman named W. B. Tyler, whom Poe claimed to highly respect. He challenged his readers to solve those two ciphers. His readers couldn't solve them, and scholars have never found any proof that this Tyler even existed. Many believe that these ciphers were written by Poe himself, hoping that nobody would solve them until after he died. Poe, as you may know, had an obsession for speaking from the grave."

"Mmm," mumbled Nikki.

"Poe eventually died, and for nearly a hundred and fifty years, the ciphers went unsolved. But then the public became fascinated with the ciphers again during the latter part of the twentieth century. A Web site and contest were established, and a gentleman named Gil Broza finally solved the last cipher in October of 2000. Think about that: Poe speaking from the grave more than a hundred and fifty years after the publication of his last book."

"I never really liked Poe," admitted Nikki. "I always thought Stephen King was scarier."

"Yeah, but you can't really compare Poe with King. Poe was a brilliant classical author who—"

"Wellington!" said Nikki sharply, gaining his attention. "How does this tie in with chapter three?"

He hesitated, then picked back up with the same enthusiastic tone as before. "Chapter three is about how the Pharisees and lawyers tried to earn points with God by following a bunch of picky rules, but Jesus was more concerned about matters of the heart. You know what the title of the chapter is?"

Another question, thought Nikki, but Wellington caught himself before she could speak.

"That's a rhetorical question, of course," he said. "The title of the chapter is 'Bloody Band-Aids and Telltale Hearts.'"

"So he used the Poe cipher," said Nikki.

"Exactly."

That established, Nikki pulled out the sheet of paper where she had recorded the capital letters from Finney's Westlaw search. "Let me read you the capital letters so you can tell me what they mean using the Poe cipher," she said.

"Um...it's not that easy," said Wellington. "It's a complicated cipher using six different alphabets to encode the text. It uses regular capital letters and small capital letters and lowercase letters and even upside-down letters, though it appears Finney tried to avoid the inverted symbols where possible. That's what made it so hard to solve—several different code letters for each plaintext letter. Frequency analysis didn't work."

"So, what does that mean?" asked Nikki, checking her watch.

"I'll need to see the Westlaw searches myself," claimed Wellington. "Just to be certain."

Nikki hesitated, a small voice urging her to be careful. There was something about giving Wellington the password to Finney's Westlaw account that bothered Nikki. It wasn't just that this would take her out of the driver's seat; it was something more than that, though she couldn't put her finger on it.

But she couldn't think of any logical reason to deny Wellington the password. After all, Finney was the one who told her to get Wellington involved in the first place. Yet her emotions were generally more reliable than her logic.

"I can meet you at the usual place on my way to work," she said. "I'll pull up the search requests on my laptop and let you look at them."

"Cool," said Wellington.

∽

Forty-five minutes later at the Starbucks, Wellington handed Nikki the decoded message.

NEED RELIGIOUS BACGROUND ON MURPHY MCCORMAC AND AVITTS

Nikki felt a surge of disappointment. She kept expecting some big revelation from Finney and instead kept getting more research assignments. It felt like her law-clerking days all over again. He would send her off on some wild-goose chase of research and never tell her why. Then, when he had all the information necessary, he would wink and unveil some dazzling resolution for the case.

But there was another issue that bothered Nikki about this cipher. She placed the paper on the table between them. "You sure this is right? Several of the words are misspelled, and the judge is usually pretty careful about things like that."

"It's the nature of Poe's cipher," explained Wellington. "There were certain letters not contained in the writing submitted by the mysterious Mr. Tyler. Since his underlying document didn't use the letters J or K, for example, there is no code text for them. In Judge Finney's book, he just substituted an asterisk for those letters, but he can't do that using the Westlaw searches since we key in on capital letters. That's why a few of the words containing those letters appear to be misspelled."

That made sense to Nikki, at least as much sense as the decryption process usually made. "What do you make of all this?" she asked, thinking out loud. "First we get this message that things are tense and Finney needs our help. Then we're told to check ties between Murphy, Javitts, McCormack, and the speedy-trial cases. Then Finney wants to know the location of the island and whether William Lassiter is connected to the show. In the meantime, Preston Randolph calls and he's all bent out of shape about what's happening on the island. And then, this morning, we get this message asking us to check the religious backgrounds on these guys."

Wellington thought for a long time, and Nikki could imagine the big brain cranking away like a high-speed computer. He stared into space, processing the bits of information they had stumbled across—the secret messages, the shows they had watched, Preston Randolph's concerns. Nikki took a sip of her drink and watched Wellington's brow furrow deeper and deeper like a software program freezing your computer until you reboot it.

"Wellington?"

He shook out of the haze. "I'm not sure what's going on, Nikki. Seems to me that Judge Finney is suspicious about the guys running this show and thinks they're out to get some of the contestants. Maybe Judge Finney wants to know if he's their target, so he's having us check their connections to the speedy-trial cases and their religious backgrounds."

Duh, thought Nikki. She didn't need a computer to tell her that. She found herself wondering why God never seemed to combine book smarts and common sense in the same package.

"Out to get him?" Nikki echoed Wellington's words. "You mean make the judge look bad and make sure he doesn't win the show, or you mean really out to get him, as in eliminate him?"

More thinking by Wellington, but this time the computer didn't freeze up. "I don't think the judge is in any real trouble," said Wellington. "Otherwise, he would have just sent a message for us to get the cops involved."

"That's what I was thinking," said Nikki. Maybe it was just Finney being Finney—figuring out a way to outsmart the reality-game producers. In that context it would make sense for Finney to inquire about their religious backgrounds. But their connections to the speedy-trial cases? Nikki had a much harder time explaining that one.

CHAPTER 48

fter the snorkeling conference, Finney raced back to his condo so
that he would have time to run some new Westlaw searches. In less
than two hours, he was scheduled to be in Paradise Court, where
the contestants would start their cross-examinations of experts from their
own faith groups, albeit experts whose beliefs varied dramatically from
those of the contestants on Paradise Island.

Finney shaved, showered, and changed, mulling over his options. He
faced the classic reality-show dilemma: Whom could he trust? Whom
could he believe? Hadji had made some good arguments, but Finney had
no reason to doubt Kareem's integrity. What was real? What was fake? Living
inside the television could play games with a person's head.

He finally made up his mind and started focusing on the types of
searches he would run to get his message across. There was so much riding
on this next message, and Finney worried that even Wellington might
not be able to figure out the key for chapter four. Finney considered several
alternatives but rejected them all. Wellington would be expecting a
message encoded according to the key hidden in chapter four. Changing
the encryption method now would be confusing, but the young man was
smart. Real smart. He would figure it out.

It was now Tuesday. Finalists would be announced Friday. Finney
would give Wellington twenty-four hours to solve the encryption. If he
didn't get some kind of confirmation by then, Finney would resort to
other methods.

He logged on to Westlaw at 9:05, local time. Court started at 10:00.
He racked his brain and typed in his first request. He would have to leave
off the dates for these requests and hope the person monitoring his com-

puter wouldn't focus on that minor difference. Unlike his prior search requests, these would contain no capital letters—an intentional clue to Wellington that this cipher was different.

christ's miracles and liberal responses to the accounts

Finney looked at a few of the documents responsive to his search request and then immediately entered another:

evidence for the evangelical view of the person and teachings of jesus

This request generated a mountain of information, none of which interested Finney in the least. He was too busy thinking up his next request.

end times and the various prophetic issues and orthodoxies

No documents satisfied this request, and Finney worried that his searches weren't making enough sense. But constructing clever searches took time, and Finney had none. He plowed ahead with his next search request.

the essence of christian teaching and ancient creeds

There. That was better. Several documents popped up. At this rate, he would barely make it to court on time. His computer started slowing down, causing Finney to worry that the people monitoring him had figured out Finney's system. He clicked to view the next document, and the page took forever to load.

"C'mon, c'mon," mumbled Finney. He clicked the same page again. Another sluggish response. He clicked the Back arrow. "This is ridiculous," he muttered.

The pain gnawing at his stomach made him irritable and impatient.

Why did the computer have to slow down now? What kind of cruel trick was this? He wanted to smash the machine into the wall.

The page finally loaded, and he breathed a sigh of relief. Exhausted. Hungry. Wired. Stressed. Finney thought up another search request and typed it in.

Westlaw started searching immediately. They were back in business. A thought hit Finney. What if the show's producers weren't even monitoring the computers? What if he could just type a message in a Westlaw search without even encrypting the text?

Too risky, he knew. When you're on the third day of a fast, you don't always think clearly.

Focus, Finney demanded of himself. He had been known to give himself some pretty good pep talks. *The cavalry will soon be on the way.*

❧

Nikki hit pay dirt on a phone call with Murphy's third ex-wife. Sheila Browning was a twenty-three-year-old actress doing commercials when she met Murphy; he was thirty-seven and an ambitious associate producer. The sex was nothing special, Browning admitted without being asked, but she fell in love with his dreams. Murphy would have his own production company. Sheila would be a star. As soon as Murphy completed the movie he was working on, they headed to Las Vegas to tie the knot.

They started fighting, said Browning, as soon as they returned from the honeymoon. "Was he abusive?" Nikki asked.

Sheila laughed. "Only when he was drunk or high or under pressure, which is to say—all the time."

"Did you report him?"

"I basically had the cops on speed dial. First-name acquaintances with half the precinct."

"Then why doesn't it show up on his record?"

Sheila hesitated. "Did you say you were a lawyer?" she asked skeptically.

Now it was Nikki's turn to hesitate. "I said I was associated with a law firm investigating Mr. Murphy."

"Oh," said Sheila. "I thought you said you were an *associate* with the law firm."

Busted, thought Nikki. But Sheila didn't seem to be bothered by it.

"If you were a lawyer, you'd know," said Sheila. "Murph would hire a good defense attorney, promise to get counseling, pay a fine, and promise not to do it again. Hollywood producers don't get records for slapping around their wives."

Sheila's caustic analysis took Nikki back a little. But she recovered quickly, asking Sheila to play the amateur psychologist and explain what made Murphy such a scum.

"His father," Sheila said immediately. "He's got serious need-for-approval issues. You know, an Oedipus complex or whatever that thing is called."

Nikki thought Oedipus was the guy who married his mother, but she let it pass. Rule number one for interrogating ex-wives: when they want to talk, you let them talk. "Tell me about that," said Nikki.

And Sheila did. For nearly twenty minutes, she trashed the men— father and son—in equal measures. According to Sheila, Pastor Martin abused his kids both physically and mentally, including his oldest son Jason, who later in life changed his name to Cameron Murphy. Nikki sensed that the reverend never really approved of Sheila, so that might have been part of the issue, but Nikki could sift the facts from fiction by conducting other interviews.

According to Sheila, Cameron Murphy was now a hard-core atheist, driven from the church by his father's hypocrisy. Cameron had tried Buddhism and also quoted liberally from the Dalai Lama—anything to make his old man mad—but in his heart of hearts he didn't really believe there was a God.

Nikki could sense she was on to something. She obtained the Reverend Martin's church number from the Internet. She called him and left a message with his secretary. She recalled the fact that he had been a vocal protester against *Faith on Trial* from day one.

She called the church a second time, her voice much huskier this time around. Nikki told the secretary that she was a big fan of Reverend Martin. "Do you know if he's taking donations for that *Faith on Trial* boycott? I'm trying to decide what to do with all this stock."

The secretary assured Nikki that the reverend was taking donations. "I'm sure he'll be returning your call right away," said the secretary. Nikki didn't doubt it for a minute.

∽

At that very moment, the legendary Murphy temper was in full bloom. He was pacing around the master control room, glancing occasionally at the huge bank of television monitors, all labeled according to the various cameras on the island, showing the different contestants as they prepared for court. On the other side of the room, one crew member sat in front of five separate computer screens, monitoring the contestants' Internet usage. The only computer in use at the time was Finney's.

Murphy had Juan Perez, the head of Paradise Island security, on his cell phone. "Why didn't you tell me you were going to lock the Hobie Cat?" Murphy snarled. "It almost ruined the entire plan."

"We've locked the Hobie Cat every night, Mr. Murphy. You asked us to thwart any escape attempts, and that's exactly what we were trying to do."

"We stay up virtually all night Sunday night going over every last detail of this plan, and then you almost screw it up at the last minute."

"Nobody informed us about this plan, Mr. Murphy."

"Don't put this on us!" Murphy barked. One of the editors sitting in front of the bank of cameras glanced over her shoulder. Murphy took a step away and lowered his voice. "You work for us, not the other way around. It's *your* job to keep *us* informed about how you're securing this place." For the next several minutes, Murphy reminded Perez about what an unmitigated disaster it would have been if Finney hadn't been dumb enough to make a run for it in the kayak. He ended with a stream of expletives strung together in trademark Murphy fashion.

"We apologize, Mr. Murphy. It was a breakdown of communication."

Not surprisingly, Murphy had a few choice thoughts about communications breakdowns as well.

CHAPTER 49

Nikki called Preston Randolph and went through the usual number of screening secretaries and paralegals before she could talk to the great man. "I found out a few things about Cameron Murphy that weren't in your investigators' file," she said. She paused a second for a compliment that never came. "Thought you might be interested."

"Okay," said Randolph.

"Abusive father," said Nikki, as if she had the court records to back it up. "When it was Murphy's turn, he abused his wife."

"How do you know this?"

"I talked to his ex-wife—something your investigators didn't bother doing."

"Good work, Nikki," Randolph said, though he didn't sound happy. She could see him in her mind's eye, scowling at the thought that his prized investigators had been scooped by a law student.

"That's just the beginning," said Nikki. "Murphy's old man is a certified fundamentalist. Used religion as an excuse to pound on Murphy. So now Murphy, the executive producer of *Faith on Trial,* hates anything to do with the Christian church." Nikki tried not to let her tone reflect how much she enjoyed telling Randolph about the things his lazy investigators had missed.

"I still don't understand why that would make him go after Dr. Kline. Seems to me that he ought to be trying to help her, not make her look bad."

Randolph had a point, though Nikki didn't want to admit it. "We haven't seen the last show yet," she said gamely. "Maybe he does."

"Maybe." Randolph didn't sound convinced. "While you've been calling ex-wives, I did have some success in tracking down the location for

Paradise Island. We called the director's cell again and had the call triangulated while we talked. It's not precise, but we think they're on an island in the Galápagos chain."

Impressive, thought Nikki. Even if Randolph did make it sound condescending—*While you were talking to ex-wives...*

"Well, between my shop and yours, we're making progress," said Nikki.

They sparred politely for a few more minutes, and then Randolph mentioned that Nikki's job application must have gotten lost in the mail because he hadn't seen it yet. *That's better,* Nikki thought. *Show some interest.*

"Maybe you should have one of your investigators run it down," Nikki teased. "But first, teach him how to use a cell phone."

This brought a moment of uncomfortable silence on the line, and Nikki wondered if she had pushed too hard. "Did Sheila tell you about Murphy's brief tryst with Buddhism?" Randolph asked.

What? The remark caught Nikki speechless. And it had been a while since that had happened. "You knew about that?"

Randolph laughed. "Of course."

"And you didn't tell me?"

"Nikki, when we first met you, we didn't know if we could trust you or not. Since you've now shared this information with me, I felt I could be a little more open with you."

"So your guys have talked to Sheila?"

"We talked to her. And we promised to pay her if she told us when somebody else called." Randolph paused for a second so that Nikki would have plenty of time to feel stupid. "And based on your questions to her, it appears you're planning to call Reverend Martin as well. Or maybe you already have. Good luck on that one."

"Right," said Nikki, realizing for the first time that she might be playing in the big leagues after all. "What else did you hold back about your investigation?"

"If you want to stop by the office again, I'll let you read the full, unedited reports," Randolph said. His voice now had an edge of authority. "But they have to stay in our office. We can't let those kinds of reports out of our sight."

A few minutes later, a slightly less cocky Nikki Moreno hung up the phone and called Wellington. "We need some new search requests to send Judge Finney another message," Nikki said. "Preston Randolph has established an approximate location for Paradise Island."

"You want me to e-mail you the requests?" asked Wellington. "Or do you just want me to do it?"

Nikki sighed. It was exhausting playing private eye with everyone. Plus, Judge Fitzsimmons was breathing down her neck for some research. If she couldn't trust Wellington, whom could she trust?

She gave Wellington the password and asked him to also tell Finney that Murphy, now an agnostic, grew up with an abusive and legalistic Christian father. She hung up the phone and started on her research for Fitzsimmons. Less than five minutes later, Wellington called back. "I sent the information," he said. "There's a new message from Finney."

Nikki felt an adrenaline surge. Maybe this time Finney would send something meaningful. After all, time was running out. "What does it say?" she asked.

"I don't know," replied Wellington. "I'm having some real difficulty figuring out the key for chapter four."

∾

Bryce McCormack received a cell phone text message from New York while taping Kareem Hasaan's cross-examination of a Shi'ite Muslim cleric. *Legal's got a problem with the Chinese water torture promo.* He cursed under his breath, turned the set over to an associate director, and stepped outside the courtroom to make a call.

They patched his call through to Zacharias Snyder, outside counsel for the network. It was Snyder's job to vet every *Faith on Trial* show prior to airing and flag any potential legal issues. He had been getting increasingly gun-shy with each show.

"I'm pulling the promo on the Chinese water torture," said Snyder. "You can't do that segment."

Bryce forced himself to remain calm. They *had* to run that segment. But he knew from past history that screaming at Snyder wouldn't help. "What do you mean—you're pulling it?"

"I'm pulling the promo, and I'm pulling the segment from future shows. I can't believe you're even suggesting we try this   you can't just torture people on the air."

Bryce could feel the heat rising—the New York suits trying to ruin his show. "And you're just now telling me?"

"They just sent me the piece," responded Snyder. "It just left post-production, which is another thing I wanted to talk—"

"We're doing the piece," McCormack snapped. "It's a crucial segment for next week's show."

"But you can't just—"

"Let me finish!" Bryce interrupted. He lowered his voice. "This isn't torture. The contestants will be within reach of a Kill button and can stop the test at any time. We've got a clinical psychologist monitoring their vital signs and asking them questions. We aren't letting anybody go longer than twenty-four hours. Plus, we picked up the idea from the show *Mythbusters,* and that show shackled *the hosts* and dripped water on them for hours."

When Bryce stopped, there was silence on the line. "Are you done?" asked Snyder.

"Yes," hissed McCormack.

"First, your promotion piece calls it 'Chinese water torture,' so how can you possibly tell me it's not really torture? Second, if we were torturing *our hosts,* that would be different. But these are our *contestants.* They didn't think this up, and they're not getting paid for it." Snyder's voice was maddeningly calm and sanctimonious. The ultimate Monday-morning quarterback. "I'm not authorizing it."

"Then get the program director for the network on the line right now," demanded McCormack, "so I can explain to her why we need new outside counsel."

CHAPTER 50

The Tuesday-night crowd at Norfolk's Finest Sports Bar was bigger and rowdier than ever. Earlier that day, Nikki had finagled her way on as a guest for a popular drive-home radio show and invited all of Hampton Roads to the party. By 8:45 the line to get into the bar was half a block long.

Nikki decided to emphasize her diva-ness tonight by accessorizing to the hilt. Aviator shades, a multicolored bandanna, and a matching Bracher-Emden bag were a start. She added tasteful chandelier earrings, chunky bangles from her wrist halfway up her forearm, a bead necklace, and fat rings on most of her fingers. Painted-on jeans, pumps, and a frilly white spaghetti-strap top completed the outfit. When she glanced with approval at the mirror on her way out the door, Nikki decided that only she could wear this much jewelry and *not* look overdone. Okay, maybe she and Beyoncé. But only if Beyoncé was having a *very* good day.

The aviator glasses went on top of the bandanna as soon as Nikki stepped inside. She smiled at the overflowing offering buckets and the people crammed into this place. She couldn't wait to hear the crowd roar with approval for their local favorite.

Unfortunately for Nikki, Byron spotted her a few minutes after she arrived and latched on like a leech. She finally managed to brush him off when she found a booth full of friends, with room for only one more to squeeze in. "Maybe we can hook up as soon as the show is over," suggested Byron.

"Maybe."

Nikki had barely started on her first drink when *Faith on Trial* began with its standard introduction of the contestants. Finney's face brought raucous cheers, Hasaan was roundly booed, and the others garnered mixed receptions.

A shining moment for Finney occurred less than fifteen minutes into the program, during Nikki's second drink, when they showed Finney standing strong in the face of temptation. Nikki was astonished to learn that Finney's temptation had occurred long before he had headed to the island. They replayed parts of it now, taped through the lens of a hidden camera.

The meeting took place in Finney's cluttered office. The young man meeting with Finney had a soft western Virginia accent that rolled off his tongue as he introduced himself.

"Thanks for meeting with me, Judge Finney. My name is William Robert Lassiter, and I'm from the governor's office." Though Finney's visitor wore the hidden camera and therefore couldn't be seen by Nikki, his accent immediately brought to mind a *Dukes of Hazzard* cast member in a business suit. Given the man's heavy accent, Nikki barely recognized Judge "Fee-ney's" name, though she certainly recognized Lassiter's name —a man who most decidedly did not work at the governor's office.

Finney had never mentioned this visit to Nikki, a fact that would have been remarkable if it were any other judge. But with Finney, privacy and discretion were paramount. So now Nikki was about to learn, along with the rest of America, at least one thing that had happened behind Finney's closed doors.

"Wheel-yum, huh?" Judge Finney said, repeating the way the kid had pronounced his own name.

"Yes sir."

"It's a long way from the governor's office," said Finney, stuffing an unlit cigar in his mouth. "Welcome to southeast Virginia, Billy Bob."

The young man hesitated for a moment. "Actually, I go by William now," he said. "Can we talk off the record?"

"Sure." Finney spit a small piece of the cigar in the trash.

"Well, as you know, there's an unexpected vacancy on the Virginia Supreme Court," William said. "And the governor really likes your ability to make the tough calls. He's narrowed his list down to three for this interim appointment, and you're one of them."

Finney looked genuinely shocked. With good reason. Nikki didn't follow politics closely, but she still couldn't imagine that Virginia's Democratic governor would appoint Finney.

"Does the governor know about my cancer?" Finney asked.

"Yes. That actually works in your favor. One of the problems with our system is that our part-time legislature only meets from January through March. The governor has the power to make interim judicial appointments and most of the time uses that power to select somebody with a prospect of being confirmed for a full-time slot once the legislature reconvenes." William hesitated, and Nikki could hear the urgency in his voice. "Can I be frank here, Judge Finney?"

"Please."

"As you know, one of the governor's key initiatives last year was an executive order authorizing state grants for stem-cell research. Several other states have already gone this route, and if Virginia doesn't act quickly, we'll be left behind. All of the best genetic scientists are already relocating in areas like California and Massachusetts."

Finney sat there impassive, his stare giving nothing away.

"A bunch of Republican senators filed suit, claiming that Governor Malone acted ultra vires by not running these grants through the budget process. That lawsuit will probably be decided by the Virginia Supreme Court this fall. Anybody who knows the justices can predict the results of the present court—a three-three split."

"So you need a sacrificial lamb," Finney interjected. "Someone conservative enough in his judicial opinions so that he won't be seen as an obvious vote for the governor's stem-cell funding. But once he does vote that way, of course, there's no way he could ever get approved by the Republican-controlled Senate in the fall."

It was vintage Finney, and Nikki loved it. Blunt. Insightful. And she knew what was coming next—unyielding.

Lassiter tried gamely to recover. "I wouldn't exactly call it a sacrificial lamb. After all, this is a six- to nine-month term on our state's highest court…and a chance to impact history."

"How do you know I'll impact it the right way?"

There was a long pause. "We don't, of course. And we're not looking for any guarantees. But we thought that your physical challenges would make you sympathetic to what the governor is trying to accomplish with this research."

"You mean my cancer."

"Yes, your cancer. But we would, of course, need to know ahead of time what your views"—Lassiter paused long enough for Finney to get the drift—"let's just say, what your judicial philosophy is on issues like the governor being able to authorize new research programs through executive orders."

"In other words," Finney said, his voice harsh, "how I might vote on the stem-cell case."

"Not really, Judge. I'm just talking about your overall judicial philosophy here, not how you would vote on a particular case."

Finney stared at the camera for a long moment, and Nikki was sure that young Lassiter had been forced to divert his eyes. "Do you know how long I've been on the bench?" Finney asked.

"Not exactly. But a long time."

"A long time is right," Finney responded, his unblinking eyes focused hard on the camera. "And in all those years I've never promised anyone how I would rule on a case beforehand. I'm not about to start doing so now."

"You da man!" somebody in the bar yelled.

"You tell 'em, Judge!"

As if in response, Finney shifted forward in his seat. "You go back and tell your boss that Judge Finney would be honored to serve his final months on the Virginia Supreme Court. But make sure you tell the governor that you don't have the foggiest idea how Finney might rule on that stem-cell case."

"I'll tell him," promised Lassiter. "And the governor would appreciate it if you kept this conversation confidential."

"I can understand why," replied Finney, and pandemonium broke loose in the sports bar.

"Fin-ney! Fin-ney!" the crowd chanted. Nikki couldn't keep from smiling. "It almost restores your faith in the justice system," Tammy, the show's host, was saying over the din. Finney had literally stared down his temptation and never blinked.

"I'll drink to that," said somebody at Nikki's table. Nikki agreed.

∾

The Assassin watched the show with a thin smile. Finney's temptation had perfectly demonstrated the beauty of reality shows. It was so hard to know what was real and what was not. Even before the show officially began, Finney had been sucked into the alternative reality created by television. All of life had indeed become a stage.

The Assassin knew that even things portrayed as *real* by the show's producers could in fact be contrived. A camera angle here, a remark taken out of context there, and reality could be warped to suit the purposes of the producers. The quest for higher ratings was the only reality that could be trusted.

What a perfect setting, this world of fun-house mirrors, for the Assassin's most dramatic job ever. It was the game within the game. And it would be over before the others even knew that they were playing.

∾

The Patient watched the temptation of Oliver Finney and then the tele-
vised cross-examinations of the contestants with great interest. He had
heard about the results last week during the taping, but it was fascinating
to watch the blow by blow.

Finney did a spectacular job of exposing the weaknesses of Buddhism,
forcing Ando to defend the extreme limits of nonattachment that require
people to turn their back on anything they might love, including family.
But Finney made a better attorney than he did a witness, stumbling some
under relentless questioning by Kareem Hasaan.

The Patient was not surprised when Javitts awarded his verdict to
Hasaan. The voting public, on the other hand, would probably go for
either Finney or the ever-popular Swami. Dr. Kline could be a long shot
if enough men voted.

The show's last segment that night featured gripping footage of
Finney's attempted escape. Only on television could a man hit the highs
and lows that Finney had experienced on this one episode, all within the
span of one hour. Finney looked desperate as they brought him to shore
on the back of a Wave Runner. Finney's scrawny frame, matted hair sticking out from under his John Deere cap, and semi-crazed eyes all combined
to form a telling caricature of the psychological toll being exacted on the
contestants. *He looks like a POW,* thought the Patient. It was good television, no doubt about it.

The Patient was fascinated with Finney's responses in the library room
after the bungled escape attempt. First, Finney established that he was free
to quit at any time. Then he claimed that he was just going for a midnight
paddle and didn't really want to quit.

But the thing that intrigued the Patient the most was the final remark
by Finney just before the commercial break. When told that he would

have to pass an exam by the island medical doctor and a clinical psychologist, Finney had a ready response: "Nobody told me that being sane was a prerequisite."

"Crazy like a fox," the Patient mumbled. He spent the next few minutes trying to get inside Finney's head, ignoring the promos for Thursday night's show when the winner of the viewers' verdict would be announced and the contestants would face the ancient Chinese water torture.

It would be interesting to see whom the contestants ultimately voted into the finals. Though the contestants didn't know it yet, one of the finalists would be determined by their own vote. Who better to observe how well people's faith held up under trial than their fellow competitors?

Well, *most* of the contestants didn't know it yet. The Patient speed-dialed the one who did.

After they chatted for a few minutes, the Patient decided it was time to pop the question. "If you had to vote today, who would it be?"

"Finney."

"That's what I thought." The Patient smiled to himself. The plan was going smoothly, almost too smoothly. "You think he suspects anything?"

"Not yet, but don't underestimate him. I think he's got some cards under the table."

"Crazy like a fox?" asked the Patient.

"Exactly."

CHAPTER 51

Nikki's first thought was that her fashion lessons were paying off. She had asked Wellington to meet her at Starbucks after the show—a convenient excuse to avoid the prospects of another night with Byron. When she arrived, she was pleased to see an untucked light-blue cotton shirt hanging loose over reasonably long khaki shorts. The kid wore sneakers without socks, but then again, they hadn't worked on footwear yet.

The harsh lights and relative quiet of the Starbucks threw Nikki off stride. After the decibel volume in the bar, followed by the tunes she had cranked up on the way to the Starbucks in the Sebring, her ears were buzzing. Or maybe it was the gin and tonics catching up to her. Finney's bizarre escape attempt had forced her to have one or two extras.

She decided that she needed a cappuccino before joining Wellington at the table. When she sat down opposite him, she realized that her first impression had been wrong. Most of Wellington's shirt was still tucked in, and he wore a V-neck T-shirt underneath that screamed of the eighties. The poor boy's instincts were all wrong.

Wellington looked up at her with bloodshot eyes, his hair sticking up from running his fingers through it. She wondered if maybe Finney's antics had caused Wellington to hit the bottle too. He had a frantic look in his eyes, and Nikki noticed the chaotic pencil scratches on his normally neat tablet.

"You okay?" she asked.

"I can't figure it out," he confessed. He rubbed his face and looked ready to cry. "I've been working nonstop since the minute I saw Finney's last message."

Nikki reached over and turned the tablet so she could see it. Wellington had made his usual charts, but as far as she could tell, he had just been writing and erasing guesses, without figuring out a single letter. It looked like one of her sheets. The letters blurred a little, partially a result of the alcohol but also due in part to Nikki's worsening eyesight. One of these days, she would have to get LASIK.

"Did you watch the show tonight?" Nikki asked.

Wellington nodded his head guiltily. "I did take a break for that."

"Oh, I didn't mean that. I just wondered if you saw Finney try to get off the island in that kayak."

"Yeah. Weird."

"It's definitely not like him," Nikki agreed. "I'm worried about him. He didn't look good. But then again, he was his usual ornery self when they questioned him afterward." She slurped on her cappuccino and noticed Wellington stare. *It wasn't that loud.*

"Something's not right with Finney," said Wellington. "We've got to break this code."

Even through the haze, Nikki could tell that Wellington needed a break. "Maybe you ought to get a little sleep," suggested Nikki, thinking that maybe she could use some herself, "and start again in the morning."

"I can't sleep," Wellington said emphatically. "Not until I figure this out."

Can we say obsession? thought Nikki. She was no psychologist, but she was pretty sure that her boy was beyond the point of being productive. You can't stare for hours at a page full of symbols and keep your focus. Her own limit was about fifteen minutes.

"You want to grab something to eat?" she suggested. "Maybe that would help."

When Wellington turned down food, Nikki knew they were in big trouble. "What can I do to help?" she asked, trying not to sound despondent.

The question brought a look from Wellington that was hard to read. But if Nikki had to guess, she assumed Wellington was thinking something like, *I'll never be that desperate.* Eventually he shrugged. "Just give me a little more time."

She tried to focus again on the incomprehensible code from chapter four sitting in front of her. She had glanced at it earlier in the day but didn't really give it a second thought, assuming that Wellington would solve it with no problem. Earlier tonight, even when she was completely sober, the letters and numbers had made no sense. Now, with a buzz going, they practically ran together.

teAJ9EBQStsWoo5tvhhtt2N16ad8tep130Y6671E8ptzt2f5DNBCC5ra8eegO2lid5ecq9

"Maybe it's another Poe cipher," suggested Nikki. "Didn't he use letters and numbers and some other stuff?"

"He didn't use numbers," Wellington said flatly. "I tried breaking it down like a Poe cipher and got nowhere. Then I tried analyzing it like a substitution cipher and then a transposition cipher and then a combination of the two. One of the problems is that the message isn't very long, so it's harder to decipher. Plus, Finney didn't just use the alphabet. He's got small letters and capital letters and numbers, so it's probable that the frequently used plaintext letters have more than one symbol representing them." Wellington took off his glasses and cleaned them on his shirttail, thereby solving one mystery for Nikki—why his shirt was half untucked. "I just don't know if this one is solvable."

"Nonsense," said Nikki. "Think about it." She took a sip of her cappuccino, hoping it would chase the alcohol away. "If Finney didn't think you could solve this chapter, he would have told you to skip to the next chapter in his last coded message."

Wellington's eyes brightened, and Nikki realized she had actually made a good point. Just like a sober person might. "You're just too caught up in these little—" She motioned at the sheet in front of her, temporarily forgetting the name for those squiggle marks. *What are they called?* "You're just all caught up in these cipher doohickeys," she said. "Think about the big picture. What clues are in the book?"

Wellington pointed at the air, as if lecturing an invisible class. "You've got a point. The cipher in the last chapter was incredibly hard—it took a hundred and fifty years to solve. But we solved it in a matter of minutes once we realized it was one of Poe's ciphers that somebody else had already solved."

"So, what famous ciphers did he drop hints about in chapter four?"

"That's just it," said Wellington. "I didn't see any."

Nikki tried to wrap her mind around this. They must be missing something obvious, something right under their noses. "What was chapter four about?"

"The Pharisees and lawyers challenged Christ to give them a sign that He was the Messiah," Wellington responded as if he had been over this point a thousand times already. "Jesus gave them the sign of Jonah, saying that just like Jonah was three days and three nights in the belly of the big fish, Jesus would be three days and three nights in the ground and then would rise again."

"I don't suppose Jonah had any ciphers?"

Wellington trotted out an "Are you crazy?" look. "Okay, that might have been the alcohol," admitted Nikki. "But I still think this is the right approach to solving this thing."

"Judge Finney says in the chapter that the case for the Resurrection is the most compelling case ever presented to a jury. Then he spends most of the chapter giving a closing argument, just like a lawyer would in court, arguing the historical proof that Christ rose on the third day, just like He predicted."

"So, what's that got to do with a code?" Nikki asked.

For the next hour, they kicked around that very question. Eventually

Wellington speculated himself out and Nikki's heavy eyelids got the better of her. She fell asleep with her head resting on an arm propped on the table. She woke when a door behind her opened and let in a muggy breeze. She gave Wellington a sheepish smile. The kid was scribbling on his pad again.

"Do you need me to drive you home?" Wellington asked. She could see the concern etched on his face and sensed that a lecture on drinking and driving was coming.

"I'm fine," Nikki replied. "It's just been a long day, that's all."

Wellington looked skeptical.

"Do you want me to recite the alphabet backward?" Nikki asked.

"Sure."

Halfway through a slow but nearly flawless performance, Wellington acquiesced.

"Be careful," he said.

CHAPTER 52

As if it wasn't bad enough to be starving half to death and facing the Chinese water torture tomorrow, the show's producers added insult to injury by placing Finney on a curfew. He couldn't leave his condo between midnight and 6:00 a.m. They had electronically wired every door and window to make sure he didn't violate his new restrictions.

"Not even to go out on my patio for a smoke?" Finney asked.

"Not even."

Because of the curfew, Finney called an end to the nightly card game at 11:00 p.m. The Swami protested loudly since he was down several hundred dollars. Though the ante was still just one buck, the betting had loosened up toward the end of the game. Horace, who had forgotten his sunblock earlier in the day and had a nasty sunburn on his round and balding head, lost nearly four hundred—a Paradise Island record. He didn't want to quit early either. Gus didn't say anything, which was par for the course. Since Finney broke even, he estimated that Gus came out about six hundred ahead.

Though no real money would change hands until the week was over, Horace looked pale under his sunburn when Finney announced his total—$817 in the hole.

"Maybe we should drop the ante a bit," suggested the Swami. "Limit the bets." Though it seemed like a nice gesture on the surface, Finney assumed that the Swami had made the suggestion because he'd been cheating all week and felt guilty about the $552 dollars he had made.

"Nah," said Horace, forcing a smile. "My luck's changing tomorrow night. I can feel it."

"No poker tomorrow night," the Swami said. "Chinese water torture."

"Oh yeah," replied Horace. "Then Thursday—our last night here. We ought to double the stakes."

The men put away the cards and rinsed out their glasses. Both Horace and Gus had quit bringing snacks once the contestants started fasting. Horace complained about it constantly, claiming that the lack of munchies affected his concentration.

"I wanted to quit early so I could take a short hike on the beach," Finney said to Horace. "Big day tomorrow."

Horace had finagled the system so he had been assigned nighttime camera duty for Finney. Gus had worked out the same assignment for the Swami, thus assuring that the foursome could be together for cards every night.

Horace picked up his camera and dutifully followed Finney down to the beach. Finney grabbed a seat in one of the loungers, and Horace sat down next to him, placing his large camera on a lounger on the other side. It was a gorgeous night, with a warm and salty ocean breeze blowing in their faces, the full moon and thousands of stars reflecting in the sea.

"Beautiful night," said Finney.

"Yep."

"Can't believe we've only got a few more days here."

"Time flies when you're having fun," said Horace.

After the two men sat in silence for a while, Horace burped, reminding Finney that he hadn't eaten in three days. Finney's stomach had now started cramping, and he felt tired all the time. At this moment he wished he could be in bed.

"I could use a brewski and a T-bone," said Horace. He was probably drooling, though Finney couldn't tell in the dark. "They haven't been feeding us worth diddly-squat since you guys stopped eating."

"Let's talk about something else."

"Okay," said Horace. Another burp. "Pizza," he said instinctively as he tasted his own burp. Then he added, "How's Swami doing it? It's like he knows every card in my hand."

The two men discussed the Swami's probable cheating techniques as they surveyed the night sky. Finney thought about the long day tomorrow, checked his watch, and decided it was time. "Think I'll wade out in the ocean a little," he said.

"Suit yourself."

Finney didn't move for a few seconds and then turned to Horace. "Do you have access to cell phones or e-mail or even snail mail?"

Horace leaned up in his chair and looked over at Finney. The pudgy little cameraman motioned toward the small of his back.

"I turned it off," said Finney. "That's why I made that remark about going into the ocean—so whoever's monitoring the mike wouldn't get suspicious."

"I'm not sure anybody monitors it at night anyway," admitted Horace. He leaned back in his chair again. "And the answer is no. I don't have access to e-mail or cell phones or snail mail. The producers have cell phones and e-mail that work through that satellite uplink somehow. But they're paranoid about the crew leaking the results. In fact, the network purposely scheduled us to shoot another two-week show on some other remote island as soon as this one is over. We don't get back to the mainland until the final show airs."

Finney considered this complication for a moment. Oh well, he knew things couldn't be that easy. Even if he could trust Horace, there was no secure way to communicate with the outside world. It's why he had already worked through Plan B. "What do you do with the raw film you shoot?" Finney asked.

Horace hesitated, and Finney could sense the little man trying to sort through his loyalties. "Uh…we make a first-edit pass ourselves and send any potentially good footage on to the team in the edit suite. They put the show together here on the island and then send it back to New York by satellite."

"Have you got a lot of footage on the tape that's in your camera right now?" asked Finney.

Horace glanced over at Finney and stared for a moment, then turned back toward the night sky, his hands locked behind his head again. "Yeah. The one in there is almost full. But I've got another in my case. Why?"

"Just wondering," said Finney. He closed his eyes and said a prayer. This had better work. "You a religious man?" he asked softly.

"I've been known to say a few prayers," Horace admitted. "I'm pulling for you, Judge, if that's what you want to know."

Not exactly, thought Finney, *but close enough.* He leaned forward in his chair and turned toward Horace. "If I asked you to put a new tape in that camera and record something as a personal favor to me, would you do it?"

Horace furrowed his brow. "Something like what?"

"What if I just asked you to trust me?" Finney replied, his voice so low it barely carried above the sounds of the waves. "What if I said that the reason would become clear in a few minutes?"

Horace shrugged. He reached over and pulled a new tape out of his camera case. "I was thinking about changing tapes anyway," he said.

Finney stood up and walked ankle deep into the water, then turned and faced Horace. "Can you tape this?" he asked.

Still sitting in the lounger, Horace turned on his camera and blinded Finney with the bright light. "Okay, Hamlet. Just keep it PG." The red recording light popped on.

"My name is Oliver Gradison Finney, and I swear and affirm that the testimony I'm about to give is all true under penalties of perjury." He looked directly into the camera, knowing that Horace was probably wondering what in the world was going on. He'd find out soon enough.

"I'm about to state certain facts based on my own personal knowledge—things I have seen and heard. These facts should be enough to establish probable cause for conspiracy to commit murder. If you're watching this tape, it most likely means that I am no longer around to testify and the conspiracy has therefore succeeded." As Finney spoke, he watched Horace stand with the camera and move a few steps closer.

For the next several minutes, Finney recounted the facts that led to his suspicions about a murder conspiracy. He started with the details of his own cross-examination and the stunning revelation that one of the speedy-trial defendants had killed an innocent young store clerk earlier this year. That revelation had been haunting him for the past week, he admitted. He could think of little else.

Then he detailed each of his Hobie Cat conversations with Dr. Kline, recounting, as precisely as possible, her alleged conversations with Bryce McCormack. He told about the staged escape attempt on the kayak and the information discovered by Kareem on Cameron Murphy's computer. He also relayed the background information that Hadji had pulled up on the various persons of interest. He detailed the conversations from the times when the contestants met together while pretending they were snorkeling. He even described, as best he could remember it, the looks on the faces of the other contestants when Kareem dropped his bombshell. Finney intentionally omitted any references to the secret messages he had been exchanging with Nikki.

Finney paused and took a step closer to the camera. "I hope I'm wrong about all this," he said. "I hope this is just a very elaborate and callous ploy designed to get the contestants off focus. If so, it has worked.

"However, based on my years of analyzing and deciding conspiracies in real-life cases, this one appears authentic." Finney swallowed and coughed to the side, then turned back to the camera. "This tape should be enough to establish probable cause for a warrant to search every square inch of Paradise Island, including all c-mails sent and received from here. I have a theory about who is behind the conspiracy but will limit this taping to the facts, rather than confuse the matter with my opinions. Motives for the conspiracy will undoubtedly be revealed if you conduct an exhaustive background search on each of the contestants as well as Cameron Murphy, Bryce McCormack, and Howard Javitts. You should pay particular attention to the religious backgrounds of those persons as well as any possible links between them and the defendants I had to release under the speedy-trial statute several years ago.

"If you're watching this tape, it probably means you're investigating my murder," said Finney, smiling wryly. "So good luck."

Horace shut off the camera and blew out a breath. "Are you serious?"

Finney just nodded.

"Unbelievable," Horace muttered to himself. And to Finney he added, "What do we do now?"

"Let me have the tape," said Finney. He reached into his pocket and pulled out a sheet of paper. It contained Nikki's e-mail and a coded letter telling her about the location of the tape. "Send this message to the e-mail address on this sheet as soon as you get off this island. Don't try to contact this person from here, okay?"

Finney had thought long and hard about the best way to proceed. If he was the target of a vendetta killing, he didn't want to alert the conspirators to Nikki's involvement and force the killer to take her out as well. It seemed that every direct communication from the island was being monitored. The best he could do would be to alert Nikki to the location of the tape as soon as Horace had a chance to send this e-mail from someplace other than the island and, in the meantime, hope that Wellington had deciphered the last message.

The e-mail and tape would be necessary only in a worst-case scenario. Finney would be dead. But, like Poe, perhaps he could speak from the grave.

"Send the e-mail message exactly as I have it on that page, Horace. It won't make sense to you, but this person will figure it out."

Horace wrinkled his face into a mask of concern. "You sure we shouldn't just call the cops?"

"How?" asked Finney.

"Maybe I could steal somebody's cell phone," said Horace.

It was tempting, but Finney knew his bumbling little friend would get caught red-handed. Besides, it wasn't necessary. "The feds are already working on it," Finney said.

∾

Though he was beyond exhaustion when he returned to his condo, Finney went straight to his computer and accessed Westlaw. Because of a long afternoon court session that bled into the evening hours, a follow-up visit by the Swami, and the nightly card game, this was the first time Finney had been alone in his condo for any length of time since he sent his message to Nikki and Wellington that morning.

He didn't want to enter new searches and run the risk of confusing Wellington, but he had to know if Wellington had deciphered the prior message. His heart raced when he pulled up the search histories, as if checking his own previous research, and noticed some new searches. Finney was confident that whoever was monitoring his computer in the control room at this hour of the night would have no idea that these searches hadn't been entered by Finney himself.

It appeared that Wellington had used the Poe cipher, continuing the pattern of responding with the same cipher Finney had used in the original message. Finney quickly wrote down the capital letters along with a few bogus notes. He logged off the computer, and took his notes and *Cross Examination* book into the bathroom stall so he could decipher the message outside the presence of the cameras.

Obviously, Wellington had not yet deciphered Finney's latest message, or he would have used the code Finney had used earlier that day. The content of Wellington's message confirmed this. He told Finney about Murphy's legalistic Christian father and the location of Paradise Island as determined by Preston Randolph but made no mention of Finney's last message. Finney finished decoding the message, brushed his teeth, and returned to his bedroom. He took off his shirt and lay down on his bed to consider this new information and his next move.

He stared at the ceiling for a while, then closed his eyes to concentrate on the puzzle set before him, including the possible wording for the search requests he would use in his next message. He thought about sending that message right now but realized how suspicious that would look—logging back on to Westlaw a second time this late at night, even though tomorrow's activities didn't really require any research. Plus, another message now might confuse and distract Wellington. No, he would stick with the original plan and give Wellington until tomorrow morning to decipher the last message. Patience. Nothing would change between now and then.

That settled, Finney began to relax, his thoughts jumbling together until he entered that land where reality and illusion merge, engulfing Finney in a fitful dream of Chinese water torture and a hellfire preacher who resembled Charles Darwin.

Before long, Finney was snoring.

CHAPTER 53

The next morning, Nikki reached Murphy's legalistic father, but the man wasn't buying her routine. "Look," she finally said, "I'm the law clerk for Judge Finney, who is one of the contestants on Paradise Island, a good Christian man like you, and I've got to ask you a few questions about your son."

"You lied to me," Pastor Martin said, condemnation riding on every word.

"Not really. I lied to your assistant. She lied to you."

"You're despicable."

"A good man could be in danger—," Nikki began. But before she could finish, the phone line went dead.

She tried calling back but couldn't get past Martin's assistant, who also accused Nikki of lying. She tried one more time, and when the assistant started in on her again, Nikki trotted out her favorite Scripture verse. Actually, the *only* Scripture verse she knew by heart. "Judge not or you'll be judged," said Nikki, and this time *she* hung up the phone.

Less than two minutes later, Wellington called. "I deciphered the next message," he said proudly.

"Tell me quickly about the code," said Nikki. "I'm running late for court." It was another white lie, but by now she had quit counting.

"You were right, Nikki. The key was understanding the link between the code and chapter four. When Jesus was asked for a sign—"

"*Wellington!* I can't do this right now." She had taken the day off to get a manicure and finish some errands that had been piling up. Fitzsimmons had made a snide comment about her work ethic, but Nikki wasn't worried. Finney would be back soon.

Right now she was on her way to the gym and didn't want to spend the entire drive listening to code-cracking details.

"Here's what it says," Wellington began, the stiff formality in his voice showing his irritation. " 'I have pc evidence of a murder conspiracy. Go to feds and get warrant. No publicity.' "

Nikki turned off her car radio. "Say that again."

Wellington repeated the message, then added, "I'm guessing that pc means 'probable cause.' "

"Um…yeah. That's probably right." Nikki pulled into the right lane and tried to focus on what this meant. "Are you sure about this, Wellington?"

"When asked for a sign to prove He was the Messiah, Jesus pointed to His own resurrection, which He predicted would occur three days and three nights after the Crucifixion. I finally realized that the small letter t, the most frequent letter in the chapter four code, was actually a sign for the cross. After that realization, I made a chart containing every letter and every number that appeared exactly three symbols after each t in the code message. That turned out to be the solution for chapter four. When I did the same thing with Finney's Westlaw searches—wrote down the letters that appeared exactly three spaces after each t in his Westlaw searches—I ended up with this message."

"Okay." Stunned, Nikki congratulated Wellington and got off the phone, collecting her thoughts as she drove. Finney really was in trouble. This was no ploy to gain a competitive advantage in a game show. Probable cause for a murder conspiracy. Nikki's stomach tied itself in knots.

Finney was counting on her. But she didn't know anybody at the FBI. She didn't even know if the FBI had jurisdiction in the Galápagos Islands. She did have a few contacts in the U.S. Attorney's office, but then another thought hit her. Of course. If anybody had connections, he would.

She dialed Preston Randolph's private cell phone and reached him immediately. Without spilling the details of the codes, she explained to

Randolph how she had received a coded message from Finney that had been deciphered by Wellington Farnsworth and that she needed to contact the FBI. Within minutes, she knew this had been the right move. Randolph told her to book the first flight to Washington DC on his nickel and take a cab to his office. He would make some phone calls to some connections he had. Nikki could meet with the feds right in Randolph's conference room.

"Better have Wellington available by telephone," Randolph said. "He'll have to tell the agents how he deciphered the codes."

It's who you know, thought Nikki as she hung up the phone. She turned around and headed back to her apartment. The gym and the manicure would have to wait.

∾

Finney sat straight up in bed, then felt his head whir. Where was he? What time was it?

Knocking. Somebody was knocking on the door. He cleared his thoughts and looked at the clock: 9:11. Blood started coursing through his veins, fueled by his frustration at sleeping through his alarm on such a critical day. Then he remembered—he hadn't set the alarm. The knocking grew louder.

"Coming," Finney yelled, then started his morning cough. He stumbled out of bed with burning lungs and with intestines that cramped in protest at the forced cleansing of his system. He managed to throw on a T-shirt while hacking and headed to the front door in his gym shorts and T-shirt, stopping at the kitchen sink to cough up a fair amount of phlegm.

He opened the door and found the Swami and Gus standing there, somber faced. Gus didn't have his huge camera, and Finney's stomach dropped. He knew immediately the news would be bad; he could see pain written all over the Swami's normally cheerful face.

"I slept in," said Finney apologetically. "Of all mornings."

"Can we come in?" asked the Swami.

"You don't have to ask."

The two men walked into the condo and took a seat in the TV room. Finney joined them, and the Swami spoke first. "They think Horace might have had a heart attack this morning."

Finney went numb, hoping this was still part of some extended bad dream. His thoughts raced to the chubby smile of his friend—the innocent vivacity that made Horace so much fun to be around. "Is he okay?" Finney managed.

"They think so," the Swami said, and Finney took a breath. "He complained of severe chest pains, and the island physician looked him over. They're trying to decide whether to send him home or not."

At that moment it dawned on a still-groggy Finney what had happened. His buddy was trying to get off the island so he could deliver Finney's message. "You think I could see him?" asked Finney.

"Probably," said Gus. "They let me talk to him this morning. He actually looked pretty good. It's probably just the pizza."

"We're supposed to be in court in about forty minutes," the Swami reminded Finney. "

Finney stood and stretched. No time to waste. "I better get ready," Finney said. "I'll see you guys in court." He headed back to the bathroom for a shower. This morning he would have to skip the shave.

Finney turned on the faucet and ran the water until he heard the front door shut. Then he went back into the kitchen and, blocking the camera with his back, slipped a sharp knife and plastic bag into the waistline of his shorts. He went back into his bedroom, picked up a thick book on Islam he had checked out of the Paradise Island library, and headed into the toilet stall. Once inside, he cut out the middle pages of the book and stuffed inside it the tape Horace had filmed last night. He would return the book to the library later today.

He put the pages he had cut from the book inside the plastic bag, sealed the bag, and dropped it into the reservoir on the back of the toilet. He replaced the lid and smiled.

He took the book back out to his bedroom and placed it on his desk, checking the clock. He had just enough time to log on to Westlaw and see if Wellington had solved his last critical message. Plus, he needed to send another message of even greater importance.

If Nikki and Wellington already had the feds involved, then Finney would try to get Horace to stay on the island. Finney now believed he was in real danger. He needed an accomplice on site more than he needed someone helping Nikki pressure the feds. Finney clicked on his Internet browser and stared at the message on the screen in disbelief: "Since all courtroom sessions except the closing arguments for the finalists have now been concluded, you will no longer need Internet research. Accordingly, access to the Internet is denied."

Finney thought through his alternatives and decided he had to trust Wellington's code-breaking abilities. Finney would operate on the assumption that Wellington had deciphered the last message and had gone to the feds with Nikki. That being the case, he would ask Horace to stay with him on the island. At least that way Finney knew he could trust his own cameraman. Somebody to guard his back.

Finney threw on his clothes and paid Horace a visit. Within minutes, the chubby little man's stomach and chest began feeling better.

CHAPTER 54

They strapped Finney into something that looked like a cross between a dentist's chair and an electric chair. He was in a stuffy windowless room in the main building on Paradise Island, the same building that housed the library. Finney, like the other contestants, had been shown this room and others like it two days ago, presumably to increase his anxiety. The room smelled like the turkey sandwiches the setup crew had eaten before they threw the wrappers in the trash. Finney wondered if the smell of food was part of the torture.

Tight iron wrist and ankle shackles bound him to the chair. He wiggled and felt the shackles rub uncomfortably against his skin. They fastened a seat belt contraption tightly around his waist and tilted the seat back. Last, they clamped a thick shackle over his neck so that he couldn't move his head more than a few inches.

"You okay?" asked McCormack.

"Do I get a last cigar?" asked Finney.

"Seems like you've already had a few too many of those," replied McCormack.

They tilted the chair back even farther, so that Finney was nearly horizontal, looking straight up at the ceiling. The end of a small hose hung about four feet above his forehead. On the wall he could see the digital clock, the figures set at zero hours, zero minutes, and zero seconds.

"As we explained before, there's a panic button at the bottom of the armrest about two inches from your thumb," said McCormack. Finney wiggled his thumb until he found the button. "That's the one," confirmed McCormack. "If you push that at any time, the water torture will stop immediately and you will be out of this round of the competition. Dr.

Andrews, the gentleman who examined you earlier this week, will be checking periodically to monitor your vital signs. We also have a clinical psychologist, Dr. Hargraves, who will be making rounds as well. The camera on this tripod will be taping the entire time, and our control center will monitor the footage. Anything you say will be heard in the control center."

"What about room service?" asked Finney.

"Okay," said Bryce McCormack, "amateur hour's over. Let's get this started so I can set up the next contestant. Any final words or predictions before we start, Judge Finney?"

Finney rolled his eyes toward the camera. "I would say myself and the Swami are the ones to watch," Finney predicted. "We're the only ones who know the key to outlasting this thing."

"We'll see," said McCormack. He turned from Finney and spoke into the air. "Let's get it started."

On cue, a drop of water from the plastic hose that ran from the ceiling to its point of suspension just above Finney fell on his forehead, close to his nose. As the digital clock ticked off the first two seconds, another drop fell. They moved the chair just a little so that the next one plunked right in the middle of Finney's forehead. He watched the next drop form...*drip*...and blinked just before it hit his forehead...*splat*.

Drip...splat. Drip...splat. This could be a long day. He closed his eyes and tried to relax.

A few days ago, Finney had done his Internet research on what he was about to experience. The ordeal would not be physically painful. Even now, the dripping water was more an annoyance than anything else. After some period of time, different durations for different people, a victim would begin dreading the next relentless drip. Increased anxiety, caused by the helplessness of not being able to avoid the next drip, would ratchet up the psychological pressure exponentially. If a person was held in place long enough, the unremitting drips would literally drive the victim mad.

Not that far of a drive for some of us, thought Finney. He was trying hard to keep a sense of humor about this.

Splat...splat...splat...splat. Though he no longer watched the drips forming, he still felt himself flinching just before each drop hit his forehead. *Splat...splat...splat...splat.* Relentless. Like your son when he's just learning to play the drums.

Tyler. Finney thought about Tyler for a few moments but quickly forced himself to dwell on something else. Finney decided to spend his first few hours refining his plan for ensuring that all the contestants, including himself, escaped Paradise Island unharmed. Small rivulets of water started running through his hair and down the side of his head. *Splat...splat...splat.* He assumed that by now Nikki and Wellington had solved his last message and procured the help of the FBI, though he would have no way of knowing for sure with his Internet access cut off. Although the code for chapter four was unconventional, Wellington was the best cryptanalyst Finney had ever seen.

Splat...splat...splat. The drops made it nearly impossible to focus on anything but the next drop of water ready to hit his forehead. *Think!*

Hopefully, the FBI would raid the island and make arrests soon. Finney's job would be to keep everyone alive until they did. *Splat... splat...splat.* If the FBI didn't show up before the finalists were announced, Finney would have to take matters into his own hands. The darker possibilities tried to torment him, like the water dripping on his forehead. What if Wellington couldn't crack the code? What if Finney had done the unthinkable—put Nikki in danger too? The thoughts made the shackles seem tighter, accentuating his own feelings of helplessness.

Splat...splat...splat. He ran through all the possibilities and gradually reassured himself. Wellington was a genius. How many times had the kid proved that? And nobody but Wellington, and possibly the feds, would even know that Nikki was communicating with Finney. Finney's instructions had been clear about that.

Splat...splat...splat.

Eventually he began to calm down again. He realized that the lack of food and the constant dripping of water had sent his mind spiraling into dark realms where it did no good to dwell. He had a plan and a backup plan. And right now the plan required that he endure this water torture. *Splat...splat...splat...splat.*

He needed something to help him relax, not make him more tense. He could pray. He could use some relaxation techniques he had learned from the Swami. He could think about simpler times with his family— vacations, amusement parks, holidays. He could think of nothing at all. *Splat...splat...splat.* He could try to fall asleep...*splat.* Nope, that definitely wasn't going to happen.

Splat...splat...splat...splat. Finney focused on his breathing. Deep, relaxing breaths.

Splat. "Are we done yet?" he asked the camera.

Splat. The stillness in the room was his reply. *Splat.* More water ran down the sides of his head. *Splat.* Some trickled into his eye even though it was closed. He couldn't reach up and wipe the water. The shackles started playing games with his mind, chaffing his wrists as he squirmed to get more comfortable. *Splat.* The quietness exaggerated the slight noise caused by the water drop hitting his forehead. He could tell that after a few hours it would seem like a sledgehammer. *Splat.* Or maybe an atom bomb.

Splat...splat...splat...splat... He resisted the urge to count.

∽

The Assassin thought the Chinese water torture was a pitiful joke. The Assassin had seen torture. This didn't qualify.

The real water torture, the Assassin knew, would come in a few days. The victim would be bound with these same shackles so that any rub marks would not be suspicious. The victim would be forced underwater and held there until he started swallowing large quantities of water, distending his stomach. Just short of death, the victim would be allowed to resurface, so that the Assassin's client could taunt the victim and order him submerged again. Five times. Ten times. It all depended on how long the Assassin held the victim under.

It would look like an accidental drowning, though the Assassin and the Client had a much better name for it in their coded messages. *Baptism*. What was it the Christian churches said? The Assassin had looked it up on the Internet. "Buried with Christ in baptism…"

A holy saying turned into a taunt.

The Assassin liked the religious overtones. It's why he had selected his own code name for this assignment: *Azrael*. How clever. Too bad the secretive nature of the assignment prevented others from appreciating the Assassin's creativity.

∾

Her flight ran late. She ended up in a middle seat. Plus, the taxi smelled like somebody threw up in the backseat last night and the air conditioner didn't work. She rolled down her window and let the wind frizz her hair. She gave the cabbie a twenty, and he claimed he didn't have enough ones to make change. She settled for two dollars in quarters.

By the time Nikki made it to Preston Randolph's office on Connecticut Avenue, she was hot, sticky, and more than an hour late. She spent a few minutes in the ladies' room to freshen up before the receptionist ushered her into the conference room. Two men in blue blazers drank coffee and huddled over thick files. They flashed FBI credentials and introduced themselves. Agent Rafferty was a bit old for the FBI—thin body and thin, dark hair. He had leathery skin so wrinkled that it seemed like somebody had left him on the spin cycle too long. His partner, Flynn, was a shorter man with prematurely gray hair and black-rimmed glasses. Nikki could tell right away that Flynn had a Napoleon complex.

"We understand you have some suspicions about what's happening on the set of *Faith on Trial*," said Flynn. He took his seat after shaking hands and immediately began scrutinizing Nikki. He placed a cassette recorder in the middle of the table. "You mind if we tape this?"

Nikki gave him a puzzled look. "We aren't going to wait for Mr. Randolph?"

"He had to leave for court about ten minutes ago," said Flynn. "He didn't know we'd be running so late."

It sounded like an accusation, and Nikki began wondering whose side Flynn was on. "Neither did I," she shot back.

"You mind?" Flynn asked again, nodding at the recorder.

This was not a good start. Nikki sensed a been-there-done-that skepticism in Flynn's voice. She had expected Randolph and the agents to be fully engaged. This was, after all, a national reality-show scandal with the life of a sitting state court judge at stake. Instead, Randolph was off to court on some other case, and these guys were acting like she was reporting a missing hubcap.

"Did Mr. Randolph say when he would be back?"

Both agents sighed in unison, like a choir of bored feds. "In an hour or so," said Rafferty.

"Could you state your name for the record?" asked Flynn, turning on the tape. "And give your verbal consent to our taping?"

"I could," said Nikki. "But I'd prefer to wait until Mr. Randolph returns."

Flynn shoved the pile of documents in front of him a few inches toward Nikki. "This pile right here is a case we've been working on for several months. We start grand-jury proceedings on Friday. I've got four more just as urgent at the office. We're here as a favor to Mr. Randolph. If there's anything illegal happening on the *Faith on Trial* set, we'll get to the bottom of it. But frankly, Ms. Moreno, we don't have time for games.

"Now, please state your name for the record and your consent to the taping of this interview."

"My name is Nikki Moreno," she sputtered. "My tax dollars pay your salaries. The life of a state court judge may be in danger, and you guys are worried about shuffling paperwork. And no, I don't mind if you tape this stuff as long as I get a copy of the tape."

"Are you done?" asked Flynn.

"I'm just getting started," said Nikki.

For the next sixty minutes, the agents asked questions and Nikki provided answers, the level of skepticism growing by the minute. They filled up two tapes with Nikki's sarcasm and the agents' cynicism. Nikki offered several times to get Wellington on the phone so he could explain some of the codes in more detail, but the agents said it wouldn't be necessary.

Nikki was about ready to throw in the towel when the door blew open and Randolph breezed into the room. "Make any arrests yet?" he asked, smiling. He shook hands with Nikki and apologized for getting caught in court.

Flynn and Rafferty both gave Randolph a skeptical look. "This isn't exactly what you described on the phone," said Flynn, his voice a combination of boredom and frustration. "Secret messages from a game-show contestant who expects us to get a search warrant just because he tells us to—"

"A judge," interrupted Nikki. "Not a game-show contestant."

"A judge," repeated Flynn, "who ought to know we need more than this."

"Oh," said Nikki, "why didn't you say so. I'll just call Judge Finney and see if he can get a taped confession on national TV instead."

Flynn extended a palm toward Nikki, as if to say, "See what I've been putting up with?"

"If it were easy, we wouldn't need the FBI," said Randolph, his voice still pleasant. Rafferty rolled his eyes.

"Can't you guys at least go to the island and shake them up a little?" Randolph asked. "If they know we're on to them, they won't dare try anything."

"The Galápagos aren't exactly our jurisdiction," claimed Flynn.

"And that's stopped you before?" asked Randolph. He grabbed a bottled water and took a seat. Nikki was grateful for the reinforcements as Randolph continued. "They're taping a show that airs all over the United States. The production crew is entirely American. The contestants are Americans. They send the show by satellite uplink to their studios in New York City. This case has FBI written all over it."

Thus began the Moreno-Randolph tag-team combination. Randolph reminded the agents of a few favors they owed him. Nikki told them again that Finney knew what he was doing and would never cry wolf. She detailed the information about Murphy's religious bias. The tag team eventually wore the agents down and extracted a promise that the agents would visit the island and ask a few questions.

"We won't be able to get down there until Friday," said Rafferty. But Nikki and Randolph both agreed that Friday would be too late. Somebody could get killed in the meantime. By the time the agents escaped the meeting, they had agreed to head to the island the very next day.

"Are you hungry?" asked Randolph after the agents left. It was mid-afternoon and Nikki suddenly remembered that she hadn't eaten since breakfast.

"Starving."

"Me too," said Randolph. "Begging always does that to me." He flashed Nikki a billion-dollar smile. "And I know just the place."

CHAPTER 55

The food was every bit as delicious as Randolph had said it would be, but the conversation left much to be desired. Randolph spent almost the entire time talking about himself—cases he had tried, verdicts he had won, cars he owned, vacation places that Nikki would have to visit sometime. But Nikki's favorite topic of conversation was sitting on the opposite side of the table from Randolph. And whenever she brought hers up, Randolph seemed to interrupt with another of his long and elaborate Randolph-centric stories.

It wasn't until after they had ordered from the dessert tray that Randolph finally turned to an interesting topic. "If you couldn't choose your man Finney, who would you say is winning *Faith on Trial?*" he asked.

Nikki pretended to think about this for a few seconds, though she already knew the answer. "The Swami."

Randolph gave her a knowing smile. "Because of his religion or because of his bedroom eyes?"

The question seemed out of character for a sophisticated man in such a fancy restaurant, but then a thought hit Nikki. *Is this Randolph's awkward way of flirting? Does he finally realize that he is having lunch with one of Tidewater, Virginia's, most sought-after bachelorettes?*

"Both."

"I see," said Randolph, his lips still curled in the slightest hint of a smile. "And what particular aspects of his religious beliefs are appealing to you?"

Nikki didn't know a thing about the Hindu religion. But she did have a lifetime of experience at changing the subject and avoiding tough questions. "Pretty much all of it. What about you? If you couldn't choose Kline, who would you say is winning?"

"That's hard to say," said Randolph, looking past Nikki to the windows that lined the far wall. "I guess I'd say Dr. Ando because Buddhism best explains suffering." He refocused on Nikki, and she noticed a tinge of sadness, something that couldn't be washed away by living the high life. "In my work, Nikki, I see a lot of clients who have suffered. I need a religion that explains that."

In my work. Nikki could tell immediately that this wasn't really about his work. She remembered Finney's cross-examination of Ando. "But how does Ando explain it? By saying suffering will always be there? By telling us to ignore it? By detaching from everything important to us, including our lovers and our families?"

Though Randolph looked surprised at Nikki's sudden animation, he couldn't have been nearly as shocked as she was. *Listen to me. I suddenly sound like some kind of comparative religion guru.*

"And your religion does?" Randolph said, chasing the sarcasm with a sip of martini.

"Actually, *my* religion tries to balance suffering by even greater amounts of partying," said Nikki, bringing the sly smile back to Randolph's face.

"I think I'm a bishop in that religion," he said.

"But seriously, Preston, Christianity at least describes an afterlife where all our suffering is over, where perfect justice is done. Buddhism just keeps recycling us so we can face more suffering and injustice."

This brought an unnerving stare from Randolph, as if he were trying to look into Nikki's soul and see if she really believed that herself. Part of her discomfort was in not knowing the answer. She took a quick swig from a nearly empty wine glass.

Randolph poured her another. "Did you know that I lost a cousin in the 9/11 attacks?" he asked.

The question shocked Nikki. And she suddenly felt silly debating religion with a man who had lost a relative at the hands of religious extremists. "No. I'm sorry."

The sadness returned to Randolph's eyes, aging the man by a good ten years. "She left behind two kids and a husband who doesn't have a clue about how to raise them alone."

"That's terrible," said Nikki. What else could she say? This was *so* uncomfortable. But it was also helping her see a different side of Randolph. An insecure side. A searching side.

"It makes you feel helpless," said Randolph. "All the money in the world can't bring her back. It's the first thing I tell my clients when they want to sue somebody for wrongful death."

And then dessert arrived. It was hard to talk of suffering while eating such delicious raspberry cheesecake, so Randolph directed the conversation back to his favorite topic—war stories from his various trials. Nikki was actually relieved.

Dessert was nearly gone when Nikki suddenly remembered to call Wellington and tell him that he no longer had to be on standby for her meeting with the FBI agents.

"How'd it go?" asked Wellington.

"The FBI is all over it," Nikki said, faking as much enthusiasm as possible.

∽

It was the little things that made Finney want to quit in the first hour. A water droplet formed on the side of his nose, tickling him, but he couldn't wipe it off. Water running into his eyes and lodging in his ears. One lousy drop at a time, yet he felt like he was drowning, the water dripping down the sides of his face and soaking his hair.

Splat...splat...splat...splat. He answered all of Dr. Hargraves's questions and told the shrink he was doing fine. A few minutes later, Dr. Andrews appeared and checked Finney's vital signs. The doctor expressed concern about the blood pressure but let the judge continue. That was the only human contact Finney had the entire first hour.

Splat...splat...splat...splat. Finney began counting. Sets of four and repeat. He estimated forty or so drips a minute. Twenty-four hundred drops an hour. He opened his eyes and checked the digital clock on the wall. He worked on the breathing techniques the Swami had shown him. He consciously thought about his heart rate, the swoosh of blood through his veins, and he tried to slow it down. *Splat...splat...splat.* When Hargraves and Andrews returned at the top of the second hour, Finney's blood pressure had improved.

The chills started in hour three. The water was colder than room temperature and seemed to grow more chilling by the minute. The rivulets flowing through his hair turned into icy spiders. His body itched everywhere. He put on a brave face for Andrews but could tell the doc was concerned. Andrews made Finney take a drink of Powerade through a straw. *Splat...splat...splat...splat.*

At three hours and twenty minutes, the headache became noticeable. Twenty minutes later, it was all Finney could think about. His mind started playing tricks on him—he pictured the drops like a waterfall that would carve canyons out of rocks over time. He imagined the indentation starting on his forehead. At three hours and fifty-five minutes, he had to consciously relax or he knew the shrink would make him quit.

Hargraves showed up and asked the same questions as before. Finney answered calmly, hypnotically. His speech had fallen into rhythm with the *splat...splat...splat.* A few minutes later, Dr. Andrews arrived and made Finney drink some more Powerade. "Not too much," said Andrews, "or you'll have to use the bathroom."

"Thanks for making me think about *that*," said Finney. "Just what I needed."

"We can make those arrangements," said Andrews.

"I'll be fine," said Finney.

"See you in another hour," said Andrews.

Surprisingly, the next few hours got better. The headache stayed about the same, but Finney fought back the chills. He even stopped counting for a while, though that didn't last long. His own compulsiveness was adding to the torture, he realized. But there wasn't a thing he could do about it.

The shackles seemed to shrink as the torture progressed, growing more and more uncomfortable. They rubbed against his neck, wrists, and ankles. The experience wouldn't be half as bad if he could just move around more.

At the end of hour seven, just as Finney was trying to calm himself in preparation for his visit from Dr. Hargraves, he started coughing. He had been hacking away periodically throughout the time in the chair, but never at the precise moment when the doctors entered the room. This time, he couldn't bring himself to stop before Hargraves walked in the door.

"We need to call it quits," suggested Hargraves, but Finney wouldn't hear of it. When the judge finally stopped coughing, he insisted that Hargraves bring in Andrews so that the medical doctor could make the call. By the time Andrews arrived, Finney had returned to a nearly vegetative state. "The vitals look fine," said Andrews. "If you want, you can stay on another hour."

The next hour was the longest Finney could remember. The water seemed to explode on his forehead—*splat, splat, splat...boom!* The chills returned with a vengeance, and the headache became nearly unbearable. The doctors consulted and agreed that Finney should quit. He begged for another twenty minutes.

He never dreamed it would be this hard to endure the water torture for eight hours. The next twenty minutes clicked by ever so slowly—five minutes, ten minutes, fifteen. How did victims of torture ever survive? At eight hours and sixteen minutes, Finney started watching every click of the digital clock, his open eyes stinging from the water. *Splat, splat, splat...* He flinched each time a new drop hit. And then, at precisely eight hours, sixteen minutes, and thirty-five seconds, he pushed the panic button.

The drops stopped immediately.

A few minutes later, Dr. Andrews entered the room. "That was a good choice, Judge Finney," he said. Andrews started unfastening the shackles and checking vital signs. "Dr. Hargraves and I were starting to worry about you."

"Who's left?" asked Finney.

"Just Ando and Hadji."

"Good," said Finney. "How's Hadji holding up?"

Andrews didn't answer for a minute as he counted Finney's pulse. Then he said, "He's totally relaxed. Seems like he could go forever."

Finney wiped some more water out of his eyes and smoothed back his hair. "Let's hope so," he said.

CHAPTER 56

L ate Thursday afternoon, Nikki received a call from Agent Flynn, her least favorite of the two FBI agents. She had described him as "the little Napoleon" when she told Wellington about him, though the phrase was probably redundant.

"We just got done talking to the show's producer and director," Flynn reported. "They answered every one of our questions. You can relax. Apparently they're just raising suspicions among the contestants as part of the reality-show game."

"And you believed them?" Nikki asked.

"Of course." Flynn ramped up the defensiveness in his voice. "They had scripts already written showing how that element would play out. Something about seeing how the contestants' faiths hold up when they're facing death."

"Did you talk to the contestants?"

"No, we didn't talk to the contestants. It tends to ruin the element of surprise when you fill the contestants in on what's happening." Nikki did not appreciate the sarcasm oozing over the phone lines. "And frankly, I wouldn't even be telling you this if I thought you still had a way of communicating with Judge Finney. But, according to the show's producer, they've suspended the Internet access for the contestants."

The comment jarred Nikki. Her only means of communication with Finney disrupted. "Why?"

"Because the contestants don't need it anymore. That part of the show's over."

To Nikki, the timing seemed too coincidental. "Did you conduct any searches?"

"No."

"Talk to any assistant producers or production crew members?"

"Ms. Moreno, we arrived unannounced on the island. We immediately began asking the producer and director questions, and they both got these snide little smiles on their faces like Agent Rafferty and I were the butt of some clever joke. Since I don't like being laughed at, I ripped into them pretty good. But then they showed me the preexisting scripts for the last few shows where all of this will be unveiled. It became clear that my partner and I were wasting our time."

Nikki could tell this was going nowhere. And maybe the guy had a point. Besides, if the show's producer or director had been thinking about offing Finney, he would have to reconsider now that the FBI was investigating.

"Did you tell them about the codes?" Nikki asked.

Flynn let the silence hang long enough to make Nikki worry. "No. We protected our source," he said at last. "Just like we promised. But they were very curious."

The phone fell silent again as Nikki considered her next move. If there even needed to be a next move. It just didn't seem like Finney would be so easily duped.

"You're welcome," said Flynn.

"Oh yeah," said Nikki. "Thanks."

∾

Thursday-night's show was a mixed bag for Finney. On the good side, it was announced that he won the viewers' verdict for the Tuesday episode. Norfolk's Finest Sports Bar exploded with approval, and Nikki couldn't wipe the grin off her face. Finney *had* done well on the cross-examination segment, but Nikki also suspected that he got a few sympathy votes based on his botched escape attempt. Hey, a victory was a victory.

The show's producers announced that Finney had designated World Changers as the recipient of his fifty-thousand-dollar prize. They showed a few clips of World Changers in action—Christian high-school and college students who spend part of the summer rehabilitating inner-city homes for the poor and disabled. Nikki nearly teared up as they interviewed a few of the residents whose lives had been changed.

She gave out congratulatory hugs for the rest of the night, even to Byron, who seemed to be at her elbow every time she turned around.

Finney didn't fare as well in the water-torture aspects of the show, dropping out after only eight hours. Patrons of the bar had mixed opinions about how hard it would be to go the full twenty-four hours, as Dr. Ando had done. Byron told anybody who would listen that he could have lasted at least three days.

As soon as the closing credits rolled, Nikki received a call. "Did you see what Finney said?" the caller asked.

Between the background noise and the poor reception, Nikki could barely hear. "Wellington?"

The reply broke up, and Nikki closed her other ear with a finger, ducking her head to get away from the noise.

"Can you hear me now?" the caller asked.

"A little better. What's up?"

"We've got to meet," said Wellington. "Did you hear what Finney said?"

∾

As a matter of protocol, the Assassin checked the offshore account one last time. It was the third bank he had used this week, transferring the funds each day. Internet banking through his secure satellite phone—the wonders of modern technology. Tomorrow he would begin diversifying the seven hundred thousand dollars, spreading it around between several different banks. He would begin investing as soon as he had finished laundering the additional eight hundred thousand that would be deposited on Saturday.

He reviewed his plan again, probing for any details he may have missed. He was not happy about having the Client involved in the hit, but the Client had insisted that this one was personal. The Client wanted to watch the victim die. The Client wanted to taunt the victim as he drew a last breath. The Client wanted to humiliate the man.

The Assassin should have doubled the rate.

The hardest part, he knew, would be making it look like an accident. But he had a backup plan for that, too. A scapegoat. How fitting, in the midst of a religious show like this, to have a scapegoat ready to take all the blame for the sins of others.

The Assassin's escape would be easy. By the middle of next week, the Assassin would virtually be a new man—facial plastic surgery, hair implants, the works. He would change his body type as much as possible over the next two months, hitting the gym every day. Big weights, low reps. Hired killers gained and lost more weight than movie stars.

The only loose end would be his client. And if the Client started getting shaky, the Assassin had been known to eliminate that problem as well. Gratis. What was that saying? "Two men can keep a secret...if one of them is dead."

It was nothing personal. The Assassin just didn't like loose ends. Made it hard to sleep at night.

He e-mailed the Seeker.

Everything is poised for completion on Saturday. Nobody suspects a thing.
    Azrael

CHAPTER 57

Nikki's enthusiasm for solving Finney's riddles had been dampened considerably by her conversation with Agent Flynn. She now believed it was entirely possible that Finney had been duped by the show's producers into thinking that a murder conspiracy was afoot when it was really just part of the show.

Wellington held the opposite view. If the agents were no longer going to help in the investigation, Finney's fate now rested entirely in Wellington's and Nikki's hands. "The judge is too smart to get suckered by a game," argued Wellington. "There's more to it than that."

He was so insistent that Nikki agreed to meet him at Starbucks after the show. Wellington had his computer up and running by the time she arrived. He motioned her over before she could even order a drink.

"I TiVoed the show and then transferred it to my computer," he said, clicking on a desktop icon. "Then I cut and spliced a couple segments I want you to see."

Another few clicks, and Wellington's Windows Media Player showed Finney being strapped into his chair for the Chinese water torture. "Listen to what he says," Wellington told Nikki.

On the screen Bryce McCormack asked Finney if he had any predictions. "I would say myself and the Swami are the ones to watch," Finney said. "We're the only ones who know the key to outlasting this thing."

Wellington hit the Stop button. "Did you hear that?"

Nikki nodded, watching as Wellington pulled up another clip. "This is the Swami," Wellington said.

The clip started playing. The Swami was already strapped into the chair, and the camera zoomed in for a closeup. "You want to know who's going to win this thing?" the Swami asked. "Sure," said Bryce McCormack's voice off camera.

"Judge Finney or me," said the Swami. "I taught him a few relaxation techniques, so we're the only ones who know the key to beating this thing."

Wellington hit the Stop button and looked at Nikki. "What do you think?"

"Sounds pretty coincidental," Nikki admitted. "They both refer to themselves as understanding the key." She tried to act calm, but a rush of excitement was crawling across her skin. "Sounds like another message from Finney."

"Exactly. Since he can't access the Internet anymore, he's using the show itself."

"Maybe," Nikki cautioned. "But how did he even know that the show would air both those remarks? I mean, they edit out a lot of stuff."

"Maybe he didn't. Maybe that's why both he and the Swami said basically the same thing, hoping the network would air at least one of them. And let's face it—a boastful prediction by a losing contestant is bound to get airtime."

As usual, Wellington was making sense. "Wonder when that footage was shot?" mumbled Nikki. She was in her thinking-out-loud mode now. "Maybe it was shot even before we got his last message."

"I doubt it," responded Wellington. "He didn't send any messages on the other shows. As long as he could communicate through Westlaw, it was safer. I think this is a recent message. I think it's a last resort."

"Let me watch them again," Nikki said.

After a second time through the clips, Nikki was still confused. "But what's the message? What's the key?"

"That's what I've been trying to figure out," Wellington said. "It's certainly not obvious. So far, I've come up with two possibilities."

"I'm all ears."

Wellington twisted his lips, searching for the best way to explain this.

"There's either a message in the words that he and the Swami used or there's a message tied in to the amount of time they spent in the chairs. I'm thinking it's probably time in the chairs, because Finney would have no way of knowing how much of what he and the Swami said would be edited out."

Nikki could sense the start of a long night. "You want something to drink?"

"Bottled water and pound cake," said Wellington.

Code breakers are such creatures of habit, thought Nikki.

∾

Nikki felt a hand gently shaking her shoulder. "Ms. Moreno."

She cracked an eyelid and tried to reorient herself. The cobwebs cleared enough so that she remembered where she was. Wellington's house. They had changed locations when the Starbucks closed. Wellington had been working on cracking any possible code formed by the amount of time Finney and Hadji had stayed with the Chinese water torture. Nikki had written down everything that Finney and Hadji said on the Thursday-night show and started looking for clues in the words. She remembered curling up on the couch for a quick nap around 2:00 a.m.

"What time is it?" Nikki asked, her voice hoarse, her eyes still closed.

"Um…I'm not really sure. Maybe about four or so."

Nikki grunted and rubbed her face. She was about to sit up when she felt a little fur ball jump on top of her, wiggle around, and then lick her face.

"Corky!" Wellington yelled, but it was too late. Nikki had already backhanded the little monster onto the floor.

Corky yelped and Nikki sat straight up, wiping her cheek.

"Sorry about that," said Wellington, rubbing the little dog's head. "He likes waking people up."

"Don't worry about it," Nikki muttered. She stared straight ahead, still waiting for her full senses to come back to her. Nobody had ever accused Nikki of being a morning person.

"Let me run Corky up to my mom's bedroom, and then I want to show you something," said Wellington.

"Good idea," Nikki managed. She checked her watch. It really was 4:00 a.m.

When Wellington headed upstairs, Nikki stumbled to the kitchen and poured a glass of water. Her mouth felt like scum. Her only goal in life was to get into her own bed as soon as possible.

She was standing against the counter finishing the water when Wellington returned. His eyes were bloodshot and his hair tousled. "You want some coffee?" he asked.

"I want my bed."

"Okay, but first let me show you what I found." His voice smacked of enthusiasm. Nikki didn't do enthusiasm when she was this tired.

"Wellington, can't it wait—"

"Just one second. You won't believe this!"

He went into the living room and retrieved his *Cross Examination* book. He placed it on the counter in front of Nikki alongside a piece of paper with all kinds of numbers and letters that blurred together. At the top were the numbers 8, 16, 35, 17, 33, 59.

"This is the amount of time that Finney and Hadji stayed with the water torture," Wellington explained as he pointed. "I've watched the tape a dozen times. They were both watching the clock at the precise moment when they pushed the panic button. That's significant, because both of them had their eyes closed for most of the time but opened them right at the end."

Nikki yawned. She could feel a long explanation coming, and she could barely keep her eyes open as it was.

"Both of them mentioned Finney's name first when they talked about knowing the key, so I wrote down Finney's time first."

"Makes sense." Another big yawn.

"So, what do these numbers mean?" But before Nikki could give Wellington a dirty look, he recovered. "That's the question I asked myself. The next two chapters in the *Cross Examination* book use letters as the ciphertext, not numbers, so I ruled out those chapters."

"Can we sit down?" Nikki asked. The couch wasn't the same as her bed, but it beat standing.

"Sure."

Wellington took a seat next to Nikki on the couch and placed the paper on the coffee table in front of them. Nikki glanced longingly at the couch pillow. "So I started looking at chapter seven, which is the next chapter that uses numbers for the ciphertext," Wellington explained. "Maybe the water torture was filmed while Finney was still using the Internet, so maybe he didn't know what chapter we would be on when the show aired. He figured he would just skip ahead a few chapters to the next one with numbers and make it easy."

Nikki leaned back and snuggled down into the couch. She felt her muscles begin to relax.

"But then I couldn't figure out the key to chapter seven and therefore couldn't even test my theory. I tried every type of frequency analysis and every other trick known to cryptanalysts. I nearly gave up but then decided to do something I should have done at the beginning—just run the sequence of numbers as a search on the Internet. Guess what I came up with?"

The words had been fading in and out, Wellington's adolescent voice putting Nikki to sleep. Ironically, it was the quiet that brought her back. "I'm sorry—what?"

"Guess what I found out on the Internet?"

"Oh. I'm not really sure," Nikki said, yawning again.

"The Beale cipher!" Wellington exclaimed. "The numbers in chapter seven have been copied from the Beale cipher."

"I never would have guessed," said Nikki. She sank lower and put her legs up on the coffee table.

"You ever heard of it?" asked Wellington.

"Sure," said Nikki, hoping to avoid another convoluted story about some super-duper cipher person. But it didn't work. Wellington started a windy monologue about the history of the Beale cipher, and Nikki could tell he wasn't going to stop and catch his breath anytime soon. She rested her eyelids and, for the next ten minutes, listened to his story. Wellington actually gave her the twenty-minute version, but she didn't hear the last half until he woke her up at 7:00 a.m. and repeated everything he had said in the wee hours of the night.

CHAPTER 58

The story began in 1820 when Thomas J. Beale rode into Lynchburg, Virginia, and checked in at the prestigious Washington Hotel. Handsome and charming, Beale spent the winter in Lynchburg, befriending the innkeeper and wooing the ladies. He left town in March, as quickly and mysteriously as he came, and he wasn't heard from again for nearly two years.

He returned to spend another winter in 1822, enchanting the town once again with his winsome personality and unmatched attractiveness. This time he left a locked iron box containing "papers of value and importance" with the innkeeper. The innkeeper placed the box in a safe and didn't think much more about it until he received a letter from Beale two months later.

"It contains papers vitally affecting the fortunes of myself and many others," Beale wrote. "Should none of us ever return you will please preserve carefully the box for the period of ten years from the date of this letter, and if I, or no one with authority from me, during that time demands its restoration, you will open it, which can be done by removing the lock. You will find...papers which will be unintelligible without the aid of a key to assist you. Such a key I have left in the hand of a friend in this place, sealed and addressed to yourself, and endorsed not to be delivered until June 1832."

Beale never passed through Lynchburg again, and his friend never sent the key. Absent the key, the innkeeper saw no point in opening the box, until his curiosity won out in 1845, more than twenty years after he last saw Beale. The box contained three enciphered pages of numbers, together with a note from Beale in plain English.

In the note Beale explained that he and some friends had struck gold

near Santa Fe during the summer of 1820. He made two trips to Lynchburg to bury the treasure and then enciphered the three notes included in
the box. The first note set forth the location of the treasure. The second
note contained a description of the treasure. The third note listed the rel-
atives of the men who should receive a share of the treasure.

For twenty years the innkeeper tried to decipher the notes without a
key, but his quest ended in failure. When he turned eighty-four, the
innkeeper conceded defeat and realized that the secret of the Beale ciphers
would die with him if he didn't tell somebody. He entrusted the Beale
ciphers to an anonymous friend, who in turn tried his hand at solving the
ciphers for another twenty years. Miraculously, he was able to solve the
second of the ciphers, revealing the description of the treasure with a
twenty-first century value of more than twenty million dollars. But he
could never crack the first cipher, the one containing the location. And so,
more than twenty years after he first obtained possession of the Beale
ciphers, the friend decided to turn over custody of the matter to the world.

In 1885 this man anonymously published a pamphlet entitled *The
Beale Papers*. He refused to reveal his own name, "to avoid the multitude
of letters with which I should be assailed from all sections of the Union,
propounding all sorts of questions…which would absorb my entire
time…. I have given all that I know of the matter [in this pamphlet] and
cannot add one word to the statements herein contained."

The pamphlet contained copies of the Beale ciphers and detailed their
history. The author also described how he had solved the second Beale
cipher after years of work. He initially assumed that the page contained a
substitution cipher, with various numbers being substituted for letters of
the alphabet. Since the code contained numbers as large as 807, the
author assumed that Beale had done what Edgar Allan Poe and numerous
others had done to defeat frequency analysis—used several different code
symbols to stand for the more popular letters.

One popular way to create a key for such a cipher had been through the use of a book cipher. In this type of cipher, a code maker would first number the words in a book or document. The first word would be number one, the next word number two, and so on. That number would always refer to the first letter of the word that matched the number.

By applying this analysis, the author of the Beale pamphlet discovered that Beale had used the Declaration of Independence as the key for the second Beale cipher. But the first Beale cipher, the one that contained the location of the treasure, did not prove so easy to crack.

And still today, more than one hundred and twenty years after publication of the Beale pamphlet, the biggest computers and brightest minds have been unable to solve the cipher that holds the key to a buried treasure worth twenty million dollars.

Until now?

∽

Even at seven o'clock in the morning, Nikki grasped the significance of this piece of history. The mention of twenty million dollars can wake a girl up fast.

"Judge Finney used the beginning of Beale's first cipher, number for number, as his key for chapter seven," explained Wellington. He looked at the page again, with a sleep-deprived trance that Nikki found unnerving. "Which means that the judge must've cracked a cipher that most cryptanalysts concluded was impenetrable."

Nikki tried to blink herself fully awake. Her boss? A millionaire? A multi-multimillionaire?

"And," continued Wellington, dejection creeping into his voice, "it means that unless we can solve the first Beale cipher, we might never be able to decrypt the message Finney sent on TV last night. The key to the Beale cipher might die with him."

"Have you got any coffee?" Nikki asked.

PART 5

VERDICT

Ladies and gentlemen, the term
"verdict"…literally means "to speak the
truth" and I charge you to do precisely that.
—JURY CHARGE, *Ware v. Rodale Press Inc.*

You will know the truth, and
the truth will set you free.
—JESUS CHRIST

CHAPTER 59

On Friday morning the contestants gathered for their day of reckoning in Paradise Court. Kareem Hasaan took his seat next to Finney, looking tense and formal in one of his custom-designed Italian suits, which seemed to hang a little looser on the man after five days of fasting. He had pulled out of the Chinese water torture after four hours, calling it "a ridiculous exercise in masochism." He told the cameras that Allah didn't subject his servants to torture in order to prove that he was god.

Dr. Ando came dressed in his traditional Buddhist robes. The man was fast becoming a legend on Paradise Island. He lasted all twenty-four hours on the Chinese water torture and probably could have gone days longer. Though he looked tired and frail, Finney knew better. It was rumored that Ando's heart rate, blood pressure, and breathing actually slowed down during the last few hours of the ordeal.

"He probably went back to his room and took a nap on a bed of nails," Gus quipped.

The Swami lasted more than seventeen hours, just as he and Finney had planned, though the Swami later confessed that his meditation techniques had failed him during the last few painful hours.

Next to the Swami sat Dr. Kline, looking stunning and rested for this final courtroom session. She was wearing a classic black sleeveless dress, with a modest silver necklace and matching bracelet. She had pressed the panic button as soon as the first drop fell on her forehead. "Rational people do not voluntarily subject themselves to torture," she said.

She has a point, Finney had to admit.

Javitts took the bench, wearing his normal dour expression. He gaveled the session to order and began by congratulating Dr. Ando for his victory in the Chinese water torture. The stoic contestant nodded humbly, and Javitts moved on to the next item.

"Today we will be selecting two finalists in a procedure that has remained a secret until this moment." Javitts surveyed the contestants and then gazed into a camera at the back of the room. "Throughout your time on Paradise Island, we have emphasized that the important thing is not whether you can defend your faith in a courtroom setting but how well you live your faith day to day. The real crucible of your cross-examination does not take place on this witness stand or even in the cross-examination room. It occurs in your interactions with others, in the challenges you face, in the unexpected tragedies nobody can explain. The question becomes: do you have something special in those times that can only be explained by faith?

"And who knows the answer to that question better than your fellow contestants?"

Finney could see where this was headed—a *Survivor*-type voting process. But, as usual, the producers of the show had a twist.

"We've looked at the voting procedures for all past reality shows," continued Javitts, his tone solemn for the occasion. "And we've decided to combine the best of those procedures for this, the ultimate reality game show. Accordingly, here's the way we will proceed.

"In a few minutes, you will be given a ballot with your name on it. Later today you will cast either one or two votes. You may vote for yourself and one other person. If you don't vote for yourself, then you cast only one vote." Javitts waited a few seconds for this to sink in. The cameras scanned the faces of the contestants.

"The contestant who receives the most votes will be one finalist. As the judge, it will be my sole prerogative to select the other. Those two finalists will stay on the island for one additional day. The rest of you will pack this afternoon and leave after lunch and one final session in the cross-examination room." Had Finney heard right? *Lunch?*

"The finalists will each give a closing argument tomorrow. After the final show airs, the viewing audience will select the winner between the two finalists, based on the same voting procedures we've established for earlier shows."

Finney was surprised at how much tension crackled in the air. His own palms turned sweaty, and he felt a coughing fit coming on. No matter how often he told himself that this was just a reality show, that his entire job was to glorify God in the way he played the show, he still wanted to win. Badly. And it wasn't just his competitive instincts. He saw this as a vindication of his faith—one bold and final stroke to reach the next generation before he passed into eternity.

Yet he doubted that his dream would ever come to pass. He had sent an encoded message to Nikki, instructing her to get the feds involved and stop this madness. Unless Wellington failed to decode that message, which Finney doubted, there would be no final session to win.

Still, Finney wanted to at least make the finals. Yes, pride was involved. And yes, vindication was involved. But if for some reason the feds never showed up, danger was also involved.

Making the finals, from all appearances, was a game of Russian roulette. Both Victoria Kline and Kareem Hasaan had allegedly discovered the same thing—a plot existed to kill one of the finalists. Even the Swami, who didn't trust anything Kareem said, agreed with Finney's analysis—a conspiracy was afoot. And the conspirators were already setting up their scapegoats.

For Finney, this danger was one more reason he wanted to make the finals. The other contestants, except for Dr. Ando, were relatively young. Kareem and Hadji both had at least a possibility of surviving their illnesses, and Kline wasn't even sick. If anybody had to be at risk, Finney reasoned, it might as well be him.

"At eleven o'clock you will return to this courtroom one at a time, in alphabetical order, to cast your ballots," Javitts continued. "At noon I will announce your verdict and select the other finalist. But before you retire to deliberate, I have one final announcement that I have been asked to make." He paused and cleared his throat. "We have the results of the medical tests performed earlier this week."

With everything else going on, Finney had forgotten all about the medical tests. But Javitts gave him no time to mull it over. "Unfortunately," Javitts continued, "there have been no changes in your various medical conditions. The God who heals apparently decided not to intervene in this show."

In his peripheral vision, Finney caught Kareem's reaction. His Muslim friend stared straight ahead without flinching, as if he had expected this news all along.

∾

By 9:00 a.m. Nikki and Wellington had shifted their base of operations to the dining-room table. Nikki still had on her outfit from the night before—her favorite pair of faded and ripped jeans, together with a sheer V-neck sleeveless silk top and matching silk camisole. She had kicked off her sandals at the door last night, and her hair was so frizzed out this morning that she tucked it all up inside one of Wellington's caps—a new ODU hat with a bill that stuck straight out. Her mouth tasted like dog's breath until she squeezed some toothpaste out of the tube in the Farnsworths' bathroom and rubbed it on her teeth with her finger.

Corky was hanging around her feet in spite of her best efforts to give him occasional kicks in the chops. Wellington was hunkered over his charts and graphs, his head nearly dropping on the table out of pure exhaustion. Nikki felt wide awake, spurred on by two cups of coffee and the thought of twenty million dollars.

She didn't bother trying to solve the famous Beale cipher on her own. If Wellington and a hundred and fifty years of the brightest minds available couldn't crack it, what chance did she have? Instead, she took an entirely different approach. She assumed that Finney had somehow solved the cipher and, as with every other chapter, had given hints about the key in the chapter itself.

She carefully read every word of chapter seven, a chapter entitled "Jesus Takes the Fifth." In it, Finney wrote about the one time when Jesus refused to answer a question from the Pharisees. When they asked Jesus where His authority came from, He answered their question with one of His own: "Where did John's baptism come from? From heaven or from men?" Since the Pharisees didn't dare answer that question, Christ refused to answer the one they had asked Him.

Finney's point: we can't expect God to answer every one of our *why* questions. Sometimes we have to operate on faith.

When Nikki finished chapter seven, she read straight through chapter eight, another chapter that used numbers instead of letters for its code.

Chapter eight dealt with Christ's response when the Pharisees asked Him about paying taxes. One phrase in particular almost jumped off the page at Nikki. In discussing the separation of church and state, Finney wrote something that couldn't possibly be a coincidence. "You can mark Jefferson's words in the Declaration—an exercise that will generate no fewer than four independent references to God."

Mark Jefferson's words, Finney had written. The key to the second Beale cipher! Nikki—on her own—had just discovered the key to chapter eight.

"Have you got a copy of the Declaration of Independence?" Nikki asked.

A tired Wellington looked at her like he couldn't be bothered. "Not on me," he said, and Nikki couldn't tell whether he was being sarcastic.

"Can you look it up on the computer?"

A few minutes later, Nikki was reading the Declaration and counting words. She felt a surge of excitement but kept her cool. It would be more fun to do it this way.

"Did you read chapter seven?" Nikki asked.

"Sure," Wellington said without looking up.

"What about chapter eight?"

Wellington put down his pencil, sighed, and gave Nikki a perturbed look. "I skimmed it," he said.

"Okay, so chapter seven is all about trusting God even when we don't understand what he's doing. Right?"

A small glint of curiosity sliced through the redness in Wellington's eyes. "Yes?" he said tentatively, like a question.

"And chapter eight is about the separation of church and state. It even references the Declaration of Independence, you know."

"I guess I hadn't caught that," admitted Wellington. Nikki thought she might burst with pride. Maybe wearing the guy's ODU hat did something magical.

"So think about it, Wellington. God doesn't always answer our questions. There are some things we will never understand. Just like there are some ciphers we will never figure out. Get it?"

Wellington knit his eyebrows as Nikki continued. *How can he not see this?* "So the judge uses a cipher for chapter seven that he knows nobody can figure out—at least nobody has for one hundred and fifty years. The first Beale cipher. Finney didn't figure it out, either, but he used it to illustrate the point of the chapter. And then, for chapter eight he uses the second Beale cipher, the one that depends on the Declaration."

"And the numbers from the water torture correspond to the second Beale cipher," said Wellington, finally picking up on Nikki's thought. "It's the only chapter that uses just numbers where we actually have a key."

Nikki nodded. It was fun being the teacher for a change. It would have been even more fun if solving the puzzle didn't require admitting that the first Beale cipher remained unsolved. *As soon as we get Finney off that island,* Nikki promised herself, *I'm going to make Wellington work on the first Beale cipher nonstop until he solves it.*

"Unbelievable," said Wellington, shaking his head. "I fell right into the classic code breaker's trap." Instead of the look of triumph that Nikki expected—after all, they *were* partners—Wellington's look was closer to shame. "I made an assumption and treated it as fact. Just like the code breakers who, for hundreds of years, thought the substitution cipher could not be cracked. They were using linguistic skills when they should have been focused on the mathematics, the frequency analysis. I was looking at chapter seven when I should have been focused on chapter eight."

Nikki wanted to interrupt him, but his rambling analysis sounded too much like a confession to cut him off. She let the silence hang there for a moment as Wellington's tired cranium processed his failure. "I don't think I would have ever thought of looking at chapter eight," Wellington admitted.

"That's why we're partners," said Nikki. "Even Einstein needed help once in a while." Nikki had no idea if it was true, but it seemed like the right thing to say.

Wellington appeared to ponder this for a moment and then make peace with it. "So, what's it say?" he asked. "Have you applied the Declaration as the key to Finney's water-torture message?"

"Here's what you get," announced Nikki. "It's PER."

"PER?" repeated Wellington. "What's PER?"

Nikki paused, extending her moment in the sun for a few more seconds. She couldn't wait to see the look on Finney's face someday soon when she got a chance to tell him she outsmarted his golden boy.

"PER is Preston Edgar Randolph," announced Nikki. "He's apparently the one behind this murder conspiracy."

Wellington's mouth dropped open—the same reaction Nikki had when she first figured it out. "How could Finney know that?" Wellington asked.

"You got me. But we've been playing right into Randolph's hands."

CHAPTER 60

Nikki felt grubbier by the minute, but she had no time for hygiene. She barely had time, at the stoplights on her way to downtown Norfolk, to freshen up her makeup. She called Wellington's cell a few times on the way—she wanted to tell him to pick up the pace—but even in a crisis of this magnitude, the boy apparently wouldn't answer his cell phone while driving.

Nikki parked in her normal spot in the parking lot of the courthouse building and tried to wave Wellington and his minivan into a handicapped spot. But the kid was unwilling to bend even the tiniest rule and ended up parking in a public garage about a block away. Nikki waited for him on the front steps of the courthouse, growing more impatient by the minute as he lumbered toward her, making sure he didn't cross St. Paul's Boulevard against the light.

"C'mon, Wellington. We don't have all day."

"Sorry."

Next, Nikki thought Wellington would have a nervous breakdown when she took his arm and forced him to cut with her to the front of the metal-detector line.

"Man, I'm starting to love casual Fridays," said one of the deputies, eying Nikki's tight jeans and sheer top.

"How many times did you vote for Judge Finney this week?" Nikki asked as she cavorted through the detectors.

"Must have been a hundred," said the first deputy.

"Double whatever he says," the other chimed in.

"He's with me," Nikki said, pointing back to Wellington.

From there, it took Nikki ten minutes to locate Deputy Common-wealth's Attorney Mitchell Taylor and another five to talk him into asking another attorney to handle his hearings that morning. In Mitchell's office, Nikki and Wellington raced through the entire saga, including the fact that phone calls to the FBI that morning had confirmed that no Agent Rafferty worked at the FBI. There was an Agent Flynn, but he had not worked on this case.

"I told them I was calling from the commonwealth's attorney's office in Norfolk on your behalf," Nikki admitted, "investigating a possible indictment for impersonating a police officer." As she described it out loud, even Nikki had to admit that her conduct had been a little ironic. She had impersonated a prosecutor to investigate someone who had impersonated an FBI agent. She braced herself for a reprimand, but Mitchell just frowned, too deep in thought to get worked up about Nikki's small lie.

"What are you asking me to do?" he asked.

"Indict Randolph. Save Finney. Get an arrest warrant." Nikki was throwing out alternatives as quickly as Mitchell rejected them with a knit brow or subtle shake of the head. "I don't know—do your prosecutor thing."

Mitchell leaned forward, elbows on his desk. "Our prosecutor thing, Nikki, requires jurisdiction. I want to help—Judge Finney is probably my all-time favorite judge—but if we don't follow the book on this one…" Mitchell grimaced. "Randolph is a powerful man. He'll never serve a minute, and we'll be facing a multimillion-dollar lawsuit."

Nikki couldn't believe she was hearing this from Mitchell Taylor. He had never shied away from a fight in his life, as far as Nikki knew.

"A judge's life is at stake!" she blurted out. "And you're worried about lawsuits."

Mitchell didn't blink. "I'm worried about making these charges stick. And doing it the right way so Randolph doesn't make us all look like fools.

To accomplish that, I need jurisdiction, Nikki. The problem here is that none of these things happened in Norfolk. You've got Judge Finney on an island who knows where—"

"The Galápagos," Nikki interrupted.

"How do you know that?" Mitchell asked.

Oh yeah, thought Nikki. *Randolph.* "I guess we don't."

"Which is my point," Mitchell continued. "We don't even know where the judge is, but we can assume it's not Norfolk. Plus, the only evidence we have that anything is wrong on that island are these cryptic messages from the judge—"

Nikki started to interrupt again, but Mitchell held up a hand. "Let me finish. We've got Randolph in DC presumably conspiring to help two other gentlemen impersonate FBI agents, but Randolph would probably just say that those men duped him, too—"

"But Randolph claimed to know them," Nikki said. "Plus, I've talked to him about it on the phone from here in Norfolk—doesn't that count for something?"

Mitchell shook his head. "That could make it a federal wire-fraud case—a phone call across state lines from DC to Virginia—but we'd have a hard time claiming jurisdiction. The impersonation took place in DC. This alleged conspiracy is taking place in DC *and* on some unidentified island."

Nikki could feel her frustrations rising, the red tape of government prosecution strangling every attempt to act quickly and decisively. Mitchell Taylor was the one person in the prosecutor's office who would shoot first and ask questions later. But even he was struggling to get through the red tape on this one.

They eventually agreed to call the DC prosecutor's office. Mitchell tried to prepare Nikki beforehand, explaining that he had good relationships with the commonwealth's attorneys in Virginia but didn't know anybody in DC. His warning turned out to be prophetic. Despite Mitchell's best efforts to explain the urgency of the case, Nikki could hear the skepticism bleeding across the phone lines in the gruff voice of an experienced DC prosecutor named Kenneth Bell. Mitchell at first pushed for an indictment on the impersonation charge, then dropped back and asked Bell to at least obtain a search warrant for Randolph's computer and office.

"Tell me again the evidence that we would present to the judge in order to get this search warrant against one of the most powerful lawyers in DC?" Bell asked.

Nikki had heard enough. Even on a good night's sleep, she wasn't known for her patience. But this morning, with little sleep, no shower, and Finney's life on the line, she couldn't help but explode. She lashed out at Bell, sprinkling her tirade with enough profanity so that Mitchell had to hit the mute button.

"You done?" he asked when Nikki finally fell silent.

She snorted in response. Mitchell took the phone off mute and asked Bell to bring Randolph in for questioning.

"Don't do that," Nikki said sharply. "That will just tip him off." She was practically pulling her hair out.

Mitchell looked at her with concern in his expressive brown eyes. The look calmed her a little, reassurance that Mitchell was on her side.

"What do you want me to do?" Bell asked. "I know you're frustrated, but you've got to give me something. I don't know how things operate in Norfolk, but in DC we can't get indictments based on coded messages."

"Let me participate in the questioning," Mitchell said.

"I can do that," Bell said after a moment's hesitation. "But I doubt that Randolph is going to voluntarily come in and answer a bunch of questions."

Nikki shook her head vigorously at Mitchell and sliced her hand across her throat.

"Can we get back to you?" asked Mitchell.

When they got off the phone, Mitchell turned to Nikki. "What was that all about?"

"Where does Randolph live?" Nikki asked Wellington. Her partner had done some quick Internet research for Nikki earlier that morning.

"Fairfax," Wellington said.

"How's your relationship with the commonwealth's attorney there?" Nikki asked Mitchell.

"Good. I know some folks in that office. But everything you've described occurred in DC."

"Give me your cell phone number," said Nikki. "And give me a few hours."

Mitchell tried to pry more details out of Nikki, but she was determined. She left his office, with Wellington struggling to keep up.

"What are we going to do?" Wellington asked breathlessly.

"Do you know how to create a computer virus?" asked Nikki.

Wellington hesitated, but they both knew the answer. "They're not that hard," he eventually admitted.

"Good," said Nikki. "I've got a plan."

Chapter 61

*S*omebody's watched a few too many Survivor *episodes,* Finney thought. To him, this ceremony felt like a cheap imitation of the grandfather of all reality shows.

Finney was the second contestant to march into the courtroom to render his verdict. He walked solemnly from the back door to the podium at the front, just as McCormack had directed. He stood there for a few seconds facing Judge Javitts. "Remember," McCormack had said, "everything should be done deliberately, as if you're moving in slow motion. That way we can build the drama when we add in the soundtrack."

"Does the contestant have a verdict?" asked Javitts.

"I do."

"Cut!" said McCormack. "Judge Finney, you've got to give us some time to change shots. You practically walked on Javitts's question that time." McCormack conferred with his cameramen. "Let's try that again, Judge. This time, count to three before you answer."

"Three Mississippi or one thousand one, one thousand two, one thousand three?"

"Take two," said McCormack.

Javitts asked the question again, and Finney waited for three Mississippis. "I do."

"What say you?" asked Javitts.

Finney counted to three again, just to be safe. But then he coughed. "Cut!"

On the third take, he got it right. "I voted for myself and Victoria Kline," said Finney.

"What is your basis for voting for yourself?" asked Javitts. To Finney, the question sounded stupid. But Javitts wore his most solemn expression yet.

"On the basis that my faith is true, it's survived the trials of these past two weeks, and plus, I'm one heckuva guy."

It looked like Javitts almost smiled at that one. "And what is your basis for voting for Dr. Kline?"

"On the basis that she's the only other contestant who would go sailing with me," said Finney.

"C'mon," growled McCormack, and the cameras stopped rolling. "This is supposed to be a serious climax to the past two weeks of *Faith on Trial*, Judge Finney. *The Last Comic Standing* is another network. This is a jury verdict of you and your peers. And jury verdicts have to have some basis in reason."

"I can tell you haven't handled many jury trials," said Finney. And this time Javitts did smile.

"Just put your ballot in the box on the judge's dais and let's get to the next contestant," McCormack said in frustration.

Finney began walking forward.

"Not yet," snapped Javitts. "We need to at least get this part on camera."

∽

After the melodramatic filming of each contestant's verdict, all were ushered into the courtroom for the announcement of results. Tammy Dietz, whom Finney hadn't seen around much lately, delivered a spiel about the procedures employed to select the finalists. It took her only two takes to get it right, and Finney wanted to applaud.

"All rise!" called the court clerk after Tammy stepped aside. "The Honorable Howard D. Javitts presiding."

"You may be seated," Javitts said.

Finney coughed as the contestants took their seats, the sound lost in the shuffle. He felt his heart pounding against his chest. It had been a while since he was on the receiving end of a verdict. He really wanted to make the finals, despite the possibility that the finalists might face danger. For one thing, he assumed that the feds would be arriving soon. But even if they didn't, he now had a backup plan.

Javitts cleared his throat and surveyed the courtroom with all the gravitas of a real judge. "As Ms. Dietz explained, I will first announce the finalist I have selected. That will be followed by an announcement of the person the contestants have chosen as the second finalist."

Javitts referred to some notes in front of him. "This is a tough decision. Getting to know the contestants these past two weeks has been a highly rewarding experience. I have developed a deep admiration for each of them. However, I may only award my verdict to one."

Javitts shifted his eyes from the cameras to Dr. Kline, and Finney took that as a bad sign. But then Finney realized that he was doing exactly what he told lawyers not to do—guess a verdict based on who the judge or jury looks at. Finney himself always looked at the losing party to see how they reacted, since that usually told him whether or not the verdict was correct.

"Mr. Hadji and Judge Finney, though they presented excellent cases, treated this experience with an attitude that struck this court as being too cavalier and nonchalant for such an important matter. Issues of faith are matters of extreme seriousness and should be treated as such."

Finney felt the gut punch of a statement made from the bench that he would have no opportunity to rebut. He wondered how many times he had made others feel the same way.

"As for Dr. Kline," Javitts continued, "she also presented an excellent case, with a high degree of professionalism. But where does her argument lead? To no god at all—modern man with both feet planted firmly in the air. I just cannot believe that this entire universe was caused by nothing."

Finney glanced at Victoria Kline. Her expression gave nothing away.

"Dr. Ando presented himself with great dignity, and his personal character gave his arguments tremendous weight. He has shown supernatural courage and peace in the face of suffering.

"But it was the unrelenting passion of Mr. Hasaan that impressed this court most. I am not necessarily saying that his religion is true and the others false. But I am saying that there can be no doubt about what he believes or about his devotion to his faith. At the end of the day, that's what this judge was looking for.

"Accordingly, I render the court's verdict for Mr. Hasaan."

Finney reached over and shook his friend's hand. Surprisingly, it was cold and clammy. "You can smile now," whispered Finney, trying to deal with his own disappointment. But Hasaan kept a straight face, though his eyes glistened with tears.

"As for the contestants," continued Javitts, "they see things differently. Their verdict, in a very close contest..." Javitts waited and Finney tensed. It was probably three seconds, but it felt more like three years.

"...is for Judge Finney."

Finney blew out a deep breath and felt gratitude flood his body. He was not, by nature, an emotional man. But now the feelings welled up without warning, a mixture of relief and exuberance and gratefulness. "Thank You, Jesus," he said softly enough so that nobody else could hear. Kareem shook his hand, and the others mouthed their congratulations. In that moment, all that Finney could think about was the respect he had for the other contestants and how honored he was to have their verdict.

The rest of the courtroom session was a blur. Flush with victory, Finney pushed aside his concerns about the danger awaiting the finalists. It was Hadji who brought it back to the forefront as the Hindu gave Finney a hug after the session had ended.

"Be careful, my brother," Hadji whispered in his ear.

CHAPTER 62

They were halfway to Richmond before Nikki dialed Randolph's cell. Wellington rode shotgun, his knuckles white from the speed, his face drained of blood by the plan Nikki had concocted. He was too scared to even lecture Nikki about talking on her cell while driving. At least she didn't break out the makeup.

God was with them. Randolph answered.

"Preston, it's Nikki. Got a second?"

Randolph mumbled something about a court hearing, but Nikki pretended he had said yes.

"Two things; I'll be quick. First, I received an e-mail from you about an hour ago claiming you were leaving the practice of law and going to work at some new company named Passion, Inc. When I dialed the 800 number, I got a porn line."

"It's a virus," explained Randolph. "It sent the same message to everyone in my Outlook database. But my secretary said the 800 number was some telemarketing group, not a porn line."

Nikki shot a sideways glance at Wellington, who quickly gazed out the side window. It was supposed to be a porn line, but her partner in crime apparently couldn't bring himself to do that.

"We had the same thing hit our computers last week at the Norfolk Courthouse," claimed Nikki. "Did you hear about that?"

"No."

"I think they call this virus Insidious or something like that. Anyway, we had our own guys mess around with our computers for about three days, and then we called this one firm that apparently specializes in this type of thing. They fixed it in about two hours."

She heard Randolph talking to somebody in the background. She wanted to reach across the line and slap him. "Say that again," Randolph said.

Nikki repeated herself and this time Randolph bit. "Can you call my assistant and give her that number?" Randolph asked. "I'm out of the office right now."

Nikki nudged Wellington and gave him a thumbs-up when he looked her way. "Okay, Preston. But I've also got something a lot more serious and really need to meet with you about this issue right away."

"Um…" She could hear the tension in his voice. "I really can't right now, Nikki. I've got a thousand things going on. I just left a hearing in federal court, and I've got two pleadings to file by day's end. Can we do it later by phone?"

"An investigative reporter called me, Preston. A friend of mine from Norfolk. He says he's going to run a story on the eleven o'clock news that you're involved in some kind of fraud with the *Faith on Trial* show. I can probably keep him from running it if I call in all my chips, but I really need to get a few things straight with you first."

"Hang on a second," said Randolph. He apparently stepped into someplace quiet, since the background noise disappeared.

"What's his name?" Randolph asked.

"Byron Waterman," Nikki replied. "Works for WVAR, a local affiliate of a major network. He's been following Judge Finney's exploits pretty closely, and I think Finney somehow managed to communicate with him."

"How soon can you meet?"

"I'm on my way right now," said Nikki. "Can you meet me someplace in Fredericksburg?"

"Fredericksburg?"

Yeah, thought Nikki. *A city where the commonwealth's attorney is a good friend of Mitchell Taylor's.* "It's an hour south of DC," she said, stating the obvious. "I thought it might save us some time."

∾

Finney exercised no self-control at lunch, gorging himself on a large roast-beef-and-cheese sandwich, french fries, soup, and two kinds of dessert. He started cramping up almost immediately.

The three contestants who didn't make the finals were told to pack their bags and report to the courthouse for one final cross-examination session. The helicopter would pick them up at four.

The feds should have been here by now, thought Finney. *Something is very wrong.* He was sure that Wellington would have decoded the message about getting the feds involved. But the message pointing to Preston Randolph was far more difficult. If Wellington and Nikki hadn't figured that message out, if they had somehow confided in Randolph about the coded messages…no, that wasn't possible. Finney wouldn't let himself entertain those thoughts. One of Nikki's messages had assured him that Randolph didn't know about their code talking. Surely she would not have involved Randolph when she went to the feds.

Maybe the feds had already arrested Randolph. Maybe they were preparing to swoop down on the island at this very moment. And even if they weren't, Finney was pretty sure that the only contestants in danger now were the two finalists. He still thought it all came down to the speedy-trial cases somehow, though he couldn't quite make that final link.

But he also knew that being pretty sure wasn't good enough, not when the price for being wrong could be the lives of his fellow contestants. He believed that Kareem had been set up when he searched Murphy's computer. The message Kareem had found—containing scenarios in which all the contestants were killed—was therefore fraudulent. Or perhaps, as Hadji suggested, Kareem had made it all up.

But one thing that didn't neatly fit into Finney's theory was the fact that Kareem had made the finals. And if Finney were wrong about his theory, the other contestants could still be in danger, and the consequences would be dire. It could happen in a thousand different ways. A staged helicopter accident. Food poisoning. A plane accident.

Unless Finney could prevent the possibility with one bold, preemptive stroke...

He found McCormack setting up for another shoot at the courthouse. Finney demanded a meeting in the library. Immediately. Bring Cameron Murphy. No cameras.

"Why should we agree to that?" asked McCormack.

"Because you want me to stick around for the finals. And if this meeting doesn't happen, I'll quit."

∽

Nikki pulled her Sebring into a spot on the side of the truck stop where she had agreed to meet Randolph. The location had been her idea. Always keep your opponent off balance by meeting on unfamiliar turf. What could be more unfamiliar to Randolph than a truck stop?

She handed Wellington the keys. "Randolph won't be here for another hour or so," she said. "He didn't know I was already on my way when I called him, and I wanted to give you time to get to his office and send me copies of any juicy e-mails."

Wellington climbed into the driver's seat, speechless.

Nikki checked to make sure Byron's T-Mobile Sidekick was in her purse. It gave her Internet access, e-mail access, and cell phone all in one. She double-checked to ensure it was on vibrate. "You've got Byron's e-mail address, right?"

It was the third time she had asked Wellington and the third time he promised that he did.

Next, she tested the hidden camera Byron had stitched into the front of her Fendi Spy bag. "Can you tell he's cut out a piece of the purse for the camera?" she asked Wellington.

"You can hardly see it," Wellington said.

But the big problem was the hidden mike and the small battery pack. Byron said the mike wouldn't pick up well from inside Nikki's purse. But she couldn't hide the mike in her sheer silk V-neck top or skintight jeans.

She tried hiding it in her bra. "Can you see the mike?" she asked Wellington.

"No," he said, though he was too polite to look very hard.

"Yes, you can," said Nikki, checking it out in the window of the car. "This'll never work."

Then she had another idea. "Is your ODU cap still in the backseat?" Nikki had thrown the hat in the back earlier, brushing her thick hair out as much as possible.

"Sure," said Wellington, fishing it out.

"I'll be right back," Nikki said. She took the hat and went into the truck stop to grab a large plastic coffee cup. She rolled the bill of the hat and stuffed it inside the cup, then placed the cup and hat under the rear tire of her Sebring.

"Back up a little," she told Wellington.

He looked at Nikki as if she had lost her mind, but then he backed up anyway, running over the hat.

Nikki retrieved it and put it on her head. This time, the bill curved like a normal hat, except it still looked brand new. Not much she could do about that right now.

Nikki handed Wellington the mike and the hat. "Will you attach the mike to the underside of the bill of that cap?" she said. "I'm going inside to get a T-shirt that will go better with my outfit. I look like a moron wearing this top and a baseball hat."

She returned a few minutes later with a pink *Virginia Is for Lovers* T-shirt. She hated pink and she hated the shirt, but it wasn't exactly the Gap in there.

She climbed into the back of the Sebring and changed while

Wellington kept his eyes glued straight ahead. She put on the hat and checked herself out in the windows again. The mike was invisible on the bill, and the battery pack was nestled under the hat.

Now her major concern was the petrified look on her partner's face. "You can do this, Wellington," she said, trying to sound confident. "A man's life might depend on it."

"I know," Wellington said. But his words came out with more of a squeak than usual. "I'll try."

CHAPTER 63

Finney arrived at the library first. He took a seat at the large conference table and mentally rehearsed his lines—Plan B, as he now called it. He forced himself to relax, focusing on his breathing and heart rate, closing his eyes to calm his nerves.

McCormack arrived next and took a seat without talking.

"Thanks for coming," said Finney.

"This better be quick."

A few minutes later, Murphy joined them. He stopped a few steps inside the door and crossed his arms. "What's this all about?" he asked.

Finney stood as well. "Have a seat," he said.

"I'll stand," replied Murphy.

Finney looked at McCormack, who simply spread his palms.

"Okay," said the judge. "Have it your way." Finney moved out from behind the table so he could pace the room and watch the reactions of both men. He had been jerked around on this island long enough. This afternoon it was his turn to uncork a few surprises.

"I'm a judge," Finney began, "and so I'm rather fond of facts. First, I'll deal with the ones you already know about. After that, I'll give you a few things to chew on as we complete our time together on this little slice of paradise."

Finney smiled at the men, who both wore serious masks. *At least one of us is going to enjoy this,* thought Finney. "First, there is a conspiracy afoot on this island for the alleged purpose of killing one of the finalists. Now, that may be part of the game or that may be real, but the existence of that conspiracy is a fact." This brought no reaction from either man, but Finney didn't expect it to.

"Second, Preston Randolph is involved in that conspiracy." McCormack's pupils seemed to narrow ever so slightly when Finney dropped that bomb, though Murphy's face remained a mask. "Third, one of the contestants has been assisting this conspiracy from the very beginning."

At this revelation, both men seemed to be working way too hard to remain unaffected. A surprise reaction is sometimes telling, Finney knew. But lack of surprise, even more so.

"Those facts you know," continued Finney, enjoying his moment on the stage perhaps too much. "Now for some facts you don't know.

"I've been communicating throughout most of the show with a person or persons who are not on the island, providing them with all the evidence they need to prove this conspiracy and obtain arrest warrants. They're prepared to go public if anything happens to me or the other contestants. They've already contacted the FBI, and the feds are now investigating. I expect indictments soon."

Finney stopped pacing a few feet from Cameron Murphy and fixed him with the Finney stare.

"You must be referring to Agents Rafferty and Flynn, who met with us at some length yesterday," said Murphy calmly, returning the Finney stare with his own trademark—a maddening smirk. "They left the island convinced that it was all a big misunderstanding."

Finney furrowed his brow and tried to make sense of this latest piece of the puzzle. *The FBI has already been here?*

"By now they should have communicated that to Nikki Moreno as well," said McCormack. Finney spun around to look at him. "So I doubt she'll be going public with these charges anytime soon."

At the mention of Nikki's name, Finney was too stunned to respond. If anything happened to her...

"Is there anything else?" asked Murphy.

"Leave Nikki Moreno out of this," Finney snapped.

"There's nothing for us to leave her out of," Murphy said triumphantly. Finney resisted the urge to strangle him.

"You're lucky we didn't disqualify you," added McCormack. "And release the videotaped cross-examination about the speedy-trial cases in the process."

Finney's head was spinning with this new information, but years of trial experience allowed him to quickly regain his composure. The FBI had paid these men a personal visit. Would they really dare try anything now?

"If I'm smart enough to make the finals, then I'm smart enough to use somebody other than Nikki Moreno as my go-between," said Finney, but the words sounded unconvincing even to him. Maybe Nikki had confided in Randolph after all. "If you think she's involved, you're badly mistaken."

"I'm sure we are," said Murphy. "Now let's get back to work."

So much for Plan B, thought Finney. It felt like he was always one step behind.

∾

Sitting across from Preston Edgar Randolph in a grimy truck stop booth with vinyl seats, Nikki learned the hard way why the man was one of the top trial lawyers in the United States. The place smelled of grease and pancakes, but Randolph, who came straight from court wearing his starched white monogrammed shirt and red power tie, seemed right at home. When she told him that the real reason she requested this meeting was to confront him with the lies he had been telling her, it didn't even knock him off stride.

"You want anything to eat?" he asked, rolling up his sleeves and motioning to the waitress.

Nikki took a pass on the food but allowed the waitress to fill her coffee cup with a black, gooey substance that looked like dirty car oil. "Can you bring out a Diet Coke, too?" Nikki asked.

"I'll take a regular Coke," said Randolph, and the waitress disappeared.

"I called the real FBI," Nikki said dramatically. Her purse was on the end of the table near the salt and pepper shakers, the ketchup, and the syrup. She had aimed the camera right at Randolph and prayed it was working. "There is no Agent Rafferty or Flynn assigned to this case."

"I know."

That's it? Confessions aren't supposed to be this easy. "You do?"

"Yes," Randolph confirmed. "I never said they were FBI, though I allowed you to make a few assumptions."

Nikki tried to replay the events in her mind. *Is that the way it came down? Assumptions? Wait a minute...*

"They showed me FBI credentials," Nikki argued. "You argued with them about FBI jurisdiction."

"My memory's different," Randolph said calmly. "And I'm pretty sure that Investigator Flynn and Investigator Rafferty will agree with me."

The man was slick—Nikki had to give him that. But also disgusting. "This is unbelievable," she said, buying time to think. She no longer had any doubts about whether Finney's message had been correct. Anybody who could lie this easily could be guilty of anything. Herself excluded, of course.

Randolph leaned forward, and Nikki instinctively slid back. She tilted her head down slightly, worried about Randolph somehow seeing the hidden mike. "Nikki, I feared for Dr. Kline's life. And I wanted to protect Judge Finney. Have you ever dealt with the FBI before? They've got so much red tape and bureaucracy that we'd still be filling out forms. We needed quick results."

The waitress reappeared with their drinks, silencing Randolph. When she left, Randolph lowered his voice and continued. "They're private investigators, Nikki. They've already been to the island and investigated. The FBI would still be opening the file."

"Why didn't you tell me?"

"I should have." Randolph admitted. "But it seemed you were determined to go to the feds, and I knew that once you did that, the private investigators would have to back off. So, instead of telling you, I just let you assume these guys *were* the feds."

That's not how it happened, Nikki knew. But Randolph either realized she might be wearing a mike or he had convinced himself of his own story. He took a sip of Coke, eying Nikki the whole time.

Why is Wellington taking so long? If he found anything, I should have heard from him by now. Maybe he got cold feet.

"So all this stuff about being contacted by television reporters—none of that is true?" Randolph asked. Somehow he was the one who managed to sound indignant.

Nikki wished she could turn the recorders and cameras off while she took her turn at shading the truth. "No. That was just a ploy to get a meeting."

"You haven't talked to *any* reporters about this?" Randolph creased his forehead in disbelief, the way he would for a hostile witness.

A sip of coffee—she nearly gagged. Who was questioning whom? *I haven't done anything wrong,* Nikki reminded herself. "That's not the point. The point is that you misled me about the FBI and who knows what else. I'm the one who should be asking the questions here, not you."

"Then you did talk to reporters?"

"I told you, I'm not answering that."

"Meaning that you did."

That did it. Now he'd made her angry enough to slap him. She was the victim, not him! But before she could move, he reached over and grabbed her hat by the bill. The mike stayed attached, but the small battery pack and cord dropped on the table.

"Which is where you got this," he said accusingly. He picked up the battery pack for a moment and studied it. "This illegal recording is over now," he said into the mike before turning it off.

Nikki crossed her arms and felt her face flush. This was not the way she had scripted it in her mind.

"What did you want me to do?" she asked. "You were lying to me."

"You have any more recording devices in the purse?" he asked.

"No." She said emphatically. It was part of the Moreno philosophy— the bigger the lie, the more confident you must act when telling it.

Except that Wellington picked that moment—the worst timing possible—to start sending e-mails. The purse vibrated and Nikki looked as startled as she might have been if the purse had actually talked. "Uh...I do have my cell phone in there."

Randolph's eyes went hard, and for the first time it dawned on Nikki how dangerous this man might be. Even in a truck stop. Even in broad daylight.

It vibrated again. "You might want to get that," Randolph said.

She knew she would have to figure out a way to look at these messages, so Nikki decided to play it casually. She pulled the Sidekick out of her purse. "It's e-mail," she said, sliding the screen into position.

"I know," said Randolph. "I don't recall that you had that at our last meeting."

CHAPTER 64

Standing outside the one-way mirror of the cross-examination room, Murphy and McCormack watched the events unfolding inside with great interest. Javitts fired questions at the Swami, who handled them with the same casual confidence he had exhibited the last two weeks. Ando and Kline had already endured their last turn in the room.

"I notice you didn't vote for yourself as one of the finalists," said Javitts.

"You noticed correctly."

"Was it because you were afraid that one of the finalists might die?"

The Swami stared impassively at his questioner as if the Swami didn't know how much of his own hand he should reveal. "What do you mean?"

Javitts smiled condescendingly. "You know exactly what I mean, Mr. Hadji. The rumors among the contestants that one of the finalists would die. Rumors planted by the producers of the show. Did they affect your decision?"

This brought a big smile and shake of the head from Swami. "You mean we've basically all been punk'd this week? It's all a big sham, this stuff about a finalist dying?"

"Yes," replied Javitts sternly. "We wanted to see how you would react."

"That's awesome, dude," said the Swami chuckling. He looked at the mirrors and gave a thumbs-up. "You guys had me going."

"And you decided your faith wasn't worth dying for?" asked Javitts.

The Swami jerked back and gave Javitts an "Are you crazy?" look that nearly made McCormack laugh. "That's not it at all, man. I decided *this show* wasn't worth dying for. My faith—now, that's an entirely different matter."

∾

Nikki scrolled through a few messages while Randolph looked on, burning holes in the top of her head with his intense stare. Right now she didn't care. Her partner had come through! It was time to go back on the attack.

"Who is the Seeker?" she asked Randolph.

"What are you talking about?" Randolph's voice was as steely as the eyes.

"Who is Azrael?"

"Never heard of him."

She held the Sidekick in front of her as she dialed Byron Waterman's office number, keeping one eye on Randolph the entire time. He glanced casually around the restaurant as if contemplating his next move.

Answer! Hurry!

Randolph stood and Nikki slid back in the booth. A sneer crossed his lips. "A little jumpy, aren't we?"

"Nikki?" asked Byron, finally answering the phone. *Thank God.*

"Did you get the e-mails?" Nikki asked. Wellington had been instructed to send any incriminating information to Waterman's personal e-mail address. Those messages would show up on both his Sidekick and his computer.

Randolph tensed, towering over Nikki, listening to the phone conversation. She felt the goose bumps of her own excitement. Mixed with fear.

"Did I get them?" Byron asked, the excitement obvious in his voice. "This is unbelievable. Huge!"

Nikki placed the phone down on the table between them.

"Can you hear me?" Nikki asked.

"Yeah," she heard Byron say, though it wasn't very clear. "But not as good as before."

"The phone's in the middle of the table," Nikki explained. "I'm here with Preston Randolph." He eyed her quizzically but didn't make a move. "If you get cut off, call the police immediately." Nikki provided the address of the truck stop while Randolph listened impassively, towering over her.

"Who is that?" Randolph asked.

"An investigative reporter for WVAR," said Nikki. "A Norfolk television channel."

"This belong to him?" asked Randolph. He detached the mike from the host and picked up the mike and battery pack from the table. He wrapped the small cord around the battery pack and put the device in his pocket.

"Yes."

"And you somehow managed to get copies of my e-mails?" And then, as if answering his own question, Randolph's eyes flashed in recognition. "The virus."

Nikki nodded.

Randolph settled back down into the booth. "You're good," said Randolph. "But unfortunately, you've played a little fast and loose with the law in the process."

Before Nikki could respond, Randolph leaned forward, closer to the phone, his attorney instincts kicking in. "As Nikki's accomplice…" He motioned toward the phone. "What's his name?" he whispered to Nikki.

She hesitated. This was so strange. "Waterman," she said softly.

"As Nikki's accomplice, Mr. Waterman, there are a few things you ought to know. And I want you to record every word of this conversation and make sure you play it for your station manager before you get any big ideas about being a hero by breaking a story about me."

He paused and pulled the mike back out of his pocket. He turned it on and placed it next to the phone. "And if the battery on your recording device wears out, Mr. Waterman, just let me know, because I'll have a backup recording."

"Are you still there, Byron?" Nikki asked.

"Yes," he answered, the noise muffled but audible. "And I'm recording every word."

"Good," said Randolph, sliding forward so his mouth was less than a foot from the mike. "You may have some e-mails to or from my computer indicating that one of the finalists for *Faith on Trial* is going to die—quote, unquote—accidentally. But relax, Mr. Waterman; it's all just part of the game. I financed the show, Mr. Waterman. The whole thing was my idea. I believed at the time, and still do, that the best test of any faith is how well it helps you deal with death. This was a reality show, Mr. Waterman. Therefore, we tried to make the threat of death seem very real...and very immediate."

Nikki couldn't believe she was hearing this. She suddenly remembered the miniature videocam and checked out the angle of her purse. She casually moved it so the camera would point right at Randolph. He was so focused on the mike that he didn't seem to notice.

"Now, I realize that this information, in itself, is a story," Randolph continued. As he did, he slyly reached over and turned Nikki's purse back toward her. A sharp look from Randolph told her to leave it that way. "And under the First Amendment, I probably can't stop you from airing it. But I'll give you three compelling reasons to wait until the final show airs before you do so. The first, Mr. Waterman, is the lawsuit I'll file against you and your station for defamation of character and invasion of privacy. I'll own that station before it's over."

He hesitated just long enough for the threat to sink in. This was Randolph the litigator trying to regain control. "The second is the lawsuit I'll file against Ms. Moreno and her accomplice for stealing my e-mail messages. Oh, I almost forgot the additional lawsuit I'll file against Judge Finney for violating his pledge not to communicate about the show with those outside the island. I think the stipulated damages for that are something like five million.

"And third, I'm about to tell you something that might cause even a calloused reporter like you to hold off. If you do, I'll give you an exclusive interview after the final show."

He pursed his lips and hesitated, as if considering whether he should really take this plunge. It seemed to Nikki that the trial lawyer veneer suddenly melted away, leaving behind a more vulnerable man. "I don't know you, Mr. Waterman, and I don't know your station manager. But I know Nikki. And I'm going to take a risk here. Despite what you've done to me today, I'm going to assume that you people all have hearts"—he paused, stealing a glance at Nikki—"and that you sometimes use them when making your decisions."

The hard edge left Randolph's voice as he continued. Nikki had to remind herself that he was a trial lawyer. Generating pity was part of the craft, like a rapper spouting rage.

"I've got an incurable brain tumor, Mr. Waterman. I'm searching for the true God. I thought maybe this show would help."

Nikki felt the air flee her lungs. *What?* The man suddenly looked so vulnerable. Just moments ago she had looked into his dark eyes and seen flashing anger. But now there was uncertainty. Randolph's.

And hers.

∾

Half an hour after Preston left the rest area, taking Nikki's hidden mike and recorder with him, Nikki was still waiting for Wellington. She had been on the phone with Byron for nearly fifteen minutes, trying to talk him out of running an exposé on the evening news. She wasn't afraid of the threatened lawsuits, but she actually believed Randolph's story. Besides, would anybody try to hurt the finalists now, with the media all over this story?

But Byron wouldn't hear of it. He didn't need Nikki's permission to go with the story, he reminded her. Even without video footage or the audio from the hidden mike, he had the phone call and the e-mails. That was enough.

After she hung up with Byron, Nikki tried calling Wellington several times. No answer. He was undoubtedly driving, and even though Nikki had talked him into breaking into a trial lawyer's computer, he was nevertheless apparently unwilling to assume the fourfold increase in odds of a fender bender that might occur if he picked up the phone.

A few minutes later, Nikki received another e-mail on Byron's Sidekick that made her think Byron might be right after all. As part of the "fix" for Randolph's computer, Wellington had made sure that every e-mail received by Randolph would be automatically forwarded, without notification, to the e-mail address for Byron Waterman. Most of the e-mails were junk. But one from "Azrael" caught Nikki's attention.

Seeker:

Things are becoming chaotic on the island. Will assume that the baptism is still a go for Saturday unless I hear from you. This will be my last communication unless you indicate concern.

Azrael

What could that possibly mean—"the baptism"? If it was just a harmless e-mail about Saturday's show, why did the sender use a code name that Randolph claimed he had never heard before? Maybe this was just another part of the charade, Nikki reasoned. But why send another e-mail now? Maybe they were going to make sure the remaining contestants "accidentally" discovered this e-mail. But if Randolph and his accomplice were trying to use this e-mail to make the contestants think their lives were in danger, why would they use a coded message about baptism?

Byron called almost immediately. "Did you see that e-mail?" he asked. "Give me one possible innocent explanation for that."

Back and forth they went. But in the end Nikki knew she couldn't take any chances if there was the slightest chance that Finney's life was on the line. She could always ask forgiveness later.

"Okay," she said to Byron. "What do you want me to do?"

"Have you watched the video?"

"Yeah. The picture's pretty grainy and you can't really hear anything. Plus, Randolph turned it away from himself during part of the meeting."

"That's okay," said Byron. "We'll use my recording of the phone call for audio. We just need the video footage for B-roll as soon as possible."

"How do I make that happen?"

"We've got a sister station in Fredericksburg. Got a pen and paper?"

After writing down directions, Nikki called Wellington one more time. After four rings, a minor miracle occurred. "Hello," he said tentatively.

"Good work on the e-mail," Nikki said. She knew he was struggling with the legality of what they had done, so she didn't bother telling him about the threatened lawsuits. She explained the rest of the events in detail, including her need to get to the television station right away.

"I'll be there in about twenty minutes," said Wellington.

"How fast are you driving?"

There was a long pause. Nikki thought she heard the sound of her Sebring accelerating. "Over the speed limit," said Wellington.

"Drive faster," said Nikki. She couldn't wait to give her protégé a hug.

CHAPTER 65

The helicopter arrived midafternoon on Friday, and the contestants started saying their good-byes. To Finney, the warm island breeze felt heavier and stickier than normal. He noticed the sheen of sweat on everyone's skin except that of the enigmatic Dr. Ando. Was the man even human?

Finney turned to Ando first, wished him the best, and expressed his great respect for the man. It was hard to think of the cruel fate that awaited this decent human being with the incurable bone disease. Ando shared his own respect for Finney.

The judge turned next to the Swami.

"My money's on you, Judge O. And you know I've got good gambling instincts."

Finney smiled, thinking about how much he would miss this guy. *So much for my strategy of avoiding friendships with the other contestants.*

"Come see me sometime," said Finney.

"Count me in, Judge O."

The two men shared an awkward moment of silence, the first time Finney had seen the Swami at a loss for words.

"Well," said Finney. He held out his Bible. "I wanted you to have this." The pages were dog-eared and the black leather cover was nearly worn off. "We never did finish the gospel of John. You might want to start there."

The Swami nodded his head slowly and seemed to be choking back a tear. Finney swallowed the lump in his own throat.

"That's quite an honor," the Swami said.

As they briefly embraced, the two card sharks took turns whispering their messages.

"Pinprick cipher, gospel of John," whispered Finney. His final encoded message contained an e-mail for Nikki, telling her where to find the tape. And a few personal things as well.

"Everything's going to be fine," the Swami whispered in return. "There's no real danger here."

After the two disengaged, the Swami moved over to shake hands with Kareem Hasaan. "No hard feelings, big man," the Swami said.

Finney turned to face Dr. Kline.

"The sailing lessons were my favorite part of the show," she said. Her face betrayed no emotion.

"Mine too."

"Good luck," she said, keeping her voice light.

"Thanks."

She hesitated for a moment, then gave Finney a quick hug. He had so much to tell her, but the other contestants were watching, the cameras were recording, and the helicopter was waiting.

She hesitated again, looking as awkward as Finney felt. "Well, better get going," she said.

Finney grimaced. He hated good-byes, but especially this one. "Make sure you follow up with Preston Randolph on that possible television career," Finney said. "You'll make a phenomenal actress."

As if to prove his point, Victoria Kline grew teary eyed, then nodded and turned away.

⌒

Twenty minutes later, Kline and the other contestants climbed off the helicopter and onto the hot asphalt landing pad on St. Thomas. A few of the islanders loaded the contestants' belongings into a taxi that resembled a double-decker tour bus, and the contestants climbed aboard. After a ten-minute nail-biting ride on the left side of the road, the contestants arrived at a luxury resort hotel for the night, compliments of the show.

Fifteen minutes after she checked in, Dr. Kline returned to the front of the hotel, checked both directions, and caught a cab to a nearby marina. The speedboat captain was waiting for her. He helped her aboard, exchanged a few pleasantries, and started the motor. He drove slowly through the no-wake zone, but within minutes had the boat skimming across the ocean at an exhilarating speed.

"How long?" Victoria yelled, straining to be heard.

"Thirty minutes, max," the captain yelled back.

"Some people just can't stay away," she mumbled to herself.

inney and Kareem showed up in the Paradise Courtroom at 5:00 p.m. They had been instructed to dress casually, which to Finney meant his John Deere cap, baggy shorts, a T-shirt, and docksiders. This time the cameras were not rolling.

"As you know, tomorrow you will be giving your closing arguments," said Bryce McCormack. "It will be your last day on the island. Later tonight you'll be given a videotape of Judge Javitts's cross-examination of the other contestant from the first week on the island. Judge Finney's tape has him admitting to negligence in the performance of his judicial duties. Mr. Hasaan's tape shows the results of a polygraph test when he tried to deny having an affair."

Finney glanced at his intense competitor. The man's neck muscles strained, veins bulging, as he glared at McCormack. If they aired this stuff, Finney would help Kareem break the slimy director's neck.

"You will decide whether to use your opponent's tape in your closing argument," McCormack continued. "If you decide not to use it, then the incident will not be aired on any of the *Faith on Trial* episodes."

Finney knew immediately that he would never use Kareem's videotape. That decision was a no-brainer. He had no doubt that Kareem would reciprocate. The show's producers had underestimated how much the contestants had bonded.

"You will be spending this evening in a special spot on the island to prepare mentally and spiritually for your final day," McCormack continued, turning first to Finney. "Judge, as you know, Jesus spent His last night before the Crucifixion praying in the Garden of Gethsemane. We've prepared a rough replica here on the island where you will be going in just a few moments. You may spend as much time there as you would like." He smirked. "Not that we expect tomorrow to be anything like Jesus's last day."

These guys are always looking for the melodramatic, thought Finney. He immediately disliked the idea. It seemed to cheapen the Passion of Christ, duplicating events just to add drama to a reality show.

"Mr. Hasaan, as you know, Muhammad's epiphany occurred in a cave outside his hometown where he went to meditate and pray for a vision of the one true God. He was sleeping in the cave when a voice commanded him to read the words on a brocaded coverlet. He began reciting scripture, and those words became the opening lines of the Koran."

McCormack paused, and Finney found one more reason why he was content not to be a Muslim. He got a garden, while Kareem got a cave.

"We have found a reasonable facsimile of that cave here on Paradise Island," continued McCormack. "That's where you will spend the evening.

"This will be a one-camera shoot at each location. Gus, you'll accompany Kareem. Horace, you'll go with Judge Finney. Just get a few good cameo shots and then you can leave the contestants alone so they can prepare for tomorrow's closing arguments and other activities."

McCormack glanced back and forth between Finney and Kareem. "Gentlemen, you'll want to be rested both spiritually and physically for what lies ahead."

∽

Horace unlocked a gate in the chain-link fence surrounding the resort property and pointed to a dirt path angling off to his left. "It's up this way about a mile," he said. Finney shrugged and followed along. If roly-poly Horace could make it, lugging that heavy camera, then Finney could surely make it too.

Fifteen minutes later, Finney decided that Horace was a lousy judge of distance. The trail climbed and twisted its way up the mountainside—

tough climbing for a man whose lungs were spotted with cancer. Fortunately, Horace was in no better shape, so they would walk for a while and take intermittent breaks. At one point Finney started coughing, bending over with his hands on his knees as he struggled to catch his breath.

"You okay?" asked Horace, his voice tight with concern. "I don't do CPR, you know."

"No problem," answered Finney. He cleared his throat. "Are we almost there?"

"Almost." It was the third "almost" in the last few minutes, and Finney was getting tired of it. His lungs burned. His stomach kept cramping. And now he had a headache.

Finney hated being sick and getting old. He had been a fair athlete in his day but now had a hard time keeping up with a chubby couch potato like Horace. After his brief coughing break, Finney trudged on. Before long, it was Horace who needed to stop for a break, and Finney actually started feeling better.

I just needed a little warmup, Finney thought.

When they reached the garden, it was almost worth it. Someone had cleared the underbrush from a small plateau carved into the side of the mountain. A rock wall rimmed the downhill side of the plateau, and bright orange and yellow flowers sprouted in clumps everywhere. The spot featured a spectacular view overlooking the small resort and miles of white sand beaches. Finney caught his breath and gazed out at the green ocean stretching endlessly toward the blue horizon. In an hour or two they would watch the sun paint the boundary where water met sky, creating a mural of orange and red.

Finney stood next to the rock wall and soaked in the sights that cascaded below him. He turned toward the camera. "How can anyone see something like this and not believe in God?"

"You got me," answered Horace, still trying to catch his breath from behind the camera.

"Oh," said Finney. "I thought we were filming."

"Sorry," said Horace. "You want to say that again?"

"Nah. Let's just enjoy the view for a few minutes."

The two men chatted for a while, and then Horace said he needed to get some video while the lighting held up. Finney took off his John Deere cap and knelt in strategic spots so that Horace could pick up the view in the background. "Aren't you going to say anything?" asked Horace. "I mean, Jesus sweat drops of blood in the Garden of Gethsemane. He probably prayed pretty loud."

The man knows his Bible, thought Finney. "But Jesus didn't have a TV camera following Him around, Horace. That's just not my style—you know that. Praying for the cameras and all."

"I know," Horace said. "That's actually one of the things I appreciate about you. Though it makes for boring TV."

A few minutes later, Horace seemed to sense Finney's desire to spend some time alone. "Well, I've got what I need, Judge. Think I'll head back down to the resort before it gets dark."

"I thought you were going to stay for some twilight shots."

"I can play with the lighting on what I've already taken," said Horace. "I've got some good silhouettes." He paused and looked out toward the ocean, looking skittish. "Think it'd be okay if I prayed for you before I left?"

The request surprised Finney. He and Horace had always been loose with the no-fraternization rule. But Horace had never asked to pray for Finney before. "Sure."

Horace put his camera down, and the two men knelt together. Finney felt Horace place his hand on Finney's shoulder. "Lord, help this man know what an inspiration he's been to Christians all over America. Give him strength and wisdom for tomorrow. Keep him safe. And Lord, if it's Your will, let him win."

Finney felt the gratefulness rise inside him, spawning other feelings that were difficult to describe. It wasn't just the sincerity of the prayer that moved him; it was the knowledge that hundreds, perhaps thousands or even tens of thousands, of Christians all over the world were praying for him. For *him*. In that moment he remembered why he was here and who he really represented.

And he coughed. Not badly, compared to a lot of his coughing fits lately, but enough to interrupt Horace's prayer. Horace waited patiently, patting Finney's back until the coughing stopped. "And if it's Your will, God, heal him from the cancer." A pause. A long pause. "Amen."

Neither Finney nor Horace stood for a few seconds, then Finney placed his hat back on his head and thanked his friend. "You're a good man, Horace," he said, standing.

"You do us proud," said Horace, standing next to Finney. Then Horace picked up his camera, said, "See ya later, Judge," and headed down the hill. Finney watched him go, turned back toward the horizon, and hit his knees in earnest.

∾

Byron Waterman was throwing a tantrum. He had a killer story—the best he'd ever produced—and the news director didn't have the guts to air it. They'd been on the phone with their outside lawyers for half an hour, listening to all the various and sundry claims Randolph might make against them. Defamation. Invasion of privacy. False light. One creative lawyer even suggested larceny related to the theft of Randolph's e-mails.

Byron laughed out loud.

By 5:30 the hand-wringing lawyers had convinced the news director to kill the story—or at least delay it so they could have more time for vetting. But Byron appealed that decision to the station manager with his most forceful argument: if WVAR didn't run the story at 6:00, their sister station in Fredericksburg would scoop them.

"It's my story," Byron whined. "The only reason the guys in Fredericksburg even know about it is because we had to use their uplink to transmit the video footage to us."

The wrangling continued for another ten minutes before the station manager decided. This was a national story with a great human-interest angle. They had dynamite audio, passable video, and smoking-gun e-mails. They could unravel the empire of a billionaire trial lawyer. It wasn't quite Watergate, but for a small-time station in Norfolk, Virginia, it was pretty close.

Being scooped was not an option. At 5:55 the station manager made her decision. "Let's run it."

CHAPTER 67

S candal rocks a popular reality show," said the woman at the WVAR anchor desk. "More from reporter Byron Waterman, live outside the Norfolk courthouse, right after this break."

On Paradise Island they were pulling the live feed down from a satellite. Murphy, McCormack, and Victoria Kline hunched around one of the many monitors in the master control room. They had spent much of the last thirty minutes on the phone trying to calm down Preston Randolph.

The news resumed with a shot of a serious-looking Byron Waterman. "Monica, WVAR has learned from confidential sources close to the show that several contestants appearing on the *Faith on Trial* reality show, including Norfolk's own Judge Oliver G. Finney, have been put in fear for their lives on Paradise Island." As Byron talked, WVAR ran video clips from prior *Faith on Trial* episodes, most of them involving Finney.

"Just today, WVAR learned that this man"—Preston Randolph's face flashed on the screen—"billionaire trial lawyer Preston Randolph, is behind many of those threats. Mr. Randolph, who has recently been diagnosed with an inoperable brain tumor, has apparently provided much of the funding for the reality show. In a WVAR news exclusive, we obtained confirmation of Mr. Randolph's involvement through use of a hidden video camera."

The station cut to grainy footage of Preston Randolph sitting in the truck stop. Waterman provided a voice-over. "In a phone call that occurred during this videotaped meeting, Mr. Randolph admitted that it was his idea to fool contestants into thinking their lives were in danger. He claims that the real test of any faith is how well its adherents can deal with facing death."

They ran a short audio clip from Randolph's phone call, the transcribed words scrolling across the bottom of the screen. Next, they cut
back to Byron Waterman silhouetted against the Norfolk courthouse. He
shook his head with a forlorn look, as if Randolph had lost his mind. "In
addition, WVAR was able to obtain copies of e-mails sent to an account
on Mr. Randolph's computer from a person code-named Azrael." B-roll
of select e-mails ran while Byron continued talking. "Though the e-mails
are vague, they do reference 'the island' and discuss a confidential plan
that would culminate on Saturday, tomorrow, the final day of taping for
the show."

The special report ended with a closeup of Byron. Of course. "Mr.
Randolph does not deny that the show intentionally made contestants
believe they were in danger. However, when we contacted Mr. Randolph
after making our decision to air tonight's segment, he emphasized again
that in reality the contestants are not now and never have been in any real
danger. He also pointed out that the contestants signed waivers at the
beginning of the show where they assumed the risk that the show might
mislead them about certain facts. Mr. Randolph said this is not at all
unusual for reality shows, and he cited as an example *My Big Fat Obnox-
ious Fiancé*, where the show misled the family of a young bride by making them think she was marrying a total loser." Waterman shook his head
again. "Just when you thought you'd seen it all...Monica, back to you."

The picture went to a split screen with Waterman on one side and the
anchor on the other. "Do we know if all the contestants are in fact okay?"
asked Monica, looking concerned.

"Yes, we do. I checked with the network that sponsors the show, and
they assured us that every contestant is fine."

"Okay, thanks, Byron. Let's hope it stays that way." The anchor
turned to the camera on her right as her head shot went full-screen. "In
national news..."

~

Murphy stepped away from the screen and pursed his lips. McCormack braced himself for the explosion. And judging from the look on Victoria Kline's face, she expected the same.

"Every news outlet in the country will be running that tonight at eleven," Murphy stated, his words slicing the air with deadly intensity.

"Probably," said McCormack.

"We can expect the usual storm to erupt over whether we've pushed the envelope too far," continued Murphy.

McCormack nodded. "We've weathered worse."

"And that publicity would be worth what? Five million? Ten million? Twenty?"

The questions allowed McCormack to relax. There would be no explosion. Murphy had immediately zeroed in on the silver—make that the gold—lining of what they had just seen. Just when the controversy from the Anti-Defamation League and conservative Christians was dying down, they had been blessed with another firestorm. "I know Randolph is going ballistic," Murphy said, a self-satisfied smile curling at his lips, "but he's not looking at it logically. We were already planning a final show where he tells the audience about his brain tumor, why he financed this show, and who he thinks won. This just lets the cat out of the bag a little earlier."

"I agree with you," said McCormack, "which worries me."

"The only reason Randolph is upset is because he's been upstaged by a small-town reporter," said Murphy.

Kline had been noticeably silent, and both men turned to her at about the same time. "Who is Azrael?" she asked.

Murphy motioned to McCormack as if he was supposed to know. "Don't look at me," said McCormack. "I figured it was one of the e-mails on your computer that Kareem was supposed to find that night they raided our apartments."

"Those e-mails were from me to Seeker," said Murphy. "I've never heard of Azrael."

The unthinkable seemed to hit them all at the same time. "You don't really think there's anything going on," Dr. Kline said. But it sounded more like a question than a statement.

"Where are Finney and Hasaan now?" Murphy asked.

"On their solos," said McCormack. "They left about an hour ago."

Victoria's face went pale. "Should we send the security guards to check on them?"

"Don't be ridiculous," replied McCormack. "Nothing's going on. If somebody on the island wanted to harm a contestant, he would have acted by now."

"Who vetted the security guards?" Kline asked, concern creeping into her voice. "They have access to every part of the island and carry weapons right under our noses."

Murphy and McCormack both shrugged.

"We're talking about two or three bogus e-mails," said Murphy. "I'm sure there's a perfectly plausible explanation."

"Why take any chances?" asked Victoria. "If there's even a slight possibility of any real danger, Finney and Hasaan are entitled to know." Victoria hesitated and sucked in a deep breath. "I came all the way back to the island just so I could be here to explain my actions to Finney when the show's over. Why don't I talk to him tonight? It's not like it's going to affect the finals."

After a brief discussion, they agreed that the point of making the contestants fear for their lives had been accomplished. They already knew that both Kareem and Finney would vote for themselves to make the finals, even if it meant danger and possibly death. Not knowing who else could be trusted on the island, they agreed that Victoria would check on Finney.

"I'll check on Kareem," volunteered McCormack.

"I'll get some background on this security outfit," said Murphy.

"And handle Randolph's irate calls while you're at it," said McCormack.

As if on cue, Murphy's phone rang. He hit Ignore. "Maybe he'll call you next," Murphy said to McCormack.

∽

Three minutes later, Azrael received a text message:

Change of plans. Strike immediately.

∽

As Finney prayed, he felt the sweat beading his forehead and sticking his shirt to his back. A fever rose within him, accompanied by a sense of urgency, a strange foreboding about upcoming events. On his knees, he listened more than he talked, feeling the presence of the Holy Spirit and that still, small voice he had learned to recognize. And follow.

This evening the voice was a distant siren, both warning him and drawing him forward. He felt fatigue deep in his bones, but he also sensed that this might be his most important hour. Maybe it was the tension of the week's events, the death threats, the pressure of national television, the lack of food—who knew? But maybe it was something more. A chance to rise above the ordinary, to beat back the flesh and strike a final blow for the kingdom of God that would be seen around the world.

He tried to understand this dark premonition that haunted him in this beautiful place. He had done what he could to ensure the safety of every contestant. He had smuggled messages to Nikki. Confronted Murphy and McCormack. Befriended Horace and others. Yet still he felt the presence of danger.

He asked God to forgive him for the pain he had caused Tyler. For putting work ahead of family too often. For not taking care of his own body, killing himself one cigar at a time. For failing to do his job properly when innocent victims were counting on him for justice—speedy justice. He asked God to comfort those who had been harmed because of one judge's negligence.

He looked up and saw the orange hues forming on the horizon— another brilliant sunset taking shape, the faithfulness of God. The sight calmed him and lifted his spirits, like a fresh gust of wind filling an open sail, pushing him forward. He steeled himself for the next twenty-four hours, said "Thank You, Lord," and prepared to stand.

Just before he did, he felt a hand on his shoulder.

Chapter 68

Victoria."

"Are you okay?"

Finney stood, blinking at the hallucination. "I didn't expect to see you here."

"I had to come back," she said simply. She had her hair in a tight ponytail, the way she wore it when they sailed. Her beautiful eyes were wary, melting away some of Finney's defensiveness. Still, she had misled him the entire time. He couldn't just pretend it hadn't happened.

"More lies?" he asked.

"How did you know?"

"Are we alone?"

"Yes."

Finney relaxed a little and moved to the stone wall. He had never learned to fear her and felt no trepidation even now. If she had wanted to harm him, she had just passed up an excellent chance.

Victoria joined him at the wall.

"It's a reality show, Victoria. We signed a release that practically guaranteed deception. I immediately suspected every contestant. Then I narrowed it down to the two contestants who didn't fit the mold—you and Kareem."

"Kareem?"

"The rest of us had terminal illnesses before we were selected. During the first few days on the island, they explained that those illnesses were part of our qualifications. But Kareem told us his liver failure was only diagnosed about a month ago, after he got a call from a plaintiffs law firm that had obtained a list of patients taking an antidepressant. My guess is that the show selected each of us a few months prior to the show, before they even told us. That's how they orchestrated my temptation. Kareem's illness didn't fit the mold. I'm not even sure he's sick."

Finney could tell by the puzzled look on Victoria's face that she hadn't considered this before. She had been looking down the mountain, avoiding eye contact with him. But now she turned to him, squinting into the setting sun. "How did you know it was me?"

"The Galápagos, Victoria. During our first conversation on the island, you said that you thought we were somewhere near the Galápagos. But when I read Darwin's journal, I realized that couldn't possibly be right. The direction of the breezes, the prevailing trade winds—here we have warm trade winds blowing from the equator; in the Galápagos they have cool trade winds blowing in from the arctic. A sailor notices those things. The vegetation, the color of the sand—it was all wrong. A scientist would have to know that, Victoria. Especially after I highlighted it in open court."

She gave Finney a thin and apologetic smile. "Guilty." She looked down and nudged a small rock with her sandal. "Yet still you sailed with me."

"I figured you wouldn't shoot me in broad daylight on the ocean," Finney said. "Plus, it was the best way to gain information."

"Keep your friends close and your enemies closer?"

"No," admitted Finney. He found a small rock from the wall to keep his hands occupied. "I actually valued the time together."

"I'm sorry," she said softly.

"It was a reality show. You've got nothing to apologize for."

She looked at him again. "Yes, I do. And I'm sorry."

"Don't worry about it," said Finney. He took a deep and awkward breath. "What are you doing here now?"

"I came to tell you what's really going on," she said. "And to make my apologies."

"Apology accepted," Finney said, glancing over his shoulder. "But I can't believe you're going to unveil for me the great mystery behind the *Faith on Trial* show and they're not even going to film it?"

"It's just us, Oliver. I promise." Victoria thought for a moment, looking at the horizon. "The threats have all just been a reality-show setup," she continued, and Finney wanted to believe her. "Just to see if the contestants would try to make the finals even if they faced danger."

"Fake death threats," said Finney, more to himself than Victoria. On the one hand, he was relieved to hear Victoria say that. But on the other hand, if it was true, it was an arrow to his pride. How could Finney the code specialist be so wrong? "I thought that myself for a while."

"Until?"

"Our clever little escape plan," Finney explained. "I knew by then that you were lying to me, and I figured that you would tell your partners about our plan. If it was just part of the show, I expected both the Swami and Kareem to find something on the computers they checked. When Kareem found something on Murphy's computer, but the Swami didn't find anything on McCormack's, I figured that Murphy had been set up. And why do you need a fall guy if there's not some seriously bad stuff getting ready to happen?"

Finney turned the rock over a few times in his hand and tossed it down the cliff. He noticed a sly smile worm its way onto Kline's face.

"Actually, that was a mistake," she said. "The Swami was supposed to find e-mails on McCormack's computer too, but Bryce forgot that the password protection for his Outlook folder kicks in ten minutes after the machine is dormant. Murphy was smart enough to remember that, so he made his machine hibernate, which doesn't generate password protection."

The irony of it struck Finney. He knew of hundreds of stories of cryptanalysts who had been thwarted because the person writing the code had made a mistake. It was an eternal problem—how can you factor in the endless variations caused by human error?

Victoria allowed him to think for a moment and then spoke softly, her voice matching the warm hues of the disappearing sun. "Can I ask you another question?"

"You can ask," said Finney in a tone that made it clear he had no obligation to answer.

"Did you somehow tip off Nikki Moreno about Preston Randolph's involvement?"

Finney mulled this question over, and his suspicions kicked in. Was he really out of danger? Or was somebody still out to get him and just needed to know how much he had communicated with Nikki? Could he fully trust Victoria? Or was she on a scouting mission for his enemy?

"Why do you need to know?"

"Nikki Moreno went to a television station, and they ran an exposé tonight on the show, including Randolph's involvement," explained Victoria. "How did you know about Randolph's part in this?"

Finney's mind flashed to the coded message he had received from Wellington and Nikki about the location of the island. Randolph had supposedly triangulated a phone call to McCormack that proved the island was near the Galápagos chain. That's when Finney knew.

"Your question assumes a fact not yet in evidence," said Finney. "It assumes I communicated with Nikki."

"No, it *is* in evidence," said Victoria. "Nikki told Randolph you had communicated with her using codes. But that's really not important. I only asked because there was something in the exposé that didn't make sense, and it's one of the reasons the show's producers allowed me to talk with you tonight."

Finney raised an eyebrow. Could things get any more convoluted on this island? "Which was?"

"Some of the e-mails to Randolph about this fake plot to eliminate the contestants weren't written by any of us who were part of the plot."

"What did they say?"

"Weird stuff, like 'I assume the baptism is still a go for Saturday.'

Another one said, 'Nobody suspects us.' That type of thing." Victoria shrugged. "We decided that if there was any hint of real danger, even the most remote hint, we ought to tell the contestants."

Finney tried to follow her reasoning. "So you're thinking that maybe Randolph really *is* going to kill somebody."

"No," answered Victoria, but before she could explain further, her logic dawned on Finney.

"You're thinking that somebody might be trying to make it look like Randolph is involved in murder in order to cover up the real killer?"

"That sounds pretty dramatic," she responded. "I'm just trying to touch all the bases. It has me a little worried—that's all." She tried to shrug it off, but Finney could see the apprehension etched in her elegant brow. He wanted to put her at ease. Plus, the fascination of an unsolved mystery had its usual allure.

"All right," he said, "I'll bite. Let's think about this. Do you have any idea which computer generated those e-mails? Is there any possible connection with the young lady killed by Antonio Demarco, the speedy-trial defendant they asked me about?"

Kline's face became determined, wearing the look Finney had seen on mothers forced to testify against their own sons. For some reason, he had hit a nerve. She swallowed and turned to face him. "They were signed under the code name Azrael, but nobody knows who—"

"Azrael?" interrupted Finney. He felt the blood drain from his face.

"Yes. And as for the young lady who died…" Victoria hesitated and looked past him, then sighed. "That's a lie too, Oliver. Demarco sold drugs again, but he didn't kill anybody."

Finney could have strangled her, but his mind raced on ahead. He would deal with his own emotions later. "Azrael?" he asked again.

CHAPTER 69

nside the cave, Kareem prepared for the Maghreb prayer, placing his prayer mat on the rock floor of the damp chamber. The cave itself was a labyrinth of similar chambers filled with limestone stalactites and stalagmites, connected by numerous entrances from one chamber to the next, some nearly closed from centuries-old rock formations. The producers of the show had left a torch at the entrance, but it was mostly for ceremonial reasons. The day before, Gus had explored the cave. This evening, he used the bright light from his camera to lead Kareem through a few openings and into a large chamber with a flat limestone floor next to a large subterranean pool.

A bat flew overhead, startling Gus, who instinctively cursed. Kareem shot him a look. "Sorry," Gus said. He swore again, but this time under his breath.

Kareem walked around the chamber, touching the walls and exploring the crevices. "You ready?" he asked Gus.

Once Gus gave him the thumbs-up, Kareem squatted next to the pool and began his ceremonial washing with the cold subterranean water while Gus recorded every move. First, Kareem washed his hands up to his wrists three times. Next, he used the bottled water he had carried with him to rinse out his mouth three times. He sniffed the clean water into his nostrils three times and then washed his face. Turning back to the pool, he washed his arms three more times, all the way up to his elbows. He passed a wet hand over his head, then washed his feet three times each, right foot first.

"Exhausting," mumbled Gus.

Ignoring him, Kareem moved to the edge of his prayer mat. He faced

Mecca and cried out in a loud voice, *"Allah u akbar"*—Allah is great. He repeated it four times, then folded his hands and quoted the opening of the Koran, feeling his skin tingle with the special significance of those verses tonight. Allah had chosen him for this task. Allah had blessed him as a finalist. His heart must be pure for the challenge awaiting him. He would not let Allah down.

He bent over three times, repeating with all the intensity he could muster: *"Subhana rabbiya al azeem"*—glory be to Allah the Great. He had never felt those words more passionately than he did right now. He sensed that much would be required of him in the hours ahead. If he survived the upcoming test, Allah *would* be glorified.

He dropped his hands to his side and cried out, *"Sami Allahu liman hamidah"*—Allah responds to those who praise him. His heart overflowed with gratitude, defying words. Then he knelt and touched his prayer rug, paying no attention to Gus as the cameraman circled around him to test different angles. *"Subhana rabbiya A'ala"*—glory be to Allah the Most High. *"Allah u akbar—"*

Without warning, pain shot into his neck, like somebody had jammed a needle—a hundred needles—deep into his muscles, down his shoulder, surging with fierce intensity throughout his body. He groaned and fell facedown, fifty thousand volts of electricity from a stun gun crippling him. He felt as if his flesh were on fire, as if every muscle had been shredded, his central nervous system fried. A scream lodged in his throat.

He realized immediately what had happened and scrambled to rise from the mat. His muscles wouldn't respond, but still he struggled to his hands and knees, tried to stand…and felt another searing jolt. This time Gus kept the gun in place while Kareem suffered and twitched, flopping to the mat immobilized. Even amid the dank mildew of the cave, the smell of burning flesh grew pungent.

"Move again, my brave friend," Gus taunted. "Allah would be proud."

∾

Azrael. The Arabic angel of death. Finney had read about him the day he prepared for his cross-examination by Kareem. It stuck with Finney because the angel seemed to symbolize the unyielding wrath of Allah. In Muslim theology the angel of death is forever writing in a large book and forever erasing what he writes. He writes the birth of a man and erases the man dispassionately when it is that man's time to die.

Azrael. Why didn't he see it before?

Finney's first suggestion was to have Victoria call resort security. But she explained that the cell phones provided by the show worked only near the resort property. It was shortwave technology, like a cordless home phone, that hooked up to a central satellite phone. There were, of course, no cell phone towers on the island. Out here and at the cave, the phones would be useless.

Out of options, Finney and Victoria started racing toward the caves—he in docksiders, she in sandals. Though adrenaline fueled Finney's body, he struggled to keep up. He followed Victoria down this hill, around that corner, cutting a new path across shrubs and rock. He stopped once from sheer exhaustion and bent over for a minute to catch his breath. At least they were running downhill.

"See that large set of rocks down there?" Victoria said, pointing to a spot about a mile in the distance.

Finney nodded.

"The entrance to the cave is about a half mile from there. Just keep following the path." She pointed down a bank, and he saw it. "I'll run ahead."

Finney started jogging again, but this time Victoria took off much faster. She was still in sight when he hit the path, but then he lost her as the vegetation grew dense. He veered off the path but then found it again.

His lungs burned, but still he ran. A man's life might be at stake. He prayed for strength.

His thoughts focused on Kareem. In hindsight it seemed obvious. Kareem's cross-examination for the so-called worst-case scenario had always bothered Finney. How could somebody know about a one-weekend affair that had happened ten years ago? That wasn't reality-show research; that was obsession. Plus, Kareem said they had first asked him questions about representing criminal defendants. The same type of thing they had hammered Finney about with regard to the speedy-trial defendants. But with Kareem, there had apparently been no specifics.

Why? Maybe somebody wanted to confront Kareem about his past sins in a general way without providing a link to a particular person? Perhaps even a particular defendant Kareem had represented?

Somebody on the show's production team sure seemed to be fixated on the issue of guilty men walking free. He recalled the background materials Hadji had discovered about the persons of interest and knew immediately who it was.

Finney could have kicked himself! He was so focused on his own cross-examination, his own humiliating history, that he didn't focus on the others. Finney was right about one thing—ratings and religion were not the motive. This was far more personal.

It explained one of the first things on the island that had really bothered Finney: the questions asked by Javitts right after opening statements. Is it right to kill? Is it right to commit suicide?

Who wanted the answers to those questions? Who was contemplating an execution? Who was haunted by suicide?

Pieces of the puzzle came to Finney quickly, like decrypting the first two letters of a code and watching the others fall into place. Only one man had control over who would be on this show. That same man knew early on that the producers wanted it to look like one of the finalists was going to die. Maybe he decided to take it one step further. Maybe he hand-picked Javitts, a man who always wanted to be a television judge, on one condition—Javitts agreed to select Kareem for the finals. Maybe this same man found an imposter to diagnose Kareem with liver disease.

Maybe he was used to orchestrating people and events, creating illusions to make the pretend seem real. Maybe this man was doing it even now, directing his most impressive show ever. But this time he was making the real seem fake.

A father loses a daughter to suicide, triggered in part by a rape. But why was the rapist free in the first place? Who was responsible for putting him on the street?

And what would a father do to avenge such a loss?

The answers, Finney believed, were in a cave that was now less than a mile away. He picked up the pace despite his screaming lungs. Victoria Kline had no idea what she was walking into.

CHAPTER 70

Finney ran most of the way, taking short breaks to catch his breath. It seemed to take forever, though it was probably no more than fifteen minutes. He was still a few hundred yards from the entrance when he met Victoria, running back toward him, breathless.

"They've got Kareem in there," she gasped. "They're going to kill him."

"McCormack?" Finney asked, jogging beside her.

"Yes." Victoria was so shaken that she didn't seem surprised about Finney's knowing. "And Gus, too. They've both got guns."

Gus? Finney kept jogging, though his body was numb from fatigue. His legs began to cramp. "What did you see?" he managed.

Between ragged breaths, Victoria filled him in. She followed the voices she heard from the mouth of the cave and crept through a couple of openings that led to a large chamber. She crouched in the shadows at the entrance to the chamber, aghast at the scene in front of her. McCormack and Gus had bound Kareem's wrists behind his back using the same shackles that had been used during the Chinese water torture. They apparently didn't want to leave any marks on Kareem that couldn't be explained. The two captors made Kareem kneel on his prayer mat while they argued about what to do next.

They had apparently put together an initial plan to drown Kareem on Saturday night and make it look like an accident. As a backup alibi, they had framed Randolph, so it would appear that he had ordered the hit on Kareem to avenge the loss of his cousin in the World Trade Center.

"Gus is apparently a paid hit man," Victoria whispered. They slowed down a little as they approached the mouth of the cave. "I'm guessing that Gus is Azrael. He was probably going to disappear after the drowning, and his e-mails to Randolph would divert attention away from McCormack if the authorities didn't buy the accident scenario. He seems upset that McCormack even came to the cave tonight—like Gus was supposed to handle this on his own."

Chaos, thought Finney. *Planning gone awry. Maybe I can use that to my advantage.*

They were now just a few yards from the entrance, and they slowed to regain their breath. "I can't believe McCormack is part of this," she whispered.

"I'm not surprised," Finney said softly.

The opening to the caves could be easily missed by a casual visitor. Three large rock structures jutting out of the ground partially shielded the jagged entrance. Victoria stopped and listened for a moment before she ducked inside. Finney had to bend over as he followed her into the first chamber.

"I hope Kareem's still alive," she said, struggling to catch her breath. "I wanted to do something but knew I needed help."

Finney followed her through a few openings and turns until they reached the chamber where the three men were located. Finney and Kline crouched down and peered around the stalagmites. Kareem was still kneeling on his prayer mat, his face dimly illuminated by the kerosene torch and the light from a camera sitting on the cave floor. Behind him stood Gus, looking disdainfully at the Muslim. Bryce McCormack stood with his back to Finney and Kline, pointing a gun at Kareem.

"Let me hear a new prayer chant," taunted McCormack. "Something like 'Allah is weak; praise be to Bryce McCormack.'"

"Never," said Kareem.

"Hurry up," snapped Gus, looking at McCormack. "We don't have time for this."

Finney inched a little closer to Victoria. "Run back to the resort and get help. I'll stall them."

Her eyes hardened, and she shook her head. "I'm not leaving," she whispered.

"Victoria, think this through—"

She put her finger on his lips. "Forget it, Oliver. Think of a new plan."

McCormack took a step closer to his victim. "You need to bow when I say bow."

Kareem spit. McCormack kept the gun leveled on Kareem but spoke to Gus. "The stun gun," he hissed.

Gus narrowed his eyes and pressed the weapon against Kareem's neck, forcing Kareem down on his face, his body twitching in spasms of pain. His moans curled Finney's stomach. Finney noticed that Gus now kept his angry eyes fixed on McCormack.

"We've got to help," whispered Victoria.

"I'll distract them," whispered Finney as he watched Kareem try to recover. His brave friend rolled to his side, hands shackled behind his back, and struggled to his knees. "You sneak in behind McCormack and get as close as possible. Grab a good-sized rock. Move on my signal."

"Which is?"

"The word 'Go!' " said Finney. "Let's keep it simple."

"You believe in an eye for an eye? A family for a family?" McCormack asked Kareem.

"Enough of this," said Gus.

"I'm not talking to you," McCormack responded. Though Finney could see only the man's back, he could imagine the look of cold hatred in McCormack's eyes. Vengeance against Kareem had taken the place of reason.

Finney quickly patched together a plan, premised on the apparent ill blood between McCormack and his paid assassin.

Finney crawled through the opening and crouched in the shadows next to the wall. He was now in the same cave as McCormack and the others, though still fifty feet away.

"My daughter is dead. She'll never return," McCormack said.

"I am truly sorry," responded Kareem. His eyes locked on his tormenter's.

"You are sorry," McCormack sneered. "You put a rapist on the street based on a technicality. And you're sorry. But sorry will not bring my daughter back."

"Nothing does," Kareem answered. "This won't either."

Finney started inching along the wall, moving closer. If he stayed in the shadows, he could perhaps move within twenty feet of McCormack before being noticed. He signaled for Victoria to begin making her way along the opposite wall. If Finney could just move close enough and make a rush at them, Victoria could possibly come in from behind.

McCormack leveled his gun at Kareem's forehead. "You have a choice. Deny your god or destroy your family, Mr. Hasaan."

Finney slid a few more inches, kicked a loose rock by accident, and froze. McCormack never turned. But Finney had another problem. He felt a cough rumbling in his chest, forcing its way up his windpipe. The running had aggravated his lung condition. He wheezed as he sucked in air. He closed his mouth and tried to choke it back. The urge grew irresistible...

"If you don't deny your faith, then Azrael will have another assignment. A year from now, he breaks into your home. Shoots your kids. Helps your wife commit suicide. If you deny your faith right now and curse Allah, I may decide to show you some mercy.

"Justice requires a family for a family, Mr. Hasaan. But I might just let your family live."

Finney couldn't hold out any longer. He was too far away to lunge for McCormack. Instead, he quickly crawled back toward the opening of the chamber. Fighting back the cough, praying for control...

"There is no god but Allah, and Muhammad is his prophet," Kareem said, his face trembling with rage and determination. "Praise be to Allah."

McCormack laughed scornfully. "See if Allah spares your wife. See if Allah saves your children."

At that moment, still a few feet from the entrance to the chamber, Oliver Finney coughed. Knowing he had blown his cover, he quickly rose to his full height and coughed loudly—a raspy, forceful, phlegm-producing cough that echoed throughout the chamber.

McCormack and Gus swung their guns in his direction, while Finney covered his mouth with his fist and kept on coughing, as if his life depended on it.

And maybe it did. After all, who had ever shot a man while he was coughing?

Chapter 71

W hat are you doing here?" demanded McCormack. The director's worried eyes flashed back and forth between Finney and
Kareem.

Finney raised his hands and took a couple of steps forward. He finished coughing and tried to stay as calm as possible. "What's going on,
Bryce?" he asked. "Was Gus trying to harm Kareem?" Finney knew it was
a long shot, but he wanted to see if McCormack might try to turn on his
partner.

"Nice try," said Gus, his voice all business. "Hands on your head,
Judge. Get over here next to your buddy."

Finney laced his fingers behind his head but appealed to McCormack
with his eyes. He saw the flash from Gus's gun out of his peripheral vision,
ducked instinctively, and heard the bullet ping off the wall behind him.
He rose cautiously back to his full height. His heart felt like it would
pound out of his chest.

"Hurry up!" commanded Gus. "Next time we don't miss."

Finney locked his fingers behind his head again and walked deliberately to the prayer mat, eying Gus warily. Two captors with guns. Kareem
in wrist shackles. Victoria in the shadows. Finney didn't like his chances.

He knelt slowly next to Kareem, keeping one eye on Gus, the other
on McCormack. He tried to read the dark eyes of a man blinded by a six-
year quest for revenge. He had no trouble interpreting the ruthless eyes of
Gus. The man played cards without emotion; he apparently killed that
way too.

Finney quickly calculated the angles, the odds, the risks.

McCormack still had his gun leveled at Kareem, but he appeared anxious, almost hyperventilating. Events were spinning out of control. Finney was still breathing hard himself, but otherwise he felt surprisingly calm. It was time to exploit the dissension between Gus and McCormack. "He's going to kill you, too," Finney said to McCormack.

"Shut up," hissed Gus. He pistol-whipped Finney across the forehead, opening a gash that spewed blood. Finney fell facedown on the mat but managed to get back to his knees, the blood dripping over one eye and down his face. He glanced up at Gus, standing a few feet away from his right shoulder. He saw McCormack take a step away from the men, backing closer to the wall.

"What about Victoria?" Finney asked Gus. "You going to kill her, too? She's already heading back to the resort."

Gus pressed the barrel of his gun against Finney's temple. "One more word, Judge Finney. One more word."

"Finney's right," said McCormack, his voice showing the initial signs of panic. "What do we do about Victoria?" He took another step back as if distancing himself from the escalating situation. Victoria crouched in the shadows behind him. Fifteen feet, maybe twenty. Finney's head throbbed with pain so great he wondered whether he would stay conscious.

Gus spoke in a monotone. "First we execute these two. Then we chase her down."

McCormack nodded, his breathing still uneven. He took aim at Kareem, holding the gun with two hands, both trembling. Maybe Finney's unexpected appearance had temporarily caused McCormack to lose his lust for revenge. McCormack had never shot a man before, Finney realized. They would need only a moment's hesitation.

But then the eyes narrowed, and McCormack seemed to refocus on Kareem. His face grew determined. Six years of hatred. Six years of thinking about his daughter's death. His own life had lost meaning, except for the purpose of exacting revenge. And Finney knew instinctively that he was out of time.

In the next fraction of a second, quicker than Finney could think rationally, he caught Kareem's eye and gave his friend the signal. Finney the code maker, the cryptologist, the man who prided himself on creating and solving the most complex puzzles and codes. With his life on the line, in that briefest period of eye contact, he resorted to a code that had never failed him before.

Oliver Finney *winked*.

Kareem ducked down and to his left. Finney spun hard toward Gus, knocking the gun away from his own temple as it discharged. Finney then grabbed Gus's wrist and lunged at the killer with every ounce of strength his tired legs could muster, yelling "Go!" at the same time. As he pounced, he heard the pop of McCormack's gun and felt the bullet graze his shoulder, causing a brief streak of pain that shot up his neck and across his brain. Finney slammed into Gus like a linebacker and, aided by the element of surprise, drove him backward and onto the floor, jarring the gun loose as Gus's skull bounced on the unforgiving limestone.

Behind him, Finney heard a dull thud and loud grunt as Victoria Kline drove her rock into the back of Bryce McCormack's head.

Finney's tackle and the blow to the head stunned Gus for a split second, but Finney had underestimated the sinewy man's strength and agility. When Finney scrambled for the gun, Gus drove a powerful fist into Finney's face, shattering the cheekbone and knocking Finney to his side, the gun just out of reach. Gus quickly grabbed the gun and staggered to his feet, while Finney found just enough strength to rise to one knee, a hand on the floor to steady himself as the cave spun, bright stars popping before his eyes. Out of his blurry peripheral vision, Finney saw Victoria grab McCormack's pistol.

Next to Finney, Gus regained his footing just as the second member of the contestant tag team delivered his blow. As Gus was struggling to his feet, Kareem had charged, hurling himself like a battering ram into the Assassin. The Muslim's head landed squarely on Gus's chin, blood spurting from the Assassin's mouth while he staggered back, tripped, and caught himself as he fell, less than an arm's length from Finney. Gus whirled around, his body in a crab-walk position, left arm braced against the floor as he swung his pistol in one smooth, quick motion up toward Kareem. Impulsively, Finney dove at Gus, throwing himself into the pistol just as the gun discharged—his torso absorbing the point-blank impact from the .22 caliber slug.

Above him, Finney thought he saw another flash, heard a slug hit bone, and saw the side of Gus's face explode, inches from Finney's own. Then there was silence, as if somebody had freeze-framed the entire scene.

When things started moving again, they seemed to go in slow motion, and the voices sounded like echoes from the end of a long tunnel. Through the fog, Finney felt Victoria rolling him onto his back, away from Gus, and shouting directions at Kareem. He heard the *whoosh* of his heartbeat in his ears, and the words of his friends faded further into the distance, though he could still feel their touch.

His stomach felt as if someone had disemboweled him. The pain only increased as Kareem pressed his shackled hands onto the wound to stanch the bleeding. Finney still had knifelike pain in his shoulder from the first gunshot wound, exacerbated by the pressure on his body being exerted by Kareem.

Victoria kneeled over him and tried desperately to resuscitate him. She pinched his nose and pumped breaths into his mouth, forcefully, methodically, as if she could will him back to life with the precious air from her own lungs.

"Don't leave us, Judge. You're going to make this," she gasped between breaths, her voice nearly hysterical. "Don't you dare die."

He wanted to fight; the flesh wanted to obey. But he could feel the blood seeping from his body and he heard another voice—softer yet infinitely stronger. He saw a brilliant white light.

"Stay with me, Oliver," Victoria pleaded. Another breath. A tear dropped on his cheek. "We've got to stop his bleeding, Kareem." She stripped off her shirt and handed it to Kareem. He stuffed it into the wound.

"Keep fighting, Oliver." Another breath. The tears falling faster. "C'mon, buddy."

"Oliver," the second voice whispered. The light grew stronger and the pain started to fade. "It's time."

In response, Finney tried to whisper the name of his Savior. He thought briefly about the ones he would leave behind—Victoria, Kareem, Hadji, even Nikki—they would all understand. Maybe one day they would follow. He floated toward the light, the voice, the outstretched hands. Nail scarred.

"No," Victoria said. She cupped his head in her hands. Placed her cheek against his battered face to feel for breath. "Don't leave."

But the other voice grew stronger, the image clearer. "Well done, good and faithful servant; you were faithful over a few things. I will make you judge over many."

The pain was gone. He ran to the light. Arms embraced him. And Oliver Gradison Finney knew that he was home.

CHAPTER 72

For Nikki, the next few days blurred together. She walked through life in a haze, too numb to appreciate the outpouring of love and grief at the passing of her judge. It was almost as if her own soul had detached from her body the day Oliver Finney died, as if she now floated above events, observing them from a distance.

She felt like a zombie at the viewing—a somber affair where she waited in line for two hours just for a glimpse of Finney's lifeless body.

"He looks good," she heard someone whisper, and Nikki almost went off on the woman. Finney had hated flattery, and to be honest, he looked terrible—the piercing eyes now closed, the ornery smile gone forever. His face looked like a wrinkled Halloween mask, and Nikki could detect the touch-up job on his cheek and forehead. She determined on the spot that her funeral would be a closed-casket affair.

The next day Nikki slipped into the funeral late, dreading the emotions it would conjure up. A pew near the front was reserved for Finney's clerks, but she didn't want to join the others. Somehow it felt as if her relationship with Finney was much more than that. Nikki had lost a father, not just a judge.

She squeezed into the back row of the balcony, away from the people she knew, preferring to deal with her emotions alone. She had seen many people cry these past few days, but she hadn't shed many tears of her own. She felt guilty for not crying more, as if she couldn't even mourn Finney properly.

The pastor handled the service masterfully, refusing to preach a sermon or even deliver a eulogy. Finney's life, he said, was its own sermon. Through it Finney spoke so powerfully that words could never do it justice. The pastor sat down, the soft music started, and the large screens were filled with images of the judge Nikki loved.

Whoever put the video together knew Finney well. It started with a court clerk calling the court to order ("The Honorable Oliver G. Finney presiding"), and Nikki almost stood out of instinct. Next, Finney banged a gavel, and the highlight film began. It made everyone laugh and most everyone cry. It ended with Finney's compelling opening statement on Paradise Island—the story of Peter's martyrdom. "Oh thou, remember the Lord," said Finney, quoting the apostle's last words.

And then the screen faded to black.

The pastor opened the mikes for impromptu testimonies about the judge, and lines formed down both aisles. The Swami made everybody laugh. Lawyers talked about a man of justice. And Victoria Kline shocked the audience when she promised everyone that she would see Finney again someday. "He taught me how to sail on Paradise Island," she said as she swallowed back the tears. "And he restored my faith in God."

The irony was not lost on Nikki. Kline, the show's handpicked atheist, was so moved by Finney's sacrifice that she testified about a newfound faith. But Randolph, the self-proclaimed Seeker who had sponsored the show, was largely unaffected by the events that cost Finney his life. "I'm still trying to decide where I come out on all this," Randolph reportedly told the press. "The prize money for the show will be split among all the religious groups represented."

It was Kareem Hasaan, however, who affected Nikki the most. He walked stoically to the podium, dressed in his finest black custom-fit suit. The entire room fell silent as he took a deep breath and stared out over the heads of those who had gathered. "The Bible says that 'no one has greater love than this, that someone would lay down his life for his friends.' On this point, the Bible is right. I loved Oliver Finney. And there is no question that Oliver Finney demonstrated his love for me." And that was it. Simple. Direct. And Kareem Hasaan returned to his seat.

After the service, Nikki climbed into her Sebring and followed the entourage to the cemetery, the emptiness gnawing at her wounded heart. She fought back tears as she approached the entrance, the road lined on each side with lawyers of all stripes, standing like soldiers in the ninety-degree heat, wearing their black and dark-blue suits, hands over their hearts.

She stayed on the fringes at the grave site as the pastor read a few verses of Scripture and spoke comforting words that Nikki was too far away to hear. Somebody sang a stirring rendition of "Amazing Grace," and eventually the crowd began to disperse. Nikki politely accepted the condolences of friends and shuffled away to a spot under a nearby tree. For some reason, she couldn't bring herself to leave yet.

The crowd had thinned considerably when he started walking toward her. He had a bounce in his step and a quick smile even as others walked slowly with their heads down.

"You must be Judge O's beautiful and brilliant law clerk," the Swami said, extending his hand. Nikki couldn't help but blush—this guy was a celebrity. "He talked about you all the time," the Swami added. And then, with a mischievous grin, he commented, "And I can see why."

The blush intensified, but Nikki ascribed it to the heat. What were the rules for flirting at a funeral? She settled for an uncharacteristically demure, "Thanks."

"Can you hold on for a second?" asked the Swami. "I'll be right back."

And before Nikki could tell him that she had voted for him, the Swami jogged off toward his car. A few minutes later, he returned.

"Judge O gave me this," he said, extending Finney's worn Bible toward Nikki. "But I wanted to give it to you."

"I couldn't take that. It's—"

"Nikki," the Swami interrupted, "let me explain first and then you can decide."

Over the next few minutes, the Swami explained the pinprick cipher and the way Finney had given the Swami this Bible the last time they were together. The Swami placed a little ribbon at the beginning of the book of John so Nikki would know where to start.

"I decoded the message," the Swami said. "It's a message for you. Part of it tells you where Finney stashed a tape that could be evidence of the murder conspiracy on Paradise Island. But the rest of it is a personal P.S., though you should probably ignore everything in chapters seven through eleven." He held it toward Nikki again, and this time she reached for it. "I thought you should have it," the Swami said, but he didn't let go when Nikki tried to take it. "In exchange for your phone number, of course."

"The judge warned me about guys like you," Nikki said with a half smile. But she gave him her phone number anyway. And then, after the Swami had left, Nikki sat down on the ground and began deciphering the message.

As the Swami had explained, the first part was mainly logistical, Finney the judge making sure the evidence all lined up. But starting in John 5, he plotted out a personal message for Nikki. She could barely finish deciphering the text as the tears began dripping down her cheeks.

Years ago I prayed for a daughter. You have been the answer to those prayers. I'm so proud of you. Love, Oliver

Her heart bursting, Nikki continued to turn the pages. And then, in the verses between chapter 7 and 11, Judge Finney's code produced a P.S.:

One more thing. Whatever he says, don't fall for the Swami. You can do better than that.

Though the tears didn't slow down, she couldn't beat back the smile. And in her mind's eye, she could see Finney plotting out the letters.

The judge, of course, was winking.

EPILOGUE

Two weeks later, Nikki sat in the second row of courtroom 3—Judge Finney's courtroom, though Fitzsimmons was now the presiding judge. On this day, however, the courtroom had been transformed into the venue for a high-profile press conference, with reporters and spectators jammed into every seat. A deadly serious Mitchell Taylor stood in the well of the court behind a mike-infested podium, facing the crowd. The television cameras recorded every word.

"This morning, a Norfolk grand jury returned indictments for criminal fraud against Preston Randolph, Cameron Murphy, and an actor named Phillip Haney for their roles in deceiving Judge Oliver Finney prior to the start of the *Faith on Trial* reality show. In particular, Mr. Haney impersonated a representative of the governor's office under the assumed name of William Lassiter, and he did so under the direction and employ of Mr. Randolph and Mr. Murphy.

"At this moment the Fairfax commonwealth's attorney is announcing similar indictments against Mr. Randolph and Mr. Murphy as well as indictments against Mr. Howard Javitts and three other defendants for their roles in deceiving Kareem Hasaan into believing he had a terminal liver disease. Jurisdiction in Fairfax is based on the fact that those deceptions, including the alleged diagnosis, occurred in Fairfax County."

Mitchell paused and set his granite jaw so squarely that nobody could doubt his tenacity. "I have no intention of entering into plea negotiations on these matters. I do have every intention of prosecuting these cases to the full extent of the law. Am I trying to send a message? Yes. And the message is this: being a reality-show producer does not give you a license to commit malicious acts of fraud."

He paused again and seemed to drink in the calm before the storm. It was vintage Mitchell Taylor, thought Nikki. Short, direct, unequivocal. It was his public side—Mitchell the prosecutor.

But Nikki had recently experienced a deeper and more philosophical side when she approached him with questions about his faith. She knew that Mitchell was a Christian, and she knew how much Finney had respected him. It seemed natural to ask Mitchell the numerous questions that accosted her as she read through the gospel of John. Mitchell impressed her with straightforward and sincere answers, admitting freely to things he did not know. She had been down this path before—searching for spiritual answers—but this time was different. She had not yet totally embraced the faith of Oliver Finney, but she was definitely on the journey.

"Any questions?" Mitchell asked, snapping Nikki out of her thoughts.

Several eager reporters jumped to their feet and simultaneously shouted their questions. Mitchell pointed to one in the second row. "Let's start here."

"What about the lies to the contestants on the island itself—making all the contestants think they were going to die, that type of thing?"

"The Department of Justice for the Virgin Islands will have to address that. Right now, they've got their hands full."

More shouted questions led to another selection by Mitchell. "Didn't the contestants sign a release and acknowledge that the show's producers might mislead them?"

"Judge Finney signed a release *after* the visit from the actor posing as William Lassiter," Mitchell explained. "As for Mr. Hasaan, a signed release does not give someone the right to put a contestant through the trauma of thinking he's got a terminal sickness. That's the kind of malicious deception that goes beyond what the parties had in mind when the release was executed."

"You haven't mentioned Victoria Kline."

"Ms. Kline has received immunity in exchange for her testimony. To my knowledge, she was not aware of the deception concerning Mr. Hasaan's diagnosis."

"Do you have any comment on yesterday's announcement by the prosecutors in the Virgin Islands?"

Nikki sat forward at the question, curious to hear Mitchell's response. The Assassin who called himself Gus had died in the cave on Paradise Island, but McCormack had survived. In the process of searching McCormack's home, prosecutors had discovered videotapes of the death of Judge Lester Madison Banks III, who suffered a heart attack in his Jacuzzi after being threatened by this same Assassin. According to the papers, Judge Banks, who lived in Florida, ruled on a case nearly eight years ago in which he released a criminal defendant because of discrimination by prosecutors during jury selection. One of the defense attorneys in the case had been Kareem Hasaan. Two years later, the freed defendant raped McCormack's daughter.

"I am assuming that the question relates to the decision of the Virgin Island authorities to allow Mr. McCormack to be extradited to Florida so he can stand trial there first," Mitchell asked.

"Yes," the reporter said. "In your view, how much is that decision impacted by the fact that Florida has the death penalty but the Virgin Islands does not?"

"That's a question you need to ask the Virgin Island prosecutors," said Mitchell, and more questions were shouted. But this time Mitchell wasn't through. Instead of pointing out the next question, he waited for silence. "I find it ironic, however, that even in Florida, if he is convicted and sentenced to death, Mr. McCormack will have the choice of the electric chair or lethal injection. That's certainly more mercy than he was willing to show Judge Banks."

And so it went, back and forth, but eventually Nikki lost interest. Her mind wandered from the scene before her to thoughts of the past. It happened with alarming frequency these days. She would think of something

Judge Finney had said or something he had done. She wished she could be with him one more time. Or just ask him one more question. Or even take one more of his sample LSAT tests.

But she noticed recently, as she read Judge Finney's Bible, that at times it almost felt as if she *was* speaking to him. She had seen so many of the words of Christ exemplified by Finney's life that the words themselves had a familiar ring to them—an almost eerie feeling of déjà vu.

She glanced to her left, to the spot on the wall that so often drew her attention lately. It was a framed head shot of Finney, unveiled earlier in the week to a courtroom every bit as packed as it was today. She drew a fair amount of strength from the picture—the piercing eyes of Finney keeping watch over the justice being meted out before him. He had an intriguing look, and considerable debate had gone on about whether he was smiling or scowling. Nikki, who knew him best, had no doubt that it was a sly and thin-lipped smile, as if he knew something the rest of the world had not yet figured out.

The key to what he knew was contained in the small plaque just under the picture. Because it smacked of Finney's religious beliefs, it had created a small storm of controversy. But Nikki had been adamant about putting it up and, with the help of Mitchell and others, was able to get it approved. Other judges, whose portraits graced the walls, had personal tributes under their pictures. Why should a tribute describing a religious man have to be censored? When push came to shove, nobody was willing to tell the grieving friends of Finney they couldn't do it.

In a way, the verse was Finney's idea, communicated in another Poe-like message from beyond the grave. But it was Wellington who had discovered it, when the kid couldn't resist solving all the remaining ciphers contained in Finney's *Cross Examination of Jesus Christ*. He had called Nikki when she was driving back to her apartment late one night, and this time she was pleased to listen to all the tedious details about how he had deciphered one of the hardest codes in the book.

The last two chapters, Wellington explained, were encrypted using the Vigenère Cipher, a code so difficult to crack it was nicknamed the Unbreakable Cipher. But that couldn't stop Wellington, of course, who couldn't suppress his excitement as he told Nikki how he had deciphered the message for the penultimate chapter. Nikki made a note to look up the word "penultimate" later.

"So, what's the message?" she asked.

Just then a driver cut Nikki off and she gave him the horn, resisting the urge to throw in a piece of her mind along with it.

"Are you driving?" Wellington asked.

"No, I'm at a NASCAR race," Nikki responded. *And I don't need another lecture about cell phones right now.*

"Right," said Wellington. "Tell you what. Call me when you get home or wherever it is you're heading."

"You're kidding, right?"

"Nope."

At first it frustrated Nikki. But almost immediately she felt a small burst of pride. It was the first time she had heard him stand up for himself. Maybe she was rubbing off on him. Maybe she could groom him for Finney's job someday after all—a code-breaking, crime-busting judge for the next generation.

"Okay," she said, "I'm pulling over." She continued driving and waited a few seconds, hoping that none of the vehicles around her used their horns. "Now, what does it say?"

" 'This is how one should regard us, as servants of Christ and stewards of the mysteries of God.' "

"That's good," said Nikki. "That's so good it's going on a plaque."

And four days later, it did.

ACKNOWLEDGMENTS

My editor thought it sounded a little crazy. "Two books at once? Fiction and nonfiction? Tied together by one mystery?" I nodded, waiting. "I think we can pull it off," Dudley said.

Turns out he was right. It was crazy.

I'm grateful for an editor and a publisher willing to take this kind of risk and a team that could make it happen. Thanks particularly to Dudley Delffs, who believed in this project from the first time we discussed it, and Steve Cobb, who was willing to put the resources of WaterBrook Press behind it. Thanks to so many others on the team: Ginia Hairston, Brian McGinley, Joel Kneedler, Melissa Sturgis, Laura Wright, Eric Stanford, and a sales team who showed passion for the idea even when it was pretty rough around the edges. I also want to thank Don Pape; every author should have such an enthusiastic advocate.

I also have an amazing group of advance readers who pore over details of the story and then refuse payment. Since they're my friends, I don't argue with them too hard about that. On this book, they brought to bear legal expertise (Michael Garnier), television production experience (Martin Coleman), scientific knowledge (Robin Pawling), local courts and culture knowledge (Mary Hartman), and good humor (all). This book wouldn't be the same without their astute insights.

I relied on dozens of books, articles, and Internet sites, but two resources stand out. Nobody knows or explains ciphers and cryptology better than Simon Singh in *The Code Book*. He manages to make the complex simple and the tedious fun. The Black Chamber Internet site referenced in this book belongs to Mr. Singh and is every bit as cool as Nikki says it is. And yes, the story of the Beale cipher, which I discovered first in Mr. Singh's book, is an actual story about a real cipher. A second book of equal brilliance on an equally complex subject is Marvin Olasky's *The*

Religions Next Door. He is respectful and fair in his treatment of other faith groups, yet he never ducks the truth. It's an approach I tried hard to mirror in this book.

It almost goes without saying, the key word being "almost," that I owe a huge debt of gratitude to the world's best and most understanding family (no lawyer hyperbole there). If you think Finney and Wellington are quirky, you should try living with me when I'm writing a book. Thanks Rhonda, Rosalyn, and Joshua for putting up with that.

And finally, to some extraordinary friends and their family members who battled cancer this past year with courage and grace—your faith in a sovereign God has been the inspiration for this story.

ABOUT THE AUTHOR

Randy Singer is the critically acclaimed author of five legal thrillers and two nonfiction books including *The Cross Examination of Jesus Christ*, the book that Oliver Finney uses in this novel as the key to his coded messages. A veteran trial lawyer, Singer teaches at Regent Law School and serves as chief counsel for the North American Mission Board of the Southern Baptist Convention. He is also a legal advisor for the American Center for Law and Justice, a public interest law firm specializing in religious liberty cases. He and his wife, Rhonda, and their two children live in Atlanta, Georgia.

Excerpt from
The Cross Examination of Jesus Christ

Cross-examination," said noted jurist John Wigmore, "is the greatest legal engine ever invented to discern the truth." Never has that engine performed more flawlessly than it did during the life of Christ, generating the most powerful truths in the history of the world. This book is the story of Jesus on the witness stand—His jaw-dropping answers that shocked the Pharisees and inspire us still.

The purpose of this book, like the purpose of any effective cross-examination, is to reveal the truth—not just what Jesus taught but who Jesus is. His character. His intellect. His mission. The astounding depth of His love. Our verdict will be a lifestyle more like His.

CROSS-EXAMINATION 101

Cross-examination, my professors stressed, is the most dangerous part of any trial. A slippery witness can decimate your case before you know what has happened. That's why you never ask a question if you don't already know the answer. The classic illustration goes something like this:

LAWYER (defending someone accused of assault): You didn't actually see my client bite the nose of the alleged victim. Isn't that true?

WITNESS: That's true.

LAWYER: In fact, at the time of the alleged incident, there were several people engaged in a fight and your view of the victim was blocked. Isn't that true?

WITNESS: Yes.

LAWYER: Then how can you be so sure that it was my client who bit the victim's nose as opposed to one of the other men in the fight?

WITNESS: Because I saw him spit it out.

By then, it's too late to plea-bargain.

Another thing to keep in mind, according to those same professors, is the difference between a dangerous witness and one who can't really hurt you very much. With a dangerous witness, sometimes the best cross-examination is no cross-examination at all.

But the Pharisees didn't go to my law school. So they hurled the most volatile questions possible at the most dangerous witness of all time without knowing what the answer might be. The explosions reverberate still.

DO WE REALLY NEED ANOTHER BOOK ABOUT JESUS?

One could argue that even a million more books about Jesus would never cover the breadth of His character or the depth of His grace. Under this view there could never be too many books about the central figure in all of history.

But I'll take a different approach. I wrote this book not just to add another voice to the choir, but to look at Jesus from a unique angle that is immensely revealing though largely ignored. It is the story of Christ under the withering fire of cross-examination, and it is organized and narrated differently than any book you've ever read.

The first and last chapters are a firsthand account of the final trial of Jesus—historical fiction based on scriptural fact. Together, those chapters tell the story of the greatest miscarriage of justice ever, bar none. I've placed you there as Pontius Pilate's primary legal advisor—the *assessore* who would have advised Pilate under the Roman legal system. The book's middle eight chapters flash back to Christ's explosive confrontations with the Pharisees, examining eight of the most intense episodes between Jesus and His critics. These exchanges, perhaps better than any others, reveal the heart and mind of Christ. We return, in the final chapter, to Pilate's court, to the verdict of the Romans, and ultimately to the cross.

I've used this organization—first-person fiction bracketing the eight nonfiction chapters—for both a spiritual reason and a practical one. The spiritual reason is this: when Christ came to town, He taught the greatest truths of all time using the two methods I've tried to emulate in this book. First, Jesus told stories. And second, He answered questions from skeptics. He didn't preach three-point sermons with soft music playing in the background. He faced relentless cross-examination. And He used fictional characters to convey life-changing truths. That's the spiritual reason the book is organized this way.

So what's the practical side of it?

I'm a fiction writer and a former trial lawyer. This is what I do; it's how I communicate. Trial lawyers are storytellers. We believe in the mantra of all novelists: show, don't tell. I want you to experience the intensity and feel the injustice of Jesus's final cross-examination. To do this, I've used fiction to make you part of the story. After all, He went to the cross for *us*.

But trial lawyers aren't just storytellers. We also love cross-examination. Why? Because it forces the jury to choose sides. Though jurors swear to keep an open mind, trial lawyers know that on a subconscious level jurors cannot remain neutral. The more intense the cross-examination, the greater the difficulty. Before the witness ever steps down from the stand, the jurors have decided whether to take the witness at his word or not.

And so will we.

You Look Vaguely Familiar...

A strange and uncomfortable thing happened as I began writing this book. The more I studied Christ's confrontations with the Pharisees, the more I recognized myself in some of these questioners.

I discovered that some of these folks really loved God but tried to show it with activity rather than relationship. A holy busyness—that felt familiar. I found men who believed that Jesus was obligated to answer all of their *why* questions. There were men so focused on winning arguments that they couldn't hear the cry of a heart. And others who would not be satisfied unless Christ showed Himself powerful through one more miraculous sign or a political conquest or another physical healing. At times I felt as if I had stepped into this book and started questioning Jesus too.

The thought rocked me like a Mike Tyson right hook in his heyday, before he traded boxing for ear biting. *I'm a lot more like the Pharisees than I ever thought.* Than I ever wanted to be. I tend to interpret Christ's words in light of my own traditions and preconceptions. I'm inclined to put my own self-justifying gloss on the stories of Jesus and the religious leaders. I may feel a need to water Him down or explain Him away or claim that He is speaking symbolically. All of this is the mind-set of a Pharisee, the nitpicking of a lawyer.

That's when I discovered this mind-bending truth: if I want to be like Jesus, I must first realize how much I am already like the Pharisees. In God's paradoxical way, that humbling realization is the first step toward becoming less like the Pharisees we loathe and more like the Savior we love. All of our mental gymnastics and convoluted questions can't make it any other way.

Tricky business, and dangerous, this road toward the mind of Christ. The devil is still a crafty cross-examiner, twisting the truth and distorting the testimony. Like Mike Tyson *after* his prime, Satan couldn't land many direct punches on Christ, but he still had a nasty bite. At the cross, hell bit off more than it could chew.

"How do you know?" you ask (violating the cardinal rule of cross-examination).

"Because three days later they saw hell spit Him out."

From: Farnsworth, Wellington
Sent: Friday, July 7, 2006 8:03 AM
To: nmoreno@aol.com
Subject: Finney codes

Nikki,

Thanks for all your efforts with regard to Judge Finney's portrait that now hangs in his old courtroom. I felt proud at the unveiling ceremony, not only because it contained the decoded message from Judge Finney's book, but because it's a fitting tribute to a life well lived. It's even got me thinking about going to law school myself (though my mom would probably disown me).

It also triggered some thinking about another way to honor Judge Finney. With all the publicity about this case and the codes we solved along the way, I thought it would be cool to set up an Internet site with a contest for solving the three chapter codes that haven't been publicized as part of our story. After all, they ran a contest for Poe's ciphers after Poe passed away, and Finney is twice the cryptographer that Poe ever was. This might be a good way to honor Finney and get the word out about his other messages.

As far as I know, I'm the only one who knows the solutions to the codes in chapters 5, 6, and 10 of The Cross Examination of Jesus Christ. I set up a Web site at www.crossexaminationbooks.com for others to try their luck. You mentioned that you would rather just have me give you the solutions, but I've been thinking about that as well. Did Judge Finney give you solutions to the LSAT questions, or did he think there was something to be gained from trying to figure them out on your own? One thing I've learned from you is to be a more independent thinker—don't give in to pressure and do what other people tell you to do, do what you think is right!

So, much as I'd like to honor your request, the codes for those chapters are on that Web site, just waiting for your finely tuned cryptanalyst talents to be applied. As for me, I'm going to spend my time working on the first Beale cipher. If I figure it out, we'll split the treasure. After all, we're still partners.

TLLW OFXP! (Think atbash cipher.)

Wellington

TWO BOOKS UNITED
BY ONE INCREDIBLE TRUTH

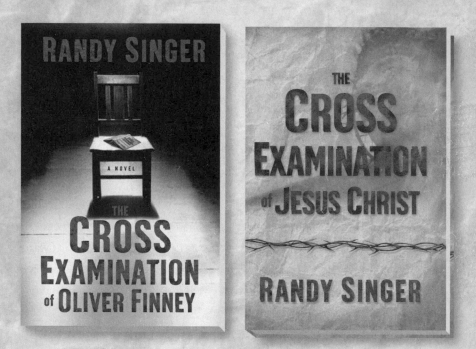

To decipher the clues in Randy Singer's suspense thriller, *The Cross Examination of Oliver Finney,* you must discover the key hidden deep in the nonfiction apologetic, *The Cross Examination of Jesus Christ.* It's a double-shot of provocative evangelism—unlock the mystery!

www.CrossExaminationBooks.com

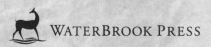